NOVUM ORBIS REGIUM
The New World Realm

Novum Orbis Regium
The New World Realm

Sequel to Τραψερς

A novel
by
W. A. HOLDSWORTH

Adelaide Books
New York / Lisbon
2019

NOVUM ORBIS REGIUM
The New World Realm
Sequel to Τραψεrςɛ

A novel
By W. A. Holdsworth

Published by Adelaide Books, New York / Lisbon
adelaidebooks.org

Editor-in-Chief
Stevan V. Nikolic

For any information, please address Adelaide Books
at info@adelaidebooks.org

or write to:

Adelaide Books
244 Fifth Ave. Suite D27
New York, NY, 10001

ISBN-10: 1-950437-43-4
ISBN-13: 978-1-950437-43-6

Printed in the United States of America

To Kris, Anna, and Sarah

Contents

7

Chapter numbering

Prologue

Prologue

"A Council was convened to decide upon the best and soundest means of withstanding the frequent and brutal raids of the northern peoples. Of their own free will, the Council invited in under the same roof the enemy they feared worse than death, the vile unspeakable Saxons, hated of God and man alike, and Vortigern welcomed them.

All the towns fell, their bishops, priests, and people mown down together while swords flashed, and flames crackled. Horrible it was to see, stones of towers and high walls thrown down with holy altars and human bodies covered with clotted blood as in some fantastic wine-press.

Some of the wretched survivors were slaughtered in heaps. Others surrendered themselves to perpetual slavery. Others emigrated overseas, wailing and singing beneath their swelling sails the Psalm, 'Thou hast given us like sheep appointed for the eating and among the Gentiles hast thou scattered us.'

Afraid, others entrusted their lives to the rugged hills and thick forests in their homeland."

– Gildas of Clyde

476 CE.

The Second rested his hands on the hilt of his sword, its leather-sheathed blade half-hidden by the dew-dampened field grass, and silently watched the dawn reveal what he'd waited a fortnight to see. With a restless smile, he called over his shoulder, "Cymry, how are the men this morning?"

"Ready to do your bidding, Second," answered the burly, war-hardened soldier as he and the Second's other two Generals walked over to stand beside him.

"Prepare the horses," said their leader, and Cymry hurried off. "Aetius, gird the men for battle." With a bow of his bald and battle-scarred head, the lankiest of the three turned to leave. "Cunneda, two columns to the south and wait for me."

"Aye," replied the General who didn't look the least bit like a soldier. His grandfather had been commissioned by the Roman Praetor of Londinium to be a sculptor at the forum, and his slight build and pallid features had found their way to his grandson. "At once," and he left his friend alone to contemplate the breathtaking view.

During the night, a heavy mist had settled into the surrounding valleys. Beyond the edge of the meadow that crowned Mons Badonicus, the Second could see nothing but a blanket of white, tinged red by the dawn. By the fates, God's good graces, or merely nature's happenstance, a chance to end three generations of war with the Saxons had been handed to him.

And so, the morn would bring battle.

The unbidden warrior within him began to awake. His pulse quickened, and his muscles tensed. Everything around him became suddenly vivid, the sounds of his men hurrying about, the scent of cooking fires, the breeze on his skin, the rustling of the grass, and the hues of color in the eastern sky. He breathed in the cool, damp air and slowly let it out.

Yes, just one more battle...for the future of Britain. They could easily wait out the siege, but to what end? To fight another day? To reach a stalemate? To negotiate peace with their tormentors? To slice

Britain into halves like a buck under the butcher's knife? No! Ambrosius Aurelianus did not die for a draw. He died so all of Britain could be free. He died to restore what once had been a civilized island.

The Second's right hand tightened on the sword's hilt as the other ran through his thick, gray-flecked hair. "A civilized island," he whispered bitterly as fragments of his island's history flitted through his mind.

Christ's apostles were spreading the Word, the Second Temple of Herod the Great brooded over Jerusalem, and the Jewish Diaspora had yet to begin when Britain became part of Rome. The Empire gave the Celtic warriors and druids of the island both peace and prosperity and nurtured their brutish villages into Mediterranean cities. The building of public forums, temples, theatres, bathhouses, amphitheaters, and villas provided good livings for mosaic layers, fresco painters, and potters. The growing population and trade with the mainland provided good livings for farmers and craftsmen. Roman galleys and roads brought wares and delicacies from the four corners of the Empire-wine from Spain, glassware from the Rhine, bronzes from Pompeii, dates from Cyprus, olives from Palestine – and provided good livings for shopkeepers and traders.

Life in Britain was life in Gaul or Africa or even Rome itself… until three generations ago when the Eternal City fell to an invader for the first time in eight centuries. Rome's great buildings were ransacked by the Visigoth-Saxons and her citizens taken captive, ransomed, sold into slavery, or simply raped and killed. So shaken was Emperor Honorius that he called home his legions from the remotest territories of the Empire, and with no means left to protect them, granted their independence.

With chilling rapidity, the pillars of Britain's civilization collapsed. Peace vanished when the Pict and Scot raids began along the northern frontiers, and nearly all memory of Rome's glories faded when the Saxons slaughtered Vortigern and the Elders. Yet, out of the dark years that followed stepped the great Ambrosius and his resistance fighters who fought to restore their once great island civilization.

"A civilization our fathers' fathers lost by their own stupidity," cursed the Second, but then bowed his head with a resigned sigh. Travelers from the mainland had told him stories of the many Saxon conquests across the channel, and he knew it had simply been a matter of time before their keels sailed to Britain, regardless of what the Council had done.

"So be it." All that mattered now was today. The old world had to pivot to the new, and if the new became theirs to create, there'd be no ancient codex of laws or mainland masters to frame their path forward. Every decision, every institution, every law, every right, and every freedom would be borne anew. They would make of their world whatever they wanted – a paradise, an Eden, a light for the world!

The thought of it was intoxicating but all that mattered now was today...surviving today. They were a thousand-man cavalry against a ten thousand-man infantry led by the Saxon warlord Oesc, who'd stormed west from Kent towards the Celtic Sea, hellbent on slicing Britain in two. But, before he'd reached Bath, the Second's cavalry had driven hard into the Saxon center, cut straight through, and headed west. As the Second had expected, Oesc gave chase all the way to Mons Baddonicus where the Second and his horsemen made their stand on the mountain's crest, and the Saxons laid siege rather than attack the high ground and risk heavy losses.

"The men are ready!" Cunneda called out as he hurried over.

"Very good," said the Second, strapping on his sword. "And my mount?"

"In front, as always."

The Second smiled and put his gloved hand on the man's shoulder. "Thank you, my friend. Now, shall we go and make peace?"

"Aye," replied Cunneda with a proud smile of his own. "For everyone." And together they walked to the waiting columns of mounted cavalrymen clad in century-old Roman armor, dented and tarnished, and held together by fraying leather straps. Mounting his steed, the Second noted the sun's position in relation to the clouds of mist , and then turned to ride back between the two columns.

"On this morn…on this day always to be remembered, he proclaimed, we shall decide our people's fate for generations to come! Only one path lies before us…to honorably vanquish our foe, to restore peace, and to turn this isle of woes into a land of hope!" The soldiers cheered and raised their swords to the fading stars. "Into the breach one last time, my noble friends, and then home to our families!"

Another cheer went up as the Second returned to the head of his column. Sliding his sword from its sheath, he raised it into the air, looked east and, just as the sun rose above the clouds, gave his final war cry and plunged down the side of Mons Baddonicus into the swirling mist.

He and his cavalrymen fell upon the Saxon camp with thundering hooves and slashing blades, striking fear into Oesc's men as they stumbled from their tents to find the horsemen of the apocalypse riding out of the blood red mist. The Second led his column straight through to the outer perimeter of the camp and turned east as Cunneda led his column west. Flanking the fleeing Saxons in both directions, the cavalrymen deftly herded their foe around the broad base of Mons Baddonicus and into a deep hollow on the far side.

All grew deathly silent as the horsemen halted, blades at the ready. The quaking infantrymen huddled below stared up in dread. In that moment, the Second knew that murder or mercy, death or dishonor, was but a command away, and his actions or inactions would color the future of his island and the peace to come. Urging his horse forward, he and descended into the hollow, alone.

"Oesc of Kent!" he called out. "Come forward and hear me!"

Barely had the words left his lips than a massive brute with long blonde, almost white hair charged out of the horde at full tilt. Oesc's gray-blue eyes were wild with bloodlust, his face crimson with rage, and his hodgepodge of animal skins matted with filth and blood. Raising his sword, the warlord cried, "Attack and honor your fathers!" But none of the soldiers dared move an inch for fear of being sent straight to Valhalla by the horsemen.

The Second turned his horse slightly to the left, the sword in his right hand dangling at his side. The warlord's blade slashed through the air and just before it struck, the Second gripped his sword's handle with all his might and swung it up in one, swift flowing arc. It met Oesc's with a thunderous clang, the force of its blow twisting the warlord's torso away from the Second. Bringing the sword down, he struck the Saxon hard on the back with the blade's flat side, knocking him to the ground, cursing with fury.

With a flick of his reins, the Second sidled over and placed the tip of his sword on Oesc's chest. "Mercy shall be granted you and your warriors!" the Second proclaimed for all to hear. "You shall be free men in the lands of my choosing! Surrender, and my promises shall be as true as the steel now laid upon your breast!"

Oesc looked about at the beseeching faces of his soldiers who moments ago had defied his order to attack, and realized he had but two choices – an honorable surrender or a noble death. Admitting to himself that he was hardly eager to see the great halls of Valhalla, he grudgingly accepted the Second's terms.

And in that moment, three generations of war ended. Tears filled the Second's eyes as his cavalrymen cheered and began chanting his name. "Artorius! Artorius! Artorius!"

"They stood alone in Europe, a new world, startling not only because it differed from the past, but because it differed from the rest."

– John Morris

α

"Men yearn for the gleam of a golden age."

– John Morris

"The association of men is founded on honor."

– James A Michener

Pointing fingers and excited conversations followed the U.S. Deputy Ambassador to the United Nations across the lobby of the Les Ambassadeurs restaurant. He heeded the attention indifferently, though it was hardly unwanted. Still, he knew it had less to do with what he was and more to do with who he was, or rather who he was related to.

With the love of his life at his side, his daughter in his arms, and his close friends T.J. and Marion Makatu following behind, William Cameron MacCrarey walked up to the tuxedoed maître d' and explained in poor French that they were there to meet two English gentlemen. Following the maître d' through the archway of the dining room, Mac – his nickname since college – came to an abrupt halt.

"Holy–"

"–shit," finished T.J., looking over Mac's shoulder.

Twenty-foot high ceilings adorned with ornate chandeliers and colorful classic scenes of gods and saints in all manner of troubles, white plaster walls, Renaissance paintings, pale red marble floors, tuxedoed waiters, linen table cloths, fine silver and china table settings created a stunning ambiance.

"Don't embarrass me," whispered his wife Marion, a bit shrewishly. A woman who never minded getting older, she was full-figured, white-haired, bespectacled, and wore one of her Sunday morning church dresses.

"Moi?" smiled T.J., a 62-year-old African-American man with a slightly receding hair line, a bit of a paunch, and wearing a stylish suit and fedora. On Mac's first day as Deputy Ambassador, the two had met in the UN offices in New York and quickly become fast friends.

Marion rolled her eyes and Genevieve giggled.

"There they are," said Mac, nodding towards the floor-to-ceiling windows overlooking the Champs-Elysees. The causally handsome man with bright blue eyes and flecks of gray in his wavy dark brown hair started forward, his daughter Cameron still in his arms.

A wave of awed excitement followed him through the dining room as though he were a ship cutting through calm waters.

As the five of them approached, Michael Abrams and the Clan Elders, Kyle Dunham and Merrill MaGeah, stood up from the table to welcome their guests. The taller and older of the three greeted Mac with an embrace.

"Lad, so good to see you," said Kyle, Keeper of the Clan Camulodunum. He wore an earthy-brown Harris Tweed jacket, dark wool-blend pants, and shoes that seemed as old as his seventy-three years. Kyle's silver hair was shoulder length and his piercing blue eyes exuded both warmth and the ability to take in all of a person with just a glance.

"And you, Keeper," replied Mac before embracing the second Elder. "Hey, old man. Been too long."

"Aye, it has," agreed Merrill, a solid-looking, fifty-nine-year-old with thick salt-and-pepper hair long enough to tie in a short ponytail. He had a belly well-rounded from years in English pubs, and wore baggy, wrinkled trousers and a frayed and faded dark-green Harris-Tweed.

"This is Uncle Merrill," Mac told his daughter as Merrill reached out for Cameron.

"Little one, y'are as cute as a button," he declared, scooping her out of Mac's arms. "Me Clan's been wondering when you're going to visit."

Cameron smiled shyly and wrapped her arms around his neck.

"Perhaps this summer," answered Genevieve. In her mid-forties, she had luxuriant copper hair cascading over her shoulders, red full lips, a radiant smile, and an easy laugh. Her dark blue, knee-length dress accented her shapely figure and set off her light blue eyes.

"Gen, this is Merrill MaGeah and Kyle Dunham, Elders of my Clan."

"So nice to finally meet you both," she smiled. "Mac's always telling stories about you."

"Don't believe him," Merrill chided. "I'm really a wonderful person."

"I know you are," she said and kissed him on the cheek, occasioning a blush. "I'm sure you both are," she added, kissing the Keeper's cheek as well.

"And this is Michael Abrams," smiled Mac as T.J. and Marion shook hands with their hosts. "I didn't know you were going to be here."

"We have some things to talk about," Michael Abrams replied, stone-faced.

"Hmmm…that doesn't sound good."

"No, it's not," answered the tall, trim impeccably dressed man with white hair, bold dark blue eyes, and the sun-bronzed skin of a well-to-do and well-traveled man of leisure.

Mac frowned before saying to Genevieve, "Michael met Kyle at university five decades ago and he's been a friend of the Clan's ever since."

"I've never met a U.S. Senator before," gushed Genevieve.

He shrugged and replied as modestly as a rich, powerful man could be expected to, "I was pleased to serve my country."

"Don't fawn over a former Senator, lass," groused Merrill. "It only means he was over-privileged at the expense of your citizenry."

"Ah, well," Michael retorted, "I'll remember not to use my over-privilege the next time you come knocking on my door for a favor."

"I've never asked you for a favor," exclaimed the Elder with as much innocence as he could muster. "'Tis me Clan that's benefitted from the wealth you stole from the people."

"I'll always help the Clan," Michael replied, "but you can fly commercial back to London."

"Ah, but where are my manners?" Kyle smiled. "Please, everyone," and he proffered the empty chairs facing the window.

As everyone sat, Merrill pointed out the window at the Place de la Concorde. "That tall, pointy thing is the Luxor obelisk," he told Cameron. "Thirty-three hundred years old, made of yellow granite and once stood at the entrance of the Luxor Temple in Egypt. It's 75 feet tall, weighs 280 tons, and on its side are funny-looking pictures called hieroglyphs that tell the story of King Ramses II, who ruled the oldest and grandest civilization of the ancient world. King Louis-Philippe of France brought the obelisk here two-hundred years ago when the rich people were being mean to us common folk."

"Hey, Professor, maybe a bit too deep for a six-year-old?" said Mac.

"Never too young to learn, eh lass?" the Elder winked at Cameron who squeezed him even tighter.

"Ohhh, you're going to pop me head off, little one!" he laughed.

She giggled and squeezed harder.

After a hearty laugh, Merrill waved an arm about the restaurant and said, "In 1778, this was the ballroom of the Hôtel de Crillon. Benjamin Franklin signed the first treaty between the United States and France right here. During the French Revolution, King Louis XVI was guillotined–"

"Merrill!" Marion gasped.

"–in the square out there. So were 1300 others, including Marie Antoinette, Danton, and Robespierre. It smelled so badly of blood that even animals wouldn't cross it."

"Merrill!" she cried.

T.J.'s chuckle over the never-ending sparring between his wife and old friend turned into a cough and a casual admiration of the ceiling frescos after one of her withering looks.

"The League of Nations Charter was signed here, too, which is important because the League eventually became the United Nations."

"Where Daddy works," she said shyly.

"Oh!" he said with feigned surprise, "you can talk." She giggled and when he asked, "Do you like castles?" her eyes lit up. "Well, not far from here is a real-life castle called the Louvre."

"Really?" she cried. "Can we go there, Daddy?"

"I was planning on it after we're done here. Perhaps Uncle Merrill would like to come with us?"

"And play docent, undoubtedly," T.J. said with a grin.

"Whether we want him to or not," added Marion.

"Why, I'd love to go with you, little one," the Elder said, "if you'll hold me hand while we're there?"

Giggles again.

"Why don't we meet you there, old friend?" Kyle told him. "You and Cameron could take a walk through the Toulieries Garden on your way."

"Aye, Keeper," Merrill replied, setting Cameron down and standing up.

Marion stood as well. "I'll come with you," she insisted, not quite trusting Merrill to do what she believed was in her surrogate granddaughter's best interests.

Merrill sighed but didn't object. "Ever have a crêpe au blé noir, little one?"

Cameron shook her head.

"Well, you're in for a treat!"

Mac kissed Cameron and promised they'd be along soon. After the three of them left, he looked from Kyle to Michael and said, "So, what's up?"

"The better question," said the Keeper, "is what's about to be up? Much is in motion and I fear something terrible is afoot,

21

something that could bring about a conflagration of the world order. But," he admitted, "I have nothing but speculation to found that prognostication upon."

"I've never known you to be wrong, old friend," Michael said.

"Nor have I," added Mac.

Kyle gave an acknowledging nod. "The first hint of trouble was Johnny Swaywell bemoaning the evils of the UN and calling Mac the Antichrist in his Sunday morning sermons."

"That didn't amount to much…did it?" said Genevieve. "Just the ranting of a televangelist interested in ratings, right?"

"I'm afraid it's not that simple, lass," Kyle answered. "Your country's far right and fundamentalists are believers, not questioners, whose political views and religious tenets are shaped by men like Michael's grandson, Jack, and Johnny Swaywell."

"Swaywell is by far the biggest contributor to Jack's Senate campaign," Michael added, "so Jack bends over backwards to ingratiate himself with the religious right."

Kyle went on, "Believers all too readily accept half-truths and conspiracy theories as gospel, especially when they're cloaked in Christian imagery. And even if they don't believe Mac is really the Antichrist, they at least believe he's a threat."

"Jack and Swaywell met with Under Secretary-General Gerhardt Schoen on at least one occasion that I know of," Michael explained, "and Schoen doesn't do a damn thing without his boss's blessing."

"And Secretary-General Boujeau just made Mac the Commander of a mission to Brazil," Kyle said. "A most unusual mission. Never in the UN's history has there been anything like it in the Western Hemisphere."

"Mac's been on Boujeau's shit list," said T.J., "ever since he captured that maniac Zeda on Cyprus, became an international hero, and went before the General Assembly to call for a Charter Amendment Conference. Now, Mac's a threat to the seven people who control the United Nations – Boujeau, Schoen, and the ambassadors from the Security Council's five permanent member states – the

U.S., Russia, China, Great Britain, and France. Without their unanimous consent, the UN General Assembly can't enact resolutions of their own, and when the Security Council unanimously does say do something, the General Assembly has no choice but to do it. Mac wants to amend the UN Charter, make the Security Council merely an advisory body, and let the General Assembly be a true democracy – one nation, one vote. For the first time since 1948, all 193 member nations would be equal. They'll be able to set policies and establish missions that could benefit hundreds of millions if not billions of people. The Security Council's power would disappear overnight, and to get his way Boujeau would have nearly two-hundred countries to cajole instead of just five."

"The Security Council member with the most to lose is the United States," Michael added, "whose UN Ambassador is Jake Tanner, the man who exiled Mac to Geneva after his confirmation hearings six years ago. Now, the U.S. has an election coming up and an incredible amount of dark money is being poured into the campaigns of thousands of far right candidates."

"Dark money?" Mac said. "Citizens United?"

"Yes, that's right," replied Michael. "Money that's impossible to trace back to its donors."

"Why this election?" said Genevieve. "President Jameson's a first-term Republican with no serious contenders from the left, and the Republicans hold both houses and half the Supreme Court. Why spend so much on ideologically stubborn far right candidates who'll make Jameson's second term a nightmare, given how moderate he is?"

"That's precisely the point," said the Keeper. "There's a coupe coming."

"The far right can't take over the party," Mac said.

"Not today," replied Kyle, "but if something were to happen between now and election day, something devastating and traumatic that shifts voters hard to the right–"

"You mean like scaring people with talk of the Antichrist?" said Genevieve.

"Aye. And what does the Antichrist foreshadow?"

It took her but a moment to understand. "The Apocalypse," she whispered.

"That's the conflagration of the world order you fear, isn't it?" said Mac.

Kyle nodded. "Many in the far right are evangelicals, and anything that hints of the Apocalypse both scares and thrills them."

"International arms sales are on the rise," Michael noted, "already above Cold War levels, but my old CIA buddies have no idea why."

"The United Nations Foundation condemned the arms buildup," Mac reflected, "but Boujeau hasn't taken action on it."

"Neither will the Security Council nations. Their arms manufacturers are making out like bandits."

"This is all about money?" cried Genevieve.

"No, lass," Kyle said ominously. "This is far more sinister than greed. Someone wants to control the United States and start a world war."

"Who?" cried Genevieve. "Why?"

"I can only speculate on who," Kyle equivocated, "and the why has many possibilities. We can only wait and hope." He turned to Mac. "For now, lad, watch your back, especially in Brazil."

Genevieve gave Mac a pleading look as if to say, 'Leave all this behind and live a nice, quiet, normal life back home in Traverse with your family.'

With an understanding smile, he squeezed her hand and turned to face Kyle. "I will."

"Choose your team wisely. The Clan will watch over your family, but where you're going, no one can watch over you."

Standing before his office window overlooking the East River, a satellite phone on hands-free sitting atop the credenza, Schoen said in German, "Calling for a Charter Amendment Conference sealed his fate." The phone converted his words into ones and zeroes, beamed them up to a network of geo-synchronous satellites, and then down again to an identical phone to be reconstituted into words once more. "MacCrarey will arrive in Brazil the day after tomorrow. Your orders are to draw him into the jungle, General."

"Ja, mein Herr," General Adolph Heinrich Mendenberg replied. He stood at attention despite being alone in his office and four thousand miles away. "But is there not a danger of his discovering our home?"

"Bring him only close enough to strike," Schoen ordered. Boujeau's Under Secretary-General was a trim fiftyish man with blonde, almost white short-cropped hair, pale blue eyes, and the faint remnant of a scar running down his left cheek.

"The settlers?" presumed the General.

"Ja."

"How many do you wish dead?"

"Enough."

"Ja, mein Herr."

"I expect to hear of the first attack by week's end," said the Under Secretary-General.

"Ja, mein–" and the satellite link ended. Mendenberg wrestled with a spate of indignation before locking the phone away in his grandfather's old mahogany desk. "Captain!" he called to his Chief of Staff in the outer room. "Gather the heads of the families together in the Opera House at once!"

"Ja, mein Commandant!" the Captain called back.

Half-an-hour later, the General stepped through the doorway and onto the landing of his Bavarian-style villa. Cursing at the stiflingly heat and humidity of the afternoon, Mendenberg stretched the collar of his freshly starched white shirt. He despised having to wear a Shutzstaffel uniform in such a place as this, but he had to set an example.

The people of Viertes Reich were going about their business in the town's square. A mother and her son passed by along the sidewalk crowded on either side by the untamed vegetation that claimed every inch of earth not occupied by the hidden city's buildings, walks, and roads. The boy – perhaps seven years old, he guessed – gave a 'Heil Hitler' salute.

Casually returning the gesture, the General made his way to the waiting car, the steamy pungent air sapping his strength and magnifying the burden of his duties – duties he never wanted, duties of leadership forced upon him when Schoen, irony of ironies, left to join forces with Boujeau at the United Nations, an international organization founded to prevent the likes of the Third Reich from rising again.

Now it fell to the General to ensure the survival of the families and protect them from the impure outside world while treating them as the genetic superiors they were. They demanded to be waited on hand and foot, and so he also had to keep the Cuari perpetually enslaved as family servants, playthings, and breeding stock. He was mayor, slave owner, judge, arbitrator, CEO, and the procurer of billions of Euros worth of war goods he himself staged in places that were little more than names on a map to him.

His reflections began to overwhelm him, and he halted. His heart began pounding, his muscles tensed into solid masses, and feelings of helplessness and despair washed over him. Balling his hands into fists, he forced himself to conjure up the picture on a faded calendar hanging in his office. A picture of snowcapped Alpine mountains. A broad valley blanketed with evergreens. A grand castle surrounded on three sides by a clear blue mountain lake and on the fourth by a quaint Bavarian village.

How he wished to be there, but his was the third generation of descendants to live their entire lives in the perpetual dusk of Viertes Reich.

"Mein Commandant?" called the Captain.

The castle faded from Mendenberg's mind. His Cuari chauffer held open the 1936 Mercedes staff car's rear door and the Captain sat waiting in the back seat.

"Another attack, Mein Commandant?"

"To the opera house," the General ordered the driver.

Mac sat quietly conversing with Lt. Sean Kelly and Taylor Johnson in the café of the San Baridiso Hotel. "Perry is stationed aboard the HMS Magellan just off the coast here," Mac told them, pointing at a map of Brazil unfurled on the table and weighted down at the corners by empty demitasse espresso cups. "Authorization codes have been loaded into GLOSAT. From deployment request to arrival at target, sixty minutes."

Sean Kelly, who Mac described to friends as a Greek god come down from Mount Olympus to walk amongst us mortals, said with the bluntness of a career non-com who'd only recently been promoted to Lieutenant, "With all due respect, Mac, is this assignment gonna be another pooch screw like Cyprus?"

Taylor let out something between a chuckle and a snort. A Cambridge-educated former Liberian diplomat, he was a tall, lithe man with a kind face and a talent for languages. "Cyprus made MacCrarey a political and media superstar. So–"

"So, they're gunnin' for us."

"So, let's be on our toes," Mac told them. Noticing a distinguished looking man walking over, he stood up from the table. "This must be our host."

The Brazilian Ambassador to the United Nations, Don Octavio Bandos, extended a hand and exclaimed in heavily accented English, "Welcome to my country! I recognized you from the newspapers, Deputy Ambassador MacCrarey."

"An occupational hazard, Ambassador," Mac said with a smile and introduced Sean and Taylor.

"I appreciate your meeting me here, gentlemen," the self-possessed Ambassador said. A bit on the heavy side and clad in an expensive Italian suit, Bandos had the classic look of a man from the Iberian Peninsula, though a bit darker in skin tone, with Basset hound brown eyes and streaks of gray in his slicked-back black hair.

Mac replied, "I just wish we were meeting under more pleasant circumstances."

"I trust the Secretary-General has briefed you on our situation?" Bandos said.

Mac was about to say, "No," when a throng of waitstaff accompanied by the hotel manager himself approached the table to fawn over their distinguished guest.

Mac turned the interruption into an opportunity to more thoroughly examine his surroundings. The nearly-empty café had subdued appointments and a retractable façade that opened out onto the sidewalk. There, several tables and chairs sat on the sidewalk beneath a green, yellow, and blue-striped canvas portico. Beyond the walk was a broad thoroughfare, and beyond that a treeless park that wrapped around the Square of Three Powers before continuing on to Lake Paranoá. On the square sat a massive building in the shape of an upside-down flower vase with dark translucent glass walls and more than a dozen cement arches curving gracefully upwards to join together in a circle a hundred-feet above the ground.

"How do you get in that thing?" Mac muttered to himself.

Bandos's cooing entourage fell silent and followed Mac's gaze outside.

"Ah!" Bandos exclaimed with no small amount of pride. "Stunning, isn't it?"

"That it is."

"Our city's cathedral – seventy meters across and supported by sixteen concrete columns, each weighing ninety tons."

"Kinda reminds me of the old Gemini launch pad at Cape Canaveral," Mac mused. "In fact, the whole city has a kind of old futuristic look to it, as if the architects had watched too many sci-fi films from the 50's."

"They probably did," chuckled the Ambassador. "It's called Modernist Architecture. It was all the rage when the city was built from the ground up in the late 50's. Visit all our architectural treasures while you are here. The Itamaraty palaces, the National Theater –"

"Perhaps on our return," Mac interrupted.

"Ah, but of course. Business before pleasure, yes?" said Bandos and ordered entrees for everyone before dismissing his admirers.

"To answer your earlier question, Ambassador," Mac said, "the Secretary-General has told us nothing of your situation."

A consummate politician, the Ambassador acted as if nothing could be more natural. "Allow me to explain, then. You see, my country has great natural resources in her interior. For decades, we have attempted to exploit them in exchange for the investment capital we need to diversify our economy. But, our trek to prosperity has had a few…side effects, shall we say. Perhaps you have heard of our Amerindian problems?"

"There have been incidents since the early 1900's of explorers, prospectors, and settlers being attacked and often killed by native tribespeople," replied Taylor.

"The aboriginal peoples are called Amerindians?" Sean assumed.

"Yes…and no," Taylor continued. "The term Amerindian is a generic reference to all of the indigenous peoples of Brazil, including millions of mixed-blood Brazilians. But, there's only about half-a-million true Amerindians left."

"Left?" said Sean.

"Left," Taylor repeated. "In the five centuries since Columbus arrived, millions of Amerindians have been wiped out by conquerors, old world diseases creating new world epidemics, and mainstreaming – the purposeful mixing of races and destruction of aboriginal languages, customs, folklore, and land."

"Mainstreaming is an act of compassion," Bandos explained. "We have given the primitives an opportunity to join modern civilization."

"Often by force," Taylor said.

Ignoring the affront, the Ambassador went on, "To harvest our great natural resources, we had no choice but to claim large tracts of land, first for timber and now to clear cut for livestock, strip mining, and agriculture. In the 1950's, Brasilia was purposefully located several hundred miles west of the Atlantic coast to encourage the development of our interior. Over the intervening decades, homesteaders, ranchers, lumber companies, precious metal extractors, and oil companies have pushed ever further inland. From time to time," he added with a dismissive shrug, "they come across an Amerindian tribe whose way of life has remained unchanged for thousands of years. They're given–" he hesitated, searching for an inoffensive word, "–a great…*opportunity* for change. But, the tribes are too ignorant to accept a better way of life, choosing instead to fight."

"Who could blame them?" Sean muttered.

"The Amerindians are filthy, backwards people, young man. We have assimilated hundreds of thousands of them over the centuries," said Bandos. "We gave them Catholicism, education, and countless amenities to make their lives more tolerable."

"Mr. Ambassador," Taylor said, "it's still not clear to me why we're here."

"Yes…of course. In the far western territories of our country, homesteaders have reached the outer edge of the Amazon basin. The further west they've gone, the more vicious and numerous the Amerindian attacks have become."

"Who's attacking who?" said Sean.

"The Amerindians are attacking the settlers, of course," the Ambassador answered impatiently. "In the past few weeks, seven villages have been attacked and more than a hundred settlers have been killed. The media has grown increasingly critical of my government, claiming it is unable to protect its people. The attacks are close enough to the border that the Peruvian President has begun creating diplomatic problems for us. To resolve the matter, our Parliament has decided to make an example of the tribe responsible. By crushing them, we will *shock* the Amerindians into assimilation and secure our frontier once and for all."

"Yeah, that'll work," Sean said irreverently. "They'll watch the nightly news on their jungle TVs and see how their brothers and sisters are being slaughtered by you and say, 'Gosh! We oughta be more like *white* people!'"

Mac held up a hand. "Sean, please. Mr. Ambassador, I still don't understand what our role's supposed to be."

"Simply to be present," he replied with a shrug. "The UN is respected for its peacekeeping and humanitarian efforts, and Brazil must do what's necessary to protect her civilized people. My government simply–"

"–simply wants us to be present so the world'll think the UN blessed your actions, no matter how reprehensible they may be," Sean said.

Bandos drummed his fingers on the table. "Crassly put…but, yes. The Secretary-General and I have an understanding."

"What are we," Sean growled, "Boujeau's lap dogs? A tiny Amerindian tribe defends itself from land thieves, the federal government decides to eradicate them, and we're supposed to just watch and smile for the cameras?"

"I will not tolerate your insolence anymore, young man!" snapped Bandos, getting up from his chair. "I am the Ambassador of –!"

"We'll be observers," Mac stated as he too stood up. "We'll be advisors, we'll reach our own conclusions, and we'll recommend whatever course of action ends the loss of life and fosters the long-term well-being of all involved. Am I clear?"

Bandos's face reddened. "Quite," he said, kicking his chair out of the way. "Your superiors will hear of this."

"I would expect no less," countered Mac.

The Ambassador gave a defiant snort and strode away.

"What now?" Taylor asked.

Mac smiled, remembering what the Dalai Lama had said when asked the same question. "First thing's first. We eat," and he sat back down.

The smug Ambassador sat in the backseat of his BMW as it sped through the streets of the capitol. "The plan is proceeding just as you knew it would," he said into his satellite phone.

"But of course," the self-satisfied Secretary-General replied, a faint French-Canadian patois tinging his words. "Mr. MacCrarey is a naïve idealist, which makes him nothing if not predictable. We proceed as planned, yes?"

"And in exchange, you will endeavor to secure Brazil a permanent seat on the Security Council. The sixth most populous country in the world should be the sixth permanent member. Yes?"

"But of course," Boujeau lied.

They flew north out of Brasilia on a cargo transport to a military airstrip along the Amazon River. There, they offloaded their Humvee and travelled upriver to a small village where a guide named Juan Luarte waited to ferry them to the frontier. He was captain of the *Purus*, a barely seaworthy ship somewhere between a small barge and a large fishing boat.

Sitting in a ramshackle open-air bar near the docks and with Taylor serving as translator, the four men finalized their travel plans over a platter of boiled fish and sweet potatoes sitting atop a large plywood cable spool that served as their table. Juan leaned over a map of the river. "It is settled then," he said in Portuguese. "We sail 900 kilometers west along the Amazon," tracing the river with his finger, "to the Jutai. Take it southwest 250 kilometers to where it is no longer navigable, and offload that…that–" pointing at the Humvee, "–*that* and from there you travel by land to Cruzeiro do Sul. I will wait on the river for your return."

"Cruzeiro do Sul is the first frontier settlement attacked," Mac explained to the others. "We'll start our investigation there. Any questions?"

Taylor shook his head.

"Nope," answered Sean.

"Let's load up, then," Mac ordered.

He and Taylor followed Juan to the *Purus* docked upstream from the café. The roar of a diesel engine sounded, and the Humvee jostled its way up the rutted, muddy road. Sean navigated the bulky truck across a makeshift ramp of old planks laid between the quay and the ship. Once on board, he and Juan lashed it down to the deck and stowed away the planks. Within minutes, the *Purus* weighed anchor and Luarte's 12-year-old son backed the ship out into the river. As the boat slowly turned upstream, the UN team members went below to settle into their quarters.

Standing in the doorway to Mac's cabin, Juan told his guests, "If you need anything, please do not hesitate to ask."

"We will. Thank you," replied Mac and the Captain left them to unpack their duffle bags. "Seems friendly enough."

"Should be for what we're paying him," griped Taylor from the cabin across the hall.

"You gotta be tougher, man," Sean called from his cabin.

"I'm telling you, the man was relentless. The longer I negotiated, the bigger his family got and the smaller his home. By the time we were done, I think he was living in a cardboard box with eight children, his parents, a sickly wife, a brother-in-law with a drinking problem, and a sister in the family way."

When they returned to the main deck, every sign of civilization had vanished. Only an occasional shanty, broken down dock, or small clearing with a pathetic crop of something or other appeared now and then along the riverbanks. The pleasant sounds of the jungle drifted across the water to mix with the low, lazy rumble of the twin inboard engines.

The whitewashed plywood walls of the bridge cabin, with its corrugated sheet metal roof, sat behind an open semi-circular bow. From there, one could see the narrow band of blue sky above the tall trees that crowded the shores. A ragged, olive green canvas canopy supported by bamboo poles shaded the aft deck from port to starboard to stern, and underneath it sat the lashed down Humvee.

A weatherworn table nailed to the heavy, rough-hewn planks of the forward deck became the unofficial office of the United Nations Mission to Brazil. There, the three of them sat with their research papers, maps, beat up old coffee pot, and four tin cups.

"Sean, give us a run down on the region we'll be traveling through, please," Mac said. "To truly understand a people, you must understand the symbiosis they have with their land."

"Brazil is the fifth largest country in size and sixth most populous on Earth," Sean began. "It has a surface area of over three million square miles and a population of nearly two-hundred million. Ten South American countries border it to the north, west, and south. Its natural resources include diamonds, gold, oil, lumber, sugar cane, cattle –"

"And coffee!" a jacked-up Taylor exclaimed, taking another swig of the dark, rich steaming brew.

"And coffee," Sean chuckled. "Brazil is the largest producer of coffee in the world." Gesturing at the river, he went on, "The Amazon is second only to the Nile in length, stretching 4100 miles from the Peruvian Mountains to the Atlantic Ocean. It's fed along the way by something like a thousand tributaries, one of which – the Jutai – we'll be sailing up. Altogether, they form a watershed covering two-thirds of the country. If you were to picture Brazil as a diamond, the watershed covers the entire top half and part of the bottom. In it lives the most diverse biosphere anywhere on the planet with thousands of mammal, aviary, marine, reptile, insect, and plant species. Unfortunately, mercury and arsenic poisoning from gold mining and slash-and-burn farming is degrading the watershed and driving many species towards extinction."

"Humankind never seems to learn from its mistakes," Mac sad sadly. "Taylor, how about a civics lesson?"

Leafing through a notebook until he came to the page he was looking for, he began, "Multi-party republic form of government with a two-house legislature. Very small military for a country its size. Low per capita income – around $3,000. Serious economic problems with a growing national debt, rampant inflation, overcrowded urban areas, and social unrest. The world got a glimpse of that during the lead-up to the 2016 summer Olympics in Rio when riots broke out. Predominantly Catholic. Official language Portuguese, though Brazil is the most ethnically diverse of all South American nations – 15% Portuguese,

11% Mestizo, 1% pure-blooded Amerindian, a third African and mulatto, 40% other European – mostly Italian, Spanish, and German."

"Germans, huh?" Mac said with a slight scowl.

"The most of any country in Central or South America," Taylor nodded. "Why?"

"For one thing, Schoen is German – *very* German," he said. His teammates laughed. "For another, as many as two-thousand war criminals escaped Nazi Germany and ended up in Argentina and Brazil, including Adolf Eichmann, Klaus Barbie, and Josef Mengele, the Schutzstaffel doctor from Auschwitz. The prisoners called him Dr. Death. He performed all kinds of gruesome experiments on Jews and Gypsies before sending them to the gas chambers."

"Real warm and fuzzy son-of-a-bitch, huh?" Sean said.

"There were plenty of Germans here *before* the war," Taylor noted. "Ranchers, exporters of iron and rubber, etcetera."

"Many of whom were supporting the Third Reich," Mac countered. He caught himself and held up a hand. "Sorry. Please continue."

"Discovered in 1500 by Pedro Alvarez Cabral, a Portuguese Naval Commander. Named after its first export, brasil, a red dye made from wood. Held by Portugal as a colony until the early 1800's when it became an independent monarchy. Became a Republic in 1891, calling itself the United States of Brazil. From 1930 to 1985, it was ruled by a series of military dictators."

"Thanks to the Nazis and the CIA," Sean said bitterly.

"Yep, pretty much," Taylor nodded. "Twenty-six states, each divided into municipalities governed by councils. We'll be meeting with a council member of Cruzeiro do Sul when we arrive who'll fill us in on the Amerindian attacks. Oh, and by the way, before Africans were brought over, Amerindians were used as slaves."

"Shit," muttered Sean.

Time on the *Purus* ebbed and flowed through the thick, humid days and inky black nights. It swam in whirlpools and stood still in tiny coves until it became almost meaningless. Only the occasional school of river dolphins arching up to the water's surface broke the hypnotic monotony. The constant drone of the engines, the rhythmic lapping of waves against the hull, the unchanging concerto of bird songs, the hum of insects, the interloping of dragonflies and the wafting nighttime swarms of fireflies furthered the wonderful, surreal illusion of an eternal, timeless world.

That changed when they traded the quiet, blood-warm, coffee-black Amazon for the clear, restless waters of the Jutai. After two days between her ever-narrowing riverbanks, the water grew so shallow that Captain Luarte had no choice but to run the *Purus* aground. Mac and his team stowed their gear in the Humvee, set the planks for the ramp, and bid farewell to the Captain and his son.

"You've been gracious hosts and skilled river men," Mac told them. "We thank you."

"May God bless you," replied the Captain.

"May your God bless you as well. We'll radio when our mission's completed."

Ten minutes later, they were standing on the shore watching the *Purus* back into deeper waters. Another ten minutes and she disappeared around the bend, the low rumble of her engines fading into the sounds of the jungle.

The tall trees and dense underbrush bordering the rutted road challenged the wide-framed Humvee, but they still reached the town of Cruzeiro do Sul by mid-day. With a mere two dozen ramshackle structures straddling a muddy creek and 200 yards of clear-cut land to the south and west to grow corn, beans, squash, and wheat, calling it a town was generous.

Stopping along what passed as Main Street at an open-air market, Mac said to the others, "Let's fill our larder."

Several villagers followed them around, hawking and gawking, while they perused the baskets of charms, blankets, handmade utensils and tools, hunting supplies, Pirarucu, caimans, monkeys, lizards, and all kinds of vegetables and exotic fruits that crowded the market's aisles. The aroma of seasoned meat cooking over an open fire hung in the heavy air and Mac suggested they get something to eat. Just then, a tall thin man with leathery skin, thinning black hair, a loose-fitting white cotton shirt and baggy trousers pushed through the crowd.

"I am Head Councilman and militia Captain Aurelio Sanchez," he announced in perfect English. His facial features and relatively light complexion bespoke a mostly Portuguese heritage.

"Councilman, I'm William Cameron MacCrarey, Deputy U.S. Ambassador to the UN," he said and held out a hand.

"Yes, I recognized you from the magazine pictures," Sanchez replied, taking Mac's proffered hand. "You have an interesting heritage, and a controversial present."

"I suppose I do," Mac replied. "May I say, Mr. Sanchez, your English is exceptional. Travelling the world as I do, I'm forever humbled by how many people speak multiple languages and master them all."

"Even here in the shadows of the Andes we understand how the nations of the world are no longer isolated but interdependent. Are they not, Mr. Ambassador?"

"They are, and call me Mac."

"Please call me Aurelio."

"Let me introduce my team. Taylor Johnson," he gestured, "fluent in Spanish, can muddle through Portuguese, and does an excellent job as my mentor. Lieutenant Sean Kelly, my military advisor and a good man in a pinch."

"Ambassador Bandos briefed me on your assignment," the Councilman said, shaking each man's hand, "and I promised my full cooperation. But, well, let us have a seat at the cantina. There we shall have a frank and honest conversation, yes?"

"They're the best kind," Mac answered, and the Councilman led the way to an outdoor bar-café.

After the proprietor had taken their orders, Aurelio told them, "We do not need you here. We do not need observers or advisors. We need an armed brigade to protect our families!"

"I have the authority to order the deployment of troops," Mac assured him, "but to what end? Claiming the land of your native peoples as your own and battling them into near extinction will irreparably damage your nation's collective psyche and make you poorer for it. Believe me, my country made the same mistake."

"I wish only to defend my families," Aurelio countered.

"As you yourself put it, Councilman, we are all interdependent. Your people, my people...*their* people. We're all citizens of Earth and want what's best for our families."

Aurelio let out a long breath. "Yes. Of course. Please understand how difficult it is to keep the proper perspective when your friends and family are in harm's way."

"I can only imagine," Mac said.

The Councilman stood up. "Let me radio Bandos that you have arrived. In the meantime, please enjoy your repast and I will return shortly."

Plates of potatoes, fish, beans, and blue corn tortillas covered the small, dingy table and the four of them ate heartily while continuing their conversation.

"When was the last attack, Councilman?" Sean said.

"Nearly two weeks ago."

"No new attacks since we left Brasilia?" Mac said with uneasy curiosity.

"I assure you, the situation has not changed. The Cuari are remorseless, fearless savages."

"The Cuari?" Taylor said in surprise. "*They're* the Amerindians responsible for the attacks?"

Aurelio nodded.

"What is it, Taylor?" said Mac.

Taylor shook his head. "The Cuari disappeared seventy-five years ago. Just after World War Two. No one's heard from or seen one since."

"They are very much alive, I assure you," said Aurelio. "They have burned dozens of homes to the ground, murdered scores of settlers, and what has our government done? They have sent you, the author of numerous amendments to the UN Charter."

Mac was beginning to get the picture.

Aurelio leaned forward. "Suppose your amendments become part of the Charter. Suppose my country brought in National Guard troops. Suppose many Cuari die. The nations bordering Brazil would be empowered by the new UN Charter to intervene."

"Yes, that's right," Mac replied.

"They could send troops across our borders, occupy the conflict areas, impose sanctions. The negative P.R. would cause trade and tourism to decline, and with it the public and private revenues my country desperately depends on. So, why do you suppose it is that my government sent you?"

They both knew damned well why. "Because if I recommend that National Guard or UN troops should be called in, then your country can say they have no choice and whatever happens is on my head."

"That is correct."

"Sounds like another pooch screw, alright," muttered Sean. "Just like Cyprus."

"Aurelio, rest assured that my decisions will be based on the best interests of all concerned, but history recommends that we leave the Amerindians in peace."

"My people wish to live in peace as well," the Councilman said, "but they'll fight to the end if they have to, for they have nothing left to lose."

"I understand."

Aurelio stood and beckoned them to follow. "Come, let's get you settled in."

They pitched their tents just outside of town, a tarpaulin hung between them to create a covered courtyard of sorts. Beneath it stood a lashed-together bamboo table and folding camp chairs. At dinner that night, Councilman Sanchez joined them to plan their tour of the settlements. When they finished, they kicked back around the campfire, talked of family and work, shared a gourd of coconut liqueur they'd bought at the market – which Mac found reminiscent of something called Arik he'd come across in the South Pacific – and soon, tall tales and the laughter of comradery among good-hearted people filled the night.

Word came in the following morning of another attack.

"In Nueve Verdes," the Councilman told the others. "Not more than ten miles to our west."

"Can you take us there?" said Mac.

"Of course. I will arrange for their Head Councilman to meet us when we arrive." Noticing Taylor, head in his hands, Aurelio added, "And I will bring us plenty of coffee for our trip, made from our own beans."

"Thanks," Taylor mumbled.

Sean gave his buddy a wry grin. "Mac and I feel fine."

Taylor muttered something in Liberian that sounded far from friendly. Sean laughed and slapped his friend on the back, occasioning a moan and another Liberian curse. "Sorry, buddy," he said rather insincerely.

An hour later, the four of them were bouncing along a two-track in the Humvee. By the time they reached their destination, the temperature and humidity were both near 100. Even with the same clear-cut farm fields to the south and west, Nueve Verdes looked even less like a town than Cruzeiro do Sul. No church, no market, nothing but shabby huts lined the two-track, and there was no one in sight but a short lean man of perhaps fifty.

Aurelio and the man shook hands and conversed in what Mac assumed was Portuguese. "This is Teo Queltico," said Aurelio. "Head of the Council."

"Taylor, please ask him to explain what happened last night."

"I doubt my Cambridge Portuguese will get us very far. What with their accents and intermixing of Amerindian and Portuguese, I hardly understood a word they said."

Aurelio passed on Mac's question, but Teo said nothing. Instead, he turned and walked away. Mac shrugged to the others and headed off after the little man. On the far edge of the pitiful little settlement, they came to a small, thatched hut and heard a woman crying inside.

"A child and his father were returning home from the forest last night," explained Teo through Aurelio. "As they crossed the open field," he pointed west, "four Cuari appeared at the edge of the forest. The father will probably survive, but his boy passed away during the night."

Mac asked if they could talk with the father. With some reservation, Teo knocked on the door to the hut and led Mac and Aurelio inside. The body of a boy no more than thirteen lay in the middle of the one-room hovel, his lanky frame tightly wrapped in a hand-woven blanket. The boy's father, a blood-soaked swath of cloth covering his lower torso, sat on the dirt floor next to his son, rocking back and forth, tears streaming down his face. Aurelio knelt down and gently kissed the boy's forehead. Mac did the same. The father gave a slight bow to the Anglo and the Councilman, who asked the father for permission to speak. The grieving man obliged with another bow and after the two had talked in whispers for several minutes, Aurelio stood and headed for the door with Mac in tow.

Once outside, he explained, "The boy and his father were hunting in the jungle. Apparently the Cuari tracked them back to the village and shot them as they started across the field. The father shot back and thinks he hit one of them."

"Why wait until they were back at the village to attack?" Sean pondered. "Why run the risk of being seen or caught in a counterattack? The forest gives you ample space to use a bow or throw a spear. And if there were four of them, why didn't they make sure to kill the father?"

Mac sensed the questions were rhetorical and encouraged Sean to continue.

"They wanted to be seen. They wanted everyone to know who killed the boy."

"The father used the word 'shot,'" noted Mac.

"You thinking the father's wound was from a bullet?" Sean said.

"It could not be," Aurelio insisted. "The Amerindians have no such weapons."

"May I see?" Sean asked.

At first, Teo adamantly refused, but Aurelio kept talking, his words growing ever more insistent, until the Councilman hung his head and shuffled back inside. A moment later, he reappeared with the grieving father. Sean carefully unwrapped the crude dressing.

"Taylor, grab my first aid kit from the Humvee, wouldya please?"

"On it," Taylor answered, glad to get away from the gore.

"Definitely a gunshot wound," Sean told the others, cleaning the torn and bloodied skin. "How the hell did a remote Amerindian tribe get a gun?"

"We're damned well gonna find out," Mac declared. "Where do the Cuari live?"

Neither Councilman had the faintest idea, but Aurelio observed, "If the father shot one of the Cuari, there might be a trail of blood to point us in the right direction."

Three-quarters of an hour later, Taylor found more than just a trail of blood.

A young Amerindian's body covered with tattoos of animal spirits and tally marks lay face down in the thick foliage of the forest floor. Strangely, he wore a pair of army fatigue pants and an ammo belt wrapped around his waist. The bullet from the father's hunting rifle had pierced the left side of the Cuari's back just below the shoulder blade.

"Punctured a lung, most likely," Sean noted, kneeling down beside the body.

"Are the Amerindian dead buried or given a ceremonial funeral pyre?" Mac asked Aurelio.

"A pyre," the Councilman told him.

"Taylor, let's gather some kindling and logs. Sean, find us a small clearing where we can build a fire."

"On it," said Sean.

"How rare is the man who can see past the prejudice and vengeance of others and do what is honorable," Aurelio said.

For Mac, it was simply a matter of honoring everyone equally. "I'm trying," he said.

"If only everyone would try," Taylor said.

When the pyre was ready, Sean and Aurelio bent down to pick up the body. Rolling it over, they took one look at the face and froze.

"Uh, guys?" called Sean. "You better come here and take a look at this."

Mac and Taylor walked over, hands full of wood and brush.

"That doesn't look like any Indian *I've* ever seen," Taylor remarked.

Though the Cuari's height, body markings, skin tone, and straight dark hair were quite normal for this part of the world, "His *face,*" Mac gaped. "He looks…he looks–"

"European," Taylor finished.

The young man staring blankly at the sky had large, round, dark blue eyes, a high forehead, low set cheekbones, and a narrow, pointed nose.

"*Northern* European," Mac nodded.

"Do all the Cuari look like this?" Sean asked.

"I've never seen a Cuari," Aurelio admitted. "They were discovered in the 1930's by a German expedition scouting locations for a rubber tree plantation, and no one's seen a Cuari since. That is, not until the attacks began on the settlements two months ago. But, I can assure you no *other* native Brazilians look like this."

"Any record of the German expedition, uh, leaving something behind, shall we say?" Mac said with a half-grin.

"Children?" replied Aurelio. "Not that I've heard of."

Mac knelt down beside the mysterious young man. "Well, whoever you were, son, and wherever you came from, it's time to go home." Then, he reached out and closed the Cuari's eyes for the last time.

That night, two families died when their homes were burned to the ground in San Benedict six kilometers to the west. The following day, another family perished in a fire and the head councilman was shot to death in the village of Monte Misme ten kilometers further on.

The mission team travelled to each town in turn to investigate, and as evening approached, Mac sent an encoded email to T.J. explaining what had happened and where they were. Stowing his laptop, he stepped from his tent and scanned the edges of the little clearing southwest of Monte Misme where they'd set up camp. The trees gently swayed as their evening shadows crept across the field, but otherwise nothing moved. The rest of the world could have been a million miles away. Sitting beside the campfire, Sean said to Taylor and Aurelio, "Nothing between our departure from Brasilia and our arrival in Cruzeiro do Sul. No deaths, no attacks, nothing. Then, three attacks, three days in a row, each further west than the last."

Taylor huffed. "Reminds me of–"

"Cyprus," Mac said, walking over to the campfire. "I doubt it's a coincidence."

"They want us out here," Sean agreed.

"Monte Misme is the western most settlement in Brazil," Aurelio noted. "Only two hundred kilometers of uninhabited jungle between here and the Peruvian border."

"Apparently not that uninhabited," Mac said.

"The Cuari don't know us from Adam, probably never even heard of the United Nations," Taylor commented. "So, who is it that wants us out here, and why?"

"I only know we must end these attacks," exclaimed Aurelio, "once and for all."

"Then, we go after 'em," Sean declared.

"Go where?" Taylor countered.

Sean pulled a black marker from his shirt pocket, grabbed the map sitting on the bamboo mess table, and made three dots. "These are the last three villages attacked." He connected them with a straight line. "Directly east to west." Then, he extended the line further west into the jungle. "With no more settlements, no one left to attack, and nowhere left to lead us."

Mac understood. "They're coming."

"Soon," Sean nodded.

Unnerved by his partners' matter-of-factness, Taylor said, "So, what do we do? Wait here like sheep in the night for the wolf?"

"But," Mac replied, "who's the sheep and who's the wolf?"

A full moon cast its silvery light on the clearing, embers from the long-abandoned campfire glowed, fireflies blinked, crickets chirped, and a gentle breeze brushed over the knee-high grass.

Four a.m.

Mac's watch.

He sat amidst a cluster of trees along the clearing's edge, his thermos of coffee nearly empty –

"Whoa!" he whispered, spying shadows moving along the far tree line – one, two, three silhouettes stealthily making their way along the edge of the clearing towards the tents. Pulling the laptop already up-linked to GLOSAT out of his rucksack, he switched the live satellite image of the clearing to thermal feed, zeroed in on the three ghostly images, and locked in each of their coordinates.

"Gotcha, you bastards." He dropped the laptop, pulled out his Berretta, and fired three shots into the air. The silhouettes stopped dead in their tracks and dropped to the ground. Red-orange flashes lit up the far tree line and bullets tore through the branches above Mac's head. Calculating their intruders' positions relative to the tents, he yelled, "Targets! Two o'clock!"

The words seemed barely to have left his mouth when Sean flew out of his tent, pistols in both hands. Before his body even hit the ground, he opened fire. Rolling into a kneeling position, he aimed above the black silhouettes and fired again until he emptied the clips. Like a runner leaving the blocks, he sprinted across the field, tossing the rifle slung over his shoulder at Taylor's tent flap as he passed.

Sean loaded a fresh clip into one of the .45's, aimed at the ground in front of the would-be-assassins, and just as he was about to squeeze the trigger, they fired back. He dove for the ground as the crack of another .45 sounded to his left.

Mac fired again and again, running full tilt across the field.

Taylor scrambled out of his tent, picked up the rifle, and knelt on one knee. Looking down the barrel, he tracked the moving shadows and fired, first over their heads and then into the dirt just behind them. The Cuari reached the tree line and vanished into the shadows of the jungle.

Mac slowed to a stop and pivoted in a circle, arm extended and Beretta in hand, but nothing moved. The world had seemingly reverted back to the moments before the attack.

"You okay?" he called out, lowering his gun.

"Yeah," Taylor muttered. "Sure."

"Woooohoooo!" Sean howled, firing his .45 into the air.

"I guess he's okay," Mac mumbled and turned back for the tents.

Backpacks packed and backed, the four men made for the tree line. Once they were standing beneath the jungle canopy, Mac said to Sean, "Alright, let's give it a try."

Taking his iPhone out of a vest pocket, the Lieutenant pressed the GLOSAT app and up came their location in degrees, minutes and seconds along with four tiny dots on a satellite image of the jungle.

"What's GLOSAT?" Aurelio asked, looking over Sean's shoulder.

"A network of communication satellites geo-synchronously or-biting above the 45th parallels," Mac answered. "I leased bandwidth on them so field offices and missions around the world can com-municate in real-time via audio, video, and text. It includes a UN database of information on member nations, missions, deployable peacekeepers and military assets that can be deployed in the field."

Sean pulled down a menu and selected VIEW. Opening another menu, he selected TRACK LOCK, another MARKER, and finally SUPERIMPOSE. Three moving ghostly shapes appeared on the screen along with another set of degrees, minutes and seconds. "GLOSAT can also track any object you mark, 24/7. Those," and he pointed at the screen, "are our Cuari."

"I'll take point," Mac said and for the remainder of the night and through the next day, the mission team tracked their would-be assassins. At nightfall, the images stopped.

"They're either home or setting up camp," Sean supposed.

"Let's dig in here, then," Mac told them, taking the iPhone from the Lieutenant. "I'll take first watch. If they start moving, I'll wake you."

At sunrise, the green ghosts set off again. Mac and his team broke camp and followed until dusk. After descending into a broad river valley, the images halted. When he could see the river through the trees, Mac held up a hand. "We'll camp here," he said, and his exhausted teammates were all too happy to oblige.

A sound woke Mac from a deep sleep, an all-to-familiar yet terribly out-of-place sound. He stumbled out of his tent, noticed the sun cresting the plateau they'd climbed down the night before, and shuffled over to where Aurelio, Sean and Taylor were standing. Staring across the river, he yawned, "Is that what I think it is, or am I still asleep?"

"That depends," Sean said, not wanting to be the one who said aloud the obvious but impossible answer. "What do you think it is?"

"Uh, well," Mac hesitated, "it sounds like, uh…traffic."

Sean nodded. "Yep. So, we're either all asleep or we'll all nuts."

"One way to find out," Mac said and waded into the river. The others followed close behind. Reaching the far bank, they cautiously headed in the direction of the grinding gears and whining engines. Twenty paces into the jungle, the trees suddenly disappeared.

"Bloody hell!" cried Taylor.

Sean grabbed his friend's arm and pulled him back from the edge of a broad trench.

Clearly manmade, five meters wide, three deep, and filled with algae-covered water, the trench ran to their left and right as far as they could see. Ahead lay a broad oval-shaped valley and at its center was the mindboggling source of the sound.

"Good God!" exclaimed Taylor.

"Like I said," Sean quipped, "we're either all asleep or we'll all nuts."

"We're nuts," Taylor decided.

"This is impossible," Aurelio said. "There are *no* settlements west of Monte Misme."

"Well," Mac replied, "that's a damned big impossibility out there."

The valley was two kilometers wide and four long, he estimated, with every scrap of underbrush long since cleared away for farming. Only the most massive trees remained, their trunks wide as a Humvee and 200 feet tall at least. They were spaced evenly apart, and their branches intertwined high above to form a vast green canopy over the entire valley. At its epicenter lay a vast city, cast forever in perpetual twilight with a well-groomed central square and a statue of a soldier. Around the square stood a theater or hall of some kind, a pub, stores with second floor apartments, a church, and a large Bavarian-style home. Vintage cars and trucks lumbered around the square and along well-groomed avenues that led into sprawling neighborhoods. Farmland with beasts of burden guided by Amerindians tilling the rich fields surrounded the city, and around the edge of the farmland stretched the broad trench Mac and his team stood beside.

On the far side of the valley were dozens of longhouses with clay-brick chimneys belching white smoke that wafted up to the canopy of branches. There, it lazily undulated back and forth like translucent waves on an upside-down sea.

A faint, bitter-sweet scent hung in the air.

"Can you make out the signs on the buildings around the square?" Mac asked Taylor.

His teammate lifted his binoculars. "They're in German," he said. "Clothiers, hunting goods, beer hall, farming supplies, groceries," and he passed the binoculars to Mac. "The statue is a soldier giving a Nazi salute. Looks like we got us a little Deutschland here."

Mac peered through the binoculars. Cuari, Mestizos, and fair-haired Caucasians went about their business, tending to their lawns and gardens, driving down streets, walking along sidewalks, and coming and going from shops just as city dwellers anywhere in the civilized world were doing at that very moment. But, this wasn't the civilized world. It was about as far from it as one could get.

The Bavarian-style mansion on the east side of the square had an immaculately manicured garden, wrought iron fence, white stucco walls cross-hatched with wooden beams, and a dark gray slate tiled roof. In front of it, a gleaming vintage jet-black touring car sat in a semi-circular driveway.

"Beautiful," Mac whispered. "Mercedes-Benz 770. Saw one at the Henry Ford Museum in Dearborn, Michigan once." He lowered the binoculars. "Aurelio, tell Bandos what we've found. Taylor, send our GLOSAT coordinates to T.J. and ask him to do some research for us. Sean, contact Perry. Tell him to ready a unit for deployment to Monte Misme. Taylor, Aurelio, and I will hike back to meet them. Keep an eye on Little Deutschland while we're gone and radio if anything out of the ordinary happens."

"Out of the ordinary?" Sean snorted. "This whole damned place is out of the ordinary!"

"Dummkopf," growled Gerhardt Schoen, punching the keypad of his satellite phone.

A moment later, the voice of General Mendenberg crackled into the receiver. "Guten morgen, mein Herr," he said.

"Fool!" yelled the Under Secretary-General. "The prey has found the hunter!"

The General's jaw dropped. "Mein Herr?"

"Secretary-General Boujeau received a call from Ambassador Bandos not 30 minutes ago. MacCrarey found Viertes Reich."

Mendenberg closed his eyes and let out a breath. "Mein Herr, it…it cannot be. I entrusted the mission to my best half breeds."

"Destroy Monte Misme!" demanded Schoen, his words so cold they gave even the General pause. "Not a soul must be allowed to live."

"But, mein Herr, the entire settlement…for just one man!"

"He is no *ordinary* man!" snapped Schoen. "*No* one must be left alive who can find our city again, *especially* MacCrarey!"

The General snapped to attention and clicked his heels. "Forgive me, Mein Herr. Your order will be obeyed. Monte Misme will cease to exist, and MacCrarey along with it."

"They had better, mein General, or *you* will cease to exist," and the line went dead.

Mac stood in the clearing, everything around him intensely vivid – the sounds and smells of the forest, the sensation of the breeze on his skin, the rustling grass, the hushed conversation of Taylor and Aurelio behind him, even the taste of the air – the legacy of his blood rising up on the eve of battle, the unbidden warrior within.

"Auto-deploy plans ready," Taylor called from the tarp-covered courtyard between the tents.

"Aurelio?" Mac called back without taking his eyes off the tree line.

"Fortifications proceeding apace," assured the Councilman as he walked over. "The settlers will work through the night, if need be. Perimeter campfires will be kept burning until dawn."

"Very good."

"The settlers are saying you're a blessing from God for giving them a chance to fight."

"If it weren't for me, they would have been left alone," Mac replied. "But, my friend, I wouldn't be any place but here with you and your people." He sensed something and stepped toward the forest. "Come on, man," he whispered.

As if obeying Mac's command, Sean materialized from the trees and sprinted into the clearing. "No more than two hours behind me!"

Mac called over of his shoulder, "Give the order!"

Taylor typed AUTO-DEPLOY into his laptop. The computer responded with ENTER AUTO-DEPLOY STRIKE CODE. He read the scrap of paper in his hand and typed 10A03Z61, then hit ENTER. Next, the computer asked for COORDINATES and he entered the location of Monte Misme – '91 degrees, 15 minutes, 32 seconds WEST; 45 degrees, 0 minutes, 23 seconds SOUTH.' Next appeared SOURCE and Taylor typed NAVY/UK/HMSMA-GELLAN and hit Enter again. A final prompt scrolled across the screen, ENTER TIMING/RESOURCES, and he punched in IM-MEDIATE, TWO, HAR.

TAYLOR, PERRY HERE, read the reply. "AUTHORIZA-TION CODE AND IDENTIFIER ACKNOWLEDGED. GOOD LUCK."

AND TO YOU PERRY, keyed Taylor, and signed off.

"Let's go," Mac told the others and they walked east through the woods to a small rise overlooking the broad field that led down to the village. Rough-hewn log barricades and trenches slashed through the crops, the excavated earth used to create hillocks. Wagons, carts, and crates blockaded every path, campfires burned all around, and lanterns lit up the village.

"Outstanding, Aurelio," Mac told him.

"My people have worked very hard," the Councilman said proudly. "A hut has been converted into an armory of sorts down by the river. Hunting rifles, ammunition, bows and arrows, ma-chetes – anything that can be used as a weapon is stockpiled inside. The outlying homes have been abandoned and the others barricaded. Boys under twelve and girls younger than sixteen have been sent downriver. Those who remain with their parents are ready to fight."

A group of settlers worked on a split-rail fence nearby and in their tired eyes Mac saw a hardened look of resolve. "Let's help them finish up and get into position."

Sean didn't have to be asked twice. "Look out!" he yelled to a man and woman trying to tip over a cart loaded with dirt, and he took off running full-tilt. The villagers cheered him on as he passed by and slammed into the cart like a linebacker sacking a quarterback and over it went.

Taylor picked up a stack of wood posts and carried them over to the settlers working on a barricade. Mac grabbed a shovel and jumped into one of the trenches. The Councilman hurried forward, dolling out orders as he went.

Finishing with the fortifications, the settlers grabbed whatever weapons they were most proficient with from the armory and filled their empty bellies with food set out by the village matrons. Wishing each other luck, they silently made their way back to the trenches and blockades.

Cracks and pops of burning logs in the perimeter fires and the rustle of wind through the trees were the only sounds. Mac circled the field, offering quiet words of encouragement to the settlers, all the while keeping a wary eye on the forest wall.

Sensing a subtle change in the air and soundscape, a surge of adrenaline coursed through him. Moisture-rich air drew deep into his lungs to fuel his tensing muscles, and every one of his senses magnified themselves a hundred-fold.

"Everybody down!" he shouted.

Thump! Thump! Thump! sounded deep and heavy from the forest.

Shockwaves from the mortars rolled across the field as red-orange streaks of fire arched overhead and slammed into the outlying huts. Burning wood and thatching blasted into the sky, showering down fire on the rest of the village. The ground shook and the air shuddered as the settlers opened fire at the trees. White smoke and the scent of burnt gunpowder hung over the field.

A thunderous, primal scream rolled out of the forest along with the *Cracks!* of return fire. Though painfully apparent they were out-gunned and out-numbered, every man and woman of Monte Misme stood their ground, firing, reloading, and firing again.

Mac drew his .45 and joined the valiant, hopeless battle. *Blam! Blam!* "Hurry up, Perry," he breathed. *Blam!*

Mortars rained down, bullets flew in every direction, bodies lay scattered on the ground, huts burned and the injured screamed. A shell exploded in a nearby trench sending pieces of dirt, rock, and settlers in every direction. The concussion threw Mac backwards, his ears ringing as he struggled to get back onto his feet.

"Come out and fight, you sons of bitches!" he shouted in anger and emptied his clip into the trees.

The firestorm from the forest died away and another primal scream sounded as the soldiers of Little Deutschland charged into the clearing, setting off an even more urgent fusillade.

Mac swapped clips and mumbled, "I gotta be more–" *Blam! Blam!* "–careful–" *Blam!* "–what I ask for."

The settlers took down one soldier after another. When they ran out of bullets, they shot their arrows and threw their spears. When they ran out of arrows and spears, they reached for clubs and machetes and steeled themselves for a final stand.

A thunderclap rolled in from behind them, and a bright white streak tore overhead. A split second later, the center of the advancing line disappeared in a deafening, blinding explosion. Chunks of earth and flaming pieces of bodies blasted into the air. Three more flashes, three more white streaks, three more massive explosions, their fading echoes replaced by a whining roar from beyond the village to the east.

Two monstrous gray Marine Harriers glided over the trees, their powerful twin turbine engines rotating downward, until the jets came to a stop in mid-air. Cheers went up from the settlers as the javelin-shaped crafts pivoted left and right, panning the battle-field and village, its streets now awash with hot, acrid gales from the turbines.

A burly blonde soldier picked up a mortar launcher and aimed it at the Harriers.

Mac took a bead on the man and pulled the trigger.

Click!

He swore, pulled the slide back, and–

Click!

He frantically ejected the clip, slid in a fresh one, pulled the slide back, and–

Click!

Realizing the chamber must be jammed, he cursed and threw the gun aside. Ripping a spear out of the chest of a dead soldier, he let out a cry and charged.

One of the pilots spotted the defiant soldier and angled his jet's thrusters back, dropped the nose down, and used the holographic image projected on the canopy's windshield to lock onto his target. The muzzle of the mortar flashed, the pilot pushed the joystick hard to the right, the port thruster roared, and the left wing rose up. The fiery shell streaked underneath and the pilot pushed the stick back to the left, locked on again and squeezed the trigger. A hail of 50-caliber, titanium-tipped machine gun shells ripped through the air. The soldier cursed, dropped the mortar tube, and ran for the trees. The bullets slammed into the ground behind him, the pilot deftly tracing them across the field until they ripped into the soldier. His torn and bloodied body skidded across the ground and crashed into the trunk of a tree with a sickeningly damp thud and cracking of bones.

The pilots continued to pivot left and right, firing at will. Their deadly hail of bullets turned one soldier after another into giant bloodied ragdolls until what remained of the line dissolved into a full out retreat into the jungle.

Another cheer went up and the pilots throttled down their engines. Once on the ground, the flight commander popped open his canopy and climbed out onto the port wing. Taking off his helmet, he jumped down and said, "Evening, Mac."

"Good of you to drop in, ol' boy," Mac replied.

"But, of course," answered Colonel Perry Spencer.

β

"God is the immemorial refuge of the helpless. They find not
only sanctuary in His arms, but also a kind of superiority."

– H. L. Mencken

"Corporations have been enthroned and an era of corruption in high
places will follow. The money power of the country will endeavor to
prolong its reign by working upon the prejudices of the people until all
wealth is aggregated in a few hands and the Republic is destroyed."

– Abraham Lincoln

Every four years, the wealthy kingmakers of the world travelled to a
tiny Caribbean island for the holidays with one purpose in mind –
to further the cause of free market capitalism. Elite CEOs, ultra-rich
business owners, and inheritors of old fortunes chose St. Martinez
for the private banks that catered to clients who wished to conduct business far away from the prying eyes of home governments.
How they made their money, what and whom they bought with it,
and how it found its way into the island's tax-havens was nobody's
business but their own. It was part and parcel to capitalism, a sur-
vival-of-the-fittest poker game where the winners stacked the deck.
To win took laws that let businessmen create marketplaces free of
regulations and put politicians in back pockets. On St. Martinez,
the most promising of those were wined and dined, praised and

preached to, and browbeaten and bribed between Christmas and New Year's. Hundreds of millions of dollars freed from campaign contribution laws by the financial Wild West of St. Martinez poured into politicians' hands like champagne into crystal flutes.

It had been a whirlwind of a week for Senator Mitchell Thomas – dinners at upscale restaurants, meet-and-greets aboard luxury yachts, invitations to parties in hilltop mansions – and all seemingly by happenstance. The final refrain of *Auld Lang Syne* died away and Secretary-General René Boujeau leaned over to say, "Mitchell, be a good chap and wait in the limousine for us? Jack and Johnny and I will be along after we say goodbye to some old friends."

Thomas blithely nodded and walked out of the ballroom. Crossing the grand foyer, he exited through the tall teakwood front doors, climbed into the waiting limousine at the bottom of the steps, and lit a Cuban cigar. After taking a long drag, he opened the minibar and took out a bottle of bourbon. When half the cigar was gone and his glass was empty, he stepped from the car and walked across the brick-inlaid circular driveway to the waist-high stone wall overlooking the city far below. Silhouettes of sailboats and yachts dotted the marina and cruise ships lit up like mini, floating cities lined the piers. Beyond the bay, the Caribbean stretched out black as the night but for the reflection of a crescent moon. He blew out several smoke rings and watched them drift away with the salty breeze.

"Mitchell!" Boujeau called out from the front steps.

"Get in! Get in!" Swaywell beamed.

"We've some good news!" Jack Abrams said as he opened the car door.

Once inside, the Reverend twisted open a bottle of Scotch. "Like one, Mitchell?"

"Bourbon," Thomas answered between puffs of his Cuban.

Boujeau rapped on the glass divider and the driver started the engine. As they drove down the mountainside, the Reverend revealed, "The people you've met this week like you, Mitchell." He took off his light tan suit jacket. "Several are high-ranking members of the CNSP, don't you know."

Thomas's face lit up. "The Christian National Separatists PAC?"

"'I will bless them that bless you and curse those that curse you,'" recited the Reverend, patting Thomas on the knee.

"The Abrahamic Covenant," smiled the Senator.

"*Genesis* 12," nodded Swaywell.

"The CNSP lives by those words," said Jack. "They're against anyone who doesn't think like they do, and they're generous to those who do. Like you."

"Me?" said the Senator.

"You were handpicked by my Under Secretary-General to run the gauntlet this week," Boujeau answered.

A tall man, and handsome in the way some men are once you take the time to consider it, Boujeau had a reputation for being cold, calculating, and intimidating. Tonight, though, he'd played up his celebrity and toned down his signature arrogance.

"Gerhardt Schoen?" Thomas said, both impressed and alarmed.

"He remembered you from William Cameron MacCrarey's confirmation hearings."

Thomas shuddered. "The Antichrist. If only we'd known then what he was, we could have stopped his confirmation and kept him out of the UN."

"But, we know now," said the Reverend, "and we *will* stop him."

"The men you've met this week were eager to find out if you're a fit," Jack explained.

"A fit?"

"They're impressed with your history. Ordained evangelical minister, former Mayor of a small southeastern Ohio town, and youngest state senator in a century. Book burnings on the Capitol steps, advocating for school prayer, opposing the teaching of evolution and sex education, passing legislation to outlaw homosexuality, closing family planning clinics, and triple-A endorsements from the Tea Party, the American Legislative Exchange Council, and the NRA. But, your willingness to listen to them this week *really* made up their minds."

"Made up their minds to do what?"

Before Jack could answer, Swaywell jumped in. "You know what dark times the 60's and 70's were. Hippies, fags, drugs, civil rights, race riots, anti-war protests, the Equal Rights Amendment, the National Organization for Women, the evil Roe v. Wade ruling, the fall of Saigon, the great Richard Nixon resigning, Jimmy Carter and the Ayatollah."

"Satan was winning," Thomas agreed.

"Satan's *still* winning," declared the Reverend. "Secular humanism is spreading like a cancer! We put women, Jews, and Hispanics on the Supreme Court and a Black man in the White House! Atheists and fags have the same rights as normal Christians. Social welfare is turning whole generations into leaches. Movies and books are filled with sex and violence. There are more single mothers than ever and more women in the workplace than men! Abortion is still legal and the government controls *everything*. Liberals want to take away our guns while Blacks and spics rape our white women and Muslims kill God-fearing Christians!"

"May God give us back our country," Thomas proclaimed.

"From your lips to His ears," said Swaywell. "America's a white Christian alpha-male nation and we'll fight tooth and nail to get her back."

"Reagan, the Bushes, Dole, McCain, Romney, Jameson – they all came to St. Martinez and won the support of the CNSP," Jack went on, "and now it wants to support you!"

Thomas' jaw dropped. He looked from Jack to the Reverend to the Secretary-General and threw back his drink. "Me?" he forced out through the burn. "They want me?"

"Will you do what they tell you, Mitchell?"

"I…yes! Yes, of course," stammered the Senator.

Like Pavlov's dog, thought Boujeau.

Swaywell poured another round for everyone. "You're the final piece of the puzzle, the last linchpin in our grand plan."

"What plan?" said the dazed Senator.

"A plan to reclaim America. A plan kept secret for *two generations*. A plan created by the retro-conservatives of the Eighties and the holy fathers of televangelism. I learned of it years ago when I was taken into the CNSP's confidence. It started in 1979 with massive donations from wealthy Republicans and offertories from evangelical churches to the Reagan campaign in exchange for seats on the GOP Leadership Council and a hard shift to the right socially, religiously, racially, and fiscally."

"Fiscally?" said Thomas. "You mean trickledown economics?"

"Yes! It's the key to everything!" Jack said excitedly. "The CNSP's whole plan! Trickle-down economics, Laffer curve economics, supply-side economics, voodoo economics – whatever you want to call it, it's a way to cripple the government and keep the poor and middleclass in their place."

Thomas looked lost.

"By convincing the masses that trickle-down economics actually helps them, we now have carte blanche to pass legislation that gives the rich *all kinds* of economic advantages. The wealthy, you see, are more likely to be contributors to Republican candidates and PACs. With their money, we took control of Congress and in 2000 and 2010 – census years – we gerrymandered voting districts all across the country to keep ourselves in power. But, still our majorities in the House and Senate are too thin to let us do whatever we want."

"Like fight against the Constitution's worst evil," said Swaywell, "the condoning of religious freedom. As we all know, America exists solely by the grace of God, yet our government allows people to have unchristian beliefs. Therefore, we must *take away* the government's power!"

"And we can do that," Jack explained, "by cutting taxes. Then, the government has to cut spending or else borrow from the financial markets by selling U.S. treasury bonds. If it borrows, its debt payments take up more of the budget and again it has to cut spending, which means fewer government programs, fewer government employees, and less enforcement of the Bill of Rights. Increasing defense spending does the same thing since it leaves less for everything else, so we prey on people's fears. We play up threats to our public safety and beat the drums of war. Communism made that easy, but after the Soviet Union fell in 1989 we had to find another enemy."

"The good Lord elected George W. Bush President, even though more people voted for Gore," said the Reverend, raising his glass, "and then He gave us Osama Bin Laden. Now Islam and terrorism are the national boogeymen."

"Praise Jesus," gushed Thomas.

"During his eight years," Jack went on, "Bush increased defense spending, cut taxes, drove up the Federal deficit, and increased the government's debt payments – everything we could have dreamed of. But, the rich got *too* greedy and Wall Street collapsed, sending us into the Great Recession."

"And that dumb Kenyan liberal Muslim Obama got elected," groused the Reverend.

"He withdrew our troops from the Middle East and by the time he left office," said Jack, "the economy was in better shape than before 9/11. The only reason we got the White House back was because we had enough control over news outlets and social media to make enough voters *think* the country was going to hell. The economy was collapsing, Whites were suffering because women and minorities get everything, Democrats were bringing terrorists into the country, the more outrageous the better."

"Jameson turned out to be a closet liberal, of course, but he's a damned sight better than that half-breed or Clinton bitch," said the Reverend.

"Amen," said Thomas.

"Now the CNSP wants Jameson out and someone who'll help them realize their agenda in," Jack said. "Things like trickle-down economics and less public spending on education, for instance."

Thomas was lost again. "Why cut funding for schools?"

Swaywell feigned shock and said, "Secular education is Satan's doorway into the minds of our young! When public schools have money, they broaden their curricula beyond readin', writin', and 'rithmetic. They add liberal arts classes," speaking the words as if they weren't meant for polite company, "like philosophy, literature, and the humanities. No liberal arts mean no liberal lies, Mitchell. Remember that," and he took another hearty, self-satisfied swig of scotch.

"You see," Jack said, "when school districts lose funding, they have to lay off teachers, put more kids in classrooms, stop buying new textbooks, cut back on teaching supplies, close and consolidate schools. When students fall behind, their parents clamor for fixes and alternatives. Like charter schools."

Swaywell gave a Cheshire cat grin. "Charters are really parochial schools in disguise, don't you know. They let us raise children in veiled religious settings. We're able to reach *millions* more kids than we can with churches alone. The teachers and administrators we hire have degrees from religious colleges or worked for parochial schools. The textbooks and teaching materials they use have a religious bent like the ones we use for home schooling. They dress in uniforms to stress conformity. They have mission statements and codes of conduct that quash independent thought and subtly infuse the morality we crave."

Jack went on, "But, children grow up and many head off to college – more now than at any point in our country's history. Polls show that young people are more likely to be 'Nones,' no religious affiliation, and vote Democratic, often because of what they learn from books and professors. So, we cut funding for public *universities*, too, making them less affordable."

"If I had my choice, *no* child would go to college," said the Reverend. "The Bible's all our young folk need. Old folk, too."

"Thanks to our efforts, college costs have risen four times faster than inflation. The costlier it gets, the more students drop out. And if they don't, they have to pursue degrees that promise big salaries so they can pay off their big student loans – degrees in STEM or law or medicine or business – *anything* but liberal arts."

"Without a liberal arts education, Mitchell," said Boujeau, "a person is less able to think critically or truly understand why things are the way they are. Their less skeptical, less likely to reject traditional values or challenge authority. And if those in authority are religious and conservative, then society as a *whole* becomes more religious and conservative."

"Ours is not to question His creation, ours is but to do or go to hell," said Swaywell, swirling the ice around in his glass before taking another sip. "The world is how He made it for a reason, but the damn liberals wanna make it soft and lazy, immoral and decadent! They wanna help every good-for-nothing loser out there! They think fags and lesbians and those transgender whatchamacallits are *normal*. If I had my way, we'd round up every sinner and bum who votes democratic and throw 'em in concentration camps!"

Boujeau and Jack silently shared a toast of commiseration over the heartless hypocrisy of a man who preached kindness, love, and the words of Jesus.

"If only we could," sighed Thomas. "If only."

Jack continued, "We've taken our battle for the minds of the people to social media – emails, texts, Facebook, tweets, websites, e-newsletters, and YouTube videos. We made our own movies, published so-called 'research' papers, even paid off elected school board members to re-write text books. We bought controlling interests in entertainment and cable companies, which bought up news stations and papers, which fired reporters and researchers, which put pretty talking heads and arguing pundits on the air, which spun stories the way we wanted them to. We funded shows on the paranormal and bizarre like ghost hunters and Bigfoot chasers. We made quasi-documentaries that mixed fact with fiction and produced so-called reality TV shows that indoctrinated the public with rude, intolerant behavior."

"But why?" said Thomas.

"To blur the line between reality and make-believe. To make people more gullible. To make rude, intolerant politicians seem like heroes!"

"The End Times are nearly upon us," Swaywell said, "and we shall see the Lord Jesus descending from heaven dressed in a robe dipped in blood. We shall watch as He reaps the vine of humanity and spills the blood of the evil upon the Earth. We shall glory in

Him as He carries the faithful home to Heaven. It is our solemn duty as Christians to bring as many of the Lord's children into the fold as we can, Mitchell, before the End of Days. We must do whatever it takes in the name of the Lord to be victorious *for* the Lord. Lie, cheat, steal, *anything!*"

The Secretary-General smiled to himself. My motto exactly, he thought.

"Praise Jesus," Thomas said, "but with the End of Times comes the Antichrist, Johnny."

"That's right. MacCrarey needs the United Nations to start his war and fulfill the prophecies of *Revelations*, a war that'll culminate in a great and terrible battle at a place the Bible calls Megiddo."

"I'll stop him, Mitchell," the Secretary-General assured him, "but I need your help. Your nation's economy is weak. Approval ratings of Congress and President Jameson are dismally low. Voters want a change and the general election is just eleven months away."

"We need more far right politicians in office to pass *all* of our, and the CNSP's, agenda," Jack insisted, "and that'll take a strong, popular far right candidate at the top of the ticket to bring people to the polls."

"We need a God-fearing man who can win the Presidential nomination at the National Convention in August," added Swaywell.

Jack launched into poll numbers, demographics, and election strategies. The Reverend tossed out Bible passages, compliments, and Amens.

"Gerhardt has set up a bank account for your campaign here in St. Martinez," said the Secretary-General. "One hundred million U.S. dollars, and the CNSP will give you hundreds of millions more."

"'And I saw heaven standing open,'" the Reverend recited. "'Before me was a white horse whose rider was called Faithful and True. With justice, he judges and makes war.'" He patted Thomas's forearm. "You are Faithful and True, Mitchell. Make war on liberal America. Be a good Christian soldier of the Lord. Heed the advice of good friends," and he gestured with his crystal tumbler to Abrams and Boujeau. "Will you do that for us, Mitchell?"

"Me?" Thomas said almost trancelike, his mind trying to make sense of everything and what it all meant. What it would mean for him, the implications, the responsibility, the power! President of the United States. Him!

He thought of the secularists and what they were doing to his beloved America. He thought of MacCrarey and how someone had to stop him. He knew the country needed a leader who would finally do what was right, someone who would make America Christian again and lead her through the Rapture. Was God calling *him* to be that person? It *felt* like He was. And why not? He'd been a good Christian, hadn't he? He'd generously tithed every week, read his Bible every day, won his struggles against temptations, fought against immorality in the world, prayed for the strength to do the Lord's will. Was it the Lord's *will* that he be President? And if it was, how could he refuse the Lord?

He said a quick prayer for guidance. And all doubt left him. Only the desire for power remained. God's power, he convinced himself. "I'll do it!" he cried. "I'll run for President of the United States!"

"Good boy," said the Reverend with another pat on the forearm

Boujeau said coldly, "Once you become President, close the U.S. borders, withdraw from the United Nations, and abandon your international agreements."

Thomas hadn't the slightest idea why and gave the Reverend a pleading look for guidance.

Swaywell said reassuringly, "Heed the advice of good friends."

Thomas nodded, "Okay."

"Get the CNSP working on his campaign," Boujeau ordered Jack before turning to Swaywell, "and announce his candidacy Sunday."

Perry said to Mac, "Let me introduce you to the Field Commander," and called out over the din of 300 Army Rangers readying for battle, "Colonel!"

A fit, fatigue-clad man in his late forties finished dolling out orders and hurried over, saying, "A proud day for the RAF, Perry."

"Just doing my duty, Chris," he replied, his attempt at modesty a poor one. "Allow me to introduce UN Mission Commander William Cameron MacCrarey. Mac, this is Colonel Christopher Stone."

"Deputy Ambassador, I've heard a great deal about you. You've really shaken up the world of politics and international relations."

"I'm trying," Mac said.

"You're succeeding, so watch your back."

"After years of dealing with Boujeau, Schoen, and the colossal egos of politicians and Security Council Ambassadors," Mac replied, "I've learned that lesson the hard way, Colonel."

"Been there, done that, sir," Stone replied. "You don't make General in peace time without learning a thing or two about politics and egos."

"Call me Mac. And, uh, you're not a General."

"That doesn't mean I don't know what it *takes* to become a General. It means I chose not to *do* those things."

"My respect for you is growing by the second," Mac said. "How'd you get stuck with this gig?"

"Perry told me what you've done the last few years, and what you're up against here. I made a few phone calls to people I can trust and arranged a training exercise for my Rangers at Palmerola Air Base in Honduras. By happy coincidence," he added wryly, "the HMS Magellan was taking on supplies in nearby San Lorenzo, thanks to Perry here. A supposed wrong turn during maneuvers and lo and behold we were dockside to the Magellan. After receiving Taylor's GLOSAT orders, we airlifted in, courtesy of the RAF."

"Does the senior brass know you're here?" said Mac.

"Nope," Stone grinned.

"Colonel, why would you risk your career for this?"

"You don't create peace by making war. You create peace by removing the political, economic, and social inequities that jeopardizes it. I believe you're doing more to remove the inequities between peoples and nations than any man alive, and I want to be a part of it."

Mac held out a hand. "Welcome to the fight, Colonel. I'm proud to have you with us."

Stone stood a bit straighter, smiled, and took the proffered hand in his. "What'll we be facing?" he said, nodding at the forest.

"Completely isolated with our back to the river, hidden by the forest canopy so no aerial intel or air support, half a mile of open field to traverse from the tree line to the first buildings, and no one inside the city to do recon for us."

Stone frowned. "Piece of cake," he muttered.

"Lieutenant Kelly," Mac said, waving Sean over, "has a sketch of the valley and a best guess at the street layout."

After helping a Ranger with his backpack, the Lieutenant ran over, saluted, and handed the map to the Colonel.

After a brief once-over, the Colonel said, "Good job, Lieutenant."

"Thank you, sir."

"Timeline?"

"We leave in fifteen, sir. I'll take point."

The Rangers camped on the ridge overlooking the valley the next evening. Field rations for dinner, lights-out at nine p.m., no campfires, and by four a.m. they were on the march again. At five, they met up with Stone's forward observers at the river, who reported soldiers hunkered down in farmhouses and makeshift fortifications around the city. Stone turned to his second-in-command, Major Robert Michael.

"Spread the units out along the trench. Have each build a log bridge to cross over. Scramble radio signals and have all units coordinate movements relative to my GPS."

"Yes, sir," Michael said.

"Beyond the trench, there's no ground cover from one end of the valley to the other," Mac reminded the Colonel. "Nothing but crops, livestock, and massive tree trunks."

"We'll be open targets in the fields," Sean expounded, "and in for a door-to-door street battle in the city."

Stone asked for suggestions and the Lieutenant didn't miss a beat.

"Crush the bastards, sir."

"Damn right we're gonna crush the bastards. But *how?*"

"You don't understand, sir," Sean replied. "I mean *really crush* the bastards."

The Colonel gave an impatient shake of his head. "Look, Lieutenant, you young West Point types don't know shit about real world battle, so–"

"Oh, boy," muttered Mac.

Sean cut the Colonel off. "I never went to West Point, *sir,* I worked my up from grunt to Master Sergeant, I've been to the Gulf on three tours, and Mac and I caught that son-of-a-bitch Zeda on Cyprus by ourselves, so if you *really* want a damned suggestion you'll hear me out."

The Colonel looked as though he could've chewed up a steel chain. "All right. Let's hear it. And it damned well better be good."

"The best way to avoid a battle is to give your opponent an honorable excuse to surrender. The U.S. wanted to avoid an invasion of Japan, so they dropped an A-bomb on Hiroshima. Truman coulda dropped it where it would've been seen without killing anyone, but regardless, the Japanese surrendered just hours after Nagasaki."

The corners of Stone's lips slowly curled into a grin. He looked across the river and said reflectively, "Massive trees, you say?"

Sean nodded smugly. "Yes, sir!"

With the sun cresting the ridge behind them, Major Michael reported, "All units ready and awaiting your orders, sir."

"Very good," Stone replied. "on your command, Mac."

"Go," Mac ordered.

The Colonel unclipped the portable radio from his belt. "All units forward! Repeat, all units forward!"

Each unit captain repeated the order and their soldiers advanced into the trees. Reaching the trench, they dropped their vine-bound log bridges across it at 100-foot intervals. Mac, Sean, and Taylor crossed over first, followed by Michael's unit and Colonel Stone. The unit Captains radioed the Major once they were in position.

"Ready, sir."

"At your leisure, Major."

Michael drew a thin, black switchbox from his backpack. A radio antenna extended from the front and two rows of 10 chrome-plated toggle switches lined the top. He threw the first switch and the perpetual dusk of the cavernous valley surrendered to a blinding red-orange flash. A hundred yards away, a massive tree trunk exploded and ominously began leaning to the right, sending Little Deutschland soldiers scampering out of bunkers and from behind barricades like rats from a sinking ship. The intertwining branches of the canopy far above slowed the tree's fall until it stopped altogether.

Mac's stomach tightened. "Come on," he willed aloud.

The sharp sound of snapping and tearing branches echoed down from the forest roof and the trunk moaned mournfully. A low-pitched *crack* boomed across the valley, the tree shuddered in its death throe, and shards of wood peeled away from the trunk with throaty thumps.

The giant tree began falling again, slowly at first, but picking up speed until it slammed down onto the field.

"Fire in sequence!" the Colonel ordered.

Major Michael flipped each switch in turn and lightning flashes filled the valley. The sound of explosions, sheering branches, and splintering wood reverberated from every direction. An enormous, crescent-shaped slice of the cavern's roof gradually fell away as one tree after another crashed to the valley floor and sunlight chased away the gloom.

Stone lifted his radio. "All units advance! Repeat, all units advance!"

Mac shouted to his unit, "Let's go!" and led the Rangers into the clearing.

Gunshots sounded as Stone's advancing troops reached the nearest barns and barricades. A familiar pounding whine sounded from above, and Perry's Harrier dropped through the gaping hole in the tree canopy.

"Let 'em know what you can do, Perry," Mac radioed.

"Roger that," replied the Colonel, leveling off 50 feet above the ground. Panning back and forth, Perry lined up the fuselage and flipped up the firing trigger's guard. "Ready."

"Fire," Mac ordered.

A sidewinder rocketed out from under Perry's right wing, bearing down on the tallest, widest tree in the valley. With a deep, thunderous *Boom!* its trunk disintegrated into a thousand flaming splinters. The branches tore free from the canopy above and the tree collapsed straight down like a giant ragdoll.

"Hang tight," Mac ordered. "Let's give 'em a minute to mull things over."

It didn't even take that long. The soldiers of Little Deutschland emerged one by one from their hiding places, hands up. White flags appeared in the doorways and windows of the town's buildings.

Cheers from the Rangers rolled across the valley as Mac radioed, "All clear, Perry," and the jet gently descended to the valley floor.

Crossing the town square, Sean said to Mac, Perry, and Taylor, "Hey, let's get a closer look," and made a beeline for the Mercedes-Benz 770 parked in front of the Bavarian-style villa.

A Ranger Sergeant was walking up the villa's front steps to knock on the front door when it unexpectedly swung open to reveal a tall, Nordic-looking man standing ramrod straight and wearing a vintage Nazi uniform.

"You don't see that every day," Sean smirked and hurried ahead of the others.

"What ist, um, dine em, uh, how do you say that again?" the Ranger asked his unit leader.

The Aryan disdainfully replied, "Ich bin General Adolph Heinrich Mendenberg."

Mac rounded the back of the Mercedes, the General looked over, and at once his face flushed with recognition and rage. He bolted headlong down the steps, hands reaching out like talons. He barreled into Mac and together they slammed into the side of the Mercedes. The passenger door caved in, the window shattered, and they fell to the ground in a tangled heap.

Mendenberg clamped his hands around Mac's neck and his world began to fade into blackness before two burly Rangers picked the General up and threw him onto the hood of the Mercedes. The forced sound of escaping breath mixed with a grunt of pain as he slid off the car and deftly landed on his feet.

Standing with Sean's help, Mac heard the General cry in German, "Go to hell, heir of Arthur!" and lunge forward.

In a swift and fluid move, Mac pulled Sean's .45 out of its holster and swung it up and around until it pointed at Mendenberg who slid to a stop, the barrel of the gun just inches from his forehead.

"If anyone's going to hell today, pal," Mac rasped, "it's you."

Flushed with rage, Mendenberg slowly raised his hands. The Rangers took him by the arms and dragged him off.

"Man, that guy was pissed," Taylor said.

"What the hell did you do to him?" Perry jibed.

"Beats me," Mac said barely above a whisper. "Maybe he doesn't like out of town guests dropping in unannounced."

Sean walked into the MASH tent they'd erected on the village green. "Up for a little stroll?" he said to his Commander.

"Sure," Mac answered, his voice still hoarse. "Just give me a sec." He finished washing the face of a Cuari girl lying on a cot and recounted, "Only 'pure bloods' got to see doctors in Little

Deutschland. The Cuari have their herbal remedies and all, but they can't cure appendicitis. She would've died for sure if we hadn't arrived when we did." He kissed her forehead. "Rest easy, sweetie," he told her and stood up. A little too quickly. He swayed and started to fall backwards.

Sean grabbed his arm. "Feeling okay, buddy?" he grinned.

"Not hardly," mumbled Mac.

"Well, I'm sure you look worse than you feel."

Mac laughed and straightaway grabbed his side, letting out a groan. "Thanks, buddy," he forced out.

"Sorry," said Sean with a noticeable lack of sincerity. "Come on."

They walked out onto the green and Mac gestured to the villa. "Who was that guy anyway?"

"Some kinda Mayor-Dictator-General dude. We've turned his home into our new headquarters. That's where we're going."

"How goes the search?" Mac said, rubbing his neck.

"The Rangers have inventoried the contents of every building and took a census of all the city's residents. Everything's being documented on laptops and linked through GLOSAT to a database T.J.'s running in Geneva."

"Find a connection between Little Deutschland and someone on the outside yet?"

"You'll see," Sean answered.

Mac walked into Mendenberg's office to find Taylor, Aurelio, and Stone waiting. The Colonel held a satellite phone in one hand and a black leather-bound book in the other.

"Found these in there," he said with a nod to an old mahogany desk.

"Seems as though the General was a meticulous record keeper," Taylor said. "The book the Colonel's holding is an account ledger of some kind. One of dozens. That burnt-wood and molasses scent in the air? They're boiling down native plants in the longhouses across the valley. Dried and ground up into a powder, it makes a drug like peyote or LSD." He picked up a different leather-bound book. "This is a ledger of shipments." He grabbed another. "Sales." A fourth.

"Bank deposits, but they add up to *way* more than the drug sales." A fifth. "Payments to companies. Hundreds of them. I recognized some of the names 'cause they're arms manufacturers."

"Holy–" Mac started to say.

"Yeah, exactly," said Taylor.

A large, dusty hardcover book sat on the credenza beside an ashtray filled with old coins and Nazi lapel pins. "That one has nothing but names in it going back centuries," said the Colonel. "A few I remember from my history classes at West Point. Politicians, an explorer or two, scientists, but the rest are a mystery, at least to me."

"Does the book list each person's birth and death date?" Mac said.

The Colonel answered, "Yeah. How'd you–?"

"Keep it safe," Mac told him. "There's someone who needs to see it. Gather up all of Mendenberg's records and begin repatriating the families of Viertes Reich back to Germany."

A deep, impatient thumping heralded the military transport helicopter's arrival. After dropping through the gaping hole in the jungle canopy, its skids barely touched the ground before the side hatch opened and Merrill MaGeah appeared in the doorway. Beside him stood a thin, ruddy-faced man in his mid-thirties looking as if he'd just stepped out of a London counting house.

"Good to see you, Elder," Mac said with a smile as his guests came down the steps.

"And you, laddy," Merrill replied warmly. "Allow me to introduce the Keeper's nephew, Colin Dunham."

The young man looked around and said with a thick cockney accent, "What's this place called, mate?"

"We've been calling it Little Deutschland, but the locals call it Viertes Reich."

"Viertes Reich? Good Lord, mate, you really stumbled into it, eh?"

Mac raised an eyebrow. "That we did," he replied as someone else appeared in the helicopter's doorway. "Genevieve!"

She ran down the steps and threw herself into his arms.

"I've missed you so much," he whispered and kissed her neck. "I had no idea you were coming."

"It wouldn't have been much of a surprise if you had," she smiled. "Besides, this way you couldn't tell me not to."

Mac laughed. "I suppose I would have." He kissed her and said, "I love you."

"I love you, too," she echoed. "Nothing could have kept me away."

"Aye," Merrill said with feigned exasperation. "Never in me life have I met a more insistent female."

Mac laughed again and looked past Genevieve to the door. "Where's Cameron?"

"With Marion and T.J.," she said.

"Oh."

"She misses you," Genevieve assured him, "but I'm sure Marion's spoiling her as we speak."

"I'm sure she is. Well, come on. Let's get you three settled in." Taking Genevieve's hand, he said to Colin, "Then we'll have a look at the book of names."

"Viertes means 'Four,'" Colin noted as he followed Mac to the staff car. "Reich means 'Order,' mate. Your town here is named the 'Fourth Order.'"

"Yes. That's right," Mac replied, opening the car door for Genevieve.

"The fourth order of what?" she said, getting in.

"According to the Nazis," answered Colin, "the First Order was the Holy Roman Empire, the Second was the Austro-Hungarian Empire, the Third was Hitler's Germany."

"And apparently this is the Fourth," finished Mac.

"These people are Nazis?" Genevieve said in surprise.

"Surly, arrogant, self-righteous," Colonel Stone quipped, starting up the car. "Walking, talking stereotypes. We took a census and gathered the personal histories of the residents," he went on loudly enough to be heard over the thrumming of the V-12 engine.

"The families are all descendants of the Third Reich's most elite party members who quietly left the country as the war was ending to avoid being tried as war criminals."

"Four generations of Germans live here now," Mac added.

"Is that what the book of names is, then?" Colin surmised. "A genealogy of the Viertes Reich families?"

"Not hardly," Stone answered. "The names go way back. Centuries. Hardly recognize any of 'em."

"Dates?" Merrill inquired.

"Birth and death," Mac said.

"You two blokes think it's like ours?" Colin asked. "In Camulodunum?"

"Aye," said Merrill darkly. "But why?"

Mac recalled, "Before Mendenberg grabbed me by the throat, he said in German, 'Go to hell, heir of Arthur!'"

"'You're' saying he knew who you are?" Stone said. "*That's* why he tried to kill you?"

Mac cringed and glanced over at Genevieve.

"Who's Mendenberg?" she cried.

Stone slid down in his seat. "Whoops," he mumbled.

"I'll explain later," said Mac, instinctively raising a hand to cover the bruises on his neck.

"But *how* did a Nazi in the most remote place on Earth this side of Antarctica know who Mac was?" Merrill asked.

"That's what Colin is going to help us find out."

Dozens of buildings sprawled across a valley nestled between green, tree-covered Appalachian hills not far from Alexandria, Virginia. The City that Swaywell Built, as believers affectionately called it, consisted of the lecture halls, administrative buildings, and dorms of Williams Jennings Bryan College, an evangelical Christian school named after the famous lawyer, three-time presidential candidate, and chief prosecutor in the Scopes Monkey Trial. There was also a small library, office buildings, a two-hundred room hotel, a convention center, and at the heart of it all, Swaywell's Church of Eternal Vigilance. In its center sat the 10,000-seat glass and aluminum cathedral with its four wings extending out in the shape of a cross. One housed the Church's administrative, foundation and program offices, conference rooms, and broadcast studios. Another contained daycare and charter school classrooms. The third a dormitory for teachers and visiting church members. And the last, a concourse of shops and restaurants. Beyond the campus, apartments and homes lined broad asphalt paths that crisscrossed the valley, along which scampered long motorized trams carrying students, congregants, residents, church officials, teachers, and visitors. Vehicles were not allowed on the paths, only in the massive parking lot next to the church where the only road leading into the valley ended.

Not unusual for a Sunday morning, the parking lot and cathedral were filled to capacity. Inside, an announcer said in a deep Ed McMahon-ish voice, "And now, from the Church of Eternal Vigilance in Alexandria, Virginia, Dr. Johnny Swaywell is pleased to present another hour of the Christian Vigil, news and its meaning as revealed by America's most noted biblical scholar. Ladies and gentlemen, heeeeerrre's Dr. Johnnyyyyyy Swaywell!"

The Reaganesque Reverend swaggered across a vast rotating stage in the center of the circular cathedral, waving to the audience. Behind him, the biggest choir this side of Salt Lake City sang, *When the Saints Come Marching In*. As Swaywell reached his multimedia pulpit, the applause reached its crescendo, mixing with cheers and the occasional 'Bless you, Johnny!' thrown in for good measure. He raised his hands into the air and with his signature smile, slowly brought them down in a prayerful gesture.

The audience dutifully fell silent.

"Dear Lord, bless us with Thy protection during these, the dark and final days before the Judgement. Help me to guide our leaders with Your wisdom and punish the wicked with Thy wrath. In Your name and the name of Thy son, Jesus Christ, we pray. Amen."

"Amen!" cried the congregation in unison and sat down.

"Welcome, my fellow Christians," he went on, his voice upbeat and rich. "Another glorious Sunday brings us another week closer to our reward in heaven. And why?" He cupped his hand to his ear and leaned forward.

"He's coming!" came the booming reply.

"Praise the Lord, He's coming. And thanks to the Church of Eternal Vigilance, His Word is spreading. Fifty million weekly viewers join us for the Christian Vigil, a hundred million members tithe each month, and half a *billion* Christians receive the Vigil e-newsletter worldwide."

Applause again filled the cathedral.

"Half a *billion* Christians," he repeated with pride. "But what does being a Christian mean?" He cupped his hand to his ear once more.

"We are persecuted!"

"Yes! And by whom?"

"God-haters!"

Swaywell nodded and bellowed, "Atheists and secularists! Those who have forsaken God and hate everything Jesus stands for! But, *you!* You *love* Jesus, don't you?"

"Yes!"

"And Jesus loves you, my children. Jesus wants us to reclaim America and I have a very special guest this morning to help us do just that. Please give a warm Crystal Cathedral welcome to Senator Mitchell Thomas!"

A respectful ovation greeted the outsider as he made his way across the stage, waving and smiling. He met the Reverend in front of two chairs and a small table with water glasses and a Bible resting on it. They shook hands, sat down, and for several minutes chatted like old friends, swapping light-hearted stories of the famous people they'd met and talking about their families.

"Well, Mitchell," said Swaywell, "I understand you have an important announcement to make."

"I do, Johnny," said the Senator, turning to the nearest TV camera.

"My fellow Christians," began the Senator, "and my fellow Americans," he added as an afterthought, "after talking with my family, consulting with the good Reverend, praying to the Lord, and searching my heart, I have decided to run for President of the United States."

The congregation sat dumbfounded. Few among them had even heard Thomas's name before this morning and most wondered why they should care. But, when the Reverend began clapping, they dutifully joined in.

For the next twenty minutes, Thomas and Swaywell discussed the issues facing America via carefully scripted banter. In a casual tone, the Reverend asked questions and Thomas reflected for a moment before giving supposedly spontaneous answers with relevant Bible passages thrown in for good measure.

When they exhausted their script, the good Reverend stood up. "Thank you for sharing this blessed news with us, Mitchell. I'm sure the good Lord will lead you to victory."

"God bless you, Johnny," said the Senator. "And may God take back America!"

That brought the audience to their feet, applauding and cheering.

"We'll be praying for you!" Swaywell said above the din, and Thomas made his way off the stage. "Remember everyone, the primary is June 8th. For those of you here today, our cathedral is precinct 12. For those of you at home, remember to vote for Mitchell Thomas in your state's primary.

"Now stay right there! My sermon's coming up and you won't want to miss what *Revelations* has to say about Mitchell Thomas, the Antichrist, and the future of America."

The organ played, the choir sang softly in the background, and donation plates passed down pews.

Over the next few days, the late-night variety shows gave Thomas's announcement a dismissive Dan Quayle/Sarah Palin/Donald Trump treatment. The conservative news media mostly kept their mouths shut and pens capped, the mainstream media treated it as a quixotic fluff piece, and Jameson's White House acknowledged nothing.

In an old Astin Martin with Clarice Ambrose behind the wheel, Cameron, Genevieve, and Mac crossed the English countryside. He'd met their driver six years before when Merrill brought him to Camleton for the first time. She'd been 16 then and terribly shy.

Now in her last year at London College, she'd talked non-stop since leaving Victoria Station. Downshifting, she turned onto a rutted dirt road followed closely by a rented Jaguar SUV carrying Merrill, Taylor, T.J., Marion, Colin, and Sean. The road switched back and forth, gradually climbing up a steep range of hills.

When they crested the ridge, Mac pointed to a clutch of old buildings far out on the valley floor. "That's where we're going. Camleton."

"Oh, how beautiful!" said Genevieve.

"It is," he said, "but after sleeping in riverboats and tents for a month, I wouldn't mind being home in Geneva."

"It'll be wonderful having you home," said Genevieve.

Cameron giggled.

"Hey, let's go apartment hunting for you two when we get back. Find you a place of your own."

"We *have* our own place," Cameron told him.

"I'm sure Marion and T.J. love having you stay with them, sweetie, but we shouldn't impose on them anymore than we already have."

"We're not imposing," said Genevieve.

Mac looked from one to the other. "Well, let's find you your own home anyway."

"We have a home, Daddy," said Cameron.

Mac's heart sank. "You mean…you went home to Traverse?"

"No!" cried Cameron. "We moved into *our* home."

"You moved already? An apartment? A house – you're renting a house?"

"No!" Cameron said with childish exasperation and Mac gave Genevieve a help me look.

She kissed him on the cheek. "We moved into *your* home."

A rush of relief followed by a feeling of complete joy surged through him.

"I hope you don't mind."

"Mind?" he said, reaching over the seat to squeeze her hand. "That's wonderful!" He brushed Cameron's cheek. "That makes me the happiest Daddy in the world."

"Yay!" she shouted and without missing a beat said, "I'm hungry."

They laughed, and Clarice said into the rearview mirror, "There'll be plenty of good English food waiting for us, little one."

"Good English food, huh?" Mac said wryly. "Isn't that kind of an–?"

"Oxymoron?" Clarice finished for him.

"Uh, well, yeah."

"You said that to Elder Merrill the first time you visited us, *and* every bloody time you have dinner at the hall!"

"I…yeah, but," Mac stammered, his face reddening. "It's just that–" He sighed. "Alright, alright. It's good food. If you're not too into flavors," he mumbled.

"Mac," Genevieve said with a chastising smile.

"Alright, alright," he chuckled.

The Astin Martin whined and rattled its way down the hillside and into the valley. Turning off the rutted dirt road onto a country two-lane, they headed north past well-tended fields, moss-covered stone walls, ancient-looking farm houses, modest orchards, and small stands of gnarled hardwoods that gave the valley a pleasant cast and bespoke of a long, gracious history.

Mac pointed up at the jagged ridge of the surrounding hills. "Up there are the remains of a broad stone wall that once circumnavigated the entire valley. Longer than Hadrian's," he said, referring to the Roman wall built across the entire width of England two thousand years ago. "It was 15 feet wide, 10 high, and had a walkway for guard patrols, forts every two miles to garrison troops, and massive wooden gates to allow troops and traders to pass. The valley was the Roman province of Camulodunum with fourteen towns, a university, a circus for chariot races and public performances, a hundred thousand Roman citizens, and a Curia – a sort of castle. The Council of Elders made Camulodunum their home province and the Curia their seat of government. That was fifteen hundred years ago."

Passing through the quaint village of Camleton with its handful of shops and houses, Clarice downshifted and turned onto a dirt path leading into a small wood. She pulled up to an old hall with an eclectic gathering of cars, bicycles, and horse-drawn carriages parked willy-nilly around it.

Fieldstones and mortar formed three of the building's walls, and rough-hewn beams framed the doorway and windows. But the fourth wall, much older and made of kiln-fired bricks, rose up to the tree branches and extended beyond the building into the woods.

"This is Clan Camulodunum Hall, and the wall there," Mac said, pointing, "is all that remains of the Curia."

Clarice stopped opposite the doors and the four of them got out just as the Range Rover pulled up alongside.

"This is where Merrill brought you to learn about your ancestry?" Genevieve said.

"Yeah. Just two weeks after I, well," he didn't want to say he'd almost killed himself in front of Cameron. "After you-know-what."

Merrill overheard their conversation as he and the others climbed out of the Range Rover and said, "I convinced the Clan Elders the time had come to bring your father home." He swept Cameron up in his arms. "Not in a millennium and a half has the tide of events been so unique, both good and bad, ebbing closer to the end and to the beginning all at once."

Sean said, "You done waxing poetic, old man? 'Cause I'm hungry."

"Me, too! cried Cameron as Merrill mumbled, "No bloody respect."

Laughing, they started for the entrance to the hall when the double doors opened wide and out stepped Kyle Dunham, Keeper of the Clan Camulodunum.

"Your subjects await, little princess," Merrill proclaimed, handing Cameron to Kyle.

Genevieve walked over and hugged them both.

"Good to see you again, lass," said Kyle.

"And you, Keeper."

He gave Marion a one-armed hug and said to T.J., Sean, and Taylor, "Y'are always welcome here, friends of the Clan."

"Thanks. What's for dinner?" Sean said.

"What a class act," drolled Taylor.

"Hearty English cuisine at its finest," the Keeper answered.

"English cuisine, huh?" Mac said. "Isn't that kind of an—"

"Oxymoron?" cried the chorus of Clansfolk crowded just inside the doors.

"Alright, alright," he smiled with a flush of his cheeks.

"Come. All of you!" declared the Keeper, and with Cameron in his arms he waded into the throng of Clansfolk. "You're newest heir!"

γ

"*The enjoyment of power inevitably corrupts the
judgment of reason, and perverts its liberty.*"

– Immanuel Kant

"*The ultimate measure of a man is not where he stands
in moments of comfort and convenience, but where
he stands at times of challenge and controversy.*"

– Dr. Martin Luther King

A pleasant fire glowed in the great hearth. A wild boar and several large pots of soups and stews hung above the flames, their delectable aromas filling the hall. The menfolk readied the tables and benches for the feast while the womenfolk prepared platters of food.

The sound of a wooden mallet tapping a keg echoed off the ancient brick wall as the Clansfolk sat down to dine, smoke their pipes, swap stories, and catch up on the latest family happenings. Kyle, the archivist and de facto leader of the Clan, gestured for the visitors to sit at his table.

"Mac says you're quite a storyteller," Genevieve said to Merrill.

Marion huffed. "If you like pompousness with your tall tales."

Several of the nearby Clansfolk snickered.

"Pompous? Me?" Merrill replied. "Shall I tell you what *you* are?"

"Whoa, whoa, whoa, whoa," T.J. interrupted, trying not to laugh. "Hold on."

"Merrill," Kyle gently admonished with the respect and love that 50 years of friendship carried with it. Not that good Englishmen spoke of such emotions.

"Aye, Keeper," Merrill replied with a half-grin.

"I was hoping you'd tell us about the Clan," added Genevieve.

"Of course, lass. Who better than a Professor of history from Cambridge University to tell the story," he proclaimed, tapping himself on the chest.

Marion gave an embellished sigh. "There's the pomposity."

The Elder leaned over to Cameron. "She's just a jealous Clansman."

"Clans-*person*, you old misogynist," Marion snapped.

"Old?" he retorted. "*Who's* old?"

"*You're* old."

"And am I the pot or the kettle?" said the Elder.

Kyle got to his feet with a sigh and said, "*I'll* tell the story. Otherwise, lass, you may never hear it."

Chuckles from the Clansfolk rolled down the tables.

"Young one, I first met your father just a few days after you were born. I told him that to truly understand our Clan he must learn about fourth century post-Roman Britain, and a man known as the Second. One need only read Gibbon's *The Decline and Fall of the Roman Empire* to learn how seemingly immortal greatness can destroy itself. Not in one self-aware, catastrophic blunder, but in countless missteps and conflicts that slowly tear apart a society. Since we have not the time, nor would me Clansfolk allow me to read Gibbon's masterpiece word for word," and several raised their mugs in jovial agreement, "I shall merely touch upon the most salient points."

Cameron didn't understand much of what Kyle was saying but was too shy to tell him so. Her mother, however, was enthralled.

"Well before the time of Christ," the Keeper went on, "the Roman Empire took as its own the ancient Greek principles of democracy. But, centuries of plundering and profiteering from the Empire's many conquests had so corrupted the Senate and Assembly that Julius Caesar decided to purify them by fire. He led his army south from Gaul – the territories from the Alps to Britain – defeated General Pompey's defending army, and conquered Rome. Once enthroned, he quickly relegated the Senate and Assembly to mere advisory bodies, united the Empire's conquered lands into a single commonwealth, instigated copious reforms, turned the old republic into an imperial monarchy, and in the process reinvented himself as Father of the Empire, Imperator, Consul, and Pontifex Maximus."

"Pontifex Maximus?" said Genevieve in surprise. "The Pope?"

"Aye," said Merrill. "The Emperors were the political *and* spiritual leaders of Rome from the time of Caesar on." He took a swig of ale. "The rituals and regalia of the emperors survive to this day in the Roman Catholic Church, the Vatican, and the Holy Father." He let out a hearty belch.

"Merrill!" Marion cried. "In front of the child!"

"Like she's never burped," retorted Merrill. "Come, lass, give us a burp, eh?"

"Merrill!"

T.J. slid down in his chair.

Cameron gave a part huff, part hiccup and fell into a fit of giggles.

"*That's* a good lass," laughed the Elder.

With an amused shake of his head, Kyle went on. "Alas, as immortalized by William Shakespeare, Caesar's reign was all too brief. At the time of his death, the Roman Empire stretched 3000 miles from Iberia in the west to Persia in the east, and 2000 miles from the Sahara in the south to Hadrian's Wall in the north."

"A mere stone's throw from our wee dale," Merrill added proudly.

"The poet Claudian wrote that the empire, 'took the conquered to her bosom, turning her subjects to citizens by the bond of affection,' and so it did with Britain. Her people were thoroughly Roman and content to be so, until 410 AD, or CE for Common Era as they say now, when the empire suffered her greatest defeat in

800 years, the Sack of Rome by the Visigoths. Emperor Honorius ordered Britain's Roman legions back to the mainland to protect the Eternal City and Britain found herself alone for the first time in four centuries.

"What little the world knows of the years that followed came from the pen of just one man, a priest named Gildas of Clyde. He wrote that not long after the Roman legions left, attacks by the native clans of Scotland and Ireland began along the old Roman frontiers. To deal with them, a nobleman named Vortigern and the Council of Elders hired Saxon mercenaries from the mainland. For a time, their decision seemed a wise one. The Britons and Saxons put down the raids, Vortigern's daughter was married to the Irish king, an acceptable border arrangement was negotiated with the Scotts, and peace was restored. Having fulfilled their purpose, the Saxon mercenaries were free to return home. But instead, they settled in the southeastern lowlands, grew in number and restlessness, and finally rose up against the Britons. Village after village fell before their onslaught. Fear reigned for thirteen years until Vortigern finally convinced the Saxon leader Hengest and his warlords to negotiate a treaty of co-existence. But, when Vortigern and the Council arrived at the designated meeting place, Hengest's soldiers ambushed them. Three hundred Elders died that day, and with them nearly all memory of Roman Britain.

"The next generation was a dark one indeed," Kyle said solemnly and told the story of Ambrosius, the resistance, Mons Badonicus, and the Second. "To this day, the Clan Camulodunum survives as testament to the Second in hopes of one day resurrecting the world he created." Kyle put his hand on Mac's shoulder. "A day we hope will soon arrive."

The Clansfolk cheered and raised their mugs in salute.

Genevieve squeezed Mac's hand.

The Keeper knelt down before Cameron.

"You, little one, and your father are the last descendants of the Second. Can you guess what his name was?"

She gave him a timid shake of her head.

"His Roman name was Artorius, but after his victory at Mons Badonicus, he wished to be known by his native name of–" All eyes turned to Mac. The Keeper stood, lifted his arms, and as one the Clansfolk cried, "Arthur!"

Another cheer and another toast.

"You've heard of King Arthur, little one?" said the Keeper.

Her eyes lit up. "Knights and magic and horses and beautiful princesses?"

"That's right," said her father, "and I was the real-life Arthur's last living relative until you were born. Now we're both his last relatives. You're Arthur's great, great, great, seventy-five times great granddaughter."

Her eyes grew wide. "I'm a princess?"

A mix of awes and gentle laughter wafted through the hall.

"You'll always be a beautiful princess to me," Mac said with a smile and hugged her.

More awes.

"Stories of Arthur were handed down by word of mouth for centuries," Kyle said, "until finally being put to paper. But, the Arthur and Camelot of those books bear little resemblance to the real Arthur and Camulodunum. Geoffrey of Monmouth's chivalrous knights were everything the lords of his time were not, Malory put them in suits of armor, and Tennyson gave them Victorian ideals. None told what life in fifth century Britain *really* was like. If it were not for the Clan's first Keeper, who kept a detailed record of Arthur's accomplishments and what life was like in the days of Camelot, all knowledge of that glorious time would've been lost to history forever."

Genevieve asked, "Why have you kept the Clan a secret all this time?"

"Our existence and mission aren't really a secret, lass," Merrill answered, "at least not in these parts. It's just that no one seems to give us much thought. They simply write us off as eccentrics living in an ancient, out-of-the-way corner of the British Isles. But, for fifteen-hundred years we've waited for the right heir to come along at the right time to bring a new Camelot to the world."

With glowing, expectant faces, the Clansfolk again looked to Mac.

All the attention was taking its toll, and he mumbled to no one in particular, "I wish they'd stop doing that."

Those within earshot chuckled.

"Not the Camelot of fiction, mind you," Kyle continued, "the real Camelot. Camulodunum. In this valley, in this *very Curia*," his hand reached out and touched the ancient brick wall, "Arthur and the men who fought at Mons Baddonicus formed the Council of Camulodunum, the descendants of whom are gathered here today."

"Whoa!" Sean exclaimed. "You all can trace your family lineage back fifteen-hundred years?"

"Aye," boasted Merrill.

"That's incredible!"

"You too, Kyle?" said Genevieve.

"The Council's first Keeper was an ancestor of mine, a historian who served as Arthur's advisor and archivist. What I am keeper of is his record of everyday life in Camulodunum, its economic, democratic, and social achievements, and how Arthur forestalled the coming of the Dark Ages to our island nation. Every Keeper since has added to that record the accomplishments and setbacks of the Clan up to this day."

"And the people you call 'friends of the Clan' are those who honor what the Clan stands for?" said Genevieve.

"Aye. Some are from families who've helped the Clan for generations and some, like Michael, are first-generation friends. They're often politically well-connected, wealthy, powerful–"

"Or poor and insignificant," T.J. deadpanned, tapping himself on the chest.

"Poor perhaps," said Kyle with a smile, "but never insignificant, and every friend is welcome." The Keeper took Cameron's hand and turned to Mac. "Remember that within you lies greatness. You'll find contentment in knowing you can achieve anything you set your mind to. But with such blessing comes great responsibility. To wear the mantle of leadership lightly, one must master circumspection, demonstrate nobility, and earn the respect of others by returning it in kind. But to become a great leader, you will have to overcome great challenges, prove your worthiness, and in so doing inspire others. Long ago, the Clan accepted the quest to found a new Camelot...a quest that can only come to pass when a worthy heir of Arthur is present in our world today...you, lad. But know this: it will neither be easy or safe. You will face those who wish nothing less than your destruction. Who want to turn the world into a merciless autocracy. Therefore, you must prevail! You must be a beacon of hope for the meek and good...the leader of all leaders of all time...the one who takes the world into a new age...a Novum Orbis Regium!'"

Amidst the pleasing sounds of happy conversations, the delicate clatter of dinnerware, and the thunking of mugs came the dull thud of Colin Dunham dropping the leather-bound book from Little Deutschland on the table. "We ready to talk about this, mates?" he said as he sat down.

Merrill gave a resigned, "Aye," and said to Marion, "Be a good lass and introduce our wee heir to the families?"

She looked from him to the book to Cameron and understood. "Children are women's work, is that it?" she snapped. Nonetheless, she called to a clutch of middle-aged women a few tables over. "Oh, Sarah, dear!" She waved, took Cameron by the hand, and contentedly led her off to be fawned over.

"Nearly ten thousand names in there," Colin revealed. "Birth and death dates. Me and me blokes looked into online newspaper records, historical databases, and genealogical archives to trace them. It turns out they're from nearly every country and period since the fifth century. Many are from our own Clan, from families that have died out completely."

"It's the book of a Keeper, alright," Kyle said grimly. "A Keeper of lineocide."

"At the end of the book there are two names," Colin added uncomfortably with a sideways glance at Mac, "from the most prominent family line, with just dates of birth."

Genevieve gasped. "No!" and tears welled up in her eyes. "Don't let them hurt her!"

"I won't, Gen. I promise," Mac said assuringly and pulled her close.

Sean got to his feet. "Neither will I."

"They'll have to kill me first," said T.J., and he, too, got to his feet.

"That goes for me as well," added Taylor.

"We shall defend her with our lives, lass," said the Keeper and everyone in the hall rose to their feet. "It is our purpose for being."

Genevieve dabbed her eyes with the back of her sleeve. "Thank you," she sniffled. "All of you."

Colin, ashamed of having caused her tears, changed the subject as the murmurs of comradery and a good meal enjoyed resumed all around them. "Guess what we found in them longhouses?"

"You already told us," Mac answered. "Drugs."

"What *else*, mate?"

Mac thought for a moment and took an educated guess. "Paintings, jewelry, first editions of classics, sculptures, gold bullion, and archaeological treasures lost since the 1930's and 40's?"

Colin's jaw dropped. "How'd you bleedin' know, mate?"

"The Nazis were thieves first and foremost," Mac replied in disgust. "Land, money, power, possessions, even people. Anything they could steal for their own selfish use."

"Especially if they could steal it from the Jews," Merrill added acidly. "The Nazis hid their ill-gotten gains in all kinds of places. Bunkers, mines, bank vaults, even the bottom of lakes."

"And in Little Deutschland, apparently," Sean said.

"Are you bringing it all back here?" Mac asked Collin.

He shook his head. "The Louvre, mate."

Impressed, Mac said, "Well done. You'll trace their provenances and return them to their rightful owners?"

"O'course, mate."

"How could we have let the Nazis do what they did?" Genevieve wondered with another sniffle.

Merrill downed what was left of his ale and wiped his mouth on his sleeve.

"Uh, oh," Mac muttered. "Now you've done it."

"What?"

"Awakened the Professor within."

"At the turn of the twentieth century," the Elder pompously began amidst the exaggerated moans and laughter of the Clansfolk. "No bloody respect," he groused. "At the turn of the twentieth century, Germany was the most powerful military nation on Earth, the United States was barely more than a third-world country, and Europe was a political and social tinderbox. Monarchy was being challenged by democracy, feudalism by socialism, capitalism by communism, patriarchy by women's suffrage, elitism by populism, corporations by unions, puritanism by bohemians, and creationism by evolution. Colonialism was at its zenith after four centuries of dividing up the world and no more lands were left to conquer. Imperialism could only continue by conquering the imperialists. The Marquess of Salisbury said, 'The living nations will gradually encroach on the territory of the dying, and the seeds and causes of conflict among civilized nations will speedily appear,' and in 1914 World War One broke out. Tens of millions of people were pointlessly slaughtered in the trenches of eastern and western Europe, wiping out an entire generation and ending with the birth of the Soviet Union in the east and the signing of the Treaty of Versailles in the west."

"Is it true the treaty set the stage for World War Two?" Sean interrupted.

"Partly. It gave the Allies the German Rhineland and the Ruhr in the west, created a new Poland in the east out of German Prussia, established a parliamentary democracy, and imposed staggering war reparations on the country's already weakened economy, creating a severe economic recession and high unemployment."

"Wait, why would parliamentary democracy be bad?" said Sean.

"'Tis a noble enough construct," allowed Merrill, "but it has a messy side as well. To work, it requires a country that's mature and committed to worthy founding principles. It took England *centuries* to evolve its parliamentary form of government, molding it to fit her people and the times. Germany had one day."

Mildred, a flirtatious widow who owned the town bakery and indulged a good deal in her creations, set a full mug of ale down on the table in front of Merrill with a wink and a grin a few teeth short of a set.

"Ah! That's a good lass," said Merrill with a pat on her plentiful posterior. He greedily hoisted the mug and gave a satisfied belch.

"What's the messy side?" said Sean.

"A multiparty system," answered the Elder with another belch. "Often, no single party gains a preponderance of seats, so coalitions of smaller parties have to be cobbled together to create a majority. The smaller parties are often made up of ideological extremists who demand concessions to join the coalition. Once they're in, they gain leverage by threatening to leave unless they get their way, shifting the coalition towards one end of the political spectrum or the other. In times of economic hardship, great social change, or threats to security, membership in smaller extremist parties grows. In truly *desperate* times, real or perceived, they can actually gain enough seats to control the coalition, dominate the country's political agenda, and appoint a new prime minister or president. That's how the Nazis took over Germany."

"Once they did," Mac said, "they demanded complete obedience. Rudolph Hess said the Nazi Party was, 'anchored in uncritical loyalty, in the surrender to Der Führer that does not ask for the why in individual cases, but in the silent execution of his orders.' The Party's members must, 'believe that Der Führer is obeying a higher call to fashion German history,' and that, 'there can be no criticism of this belief.'"

T.J. snorted. "Swap a few words and you'd have a Sunday morning televangelist sermon or a Tea Party stump speech."

"The German parliament gave Hitler emergency powers to deal with the economic crisis facing Germany during the Great

Depression. He immediately began a massive arms build-up, banned secular organizations, burned books he considered threatening, mixed nationalism with religion, outlawed opposing parties, stacked the courts, murdered political rivals, took over the media, and spread conspiracy theories that Jews were stealing what was rightfully theirs, that good German Christians were victims, that the Allies of the Great War wanted to destroy the Fatherland, that the Versailles Treaty was a chain around the peoples' necks, and that Aryan's were descended from antediluvian super warriors who deserved by genetic right to rule–"

"Aunty who?" snickered Sean.

"Pre-Flood," said Mac. "Before Noah. Aryan's were supposedly created by God to be the master race sitting atop an evolutionary hierarchy. In Hitler's world order, the Jews and Gypsies were at the bottom, little better than vermin, making it all the easier to first enslave and then exterminate them."

"Why has there always been such bad blood between Jews and Christians?" wondered Sean.

"Read James Michener's *The Source* for your answer," replied Mac.

"How 'bout a dust jacket explanation?"

"It began with Rome's occupation of Israel," answered Merrill, "when Jews took to violence to force the Romans out. One group, for example, called the Sicarii, would stab unsuspecting Romans at public gatherings and then disappear into the crowds."

"Now the Jews have their own nation, the Palestinians call *them* occupiers," said Sean, "and radical Muslims go into public places and blow themselves up."

"Or drive cars into crowds," said T.J., "or shoot people on the street or stab them on subways."

"Jews and Romans, Arabs and Jews," Taylor grumbled. "Round and round we go."

"'Let he who is without sin cast the first stone,'" Mac agreed and turned to Merrill. "But, back to Sean's question."

"In 66 CE," the Elder continued, "a generation after Jesus' crucifixion, the Jews rose up en masse against the Romans and drove them out of Israel, only to have Titus return in 70 CE with four Imperial legions to destroy Jerusalem. The Temple of Solomon was razed to the ground and its most sacred relics, including the Ark of the Covenant, were carried off to Rome. The Jews were banished from their homeland and the Great Jewish Diaspora began. To every corner of the Empire they went, and wherever they settled they were resented as outsiders who looked and acted differently. By the time Rome faded away and Christians ruled the lands of the old Empire, Jews had been restricted to certain trades, forbidden to own property, and cloistered in city ghettoes. Smart, tenacious, and industrious, they became businessmen, lawyers, accountants, doctors, importers, exporters, and bankers. Successful and wealthy, they were stereotyped by their enemies as stingy and greedy. Time and again, *John 8* would be trotted out and a mob would ransack Jewish homes and businesses."

"I'm a little rusty on my Bible," admitted Sean. "What's *John 8?*"

"'Ye are of your father the devil,' referring to the Jews who turned Jesus over to Pilate. Christians called Jews Christ-killers and made up wild stories about them, the two most slanderous being the 'blood libel' and 'host desecration' myths."

"Which are?" said Sean.

"The blood libel myth claims Jews need the blood of Christian babies to salve the oozing sores God gave them for murdering Jesus, to ease the labor pains of Jewish mothers, to give sight to Jewish babies born blind, and to make Jewish adolescent girls fertile. The host desecration myth claims Jews take unleavened bread after it's transubstantiated into the body of Christ and desecrate it.

"Then, in 1903 *The Protocols of the Elders of Zion* was published. It claimed there was a Jewish plot to subvert the morals of Gentiles, control the press, and manipulate the world's economies. Henry Ford printed 500,000 copies of it and sent them around the U.S. When Hitler came to power in 1933, he used the *Protocols* in his propaganda and many German teachers made it assigned reading."

"Thank God the world'll never see another Hitler," Sean said.

"Don't be so sure, lad. The parallels between the far right in your own country and the rise of German Nazism are far more than superficial and quite disturbing."

"No way, not in America."

Merrill happily considered that a challenge. "It happened before and it is happening again, and I shall give you but the merest of parallels. After World War One, Hitler became disillusioned with what he saw happening to the Germanic people. He began studying the successes and failures of various political movements and came to the Machiavellian conclusion that success depended on learning the art of propaganda, creating a mass movement, appreciating the value of spiritual and physical terror, and having no compunctions about lying and slandering adversaries. Is that not what your far right is doing?"

Sean was about to answer, but Mac said with a half-grin, "Don't bother. He's on a roll."

Merrill went on as if casting pearls to the swine. "Hitler demeaned whatever peoples and races he believed inferior and promised a utopic future of white Aryan domination, plentiful jobs, prosperity, and respect from the Germany's newspapers and radio stations to manipulate public perceptions. William L. Shirer, who was a foreign correspondent in Germany at the time, said, 'notwithstanding the opportunities I had to learn the facts, a steady diet of falsifications and distortions made a certain impression on one's mind and often misled it. The facts of life had become what Hitler and Goebbels, with their cynical disregard for truth, said they were.'

"Your far right berates the media for its supposed liberal bias yet controls a large slice of the media market itself. Fox News, countless web and social media sites, radio talk show hosts and authors like Rush Limbaugh, Glenn Beck, and Ann Coulter. It uses its media channels to mislead, redirect, and convince its consumers to disregard valid, verifiable facts when they contradict the conservative mantra. America's far right has pulled a growing class of citizens away from reality with a psychological war fought on three fronts – economic, theo-social, and fear. Economically, 30-plus years of

pro-business, 'trickle-down' Reaganomics has let big business deci-
mate your manufacturing base and leave many Americans financially
behind. Real incomes have stagnated and for the first time ever, a
generation of Americans will be worse off than their parents. So the
far right blames the Left, says the nation's money and power is being
taken away from white men and given to minorities and women.
The far right promises great paying jobs if only taxes were lower.

"Theo-societally, the far right claims its members are nice, mis-
understood, victimized, God-fearing people pitted against selfish,
demeaning, immoral, good-for-nothings. The far right says America
used to be a lily-white Christian paradise until foreigners, liberal
legislators, and activist judges bollixed everything up.

"H. L. Mencken wrote, 'The aim of practical politics is to keep
the populace alarmed by menacing it with an endless series of hobgob-
lins, all of them imaginary.' Your far right is Mencken in Machiavellian
practice. Newt Gingrich and his doppelgangers created a make-believe America of terrorists around every corner, minorities killing white
people, rampant crime, a collapsing economy, a liberally biased news
media, and an evil federal government on the verge of martial law.

"Hitler's war machine depended on free enterprise and the support of industrialists, so he dissolved trade unions, put an end to
collective bargaining, and set wages according to employers' wishes.
Your far right wants to eliminate regulations, give corporations free
reign, lower taxes, and end collective bargaining, right to work laws,
and the minimum wage.

"Hitler used his Brownshirts, the Sturmabteilung, to violently
disrupt meetings of opposing parties, threaten Jews and commu-
nists, and bend the people to his will. The Stormtroopers of today
are white supremacists, militia groups, campaign rally thugs, and
anti-government nihilists who've created an entire subculture and
on-line world where weak-minded and insecure peoples can com-
miserate, indulge in every conspiracy theory, and reinforce their hatred of minorities, liberals, and Jews.

"Hitler Nazified the schools – textbooks were rewritten, curricula were changed, and teachers who failed to go along were cast

out. Your far right cuts school budgets, breaks teacher unions, channels taxpayer money into charter schools that blur the separation of church and state, takes over school boards, and alters textbooks.

"Hitler vilified the Jews, Slavs, and Gypsies. The far right vilifies Hispanics, Blacks, and Muslims.

"Hitler said it was the 'moral and patriotic duty' of German women to bear children for the Reich and sent young women to schools where they learned to be good Nazi wives and mothers. Your far right revels in misogyny, belittles strong successful women, refuses to pay them as much as they pay men, attacks Planned Parenthood, and restricts women's rights to control their reproductive life.

"And that's merely scratching the surface, lad. Sooner or later, a delusional, xenophobic, racist, misogynistic, megalomaniacal, master propagandist will either become President, or become the Geppetto of a Pinocchio President."

"God forbid," said T.J.

"Can we get back to the ledgers, blokes?" Colin said impatiently.

Mac nodded distractedly, still reflecting on Merrill's comparisons.

"Someone out there is as rich as Midas," began Colin, "and as powerful as Zeus."

That drew Mac's full attention, and everyone else's.

"The drugs from them longhouses were shipped down river to cargo ships bound for Europe and North America, but their sales only accounted for two-percent of the total revenues documented in the ledgers. The rest came from sales of oil, gas, uranium, precious metals, gemstones, phosphates, copper, all kinds of natural resources, shipped from third-world countries and sold on black markets. Hundreds of billions, perhaps *trillions* of Euros were wired to holding companies, who wired it to other holding companies, who wired it to *others*, all of whom existed only on paper. Eventually, the money found its way into secret Viertes Reich bank accounts and used to buy war goods that were documented in still *more* ledgers."

"Michael told me that international arms sales are on the rise," Mac mentioned. "They're already above Cold War levels."

"Was *all* the money spent on war goods?" said Taylor.

"Mostly," Colin replied, "but someone's still sitting on enough cash to make him the richest bloke in the world."

"Who controls the military hardware?" asked Sean.

"That's where it gets *really* bonkers, mate. The arms stockpiles are in 23 third-world countries, all of which have two things in common – each has an IDA loan, and each has a military dictator."

"What's the IDA?" said Genevieve.

"The International Development Association," answered Mac. "It makes loans to third-world countries with low per capita incomes."

"Right," said Colin, "and they're supposed to pay the loans back over 40 years, but they're so big and the countries so poor that they rarely even make *payments*. And that's what those 23 countries did, defaulted. Twenty-three countries that just happen to have the same natural resources that were sold on black markets."

"Boujeau and Schoen worked together at the IDA back in the early Eighties," T.J. revealed.

"Shit," muttered Sean.

Mac recalled, "Kyle talked of a 'conflagration of the world order' and now someone controls a fortune in cash, 23 third-world dictators control a massive armory of advanced weapons, Mitchell Thomas is running for President, dark money is being funneled into the campaigns of far right candidates who hate the UN, I'm being called the Antichrist, a bunch of Nazis hidden away in a jungle for three-quarters of a century killed hundreds of settlers just to force a UN mission to Brazil, and Boujeau named me the Mission Commander."

"But why be afraid of Mac?" implored Genevieve. "He's just one man."

"Arthur was just one man," Merrill replied. "Camelot was just one place, yet a millennium and a half later the world still dreams of both."

"If Mac prevails at the Charter Amendment Conference," observed Kyle, "the General Assembly will become the most influential political body in history and its leader potentially the most powerful person on Earth. There are many who would lose much if that were to happen, many who would do anything to prevent it. Therefore, our path is clear."

Genevieve's heart sank, but still she asked, "And just what would that be?"

"The Charter Amendment Conference takes place in September," Kyle explained. "The United States will hold its Presidential election in November, and the United Nations holds its election for Secretary-General in February."

"So, I announce my candidacy at the conference," said Mac, half as a question, half as a statement.

Kyle nodded. "Aye."

"My god, Kyle," Genevieve cried. "Secretary-General? Why not just put a target on his back and be done with it?"

The Keeper remained silent. There were no words of comfort he could give her.

"Forget all this," she begged Mac. "Come home with us. We'll have a nice, quiet life in Traverse and all this will become just a memory."

Mac took her hand. "That would be wonderful, Gen."

A sense of hope rose within her, and just as quickly she felt the pangs of guilt.

"It would be a dream come true," Mac admitted. "But, after everything the Clan has done, after all these centuries, what the world is facing, I can't turn my back and walk away. I love you very much, Gen. Cameron, too. But, being Arthur's heir means I have a role to play, a destiny to fulfill, even if it means my own death. My life has never really been mine alone. It belongs to the Clan, to Arthur, maybe even to the world. I know it's terribly unfair of me to ask, Gen, but please understand, and please don't give up on me."

Genevieve wiped her eyes and said softly, "I can't lose you again. I can't go through that pain."

Mac's heart sank.

"So, you better live," she told him, "and someday, you better take us home to Traverse."

He let out a long breath. "Well, that's certainly the plan," he smiled.

The Secretary-General set his teacup down on the conference table. "MacCrarey is even more of an international hero now than he was after Cyprus," he said, a dangerous edge to his voice. He stood and walked over to the plate glass window. His office on the 39th floor of the United Nations Secretariat Building had a magnificent view of the East River and Upper East Side of Manhattan. "Your General Mendenberg is in The Hague. Viertes Reich has been discovered. Our black-market revenues and arms purchases are at an end. And MacCrarey is still alive!" He paused, purposefully prolonging the agony of his second-in-command. "There is something about him you've underestimated."

Schoen stood ramrod straight, eyes staring straight ahead, his chiseled face hard as stone. "Arthur is inside MacCrarey, and I have never underestimated him."

Boujeau slowly turned around. "Enough of your fairy tales, Gerhardt," he hissed. "No more excuses, no more failures, and no more Arthur. Just rid me of MacCrarey once and for all."

"Ja, mein Herr. I will find an assassin and–"

"You tried that before and *failed.*"

"I will not fail this time, Mein Herr."

Boujeau walked back to the table. "Be sure you don't. I will not tolerate another failure. Not with the Charter Amendment Conference staring us in the face."

"Ja, mein Herr," Schoen repeated with a click of his heels.

"How is our special shipment progressing?" the Secretary-General asked.

"Well," Schoen replied. "Finding plans was easy enough. One can even find them on the Internet, believe it or not. Finding people to *build* one is another story. But, I was able to find a Russian physicist and an American nuclear engineer who valued a comfortable and early retirement far more than patriotism."

"And when does the *Shkhara* leave port?"

"June 1st, mein Herr. From Poti."

"Very good. Oversee its loading and arming personally, Gerhardt. Understood?"

"Ja, mein Herr. Now, if I may discuss another matter?"

Boujeau waved a dismissive, impatient hand and sat down.

"Swaywell and Thomas have drawn down our St. Thomas account considerably," explained Schoen.

Another dismissive wave of the hand. "Inconsequential."

"How can we guarantee the money will get the results we need? How can we be sure Thomas and enough other far right candidates will win?"

"The Reverend Swaywell preaches constantly of the coming Apocalypse and the Antichrist. Conservative news networks and pundits see threats and conspiracies around every corner. Social media spins the crazy and ignores the sane." A dark smile crossed Boujeau's face. "Thomas is an evangelical puppet and our special shipment, our catastrophe of Biblical proportions, will soon arrive."

It had taken nearly four decades to reach their final objective. Boujeau would win re-election in February, their puppet would be in the White House, a great blitzkrieg would be unleashed, and his glorious Fourth Order would finally come to pass.

A serpentine leer crawled across Schoen's face as a wave of physical pleasure crashed over him. But then, unbidden into his mind, came the image of William Cameron MacCrarey. A dull disquiet settled over him and the muscles beneath the pale skin of his face tautened. "Damn you," he hissed.

The soft sound of creaking boards brought him back to the moment. He spun, ready for a fight, only to find the ship's captain approaching.

Slowly turning back around, Schoen raised his binoculars and surveyed the bay. To the west stretched the Black Sea, its horizon dotted with oilrigs and tankers slowly coming and going from massive docks along the bay's north shore. An eclectic array of passenger and cargo ships crisscrossed the waters between him and the city of Poti, Georgia, at the mouth of the Rioni River to the east. From there would come his long-awaited shipment.

The creaking of the boards stopped. "I've waited a week," the *Shkhara's* grisly sea dog of a captain rasped. "Where the hell's your boat?" The old man had dark, weather-worn skin, long stringy gray hair, and a burned-out cigar stub stuck in the corner of his mouth. The pungent scent of ouzo hung about his threadbare and filthy uniform like a vale.

The Under Secretary-General didn't answer. To have done so would have been beneath him.

Waving the rolled-up nautical chart Schoen had brought with him on the seaplane, the Captain warned, "Don't expect your shipment to make it there by the end of July."

The Under Secretary-General continued to ignore him.

The Captain poked Schoen in the back with the chart. "Did ya hear me?" he barked.

Schoen dropped the binoculars, slid a knife out of the sheath hidden under his left sleeve, and in one fluid motion, loosed a mad slash at the Captain's face. The old man jerked his head back, raising his arm in time to block the attack. The blade sliced through the grease-stained sleeve and cut deep into skin and muscle.

"You crazy bastard!" cried the Captain, backing away.

The Aryan took a step forward, tensed for a counter-attack, his knife at arm's length.

The wizened seadog had been around the world enough times to recognize the longing to kill in Schoen's eyes, and to know there was no shame in walking away. Cursing under his breath, he made his way back down the dock to the gangplank and up to the ship's main deck, all the while trying to stanch the flow of blood from his forearm with his left hand.

A small cargo vessel rounded the stern of a passing ship with two, quick blasts of its horn. Schoen wiped the blade on his pant leg, slid the knife back into its sheath, and followed the trail of blood to the gangplank.

The ship's deck crane lifted rope-baled bundles of crates out of the smaller ship and swung them up and over the *Shkhara's* railing to lower them through an open deck hatch. Schoen crouched along the hatch's edge waiting for the last bundle to drop into the hold, and then leapt out, caught the crane cable, and rode it down into the hold. When the bundle had settled on the hold's floor, he pulled out his knife and sliced through the netting. Reading the stenciling on each box, he found the only one with German rather than Cyrillic lettering, and with a crowbar pried open its plywood side to reveal a skeleton of wood beams holding in place a long, drum-like, brushed steel cylinder. Taking a small screwdriver out of his vest pocket, he unscrewed the cover plate of a small black box fastened to the cylinder's side. From another vest pocket he withdrew a satellite phone and broke open its casing. With practiced efficiency, he hardwired its receiver into the black box's circuitry, set the phone inside, and screwed the cover plate back on. After hammering shut the crate, he climbed up the crane cable with the lithe strength of a man half his age, fastidiously brushed himself off, and causally made for the gangplank.

The Imperial Fund was one of thousands of 501(c)4 non-profits founded since the 2009 Supreme Court ruling in *Citizens United for Freedom vs. the Federal Election Commission*. The Court had ruled that under the Constitution, non-profits had free speech rights like human beings did. Even *more* free speech rights, in fact, since they could spend any amount of money they wanted on political candidates and lobbying while real people had to obey spending limits set so as not to unduly sway elections. *Citizens United* brought billions of dark dollars – money from donors whose names were kept secret – into the coffers of political parties and candidates, an amount exponentially more than all the contributions of real people combined.

"As you can see," the Fund's Nixonian CFO began, "we have quite a nice bottom-line."

His attractive administrative assistant – the 'office girl' he called her – set a tray of pastries on the polished redwood table and turned for the door. Swinging his laser pen from the Mt. Everest-like graph on the screen to *her* bottom line, the men around the table – and they were all men – watched admiringly as she left the room.

Most of the Imperial Fund's Board of Directors were members of the Christian National Separatists Political Action Committee who wrote eight-figure checks to the Fund every four years, and this election season was shaping up to yield the best return on their investment since Reagan. The ROI they wanted was to abolish corporate taxes, labor unions, government regulations, and countless other things they felt hamstrung their free exercise of capitalism and the power they believed should be theirs.

And the upstart Senator from Ohio they'd met on St. Martinez over the holidays promised to be a pliant candidate and a perfect puppet President.

Swinging the laser pen from his secretary's assets to Mt. Everest again, the CFO paged the PowerPoint to the next screen. "The Secretary-General's contributions this year have been most generous." As if on cue, his cellphone rang. "Excuse me, gentlemen," he said, extracting it from his suit coat pocket. "Speak of the Devil," he chuckled and pressed Accept. "Yes, sir?"

"You may proceed as planned," said René Boujeau.

"Very good, sir. And may I say on behalf of the Board–"

The line went dead.

Flushing slightly, he cleared his throat and announced, "We've the green light to proceed, gentlemen," and began punching in another number.

After several rings, a gruff voice barked into the receiver. "What?"

"Is everything ready?" said the CFO, his voice suddenly void of all pleasantness.

"Oh! Uh, yes, sir," the now-respectful man replied. "Been workin' double shifts, just like you asked."

"Ship everything. Now," ordered the fund manager, and then he promptly hung up.

His instant smile returned. "Our warehouse across the Hudson will deliver everything to the Hoboken post office tomorrow morning, two months to the day before the Republican National Convention begins."

"Why the government?" groused a board member. "Why not a private carrier?"

"Well," the CFO hesitated, "I hate to admit it, but the U.S. Postal Service is still the most cost-effective and efficient game in town. And the most accommodating. After all, it isn't every day you mail 48 *million* copies of a DVD."

The other Board members chuckled, and the protestor grumbled, "Yeah, well, the government can't do anything as well as a business can."

Minimizing the PowerPoint, the CFO clicked a video icon and up came the pseudo-documentary about to be mailed to homes all across the country. The words *Satan's Chosen* appeared over a background of flames. Dark, ominous music played as a video appeared of the second plane flying into the World Trade Center. Pictures of people jumping to their deaths from a hundred floors up flashed by. Footage of the terrorist attacks in Paris, Jerusalem, Boston, San Bernardino, Dallas, Bagdad, Cairo, London, and Orlando came next, complete with burning buildings, sirens, screaming bystanders, and bloodied, charred and dismembered bodies. The video segued to images of ubiquitous Arab children, women in headscarves, and fatigue-clad young men holding rifles and screaming words of praise to Allah. A vitriolic speech by a Grand Imam demonizing the West morphed into a crowd of Muslims chanting, "Death to America." Pictures of mosques in American cities panned across the screen as a Muslim cleric read passages from the Koran, calling for the merciless slaughter of infidels. Clips of Democratic politicians praising freedom of religion, vilifying President Jameson, bemoaning NSA spying, and decrying torture played one after the other. Pictures of immigrants crowding southern border crossings slid across the screen. Former President Obama appeared, proudly declaring that all American troops had been withdrawn from the Middle East, followed by videos of ISIS beheadings and mass graves in Syria. A news clip of the Iran nuclear limitation agreement signing played next, followed by videos of uranium enrichment plants, rockets streaking from Gaza into Israel, and Netanyahu calling Obama an Arab sympathizer. A 1950's clip of a mushroom cloud rising into a perfectly clear blue sky played as snippets of sermons by well-known televangelists could be heard in the background. The preachers damned Islam, warned that the Holy Land would be overrun by Muslim hoards, and blamed liberalism for everything from 9/11 to homosexuality. Next came a stump speech by a far right Presidential candidate telling a room full of cheering supporters that every immigrant should be electronically tagged and if they so much as sneeze they should be deported. That was followed by Johnny Swaywell standing on his circular stage predicting a terrorist attack on America's Heartland so bloody and horrific that it would lead to the End Times. The sound of his voice reading the words of *Revelations* could be heard while pictures flitted across the screen of hurricanes, earthquakes, tornadoes, floods, droughts, fields of failed crops, swarming flies, slaughtered cattle, aborted fetuses, men kissing men, teenagers shooting heroin, police officers dead in the streets, and finally the Antichrist, William Cameron MacCrarey, standing beside the flag of the United Nations.

The screen faded to black, the lights went on, and the men seated around the table gave a self-congratulatory round of applause. The CFO said smugly, "The DVDs will arrive at voters' homes by week's end."

Mac stood on the deck of his condo gazing up at the stars and wondering, as he'd done so many times in his life, whether anyone was looking back. With a sigh, he looked out from his vantage point atop the ridge of Mission Point – the peninsula that divided Grand Traverse Bay into its eastern and western halves – at the twinkling lights of Traverse lining the bay's southern shore.

Traverse was a typical, though touristy northern Midwestern town and he loved being here with Genevieve and Cameron. They made his house feel like a home for the first time. Unfortunately, they could only stay a week this summer since he had his hands full preparing for the Charter Amendment Conference which started in a month.

For now, though, he was where he most wanted to be, the place he'd made his home and where he'd met Genevieve on a sunny July day nine years before. The Cherry Festival was in full swing and downtown Traverse was packed with people and street vendors. A dozen blocks up Union he finally found a parking space for his 1968 red Mustang convertible and then walked back through town. He made his way through the crowds to the marina and out to the end of the breakwater. From there, he could take in the whole beachfront with a glance.

The festival bandstand and carnival midway competed with volleyball nets and sunbathers on the beach. Speedboats, sailboats, parasailers, and jet skiers crisscrossed the bay all the way out to Lake Michigan. Cabin cruisers from all over the country filled the births of the marina and craft tents and food trucks lined the street running between the beach and downtown.

A breeze carried the scent of grilling hamburgers, corn dogs, caramel corn, and cotton candy out to the breakwater, and with a growl from his stomach, he headed back into the fray. In line at a fresh-squeezed lemonade stand, he noticed a woman he guessed was in her mid-30's at a nearby game booth. The breeze from the bay gently blew her long auburn hair about her shoulders. She had bright blue eyes and wore a copper sundress that accentuated her shapely figure.

He bought two lemonades and walked over as casually as his racing heart would let him. Handing her one of the drinks, he said, "Hi. I'm Mac," a bit too business-like he decided. Her smile said this sort of thing happened all the time and, "I'm Genevieve," conveyed in two words that he didn't have long to prove himself. So, he started up a conversation and led her along the midway past the booths and rides. They talked and laughed until the afternoon became evening and they found themselves at a romantic dockside bistro. Afterwards they took a bottle of wine and two plastic cups out to the beach and watched the sun set over the bay.

"She's asleep," Genevieve said as she came through the sliding door from the living room. Noticing the dreamy look in his eyes, she said with a smile, "What have *you* been thinking about?"

"How lucky I am," he said and kissed her.

"Mmmm. Good answer."

"A glass of cherry Port, my dear?" he said with his best imitation of a stuffy, high-born Englishman.

She placed her hands on her shapely hips. "Wine, moonlight, a sleeping daughter. Are you trying to take advantage of me?"

"Take advantage? Never," he said, taking the bottle of Port out of the ice bucket sitting on the patio table. "Get you in bed? Oh, yeah."

She giggled and wrapped her arms around his waist.

"I love you so much," he whispered. "I always have, and I always will."

"I love you, too," she echoed softly. "It's the easiest thing I've ever done."

He kissed her again and twisted the corkscrew into the bottle. "We have great wines here, don't we?"

"And cherries and apples and peaches. I just wish the summers lasted longer."

"Yeah, me, too." *Pop!* "We're half-way between the North Pole and the equator, and the 45th parallel runs through all the great wine regions of the world, even France. The length of the days during growing season, cool nights, moist air rising up the hills from the bay, the contrasting seasons, and rich soil makes Traverse the ideal place for growing grapes."

He poured two glasses of the rich red liqueur, picked them up, and led her to the railing. At the end of the bay, a ship slowly crossed the horizon of Lake Michigan.

"Ocean freighter," he noted.

"How do you know?"

"Great Lakes ore boats are low and long." Pointing at the horizon, he said, "Her running lights are high and clustered together."

"Whenever I see a ship like that I wonder what ports of call her sailors have been to," Genevieve mused. "What exotic places they've seen, what fascinating people they've met."

"You're such a romantic," he said, handing her a glass.

"Look who's talking," she said with a smile, and they drank their wine in silence, watching the ship sail east.

Viktor, the *Shkhara's* communications officer, leaned against the rusty, portside railing watching the distant lights of Traverse. He took a drag on his Turkish cigarette and day-dreamed of a girl waiting for him back home in Poti. Just this one last trip, he'd told her, and they'd have enough money to get married. They'd never be apart again, he promised. Tomorrow, he'd jump ship in Chicago to buy a ring and when next he sailed into Poti, she'd be waiting for him on the quay. He'd run down the gangplank, fall into her arms, give her the ring, and ask her to marry him. With a wistful smile and a sigh, he flicked the cigarette butt into the lake and took a last look at the city lights before heading below for the night.

The following afternoon, the first mate of the *Shkhara* reached for the radio mic. "Skyline, sir," he announced.

Out on the main deck, the grisly old captain halted his berating of the chief engineer, looked past the bow, and unclipped the radio from his belt. "On my way," he growled.

No sooner had he walked through the doorway of the bridge than he ordered the young communications officer to, "Call the Secretary-General!"

The 20-something's face paled. "Aye, Captain," Viktor replied, turning back to his console. "Mother of Mary," he whispered, "the Secretary-General."

"The cell," the captain reminded him impatiently. "Call him on the *cell,* and patch him into the cabin speaker."

"Aye, Captain," replied the young man anxiously. "Of course." He rummaged through the console drawers, found the phone, and peeled off the crumpled piece of paper taped to it. Then, he plugged one end of an audio cord into the phone's jack and the other end into the console's speaker port. He flipped the ON switch and read the number scribbled on the piece of paper the captain had given him with the warning, "You'll be fish bait if you lose this." He dialed the number, pressed SEND, and turned to the captain.

Through the bridge speakers came a single ring followed by a click and the booming voice of Secretary-General René Boujeau. "You can see the city, Kalla?" he said.

"Aye, sir," the captain answered.

Viktor had never heard the captain so deferential before.

"What is the tallest structure you see?" said Boujeau.

"B'Alna?" the captain asked his First Mate.

The captain's oldest and most trusted shipmate lifted his binoculars. "Two black towers with radio antennas atop each."

"The one to the left is the Willis Tower, Kalla," said Boujeau. "Some still call it the Sears Tower. Fourteen-hundred feet high, the tallest building in the Western Hemisphere for 13 years before the Americans rebuilt the World Trade Center. Set a course for it and anchor as close to shore as you can. Understood?"

"Aye, sir. But–" He hesitated

"Yes?" Boujeau said impatiently.

"Sir, the docks are to the south. Where are we to off-load our cargo?"

"I'll disperse your cargo myself, Kalla. Do not worry."

"Sir?" said the captain.

"Let me know when you are at anchor," Boujeau ordered and unceremoniously ended the call.

The Secretary-General read reports, made notes, sent emails, but never made a call and never left his desk. When the glowing red dot slowly moving across the GLOSAT satellite map on his computer screen finally stopped, he put aside his papers and increased the resolution. Lake Michigan's coastline and the streets of Chicago's Loop came into focus.

His office door quietly opened and closed. The Secretary-General didn't look up. He didn't have to.

"Apparently you were watching your screen, too, Gerhardt," he said. "Hard to imagine, isn't it? After all these years?"

"Ja, mein Herr. After all these years," Schoen answered distractedly before eagerly saying, "May I, mein Herr? Bitte?"

The twitching of his partner's fingers made the Secretary-General chuckle deep and slow. "I imagined you'd want the *honor.*"

He opened his desk drawer and took out the twin to the cell-phone sealed inside the crate with German stenciling on its side. Tossing it to Schoen who caught it one-handed, Boujeau watched the man in morbid amusement as he hungrily dialed a number from memory. With every press of a key, his breathing quickened with ravenous intensity as if some pent up carnal desire was about to be released in one, great eruption.

"Hi, Hon!" Bob Derry said as he knotted his silk tie into a half-Windsor. The phone on hands-free, he stood behind the desk in his 86th floor Willis Tower office watching his reflection in the floor-to-ceiling window. "I'll be leaving right after my meeting."

"You told me that last time," his suburban housewife gently scolded, "and you didn't get home 'til the boys were in bed."

"Promise. I wouldn't miss our date night if the world was coming to an end."

"I made reservations for us at that little Italian place you like so much," she told him, her words tinged with an alluring nuance.

"Aw, that's great, hon. Meet me at the station in Downers Grove?"

"I'll be there by 4:30. The boys'll be with me."

"Your sister knows she's got 'em overnight?"

"Uh-huh. Oh! Guess who I ran into at the store?" and off she went on the morning's happenings.

Bob finished with his tie, giving an occasional, "Uh-huh," as he daydreamed of their night alone together and stared out at the great lake. "Hmmm. That's odd," he muttered.

She stopped in mid-sentence. "What is?" she asked, a bit offended.

"Oh, sorry, hon. Um, remember that marina my boss has his yacht at?"

"Near Grant Park," she answered.

"Yeah. Well, a huge ocean freighter's anchored off its breakwater."

Eight-hundred miles away, Schoen pressed the last number. The cellphone's digital signal beamed up to the nearest geosynchronous GLOSAT satellite and daisy-chained through two others before streaming down to the cell's twin secreted away in the *Shkhara's* hold. The twin came to life, a circuit closed, and a jolt of electricity ran down the wire leading not to the phone's speaker, but to a firing circuit. A charge of gunpowder exploded, sending a marble-sized ball of plutonium-241 careening down a carbide steel barrel into a basketball-sized sphere of the same highly radioactive element. Combined, the plutonium surpassed its critical mass and the temperature in the magnetic holding chamber rocketed upwards. The atoms' nuclear bonds tore apart in a chain reaction, unleashing titanic amounts of energy in a blinding, cataclysmic explosion! The searing heat vaporized everything in the blast wave's path. The *Shkhara*, her crew, the lake water, the marina, the shoreline, Grant Park, museums, hotels, apartments, offices, stores. Block after block of The Loop disappeared, the ashen remains of buildings, furnishings, cars, buses, trucks, park benches, street lamps, asphalt, cement, and human flesh rising up in a massive black mushroom cloud that turned day into night.

The blast wave rushed towards the tower and Bob Derry had just enough time left in his life to utter the words, "Oh, my God!" before the window blasted inwards, shredding his body into bits of bloodied flesh and bone.

The tower's steel exoskeleton buckled under the intense heat and crushing force. Ever so slowly, its top half began to lean as if bowing in submission to the evil destroying it. Its rivets sheered, the weight-bearing I-beams snapped like twigs, and the massive super-structure with thousands of hapless souls inside fell like the hand of God onto the city below.

δ

"Where fear is present, wisdom can not be."

– Lactantius

*"No passion so effectually robs the mind of all its
powers of acting and reasoning as fear."*

– Edmond Burke

"We will not be driven by fear into an age of unreason."

– Edward R. Murrow

It would take days for the dust and ash to settle, weeks for the death toll to be tallied, months for the economic, emotional, and political tolls to play themselves out, yet it would take mere minutes for the most Machiavellian of Americans to decide who was to blame.

Before the day ended, a video clip from a DVD mailed to tens of millions of homes just weeks before played over and over on national news networks and social media sites. In it, the Reverend Johnny Swaywell predicted a horrific terrorist attack on America's Heartland that would herald the End Times.

"In the immediate aftermath of the nuclear bombing of Chicago," Jan Roberts, a well-dressed attractive woman with auburn hair, large brown eyes, and a shapely figure, reported from the network's Washington, D.C., studio, "all aircraft were grounded, cargo and passenger ships were ordered out of port, the coasts were blockaded by the U.S. Navy, commercial trucking was halted, and all border crossings were closed. In the weeks since, little has changed. Our nation's commerce has ceased, and her people remain in shock.

"Homeland Security is now reporting that a Georgian ship named the *Shkhara* was responsible for transporting the nuclear weapon that laid waste to the Chicago Loop, killing half a million people in a matter of seconds and surpassing Hiroshima, Nagasaki, London, and Dresden combined to become the deadliest bombing of all times. According to the White House, crucial information provided by UN Secretary-General René Boujeau led to the arrest yesterday of two scientists suspected of building the bomb. The scientists had never met, nor directly communicated with the individuals who paid them, however. Therefore, those ultimately responsible may never be known. Even though neither scientist is Middle Eastern, conservative media pundits and far right political figures continue to blame Muslim extremists for the bombing.

"As was the case after September 11, anguish and fear have found their outlet in hate and cruelty. Public brawls, the burning of homes and mosques, even murders of Muslim-Americans and immigrants have been reported across the country. The latest occurred last night in Dearborn, Michigan, when a Mr. Kindar Kapani left his daughter's home after babysitting his grandchildren. He happened upon a roving mob that beat him unconscious, hung him from a nearby weeping willow, and pinned a crudely written sign to his jacket that read, 'God Bless America, God Damn Muslims.'" She paused. "Mr. Kapani and his family were from Bombay, India. He was Hindu.

"In a press briefing today, President Jameson urged Americans to refrain from violence and instead help those in need. While he encouraged individuals to be cautious, he said the country needs to get back to business as usual and promised to send Congress a stimulus package to spur the faltering economy. Stock markets around the world, which lost half their value in the wake of the attack, remain down despite Jameson's promise, and experts are now predicting another Great Depression.

"The President, a moderate Republican, is known for his dovish foreign policy and timid government agenda. His approval rating is now in the mid-twenties, second only to George W. Bush for the record low. Sources within the President's own administration are privately saying that Senator Mitchell Thomas could give Jameson a run for his money at the Republican National Convention in Detroit two weeks from now.

"According to a poll, a majority of Americans say they're willing to close the borders, deport foreigners, and suspend civil liberties to ensure greater security. Nearly half of those surveyed said immigrants and even first-generation-Americans should be forced to register where they live and even be electronically tracked by Homeland Security. A third of those surveyed supported mass internments akin to what Roosevelt and Congress did to Japanese-Americans during World War Two."

The doorbell rang.

"On the international front–"

Snuggling on the couch with Cameron, Mac muted the TV.

"Be right back," he said, kissing the top of her head.

The front door flew open and a familiar voice bellowed, "We're here!"

"Uncle Merrill!" Cameron cried, jumping up and spilling a box of crayons and a princess coloring book onto the floor.

"Come here, m'darling," beckoned the Elder, and she ran into his open arms.

Kyle appeared in the doorway as Mac reached the foyer and Genevieve came down the hall.

"Always keep your doors locked, laddy," scolded Merrill.

"Yeah, maybe then I could keep you out," grinned Mac.

"Oh, ho! Feisty are we, eh wart?" he retorted.

Mac laughed and gave both Elders a hug. "Welcome, Keeper."

"Good to see you, lad," Kyle answered. "Although I wish it could have been under better circumstances."

"We're still glad you're here," Genevieve said and kissed them both on the cheeks. "Can I get you something to eat and drink?"

"That would be welcomed, lass," Kyle replied. "Thank-you."

They enjoyed a casual repast on the deck and a local wine libation while sharing the latest happenings of family and Clan. Mac took advantage of a momentary lull in the conversation to ask, "How did you get here? Commercial flights are still grounded. That's why we haven't flown back to Geneva yet and why the Charter Amendment Conference has been postponed. No one can get to New York."

"Friends of the Clan," was all the Keeper said, taking out his iPhone and placing it on the patio table.

He pressed Play and a YouTube video of Johnny Swaywell appeared on the tiny screen.

"America was founded by Christians seeking religious freedom," the Reverend declared as he paced back and forth across the massive, rotating stage in his Crystal Cathedral sanctuary. "Our great nation held a special place in the Lord's heart," and he pointed an accusing finger at the camera. "But not anymore!"

Uneasy murmurs wafted about the cathedral.

"Are you surprised?" he challenged. "Can you really be asking yourselves 'Why?' The answer should be obvious. He *loves* us. A shepherd never gives up hope of finding his lost lamb and God shall never give up hope that we shall find our way back to Him. The Lord destroyed Chicago as a message to us, a warning! He's telling us the end is near. *The* end. The end *times*. The times of *Revelations*. Unless you repent and beg God's forgiveness, unless secularists and sinners change their evil ways, we shall suffer unspeakable horrors. Only true Christians shall survive unscathed and see the Lord Jesus descend from heaven to reap the vine of humanity and carry the faithful home with Him to heaven."

Kyle stopped the video. "The sermon went on for another twenty minutes. Claims of the end times are nothing new, of course, but in the DVD that was mailed out last month, Swaywell virtually *predicted* what happened in Chicago. Now preachers all across your country are calling it a message from God, conspiracy theorists and opportunistic news commentators are cherry-picking events and tying them to Revelations. A civil war, an earthquake, a flood, an outbreak of disease, anything they can think of. Politicians are ginning up fear of more attacks, and social media is fanning the flames to the point of mass hysteria."

"It's the Salem witch trials and the Red Scare on steroids," said Merrill. "Violence is on the rise, militia membership and church attendance are up, a mentality of, 'If you're not with us, you're against us' is taking hold, and your country's turning to the political right for cover and God for comfort."

"Man never learns from his mistakes," replied Kyle. "We let irrational fear have its way time and again."

Mac nodded, recalling, "In the War of 1812, the White House and Congress wanted carte blanche to do whatever they wanted in the name of national security. They passed the Alien and Sedition Acts to imprison anyone who defamed the government, expel people not born and raised on American soil, and make it harder to become an American citizen. In the Civil War, Lincoln suspended the Constitutional right of citizens to a fair and timely trial before their peers and imprisoned anyone suspected of Confederate sympathies until the end of the war. In World War I, Congress passed the Espionage and Sedition Acts to arrest whoever the government thought was a threat, even those doing nothing more than *talking* about treasonous acts. In World War II, Roosevelt and Congress imprisoned 120,000 Japanese-Americans. During McCarthy's Red Scare, 3,000 people were ordered to appear before the House Un-American Activities Committee based on nothing more than hearsay evidence, ruining many of their lives in the process.

During the so-called 'War Against Terror,' Bush imprisoned thousands of Arabs without trial and tortured hundreds of them. During Obama's presidency, suspected terrorists were summarily executed by drone strikes."

"All of which weakens democracy and degrades respect for constitutional rights," Kyle said with more than a hint of ire. "Jameson's approval ratings are abysmal. Radio and TV are awash in campaign ads for far-right candidates paid for by Super-PACs. Religious schools like Swaywell's William Jennings Bryan College have suspended classes and sent their students out campaigning alongside throngs of Churchgoers to drum up support for far right candidates. The Republican National Convention gets underway in two weeks and the raw emotions of the delegates will hold sway over state rules for casting votes." He paused and sighed. "Mitchell Thomas will win the nomination, and with him at the top of the ticket in November to draw voters to the polls, the far right will carry everything from Congress to city councils."

The doorbell rang again.

"I'll get it!" Cameron called from the living room.

Mac could hear the sound of tiny feet running across the floor and a door opening. By the time he reached the foyer, she was hugging Dr. Angela Fuentes.

Despite his surprise, Mac gave her his usual, "Hey, what's up, Doc?" and a hug. They'd met six years before during his two-week court-mandated observation period at the State Hospital in Traverse after his suicide attempt. A psychiatrist in her mid-thirties, she had the high cheekbones, dark brown eyes, and mocha skin of those lucky enough to be of mixed Spanish and Native American heritage. Her lustrous shoulder-length black hair was tied back in a ponytail and she wore a flowery blouse, blue jeans, and high-heels.

"Don't close the door, honey," she said to Cameron. "Someone just pulled up."

"Not sure what brings you here, Angela, but the others are in the kitchen."

She took Cameron by the hand. "Walk with me, honey?"

"Okay!" she said, bouncing up and down on the balls of her feet.

"Be there in a sec," said Mac as Merrill sidled up beside him. "What are you up to, old man?"

"Trust me, laddy."

"I hate it when you say that," Mac mumbled, stepping out onto the landing as Dwight, Mark, Duron, Robbie, and Damon got out of a Lincoln SUV. "Hey, guys," he called.

"How you been, man?" said Robbie with a hug as he walked in.

"Couldn't be better."

"Why are we here, dude?" asked Duron.

"Beats me."

"Any reason to come to Traverse is okay with me," Dwight said.

"No doubt," Damon said. "Even if we do have to see Duron."

"Ha, ha," Duron drolled.

"Everyone's in the kitchen," Mac told them. "I'll order us some takeout from that French bistro downtown. Micro-brews in the frig, booze in the pantry, make yourselves at home," he added, knowing full well his old friends would have done so anyway.

A second car pulled up. "Ah! The Professors," Merrill smiled conspiratorially.

Dr. Jay Michener, a sociobiologist from Penn State, Dr. Robert Ingersaul, an archaeologist from Yale, and a third man Mac didn't recognize came up the walk.

"Good to see you again," Dr. Michener said warmly.

"And you, Professor," Mac replied.

"Been doing some wonderful things at the UN," said Dr. Ingersaul. "Glad we were able to help with your nomination all those years ago."

"So am I," Mac grinned.

"May I introduce Dr. Alberto Galatea," Dr. Michener said, "Professor of Physics from the Università de Firenze."

"Nice to meet you, Professor. Please come in. All of you. I'll get a fire started and we can sit out on the deck."

Their favorite drinks and full plates in hand, Mac and Genevieve's impromptu guests were laughing and talking on the deck, the heat from the stone fireplace fending off the night's chill, and the lights of Traverse lining the bay below like a strand of pearls on black satin.

"To our host," toasted Duron.

"Here, here!" said Robbie and, everyone lifted their glasses.

"Secretary-General," Duron said. "What's up with that?"

"Crazy, huh?" chuckled Mac.

"I can certify he's not crazy," said Angela, "just grandly delusional." Everyone laughed.

The Keeper stood and walked over to the fireplace to warm his hands. "Within Mac lies a greatness the world has rarely seen."

The small talk and friendly arguments waned into silent anticipation.

"He has learned much, been steeled by the ordeals he's endured, and now is poised to become Secretary-General of the United Nations. To prepare him for what lies ahead, and to help him become the noble leader the world so desperately needs, I have invited you here tonight to engage in a debate of the most pressing societal, religious, and scientific questions facing the world today." Searching the faces of all present, he proclaimed, "Such is the quest I set before you all. Do you accept?" Affirmations in both gesture and word were his answer. "Then let us begin with this. What are the qualities of a great leader?"

"Simple. Honor and duty," said Dwight, an academic-looking 53-year-old African-American with a receding hairline. He was a bit taller than Mac and usually better dressed.

"Fortitude," added Mark, the most gregarious and jovial of Mac's friends, not to mention the tallest, with thinning blonde hair, dark blue eyes, and office-casual attire.

"Strength of character," declared Robbie, an imposing and intense man twice as broad as Mac but the same height with intelligent hazel eyes, a full head of thick brown hair lined with gray, and who dressed in the wears of half-a-dozen New York designers.

"Kindness and compassion," Angela said in counterpoint.

"Justice and humanity," suggested Damon, a bald Scandinavian-looking man nearly as broad as Robbie and as tall as Mark with the latter's style tastes.

"Loyalty," added Duron, Mac's oldest and dearest friend, who dressed a bit earthier than the others and was outgoing to the point of wearing his heart on his sleeve. He had thinning brown hair, dark blue eyes, a graying goatee, and wire-rimmed glasses.

Merrill gave a dramatic sigh. "Not a mention of chivalry."

"Already a given, old man," said T.J.

"Now, everyone," said the Keeper, "keep those traits in mind while Merrill sets the stage."

"Not *another* history lesson," Mac sighed.

"My, aren't *we* funny," drolled the former Professor.

The others laughed again and so began the evening's enjoyable and thought-provoking conversation. The time passed swiftly by, and soon Genevieve announced it was someone's bedtime.

"Say goodnight, sweetie," she said, getting to her feet.

"Aw!" Cameron moaned. "Can't I stay up a little longer?"

"Say goodnight, young lady."

"Aw!"

The next-to-last heir of Arthur reluctantly said goodnight to everyone, taking a purposefully long time with her hugs, the last reserved for Uncle Merrill.

"Goodnight, little one," he said, bear hugging her until she giggled.

Genevieve led Cameron to the sliding glass door and a chorus of "Goodnight!" ushered her and her mother inside.

"Now, where was I?" Merrill reflected, though he knew exactly where he'd been. "Ah, yes. Post-World War America. The 1950s. A time of stability, modest prosperity, religiosity, and traditionalism. But by the end of the decade, the winds of change were in the air. Forcibly desegregated schools, the Supreme Court striking down prayer in the classroom, the wizened old Eisenhower warning of the military-industrial complex, a young east coast intellectual with a glamorous wife moving into the White House, the Cuban missile crisis,

Kennedy's bloody 1963 assassination, an archetypical Texan sworn in as President hours later, the passing of the Civil Rights Amendment, Betty Friedan and her *Feminine Mystique*, the Pill, women's lib, an escalating war in Vietnam, the poor sent off to die in a faraway jungle, the sons of the rich sent off to college, a growing culture of sex, drugs, and Rock 'n Roll, Robert F. Kennedy and Martin Luther King shot dead just two months apart, the Democratic National Convention imploding two months later, a paranoid cold-warrior winning the White House, anti-war and race riots, college students shot dead at Kent State by National Guard troops, pulling out of Vietnam in disgrace after burying 60,000 American soldiers, Woodward's and Bernstein's uncovering of Watergate, a President resigning from office for the first time, Roe v. Wade legalizing abortion, the Equal Rights Amendment failing, divorce rates and single-mother households rising, the Arabs embargoing the world's oil, Carter's 'malaise' and 'stagflation' choking the economy, the Soviet Union invading Afghanistan, Three Mile Island melting down, the Panama Canal stolen by a dictator, and the U.S. embassy in Tehran seized by Muslim radicals." He paused for a moment to let the events of a tumultuous twenty years settle in. "America was psychologically and emotionally punch-drunk by 1979 and no one seemed quite sure what to do or where to go. No one, that is, but people of faith and tradition whose social values and beliefs were still anchored in the 1950s. In their minds, America had gone off the rails and become a nation they couldn't relate to anymore and didn't approve of.

"Enter Ronald Reagan and his 1950's Morning in America time machine. For the first time since Lincoln freed the slaves 115 years before, the Republican Party carried nearly every state of the former Confederacy in 1980 thanks to the votes of seventy million religious conservatives. Trickle-down economics came into existence, the Red Scare miraculously resurfaced, the arms race accelerated, and the materialism, superficiality, and greed of the 80's and 90's choked to death the free-love hippie idealism of the 60's and 70's."

"Billy Graham meets Dirty Harry meets Gordon Gekko," said Damon.

NOVUM ORBIS REGIUM - *The New World Realm*

"Aye," Merrill grumbled, "and it proved a potent political triumvirate. In the 40 years since, only two democrats have won the White House, and for the past 30 years, Republicans have held one or both houses of Congress."

"If the far right's so politically successful, why do its followers still claim to be victims?" Mark said.

"A brilliant strategic move, don't you think?" answered Merrill. "With Big Religion on its side, the far right can claim the moral high ground. By demonizing Big Government, they can bemoan anything the government does. By claiming its constituents are economically and socially disadvantaged, they can claim that lower taxes and smaller government will solve their problems. With tortured logic, they can twist gay marriage, Happy Holidays, birth control insurance, school prayer, the ten commandments, and teaching evolution into infringements on their religious rights. By making people feel like moral and social outcasts, the far right's created the most reliable voting bloc in the country. Angry white men."

"But, doesn't that voting bloc see how counterproductive it is?" Mark argued. "They're only hurting themselves. A blue-collar worker who can barely feed his family and keep a roof over his head votes for politicians who support anti-union legislation, deregulation, tax breaks for the rich, no universal healthcare, letting businesses end pensions, and keeping the minimum wage low. A person who sees himself as God-fearing and kind votes for politicians who take away government support for the downtrodden, throws immigrants out of the country, jails people for years over offenses that pose no public threat, takes away the voting rights of the poor, builds up the military to unimaginable levels, supports the death penalty, and justifies invading third-world countries on the flimsiest of evidence. Struggling young couples vote for politicians who eliminate funding for family planning, kill healthcare plans that cover birth control, let businesses send good paying jobs overseas, and cut food stamps and welfare."

"Machiavellian, isn't it?" Merrill replied. "The far right's created a world where the conservative elite get everything they want without giving anything back to the people, and the largest wealth gap between rich and poor in American history. All because of a dinner meeting in 1976."

"What are you talking about, dude?" said Robbie.

"Donald Rumsfeld and Dick Cheney had dinner in 1976 with Wall Street editor Jude Wanniski and economist Art Laffer," the Elder explained. "Laffer sketched a graph on the back of a cocktail napkin showing how lower taxes for the wealthy and businesses would lead to expansion and more jobs. The graph became known as the Laffer Curve and Reagan bought into it hook, line, and sinker. It's also called supply-side economics, voodoo economics, and trickle-down economics, the latter derived from Will Rogers's 1932 quote that the nation's, 'money was all appropriated for the top in the hopes it would trickle down to the needy.'"

"Since then," Dwight, who had a Harvard MBA, spoke up, "two generations of Americans have grown up thinking trick-le-down economics is *real* when it's malarkey! Businesses are profit- and demand-driven, not *supply*-driven. They *adjust* supply to match demand and maximize profits. They keep inventories low, prices up, and employment down. They open or close plants, run more or fewer shifts, run up overtime or lay off workers. Too few goods on the market and prices go up. Too many unemployed workers and wages go down. High prices and low wages equal big profits, so supply is kept *low* and unemployment is kept *high*. Simple Keynesian macroeconomics. Our policies need to be ori-ented towards *demand*-side economics. Demand increases when there are plenty of good paying jobs, companies come up with new and innovative products, and consumers believe in a secure future. Good paying jobs come about when demand increases and sales go up. Higher sales and good paying jobs raise tax revenues. Higher tax revenues enable the government to do more for people and businesses."

"Yet," said Merrill, "your businesses are sending jobs and man-ufacturing overseas, paying undocumented immigrants under the table, keeping wages low, and taking away employee benefits."

"Plutarch said an, 'Imbalance between rich and poor is the oldest and most fatal ailment of all republics,'" Mac noted. "James Michener said–"

"No relation," Dr. Michener smiled. "Unfortunately."

Mac chuckled and went on, "James Michener said, 'We are not exempt from the universal law of obsolescence.' If we continue 'to shower largesse on the already rich at the expense of the bottom of the population, violence is bound to result.'"

"You gotta book of quotations over there?" Damon chuckled.

"You threatening revolution, dude?" said Duron.

"No," Mac said to Damon, "and yes," to Duron.

"Bring it on, Bro," said Duron. "We'll put you Democrats in your place."

"Fuckin'A," said Robbie, fisting-bumping his pal.

"Classy. Real classy. You kiss your mama with that mouth?" Damon said.

"Democrats are greedy, lazy, atheists," Robbie groused.

"Such a warm, fuzzy person you are," muttered Damon.

"Careful, Robbie. Your ignorance is showing," said Dwight.

"Yeah? Well, your epidermis is showing."

When the laughter subsided, Mark pointedly asked Kyle, "Tell me again how lecturing and arguing is gonna help Mac?"

"If Mac can come to appreciate the subtleties of our political, social, and economic systems," answered Kyle, "if he understands our social evolution, moral failings, and political mistakes; if he can navigate the ethical conundrums facing the world; if he learns the key lessons of history, science, and sociology; then he can craft a philosophy of leadership for any nation, even a *single* nation comprising *all* the world's peoples. A one-world government, a *Novum Orbis Regium* without national rivalries, without prejudice or wont, and without discrimination, desperation, and despotism."

"If we're gonna do all that, then I'm gonna need another beer," Duron said sardonically and got to his feet.

"Get me a beer, too, dude?" said Robbie, handing over his empty.

"I'll tell you what," said Damon as he, too, got up. "I'll get everyone a beer if you two hear me out."

Duron stood there for a moment. "Alright," he said cautiously.

"There's been a lot of derogatory talk by the far right about the media being too liberal," began Damon.

"Oh, geeze," Robbie moaned.

"But all the media is doing is reflecting the polarization of society. The right's becoming more conservative and the left's becoming more liberal. Even if the media stayed dead center, folks on the right would perceive it to be drifting left and vice versa. The real problem is that most news outlets have been bought up by entertainment companies more concerned with advertising dollars than journalism. Too many cable and radio news shows are little more than arguments between talking heads and barely qualified pundits. Too many feature GQ and Cover Girl reporters covering fluff pieces and soap opera controversies to increase viewership and ad revenues. Real, honest, hard-hitting journalism is becoming harder to find, especially as experienced journalists at reputable news outlets are being let go to increase profits. Complicating matters is the Internet, with its thousands of extremist websites, conspiracy theories, half-truths, and boldfaced lies getting repeated over and over on social media until no one knows what's *real* anymore."

Duron and Robbie waited for the hammer to fall.

"That's, uh," Damon said awkwardly. "That's it."

Duron shrugged. "Too little fact, too much noise, too hard to find the truth. I agree."

Robbie nodded. "Media companies putting profits before principles."

Damon shook his head, muttered, "Holy shit," and turned for the sliding glass door.

Dwight remarked, "No party does their members any favors by leading them around by the nose with simplistic solutions, untruths, and slanderous attacks."

"Leonardo da Vinci wrote, 'The greatest deception men suffer is from their own opinions,'" commented Mac. "Sigmund Freud talked of mass psychology, and Edward Bernays said, 'If we understand the group mind, is it not possible to control and regiment the masses according to our will without their knowing it?'"

"Bush must have studied Bernays," griped Mark. "How else could we have been duped into the Patriot Act and invading Iraq?"

"The only Béarnaise Bush knows is what he puts on his Texas Longhorn steaks," Mark quipped.

"Nazi propagandist Joseph Goebbels called radio, 'The most influential and important intermediary between a spiritual movement and the nation, between the idea and the people,'" Mac recounted. "Now, we have radio, TV, and websites. People can indulge every whim, ideology, and bias they have. They don't have to think for themselves or ever challenge their beliefs. They can avoid inconvenient truths and mollycoddle their minds into believing they're right and everyone else is wrong."

Genevieve slid open the glass door, and Merrill stood up.

Not to be out done in the art of chivalry, Kyle, Mac, and his friends followed suit.

"My! What gentlemen," Genevieve said as she stepped aside for Damon who had his arms full of beer bottles.

"I should say so," Angela giggled.

"Aw, gee guys, you didn't have to stand up for little 'ol *me*," said Damon as he began passing out the micro-brews.

"Facts are the only basis upon which wise decisions are made," the Keeper said, "and facts come from science and unbiased observation."

"Tell that to the politicians who think rape can't cause pregnancies," Genevieve said bitterly as she curled up next to Mac.

"Or abortions cause mental illness," added Angela.

"Or global warming is a liberal conspiracy," said Dwight, "or evolution is a hoax, homosexuality can be cured, more guns make us safer, and war can end terrorism."

"Carl Bernstein published an article in *The New Republic*," T.J. noted, "entitled 'The Idiot Culture.' He said journalism used to be about common sense, respect for the truth, and a duty to tell the public what they needed to know, even if it's not what they wanted to hear. It used to be about knocking on doors, interviewing people, asking tough questions, sifting through records, and verifying facts. That's how he and Bob Woodward uncovered the Watergate scandal. But these days, the media is, 'the social and political equivalent of the *porn* business. The weird and the stupid and the coarse are becoming our cultural ideal.'"

"Sleazy liberals," grumbled Robbie.

"Anti-science, ignorant, racist conservatives," countered Damon.

Duron threw his arms up, sloshing half his beer onto the deck in the process. "Why do you liberals always call us racist? We're not racist. We just tell it like it is!"

"Do the militia, Alt-Right, and neo-Nazi types belong to your party?" Damon argued. "And whose party failed to pass immigration reform? Whose party said liberals wanted Ebola to come to the United States 'cause southern whites deserved it for enslaving blacks? Whose party called Central American children crossing our borders disease-ridden gang members? Whose party makes cops out to be saints, even when they kill unarmed black men in the streets? Whose party members called Obama a half-breed? Whose party members bought up all the guns and ammo after Obama was elected? Whose party won't pass gun legislation because they have an irrational fear of the government and people of color? Whose party–"

"Stop!" Robbie yelled. "*Yeah*, we got jerks in our party, but so do you!"

Damon stood there for a long moment. "Well," he muttered, "I'm not about to argue that point."

"We *do* need guns," Duron argued. "Our cities aren't safe and crime's spreading into the suburbs."

"'From my cold, dead hands,'" grinned Robbie, channeling Charleston Heston and fist-bumping Duron.

"The Constitution says we have a right to bear arms," Genevieve conceded, "but we have 35,000 gun deaths in America each year!"

"The number of auto-related deaths is about 35,000 a year, too," Robbie pointed out. "Should we get rid of all our cars?"

"The number of auto-related deaths in 1950 was 35,000 a year," she pointed out, "but we have three times the population and millions more cars. Why do you think that is?"

Robbie opened his mouth, thought for a moment, and closed it again.

"Because the government regulates who can drive," she answered, "how cars are built, what safety equipment they have, when to recall them, what the speed limits should be, etcetera, etcetera. So, why shouldn't we regulate guns, gun makers, and gun owners the same way?"

Robbie answered half-heartedly, "The right to *bear arms* is in the Constitution, not drive cars."

"Just about everything is *not* in the Constitution," she said. "Should we stop doing everything? Or should we make everything as safe as possible?"

"I agree, Gen, but gun regulations get blocked by politicians graded by the NRA on their gun rights record," Dwight said. "The better their record, the bigger the political donations. The American Legislative Economic Council gives legislators drafts of bills to take back to their capitols for a vote, bills giving arms manufacturers tax breaks, bills to open-carry in public places like schools, bills to–"

"Oppose green energy," Damon said, "give more money to charter schools, ban gay marriage, basically whatever the far right and Bible-thumpers want."

"There is no such thing as gay marriage," Robbie retorted. "The Bible says marriage is between a man and a woman, not two dudes or dudettes. If they want to get hitched, let 'em have a civil union."

"A civil union isn't a marriage," countered Angela, "it's a legal document. You're using the old separate-but-equal argument. Straight and gay couples can ride the same bus, but the gays have to sit in the back."

"Hey, don't try and make this out to be a racist thing again. It's *totally* different."

"No, it's not. It's exactly the same thing."

"It's immoral," argued Robbie. "It's a sin. It's evil!"

Angela took a deep breath and counted to ten. "There's no such thing as *evil*," she said as calmly as she could, "only what people *call* evil. Like crime – theft or robbery or gang violence or whatever – all of which have their roots in desperation. People with nothing left to lose care little about the law. For them, it comes down to survival. Even a jail cell with three square meals a day and no worries about paying bills or getting healthcare looks good if you're destitute enough. We should be asking ourselves, 'Can most criminal acts be stopped?' and the answer is, 'Yes, by taking away the economic inequities and social barriers that cause them.'"

"But, there's still evil. The Bible says so."

"The Bible says there are burning bushes," said Dwight, "people living in whales' bellies, water that turns into wine, angels *de*-scending from heaven and men *a*-scending to heaven like there's some kinda holy elevator in the sky. Is all *that* true, too?"

"Evil is a simplistic explanation for negative psycho-social behavior and random natural events," Angela explained. "Evil implies a malevolent, supernatural power. But, everything has a rational explanation. Even terrible things. Remember Timothy McVeigh?"

"Yeah. The Oklahoma City bomber," answered Robbie. "Why?"

"McVeigh was a corporal in the army, fought in the Gulf War, and earned a Bronze Star. Sound like a good guy? After the war, he imbibed in the paranoia of militia groups, read *Soldier of Fortune* magazine and white supremacist hate books, watched the ATF and FBI screw up and kill all those people at Ruby Ridge and Waco, and decided to strike a blow for justice. Still sound like a good guy? He loads up a truck with explosives, drives it to the Murrah Federal building in Oklahoma City, and detonates it. One-hundred and sixty-eight people died in a matter of seconds, including 19 children in a daycare center. Six-hundred more were injured. So, was he a good guy? Was he evil? No. Neither. People get screwed up by what happens to them, what they're taught, and what they hear and read. That's why they end up doing bad things. If we don't learn how to stop creating the McVeigh's of the world, then it's just a matter of time before we have another one."

"Yeah, well, he was executed," Robbie said coldly, "and we oughta kill everybody like him."

"Careful," Angela warned. "Don't make a martyr out of someone that others will rally around and avenge."

"Then, kill them, too."

Angela looked at him for a good long moment. "Freud would have a field day with you."

After a tension-breaking spate of laughter from the others, Robbie sighed and said, "Sorry. Sometimes it's hard to stay objective."

"So, how do we stop creating McVeigh's?" said Mark.

"Engagement and empowerment," answered Angela.

"Democratic socialism," Damon added.

Duron gasped in feigned shock. "Communism?"

"No. Communism is Marxism. Socialism is an even playing field."

"Karl Marx was a nut job," Duron said. "An angry, argumentative, borderline sociopath."

"I agree," said Damon.

"Excuse me? Did you just say you *agreed* with me?"

"Yes," laughed Damon. "Marxism predicts that companies'll coalesce wealth, suppress wages, and influence laws in their favor to such an extent that the working class'll finally revolt." He paused. "Well, I guess that part's true."

Duron growled.

"Look, Marx was a horse's ass, but up until World War II lots of people thought communism would lead to an egalitarian utopia. The Soviet Union, though, proved Marxism was nothing but old-fashioned fascism with an anti-religious twist."

"Like liberalism," Robbie snickered.

"Liberalism is social and economic equality with a live-and-let-live twist," Dwight rejoined.

"And yet you support abortion," said Robbie. "Murder!"

"Abortion is a choice that only a woman can make for herself," Damon answered, "regardless of how you or I feel about it."

"It's not a choice women *want* to make," Genevieve said reprovingly. "We need to *avoid* unwanted pregnancies in the first place. We need to ensure access to family planning services and inexpensive birth control, but the country's going in the opposite direction. The

Hobby Lobby ruling by the Supreme Court years ago let companies deny insurance coverage for birth control if it went against the *owners'* religious beliefs. As if the company was an extension of the owner and therefore guaranteed the same rights. Like the company is a person!"

"There's legislation pending in the House, again," said Angela, "to de-fund Planned Parenthood because it provides abortions. But, that's only 12 percent of its budget and spending federal dollars on abortions is already illegal. The other 88 percent is spent on women's healthcare, birth control prescriptions, STD prevention, mammograms, cervical cancer screenings, and counseling. Defunding Planned Parenthood will do nothing but increase illnesses and unwanted pregnancies."

"And crime," Mark said.

"Excuse me?" said Damon.

"Read *Freakonomics*. More unwanted pregnancies lead to more crime."

"How?"

"Back in the 80's, Congress lengthened prison sentences, built more prisons, hired more cops, and the violent crime rate decreased. *Freakonomics* showed that all those things combined accounted for just 55 percent of the drop. The other 45 percent came from societal change."

"And what was the change?" Duron said dubiously.

"Roe v. Wade," Mark answered.

"You've got to be kidding?" Robbie said in disgust.

"Abortion was legal in the U.S. until the early 1900s, then illegal until 1972 when Roe v. Wade was passed by the Supreme Court. Justice Blackmun said of the ruling that, 'by denying this choice, maternity may force upon the woman a distressful life and future. Mental and physical health may be taxed by childcare. There is also the distress, for all concerned, associated with the unwanted child.' When abortion was illegal, only the daughters of well-to-do families could arrange for a private and safe abortion. The poor had little choice but to bring their babies to term and raise them amidst racism, poverty, and classism. But, after Roe v. Wade any woman could have a safe, affordable abortion. The ones who did were often young, less educated, and unmarried. More than half of their children would have grown up in poor, single-parent households, two factors statistically correlated with crime."

"So, you're saying the children who weren't born after 1972," said Duron, "weren't around to commit crimes."

Mark nodded. "And they would have reached adulthood in…?"

Duron did the math. "The 90's."

"Which is when the violent crime rate dropped."

"No way!" Robbie said.

"Hey," Mark said with a smile and a shrug. "Statistics don't lie."

Robbie huffed and said, "There are lies, damn lies, and *statistics*."

"What I *hope* Mark is saying," Angela interposed, "is if we avoid unwanted pregnancies, deal with poverty, improve education for the poor, and make being a single-parent less burdensome, *then* we'd have less crime."

"If we also improved living conditions," Mark added. "Many poor people still live in old homes and apartments with lead paint, for example. Abnormally high blood lead levels can cause learning disabilities, lowered intelligence, and behavioral problems in children. In 1973, lead in gasoline, paint, plumbing materials, food containers, playground equipment, and household products was banned, which helped lower crime levels by the 90's as well."

Duron said impatiently, "We shouldn't kill babies *and* we shouldn't poison them *and* we shouldn't let them live crappy lives in crappy homes."

"Exactly," said Mark. "So, educate our teenagers on abstinence *and* birth control, make it easy for women to get it, take away any stigma from using it, provide free childcare for working mothers, mandate livable wages, increase funding for public education, and subsidize continuing education for adults."

Angela nodded. "College needs to be more affordable and the quality of our public education system needs to remain high."

"Turn it over to private charter schools, then," said Robbie.

"Hell no," said Dwight. "Charters take away the money and smart, well-behaved kids and leave the rest behind in underfunded schools with disciplinary problems, kids that need extra attention, no peer role models, and no resources!"

"Plus, Charters are religious schools in disguise," said Damon.

Mark looked at his friend as if he were crazy.

"Look at the owners. Look at the teachers. Look at the mission statements and mottos. Look at the dress codes and uniforms. Just scratch the surface and you'll find a parochial school."

"You say that like it's a bad thing," Robbie scoffed.

"Separation of church and state, man," said Damon. "Every religion and no religion have to be respected. The Establishment, Free Speech, and Free Exercise Clauses of the Constitution say the U.S. government can't endorse a religion, which includes giving tax money to religious schools and charter schools are religious schools in disguise!"

Duron shrugged. "Then repeal the First Amendment and make Christianity the nation's religion."

"The far right would love that," said Damon.

"Isn't America already a Christian country?" Dwight said cynically. "'In God We Trust' was put on our currency during the Civil War and on postage stamps during the fundamentalist period leading up to the criminalization of alcohol, drugs, and abortion after World War I. 'Under God' was put into the Pledge of Allegiance during the Red Scare of the 50's. The President says, 'So help me God,' when he takes the oath of office, even though the Constitution says, 'no religious test shall ever be required as a qualification to any office.'"

"Maybe Americans *want* a Christian nation," Duron posed.

"Maybe America was founded as a Christian country and we gradually drifted towards secularism," added Robbie. "Maybe we need to go back."

"Always backwards with you people," Damon said angrily. "Liberals talk of how great America *can* be. Republicans talk of how great America *used* to be. 'We need to make America great again,' and all that crap."

"If you look for the word 'Christian' in the Declaration of Independence, the Constitution, or its amendments," Dwight commented, "you'll never find it. And if you look for a reference to God, you'll only find it in three places."

"Bull," Duron scoffed.

To prove his point, Dwight began reciting from the Declaration of Independence. "'When in the course of human events–'" Robbie joined in, "'–it becomes necessary for one people to dissolve the political bonds which have connected them with another–'" Damon and Duron followed suit, "'–and to assume among the powers of the Earth, the separate and equal station to which the Laws of Nature–'" then Mac and Mark, "'–and of Nature's God entitle them, a decent respect to the opinions of mankind requires that they should declare the causes which impel them to the separation.'"

Everyone laughed and applauded.

"You all must have gotten A's in civics class," Angela teased.

"Dwight did," Damon replied with a grin. "But, Duron flunked."

"Always the comedian," said Duron, a summa cum laude graduate of Michigan.

"What are the other two references?" Robbie asked.

"'We hold these truths to be self-evident–'" Dwight began reciting again, guessing correctly the others would join in. "'–that all men are created equal, that they are endowed by their Creator with certain unalienable Rights, that among these are Life, Liberty and the pursuit of Happiness,' and," Dwight concluded, "'We, therefore, the Representatives of the United States of America, in General Congress, appealing to the Supreme Judge of the world for the rectitude of our intentions, do, in the name, and by authority of the good people of these Colonies, solemnly publish and declare, that these united Colonies are, and of right ought to be free and independent states.'"

Duron said smugly, "There you go. God."

"Ah!" Dwight said. "All three references came from the Declaration of Independence which was meant to incite revolution. It didn't serve as the foundation of our government or our laws. Further, the terms Nature's God, the Supreme Judge, and their Creator could refer to a deity of *any* religion – Judaism, Christianity, Islam, Hinduism, Buddhism, even Nature or pagan religions."

"Our founding fathers weren't pagans," Duron argued. "They were–"

"Deists," said Merrill. "The Declaration of Independence was written by men of the Enlightenment. Believers in William Paley's Watchmaker God."

Mac understood. "A God who wound up the Universe and set it in motion, rather than a God who's tinkering with life day in and day out. Our founding fathers believed it was up to us to make of our world what we will and wrote the Constitution to balance personal freedom with personal obligation to our nation, a Constitution that doesn't mention God."

"The Constitution doesn't endorse a *secular* government," Robbie pointed out.

Dwight half-agreed. "It gives the right of private religious expression to the people and creates a government without religious affiliation. Not Christian, not anything."

"President Adams negotiated a treaty with Tripoli in northwest Africa not long after the Constitution was ratified," Merrill noted. "Since Tripoli was a Muslim nation, its leaders had serious reservations over signing a treaty with a Christian nation. Adams assured them that, 'the Government of the United States of America is not, in any sense, founded on the Christian religion.' Tripoli signed the treaty and Congress unanimously adopted it, only their third unanimous vote of the hundreds taken up to that point."

"The nations of our ancestors had state religions," argued Duron. "Lutheranism, Anglicanism, Catholicism, etcetera."

"Aye, they did. Religion used to be almost indistinguishable from government. But today, laddy, only a third of all nations have State religions. Thirty Catholic, 29 Muslim, five Buddhist or Hindu, and one Jewish."

"A society needs to have a foundation of moral behavior," Robbie contended.

"Yes, of course," said Angela. "But moral behavior is simply that which is necessary to live together in peace. Conformity and cooperation are part of who we are. It's part of our nature by virtue of being social animals."

"You're saying with or without religion we'd be moral beings?" said Genevieve.

"Yes, though religion, if it's taught in a loving, all-inclusive way, can *help* us be better persons."

"So can a broad education," said Kyle. "One that incorporates history, philosophy, psychology, sociology, art, poetry, music, world religions, and the physical sciences."

Mac recalled the amazingly diverse books Kyle and Merrill had given him to read when he started at the UN nearly seven years before. "A broad education lets us clearly see what's right and wrong, what we ought to stand for and against, how brief our time on earth is, and the importance of illuminating ideas."

"Without such an education," said Angela, "we spin our wheels, stick to the status quo, go along, and remain followers. We become workaholics or under-achievers or sports nuts or hunting fanatics or alcoholics or addicts or Internet junkies or conspiracy believers or paranoiacs or champions of lost causes. In short, we waste our lives on the mundane and meaningless."

"Sheep forever driven by the Shepherd," Mac mused. "Rudderless ships carried away by the winds of fate."

3

"*These are the times that try men's souls.*"

–Thomas Paine

"*They who would give up liberty for temporary
security, deserve neither liberty or security.*"

–Benjamin Franklin

"*If it be admitted that a man possessing absolute power may misuse that
power by wronging his adversaries, why should not a majority be liable
to the same reproach? The power to do everything, which I should
refuse to one of my equals, I will never grant to any number of them.*"

–Alexis de Tocqueville

"*Simplicity is always more appealing than complexity, and
faith is always more comforting than doubt. Both religious
faith and uncomplicated explanations of the world are
even more highly valued during times of great fear.*"

–Vice President Al Gore

"We must do anything and everything to win!" Swaywell decreed in
his final sermon before the convention. "Everything's at stake! Our
nation shall fall, and the Devil enthroned if God is not victorious in
November! So, be not afraid, my children. Do what must be done,

for it shall be with His blessing. If it isn't, then His mighty hand shall stop you."

To "do what must be done" required money, so the riches of the CNSP, Super PACs like the Imperial Fund, and churches rained down upon Thomas's campaigners like manna from heaven. They gleefully launched a massive political assault in the halls of Congress, local campaign offices, and hotel rooms of delegates to the Party's National Convention in Detroit. Their weapons-of-choice were cash bribes and political threats, their unethical behavior justified by seeing themselves as soldiers of Christ fighting a holy war.

And the Lord's mighty hand never stopped any of it.

On the last night of the Convention, fundamentalist, Alt-Right, and neo-con speakers touting family values, immigrant deportations, white rights, free capitalism, small Government, and theocratic nationalism whipped the delegates into a frenzy. In the final hour of primetime coverage, hundreds of 'St. Thomas' and 'America Over All' signs miraculously appeared on the convention floor.

Chants of "Thomas! Thomas! Thomas!" echoed from every corner as President Jameson, the de facto nominee a mere month earlier, walked across the stage to make his concession speech.

What the hell happened? he wondered, his face crimson with indignation. "Thomas! Thomas! Thomas!" He began reading from the teleprompter, but the chanting continued. "Thomas! Thomas! Thomas!" He motioned for the audience to quiet down. "Thomas! Thomas! Thomas!" He tried yelling but, if anything, the chants grew louder. His humiliation roiled into fury and he slammed his fists down on the podium, flipped off the delegates, calling them every name in the book, and stormed off the stage, cursing all the way.

Laughter and cheers followed his retreat as the massive TV screens on either side of the stage switched to a camera feed of Senator Mitchell Thomas making his way through throngs of elated delegates. Though his grand procession to the stage was purposefully drawn out, the enthusiasm of his followers never waned. Bounding up the steps like a cocksure prizefighter, he confidently made for the podium.

Genevieve set a bowl of warm oatmeal with milk and honey down in front of Cameron

"Thanks, mommy," she said with a quick smile, her eyes never leaving the *Magic Treehouse* book she was reading at the dining room table.

Genevieve kissed the top of her daughter's head. "You're welcome, sweetie."

From the far side of the living room, the host of the BBC's morning news show said, "Let's go to Jan Roberts, reporting live from the Republican National Convention in Detroit," and the image cut to the inside of the mostly empty Gordie Howe Arena. The stadium floor behind Jan was littered with confetti and abandoned signs.

"It's on!" Genevieve called.

"Coming!" Mac called back from the bedroom, finishing with his tie.

"Thank you for joining us, Jan," the host began. "What time is it there in Detroit?"

"Nearly 3 a.m. eastern, Seamus," said the tired-looking reporter.

Coming down the stairs, Mac slipped on his suit coat.

"Morning," he said giving Cameron a hug. "Sleep OK?"

"Uh, huh," she said without looking up.

"Good," he said with a chuckle and glanced at the TV.

"The most telling part of his acceptance speech," Jan Roberts was saying, "was this."

The screen switched to a video of Senator Thomas on stage addressing an arena packed with raucous delegates. "The power to rule comes not from 'We the People' but from the divine will of God. We have no obligation to heed the words of our Constitution, the rhetoric of our politicians, the lies from the liberal media, the Godless rulings of our courts, or the advice of so-called experts and scientists. Our duty is to heed the teachings of the Father, the Son, and the Holy Spirit, to whom America owes its bountiful blessings. I stand before you tonight, a nominee for President of the United States, not because of you the delegates, not because of the voters, but because of our Holy Father who saw the peril of our decadence and wished to save us. Out of love, He reminded us of the consequences of our acts by letting His children in Chicago die for our sins."

Cheers resounded throughout the arena and Thomas raised his hands to heaven.

"Lord, I shall be Your St. Paul, Your minister, Your avenger, Your persecutor of evil, and my power shall be Your power, my words, Your words. In the holy war to come, I shall fear no evil, and I shall do what must be done to create the Holy Land of America!"

The delegates erupted in a fit of ecstatic screams and applause. "I accept the nomination for President of the United States to bring America home to Him!"

Jan Roberts reappeared, her tired face slowly reconstituting itself into an impassive mask of journalistic composure. "Presidential-nominee Mitchell Thomas and his Vice Presidential-running mate, second-term Virginia Senator Jack Abrams, are expected to begin campaigning today."

Genevieve picked up the remote and switched the TV to *Sesame Street*. "If they elect him President–" she said under her breath.

"Then everything Kyle predicted will come true," Mac said with a resigned nod.

In the nearly three months between the National Convention and Election Day, televangelists like Johnny Swaywell eagerly spread the political Gospel of Thomas, churches sent tens of thousands of parishioners out on the campaign trail, and SuperPACs filled the airwaves with ads. On election night, Thomas and the far right swept into office at every level of government.

Just before midnight, Mac picked up the phone and dialed a number from memory.

"You watching?"

"Aye," replied an unusually reserved Merrill. "If you still announce your candidacy–"

"I've given my word," Mac told him.

"*If* you announce your candidacy now," Merrill insisted, "the stakes will be monumental. Those in power will do anything, *anything* to stop you."

"I know," Mac said with cold resignation.

"The Clan will try to protect you, laddy," the Elder promised, "but–"

"I know," Mac repeated, fully aware that the Clan's protection would be of little use. "I'm not afraid."

"You should be," warned Merrill.

"I know that, too."

"Is there anything I can do, lad? Anything at all?"

"Actually, yes."

"Aye?"

"I'm giving you power of attorney to handle my financial matters. My paycheck will be direct-deposited into a Clan account. Take half and give it to charity – Doctors Without Borders, the Children's Volunteer Organization, Plan USA, that sort of thing. Take the other half and invest it in a trust fund for Cameron."

Merrill closed his eyes. "What will you live on?"

"My savings," Mac replied simply.

"You mean your retirement," said the Elder.

"You and I both know I may not be around to retire. So, I'm asking you, as a friend and a Clansman, please do this for me. Okay?"

"I respect your chivalry, lad, but this feels like tempting fate."

"Merrill, please do as I–"

"But, I will honor your request. And if anything happens to you, know that Kyle and I, the Clan and your friends, will all look after Genevieve and Cameron as if they were our family."

"I know. Thank-you."

The Whiffers, as the White Freedom Nation militia members were not-so-affectionately called around town, never set foot in a government building. So, once a week Postmaster Lars Robinson walked across the street from the U.S. Post Office during his lunch hour to drop their mail off at the General Store. A pale blue prairie sky and unusually warm fall weather made his short walk this week particularly pleasant.

The tinkling of a bell suspended above the door announced his arrival.

"Mornin' Russ," Lars said. "Got some mail for the Colonel."

"Damned Whiffers," muttered Russell Bosley from behind the counter. "Give this place a bad name."

"First amendment, second amendment. Whadya you gonna do?"

"You ever try and deliver the mail out there?" said Russ.

"Yeah, once. *Just* once," Lars answered. "Drove up to the gate in my U.S. Post Office Jeep and before I even came to a stop someone shot out my passenger window."

"Damned nut jobs," Russ grumbled. "All of 'em."

"Give these to the Colonel on Sunday for me?"

"Sure thing. How's your wife feeling?"

"Better, thanks," answered Lars. "Oughta make it to the church social tomorrow."

"Millie and me'll be there, too. Look forward to seeing her again."

Lars turned to face the big plate glass front window. His Post Office sat across the road, and beyond it along the horizon he could see the Black Hills. "The Whiffers sure gotta nice piece of land up there, though. Great view of Devil's Tower."

"Devil's Tower? Why, that's forty miles from here, up to the Montana state line."

"Yep. Right along the 45th Parallel. Halfway between the equator and the North Pole."

"Pretty amazing, huh?" Russ said.

"Yep. Pretty amazing," replied Lars. "Well, better get back to work. See you and the missus tomorrow. Thanks again."

Just before noon on Sunday, Colonel Randall Joseph Collins, second in command of the White Freedom Nation, rattled into town in a beat up old F150 trailing a cloud of road dust behind him. A bumper sticker on its back gate read, "God, Guts, and Guns Made America Free," and a 12-gauge shotgun rested in a gunrack mounted in the rear window. Flying from a pole anchored to the side of the truck bed was a white flag with a red Christian cross in the center overlaid by a black Nazi swastika, its spidery legs tapered down like daggers and blood dripping from their tips.

Backing into a parking space in front of the General Store, the ruddy faced, pot-bellied Collins looked warily up and down Main Street before stepping out of the cab. With one more anxious look, he slammed the door shut and hurried inside, abruptly stopping to survey the aisles for danger.

Russ appeared in the doorway of his office to see whose arrival the bell had tolled. "Mornin', Colonel," he said none-too-warmly, thinking for the hundredth time how the Whiffer looked like a chubby child playing make-believe soldier, but for the Colt revolver at his hip and the hair-trigger look in his eyes.

The Colonel – a rank bestowed by the White Freedom Nation's leader – warily approached the counter, one palm on the Colt's handle, the other passing Russ a list of groceries and hardware items.

A bottle crashed to the floor behind Collins and he spun, the revolver half out of its holster.

"Oops! Sorry Russ," Laura Faraway, Crook County's Black Hills Princess two years running, apologized from one of the aisles, her tone more annoyed than sincere.

Collins exhaled, released the pistol grip, and slowly turned back around.

"She breaks more in one day than I sell in a week," Russ griped and waved the list at the Colonel. "Gimme a few minutes. Got some mail for ya, too," he said, and walked into the back room.

Collins watched Laura Faraway sweeping up the broken glass, recalling how his son Willie was sweet on her, though she'd never given him the time of day. If only his son had lived to see the war of Revelations that Reverend Swaywell said was coming. She'd have wanted Willie then, by God. She'd have needed him, done anything he wanted her to do.

"Laura! Gimme a hand!" Russ called.

With an annoyed sigh, she dropped the broom in the middle of the aisle and moped towards the door of the store room.

The front door opened with a tinkling of the bell and Collins spun around again, pulling his Colt on an elderly man with a cane. The would-be customer stopped in his tracks, eyes wide with shock, and slowly backed out the door.

Collins leaned back on the counter and lowered the Colt to his side. Again, the front door opened, and this time U.S. Postmaster Lars Robinson walked in. The Colonel's shaking hand holding the revolver slowly rose up.

"D…don't come any closer, Lars," he stammered, "I, I swear I'll…shoot!"

Lars raised his hands in a bored sort of way. "Randy Joe, you really think I wanna do anything to you? I've known you since we was twelve, for chrissakes. I don't give a damn what you all do out there. Just leave us alone and we'll leave you alone. Alright?"

"You *won't* leave us alone! You damned Feds keep takin' away our rights and tryin' to make us think things we don't wanna think and throwin' us in jail and takin' our guns and, and tryin' to *kill* us!"

"Jesus, Mary, and Joseph," Lars muttered. "What you been smoking out there, Randy Joe?"

"That liberal Muslim nigger President started spyin' on us 'cause he wanted revenge on decent white folk and Jameson's cuttin' deals with the Jews and Arabs, and that son-of-a-bitch Antichrist," he said painfully, "that evil bastard MacCrarey, he killed my boy. Now he's startin' Revelations."

Lars grimaced. "I'm real sorry about Willie, Randy Joe. Only met him once, but he seemed—" the Postmaster couldn't honestly say he thought much of Willie, "–seemed like a good White Freedom Nation member."

"He was a child of God, he was. Died doin' the Lord's work. But, Satan was watchin' over MacCrarey the day he killed Willie. Shot him dead in the street, like he was one of them nigger gang bangers."

He paused to dry his eyes with a sleeve and Lars lowered his hands. "Sorry about Willie, Randy Joe," he said again and backed out the door.

Collins stopped at the edge of the trees and leaned forward with his hands on the steering wheel. He loved to look at the fifteen-foot high barbed wire fence that ran a good 100 yards to his left and right. Beyond stood the fourteen wooden, one-story buildings he called home – the White Freedom Nation compound. This ritual moment of reflection made leaving bearable.

He'd grown up here and rarely ventured off White Freedom Nation land. None of them did. Having a thousand acres of rolling prairie, of course, hardly made staying a hardship. Back in the days of the Great Ronald Reagan's reign, General Cobb's father had claimed the land by sending a letter to the Federal Bureau of Land Management citing the Homestead Act of 1862 and claiming 80-acre tracks of land for each member of White Freedom Nation. The Bureau never replied, and enough time had since passed for common law adverse possession to give them legal title. At least that's the way they looked at it.

But they knew it was just a matter of time before the Feds came. No worries, though. They were ready. They'd always been ready thanks to Reagan's Home Defense Front program. When the first George Bush was Vice President, he was in charge of giving whoever wanted to form a HDF everything they needed to get ready for the communist invasion. Money, offices, uniforms, weapons, training, everything.

But, when the Berlin Wall came down, half a century of Red paranoia evaporated as if it had all been made up. The USSR fell, that sleazebag Clinton got elected, and the Feds turned their backs on militias like theirs. Most refused to disband, of course, choosing instead to arm themselves since there'd always be someone to fear, even it was the Feds themselves.

Collins threw the truck into gear and drove up to the front gate. Two privates ran over, rifles over their shoulders, and swung open the gate. The Colonel called through the window as he passed, "Follow me to the Hall and unload the supplies!"

"Yes, sir!" they said in unison, hurriedly closing the gate behind him.

Pulling up to the gymnasium-like building affectionately called Freedom Hall, Collins offered a prayer of thanks for a safe return from the immoral, decadent world of free thought before grabbing the mail on the passenger seat.

Inside the wood-planked foyer, he hung up his coat and gun belt on a wall hook and called to the open office doorway down the hall, "Got the mail, Boss!"

General Jonathan Robert Cobb, Jr. got up from behind his army-surplus desk and followed his second in command to the meeting/mess hall. The Colonel dropped the bundle on one of the dozens of long wooden tables, and together they sorted through the envelopes and packages, their stomachs growling thanks to the mouthwatering aroma coming from the kitchen where their womenfolk were preparing lunch.

"Any troubles, Randy Joe?" the General asked. Beer-bellied and stubble-cheeked, the 57-year-old man with a graying buzz-cut, pale skin, and small blue eyes could have been Collins' twin.

"They was spyin' on me," the Colonel answered.

"You *always* say that," said the General.

"That's 'cause it's always true! Lars come in and threatened me 'til I pulled my gun on him."

Cobb knew Lars wouldn't hurt a fly, but said anyway, "You okay?"

"Yeah. He just turned-tail and–" Collins froze, his eyes fixed on the letter in his hand.

"Whatcha got there, Randy Joe?" Cobb said eagerly. "Something from the Reverend Swaywell again?"

The Colonel slowly extended his arm for Cobb to see the seal of the United Nations embossed on the envelope. "It's addressed to me," he whispered. "To me! Why?"

Cobb took a step back. "Open it."

Collins carefully did as he was told, pulled out the note, and read it. When he got to the 'Truly Yours in Christ' at the bottom, his jaw dropped.

"What?" Cobb said snatching the letter out of his friend's hands.

"'Dear Colonel Collins,'" he read aloud. "'I heard from my good friends the Reverend Swaywell and Vice President Abrams of your terrible sacrifice. Please accept my belated condolences for the death of your son and know that whatever God wills to happen is for His greater glory. While I am sure you are comforted in knowing he died in service to his country, I know your soul will never be at peace until your son's killer is brought to justice. Given your sacrifice, I hesitate to ask for your help again, but I must. You see, we have unfinished business, you and I. The Antichrist William Cameron MacCrarey, the murderer of your son, the heir of a king born under the empire that killed our Lord Jesus Christ, still lives. He is plotting to overthrow Secretary-General Boujeau and take over the United Nations, but you and I can stop him. I have the power to hand you justice and you have the power to be God's mighty sword on Earth. Call me at my private number below and I will explain what the Lord has in store for you. Your fellow soldier of Christ–' dear God! '–Under Secretary-General Gerhardt Schoen!'"

"He wants to help me kill MacCrarey," the awed Colonel said.

"But, he's in charge of the United Nations," the General cautioned.

"MacCrarey killed Willie," Collins said, more to himself than to Cobb. "I can avenge my son."

"What if it's a trap, Randy Joe? What if Gerhardt Schoen wants to kill you?"

Collins stared at the letter a good long while before finally making up his mind. "I got no choice, Jon Bob. God wants me to. I knows it."

Mitchell Thomas stood behind a podium adorned with the Presidential seal, fielding question after question from a reporter in the front row. Frustrated with being ignored, one of the newbies in the back of the White House press room leaned over to Jan Roberts.

"Who *is* that guy?" he said, referring to the tall, strikingly handsome reporter.

"He started showing up at press conferences right after the election last November," she answered, never taking her eyes off the President. "Thomas calls him Brett, but there's no Brett registered with the White House press corps. I took a picture and sent it to Research and it turns out he's a former male model. GQ kinda stuff."

"No way! He's a plant?"

Jan nodded. "Probably gets a list of questions from Vice President Abrams beforehand, then Thomas calls on him, Brett asks the question–"

"And the President gives his rehearsed answer like it was off-the-cuff," said the cub with a shake of his head.

"On the campaign trail, Thomas couldn't answer a question on the fly to save his life. Claimed the liberal media kept asking gotcha questions to make him look bad."

"He didn't need the *media's* help," muttered the newbie.

"That'll have to be the last one, gentlemen," the President announced.

"Like there aren't any female reporters in the room," Jan grumbled.

"I've an important meeting to get to. My Vice President and Secretary of Homeland Security will take it from here."

"Mr. President!" several reporters called out, but with a wave of his hand he disappeared through the dark red curtains behind the dais.

The Reverend-Secretary opened a laptop on the podium and two, large flat screen TV screens mounted to the walls on either side of the stage lit up.

"These are the Administration's plans," he said in a don't-challenge-me tone.

Jan scanned down the list of federal departments and what Thomas planned to do with them.

"Oh my god," the newbie said under his breath.

The further down Jan read, the sicker she felt. Halfway through, she dropped her notepad and pen.

Department of...	Plan...
Agriculture	End domestic subsidies to farmers
	End exports
	Quadruple tariffs on imported food goods, crops, and livestock
Commerce	Complete deregulation of all markets and industries
	Withdraw from international free trade agreements
	Ban worker pensions and other benefits paid for by employers
	Ban consumer lawsuits against businesses
Civil Rights	Eliminate
Corrections	Reinstate mandatory prison sentences and zero-tolerance laws for drug and other crimes
	Increase prison funding and construction
	Increase funding for police departments
Defense	Double funding and shift from offensive to defensive domestic weapon systems
	Withdraw all troops from foreign soil
	Close all overseas bases

Education	Divert tax revenues to religious and charter schools
	Ban teachers' unions and teachings contrary to Biblical beliefs
Elections	Declare voter fraud a capital crime, punishable by life imprisonment, and limit the number of polling stations in urban areas
	Require photo ID and birth certificate to register to vote
	Registration must take place at a state capitol at least 90 days before Election Day
Energy and Science	End tax subsidies for so-called 'green' technologies
	End funding of the National Science Foundation
	Rescind legislation designed to reduce carbon emissions
	Increase tax subsidies for domestic nuclear, oil, and coal production
EPA	Eliminate
FCC	Ban funding of PBS and NPR
	Monitor all print, web, social, and news media for liberal, seditious, and terrorist activities
	Legalize government censorship for national security
	Shut down anti-government websites and social media

Health and Human Services	Eliminate Medicare/Medicaid Ban ObamaCare-style insurance schemes Eliminate social welfare programs (WIC, food stamps, group homes, child care centers, et cetera) Divert funds to private and faith-based service providers Support anti-abortion, pro-abstinence education Support LGBT corrective counseling Restrict foster care and adoption to heterosexual Christian families Ban federal funding for birth control and Planned Parenthood
Housing and Urban Development	Eliminate
Homeland Security	Close all borders Halt the issuance of visas Ban all forms of gun control Allow guns in all public and private buildings Lower the legal age of gun ownership to 15 Militarize police departments with army surplus weaponry Allow wiretapping and home searches without a warrant Pass an Anti-Sedition Act Allow indefinite detainment, or deportation, of non-citizens, suspected terrorists, and seditious felons

Interior	Privatize national parks for commercial development and oil / mineral mining
Justice	Empower the President to appoint judges at all levels of government
	Require a religious oath of office for all elected and appointed officials
	Criminalize discrimination against Christians
	Ban the ACLU
	Ban quota systems for minorities
	Ban civil rights and discrimination lawsuits
Labor	Eliminate
	Repeal Fair Labor Standards legislation
	Eliminate minimum wage
	Ban labor unions
Social Security Administration	Eliminate and shift funds to Defense Department
State	Withdraw ambassadors from foreign capitols
	Withdraw U.S. from all international treaties
	Withdraw U.S. from United Nations
	End foreign aid
Treasury	Deregulate financial / banking industry
	Replace all forms of taxation with fines, usage fees, and service charges

Jan sat still as a statue. All through her career she'd kept an open mind, looked at every issue from different perspectives, never joined a political party, and stood fast to her journalistic integrity. She believed people ought to help those in need, always do what's right, and respect the opinions of others. What she saw on the screens and what had been happening since the election was so contrary to everything she held dear that tears welled up in her eyes. The country was growing ever more cynical, self-absorbed, cruel, vile, and polarized. She wanted to scream. She wanted to run away and never look back. But, she knew, giving up an appendage would be easier than giving up journalism. Its nobility, its responsibility, its David-and-Goliath ethos was in her blood, and to run away would be an anathema to her. What this government wanted to do to America, its lack of respect, lack of common decency, lack of inclusivity and generosity, had to be stopped and it was up to journalists like her to do it. She had to hold a mirror up to society and ask, "Is this *really* what you wanted to become?"

But, how to do it? How to–

And an idea began to form in her mind. A simple, elegant, quixotic idea. A tingling rush of adrenaline-fueled excitement ran from her finger tips to her toes.

She wiped the tears from her eyes, picked up the notepad and pen from the floor, and began writing.

The President poured himself a cup of coffee and settled into his armchair in the Oval Office for some Deuteronomy. Despite what he'd said at the press conference, there'd been no meeting to go to. There rarely was. Jack, Jake, and Johnny took care of everything for him.

Such good men they were. "Good Christians," he said to himself.

Someone knocked on the door and entered without waiting for permission.

"Speak of the devils," said the President.

"You shoulda seen their faces when the screen lit up, Mitchell," Tanner beamed as the three of them sat down opposite the President.

"We've been calling members of Congress since the press conference ended," Abrams said, "and both Houses are with us."

"We'll get our PACs, preachers, and PR guys spinning our agenda by day's end," Swaywell promised. "TV commercials, mailers, news interviews, the whole shebang."

"It's time we start making plans for a Constitutional Convention," Abrams announced.

"Sure," said Thomas, hoping he wouldn't be asked to offer any ideas of his own.

"First, we—"

"Pray," said the Reverend. "For the Lord's guidance."

The President dutifully bowed his head.

Tanner rolled his eyes at Abrams who grinned as they both looked down at their shoes.

"Lord Jesus, Your agonizing death was Thy Father's gift to us that we might be saved. Give us Thy strength so we may prove our worthiness to You, and bless this man," he gestured to the President, "so that he may make America strong again, and on the day of final judgment, bring us home to You in heaven. Amen."

"Amen," the others echoed.

"Johnny, *how* can I prove *my* worthiness?" said the President.

The Reverend-Secretary gave a nod to Jack and said, "By convincing everyone that we need to change the Constitution." He took a well-worn leather-bound book out of his valise and opened it to a dog-eared page with a picture of a particularly gruesome crucifixion of Christ. He handed it to the President and tapped the opposite page of text. "Read this."

Thomas read the title aloud. "'*The Devine, Morall, and Martiall Code*, by Sir Thomas Gates.' Spellings not too good." He looked up. "Is it?"

"It was good in the seventeenth century," Swaywell told him. "Read."

"'He that upon pretended malice, shall murder or take away the life of any man, shall be punished with death,'" the President read haltingly.

"'He that shall take an oath untruly, or beare false witnesse in any cause, or against any man whatsoever, shall be punished with death.

"'He that speake impiously or maliciously against the holy and blessed Trinitie, that is to say, against God the Father, God the Son, and God the holy Ghost, or against the knowne Articles of the Christian faith, shall be punished with death.

"'He or she that can be lawfully convicted of Adultery shall be punished with death.

"'He or she that shall commit fornication shall be whipt three times a weeke for one month.

"'He that useth unlawful oaths or take the name of God in vaine shall have a bodkin thrust through his tongue.

"'He that uses traiterous words against his Majesties Person or royall authority shall be punished with death.

"'He that does not hold any Preacher or Minister in reverent regard shall openly be whipt three times three several Saboth days.

"'Every man and woman duly twice a day upon the first tolling of the Bell shall upon working days repair unto the Church to hear devine Service or they shall be whipt.

"'He that detracts, slanders, mutinies, disobeys, or neglects the commandments shall upon the fi rst time so off ending be whipt three severall times, for the second condemned to the Galley for three yeares, and for the third punished with death.

Thomas looked up and handed the book back to the Reverend-Secretary with a misty sigh. "If only *we* had such laws."

"We *did*," said Swaywell. "Our forefathers wrote *The Devine Code* three hundred years ago in Jamestown, Virginia. They came here to create a nation where they could worship God however they pleased. A century later, the Massachusetts Constitution said the right to hold office and enjoy equal protection under the law was reserved for Christians who lived by the Ten Commandments," and he began reciting them. "'You shall not take the name of the Lord your God in vain, nor curse a ruler of your people. You shall have no other gods before me, lest ye be utterly destroyed. Remember the Sabbath day and keep it holy. Honor your father and your mother. Whosoever strikes his father or mother shall be put to death. You shall not commit adultery. You shall not steal. You shall not kill anyone but slaves or thieves, lest ye be killed. You shall not bear false witness against your neighbor. You shall not covet your neighbor's house, wife, or servant.'" Swaywell leaned eagerly forward in his chair. "Mitchell, use the Constitutional Convention to make the *The Devine Code* and the Ten Commandments the law of our land once more."

Knowing the sort of power that would give the administration, Tanner all-too-gladly went along. "We could subtly re-craft our amendments, work *The Devine Code* and Commandments in, then use our PR and pulpit machine to gin up public support before the Convention, and maybe Article 5 the state legislatures."

"Article 5?" said Thomas.

"Article 5 of the Constitution says amendments have to be ratified by two-thirds of Congress and three-quarters of the states. Since we hold a supermajority in both Houses and four-fifths of the states' legislatures, we can ratify anything we damn well please. If we pass the amendments we want, we'll have the iron-fisted control over the country we've dreamed of since Reagan." His enthusiasm faded somewhat as he added, "But only for a while. We still have the longer-term problem of demographics. Our Party is getting older and whiter while the nation's becoming younger and colored. They're the kinda people who vote Democratic. Within a generation, whites'll make up less than fifty-percent of the population. To keep whites in power, we'll have to raise the voting age, set strict citizenship quotas, oppose immigration, ban birth control and abortions for white people, make interracial marriage illegal again, and reinstate the three-fifths clause."

"The three-fifths clause?" interrupted the President.

"Article 1, Section 2 of the Constitution says a slave only counts as three-fifths of a person. The exact language is, 'Representatives and direct Taxes shall be apportioned among the several States according to their respective Numbers by adding to the whole Number of free Persons, including those bound to Service for a Term of Years and three fifths of all other Persons.' The fourteenth amendment invalidated the clause after the Civil War, but we can use the Constitutional Convention to re-define 'free persons' as anyone who can trace their ancestry back to a free-born European and define everyone else as 'three-fifths persons.' That'll weaken the voting strength of non-Whites and immigrants for generations!"

Jack listened contentedly. Swaywell's Christian-centric practicality, Tanner's neo-con winner-take-all mentality, and Thomas' malleability would wear thin with voters soon enough, he knew. Their favorability ratings would tank and by the end of their first term the Party would be searching for someone new. Someone more moderate, someone Presidential looking, someone with a good name and a prestigious record of public service. Someone like a young Senator from Virginia.

President Abrams. That had a nice ring to it.

"Hell, maybe we'll add a clause outlawing liberal ideas," Tanner chuckled. "Or maybe liberals themselves!"

Swaywell laughed. "Remember when I said it's too bad we can't round up secularists, Mitchell? And anyone else we don't like and put 'em in concentration camps somewhere?"

The President laughed, too, but then went suddenly still. His face lit up and he said in awe, "Revelations is coming, and God'll reap the immoral from the earth. Right, Johnny? In the end, only the virtuous will survive, only *they* matter to God. Why waste another minute of time or dime of taxpayer money on people who'll be gone soon? Why shouldn't we help God get rid of them now? Maybe that's what He *wants* us to do. Maybe He's making us talk about it right now! Maybe He wrote Revelations about us!"

After an uncharacteristically speechless moment, Swaywell stammered, "You…I never…*my God*, could it be?"

"Wait, what?" spluttered Tanner. "You're saying…you mean like Roosevelt sending Japs to detention centers? Stalin sending dissidents to Siberia? Hitler gassing the Jews?"

Swaywell's eyes were wide as saucers. "We'd have to be really careful. Keep it secret. Use Homeland Security agents, night time raids, things like that. Put 'em somewhere out of sight."

"*Way* out of sight," Tanner said mockingly, still not believing they were actually having this conversation.

"We don't want anything coming back to hurt us in the next election," Swaywell went on.

Stunned, Jack cried, "Whoa, whoa, whoa! You're kidding, right?"

"Somewhere they can't corrupt America anymore," the Reverend-Secretary continued as if he and Thomas were the only ones in the room.

"Another country," said Thomas.

"Damn well better be another *continent* if you're gonna do it," grumbled Tanner.

"Yes!" cried Swaywell. "Another continent!"

"You…we," Jack faltered. "We're not seriously thinking about this, are we?"

"Yes!" said Thomas, his face aglow, "and I know exactly who can help us!"

A wave of anxiety swept over Jack. "No!"

"Gerhardt Schoen!" beamed the President.

"Shit," Jack said under his breath.

Jan Roberts wrote all through the press conference. She wrote in the cab on her way home. She wrote all evening and late into the night. Vignettes and themes poured out onto sheet after sheet.

She researched stories, downloaded news clips and articles, made notes, and jotted down the names of who she needed to interview. It might take months, she knew, but once she had everything together, she'd find a network to broadcast what might be the most important documentary in a generation.

Then, she'd sit back and watch what happened.

She poured another cup of coffee, smiled with contented satisfaction, and started writing again.

F

"A country isn't a rock. It isn't an extension of one's self. It's what it stands for…when standing for something is the most difficult."

– Judgment at Nuremberg

"The human psyche has two great sicknesses: the urge to carry vendetta across generations, and the tendency to fasten group labels on people rather than see them as individuals."

– Richard Dawkins

"I have found that a man without a firm moral foundation is like a ship without a rudder. He can not be depended upon to remain upright in a storm."

– James Michener

While he made dinner for his guests, Mac listened to the BBC news on an old transistor radio. "And this just in from the States," said the tinny voice of the news anchor. Mac turned up the volume. "It's been a year since President Thomas and his cabinet announced their stunning domestic agenda, and the impact on American jurisprudence and society has been nothing short of a retrograde revolution. Federal courts are now barred from hearing freedom of religion cases. Americans can be stripped of their citizenship after committing even minor felonies. Legal immunity has been granted to law enforcement officers and soldiers for any acts of violence committed against citizens in the line of duty. People who default on bank loans or face 'terminal unemployment' can be sent to work camps. Teachers can be imprisoned for teaching subjects not sanctioned by the government."

Mac cursed.

"Jews, Hindus, Muslims, gays, lesbians, and 'anyone of immoral character' are now banned from government and military service. Homeland Security has been granted unheard of peacetime powers, including the ability to deport foreign-born citizens without judicial review or hearing.

"Foreign leaders, Nobel laureates, human rights activists, noted historians, and respected scientists have denounced the United States and begun referring to its government as the Dark State.

"More news at the top of the hour. This is the BBC." Mussorgsky's *Night on Bald Mountain* started to play.

Mac reached for the wine glass on the counter, downed its contents, and as he set it back down noticed a stack of unopened letters. Some, if he was lucky, were from well-meaning but deluded folk pleading with him to turn away from Lucifer or Satan or whoever, and receive Jesus into his heart. If he wasn't so lucky, they were more death threats against him and his family. Such was the life of the supposed Antichrist. With a growl, he scooped the letters up, tossed them into the wastebasket, grabbed the wine bottle, and took a swig. Pouring the rest into a saucepan of sautéing cubes of beef and chunks of onions, carrots, and potatoes, he stirred them until they were ready and scooped them into a serving bowl. Picking it up with one hand and a bowl of Michigan salad with the other, he walked into the dining room where Genevieve, Merrill, Kyle, Dr. Angela Fuentes, T.J., Marion, his old school chums, Petra, his daughter Katrina, and Drs. Michener, Ingersaul, and Galatea were chatting around the table.

"A reporter in Detroit filed a story saying the recent rise in homelessness and crime was due to funding cuts to social programs," Robbie said to Duron. "The next day he was charged with sedition."

"That's terrible," Marion cried. "Journalists are going to be scared to report *anything*."

"That's what the White House wants," said Damon.

Mac passed the salad bowl to Merrill and the Beef Bourguignonne to T.J.

"Speaking of the White House," Mark mentioned, "Thomas is on track to beat Roosevelt's record for the most executive orders. Reagan and Clinton had 400 a term. Johnson, Nixon, Carter, Bush the Second, and Obama had over 300. FDR had nearly 1,000."

"What EOs has he passed recently?" said Genevieve.

"Mandating the Lord's Prayer at public gatherings, banning the American Bar Association from vetting judicial appointees, and allowing corporal punishment of students."

Damon huffed. "A lawsuit was just filed against a church-run youth home for torturing children. The pastor said his teachers were driving Satan out of the students' heathen souls. So, Congress passed a law forbidding legal action against faith-based organizations and charter schools."

"It also passed a law to charge women who abort their babies with murder," Dwight added.

"I heard the Supreme Court could rule this month that the life of the mother can't be used as a reason to have an abortion," Angela said dejectedly. "Their so-called 'logic' is that God decides whether a woman gets pregnant, so He'll decide whether she lives or dies."

"Men are such fools," Marion snapped.

"Hey! Sitting right here," said Robbie, taking a basket of rolls from Mac.

A defeated-looking Duron held his head in his hands. "This is gonna be a long evening," he muttered.

Damon sensed his friend was having second thoughts about the hardline political and social positions he'd taken in the past and gave him a good-natured punch in the arm. "Chickens coming home to roost?"

Duron just shook his head. "I was at a post office last week and on the wall was The Ten Commandments and something called *The*

Devine, Morall, and Martiall Code. I asked the postmaster what was up, and she said every government building had to post them."

"Everything's going evangelicalish," Robbie said. "Even the U.S. Attorney General's Office. It's only hiring lawyers from religious schools now."

"Hey, you guys heard of Patriot Scouts? For people who think the Boy Scouts are too immoral?" Mark said.

Duron sighed. "My church is sponsoring a troop," he admitted.

Damon said, "How about Freedom Patrols?"

Duron closed his eyes and answered weakly, "Yeah. Some guys from the plant are in one. They roam around town in the evenings looking for people listed as security threats on the Homeland Security website. But, from what I can gather, anyone they decide is of immoral character will do."

"Do they have the authority to arrest them?" said Genevieve.

Duron gave a nod. "They take 'em to Homeland Security Offices, which I hear are swamped."

"So are hospital emergency rooms," added Damon, "patching up the cuts and broken bones of 'immoral characters.'"

"I heard a high school teacher was reported to Homeland Security by the Patriot Scouts who were in her World Religions class for saying every religion, even paganism and secularism, were equally valid," Dwight mentioned.

Damon grumbled, "Soon our schools'll be nothing but seminaries and sports camps."

"She got fired without a hearing or anything," Dwight added, "and blacklisted on the Homeland Security Office website. She'll never teach again."

"I heard she was reported missing," Angela added.

Genevieve gasped. "She was killed?"

"No one knows. Just disappeared without a trace."

Duron hung his head.

"You okay, buddy?" said Robbie.

"I can't believe this is happening," said Duron. "I didn't want anyone to be hurt, I just, I don't know, just wanted America to be better. Like I thought it used to be."

"I know, man," Robbie sighed. "I know." Another sigh. "Well, Kyle, I assume we're here tonight for another debate?"

"Aye," said the Keeper, "on science and education, then we'll meet once more to debate religion."

"Oh, geeze," Mark said.

"Piece of cake," Dwight smirked.

"Yep, that couldn't possibly cause any arguments," added Robbie.

"I'm sure we'll make quite an evening of it," Kyle smiled. "T.J., if you would be so kind?"

T.J. took a deep breath. "O-kay. Here we go. Thomas wasn't in the White House a week before he appointed a former Republican National Committee Chair as the Corporation for Public Broadcasting's Director, who sold off its assets and trademarks like Sesame Street. Congress gave the revenues to Vigilance Academy, LLC, a chain of charter schools owned by Reverend-Secretary Johnny Swaywell."

"Bye-bye Big Bird," Angela said irritably.

"Bye-bye public education," quipped Damon.

"The far right's been gunning for PBS and NPR since the 80's," Mark said. "All part of their war on intellectualism. Public schools, journalism, literature, the arts, they're all under siege."

"Why? A broad education enriches a culture," Petra said, mixing his English with Swiss-German.

"Indeed," agreed Kyle.

Merrill said, "The far right despises intellectuals. Shakespeare said, 'the truth will out,' and the educated can better discern the truth, select relevant facts, and then dispute far-right propaganda. Therefore, the far-right believes the greatest challenge facing *religion* is science and public education."

"The conflict between science and religion has simmered since the Renaissance," explained Merrill. "Over the past century, science has advanced by leaps and bounds, creating not only new technology and products, but new ways of looking at life and society that conflict with traditional ideals and Biblical teachings."

"And the greatest conflict," said "is the debate over why we're here."

"We're here 'cause our parents got busy," Damon sniggered.

"No kidding," T.J. deadpanned.

"But why do we have parents?" challenged Dr. Michener. "Why are their people? Why is there an Earth?" He turned to Dr. Galatea. "Why?"

"You really want me to answer that?" he replied with an Italian lilt. Looking as though he'd just stepped out of a Ralph Lauren Polo ad, the Professor was tanned, dark-haired, and fashionably dressed. After a general assent from the others, he said, "Let us begin, then, with the very big, the very small, and their interrelation."

"Their interrelation?" Mac said. "You mean the Grand Unifying Theory? Einstein spent the last half of his life trying to come up with a single formula that merged all the different forces of physics."

Always the joker, Mark grinned and said, "Yeah, 'cause he knew in his G.U.T. that all the forces had to fit together." The others moaned. "Tough crowd," he muttered.

"Einstein failed," said Mac, "and so has everyone else who's tried."

Dr. Galatea nodded. "Sì. Many times we thought we had the problem sucked, only to be–"

"Licked, Alberto," said Dr. Michener, holding back a laugh. "Had the problem licked."

"Ah," the Professor said, red faced. "Perhaps I should stay away from American idiots."

"Stay away from Republicans then," Damon muttered.

"Ha, ha," Robbie drolled.

"Idioms," Mac corrected. "American idioms."

"Idioms," echoed the Professor. "Let me begin again. Physicists have learned much, but every time we think we have a solution to the Grand Unifying Theory, something new challenges our fundamental beliefs, such as the Dark Energy, Dark Matter controversy of recent decades. But, let me share with you what we *are* sure of." With his palms down, he held his hands still above the dining room table. "Imagine for a moment a still pond. Now, imagine throwing a pebble into it and breaking the calm." He fluttered his fingers in the air. "Ripples get sent out in every direction. That's what happened in the Big Bang 15 billion years ago. Something splashed into the space-time continuum sending waves of energy expanding outward into the emptiness of space, waves that continue even to this day."

"The hand of God," said Robbie, touching the wine in his glass with a finger, "creating the universe."

"Any physicist worth his salt will admit we do not know what came before the Big Bang. Neither do we know what, or who, caused it. All we can do is study its effects, the very first being the creation of quarks, little ripples of energy that came together as the early universe cooled to form protons, neutrons, and electrons. These, in turn, came together to form hydrogen atoms. One neutron, proton, and electron held together by nuclear and electromagnetic forces. The hydrogen atoms were then pulled together by their gravitational attraction to form massive spiraling clouds. The denser the clouds became, the more often the atoms slammed into each other, bringing $E=mc^2$ into play and converting a fraction of their mass into heat-energy. The clouds became hotter and hotter, making the atoms move faster and their collisions more violent, until finally they began fusing together to form helium, the next element in the Periodic Table. The fusions released even *more* heat-energy, the dust cloud eventually began to glow, and the first star was born."

The Professor's face seemed to glow as well with intellectual passion as he spoke.

"When the star reached hydrostatic equilibrium – the outward pressure of the star's heat balanced with the condensing force of gravity – it stabilized until all of the lighter hydrogen fused into heavier helium. Then, the inward force of gravity overcame the heat's outward force and the star condensed again. The helium atoms drew closer, collided more often, released more energy as heat, and pushed the atoms faster and faster until they, too, fused together, this time to form beryllium, the next heaviest element in the periodic table. Hydrostatic equilibrium re-established itself, the helium atoms were eventually consumed, and the gravitational forces took over, collapsing the star. The beryllium began heating up and *again* the fusion cycle started.

"In this way, the star climbed up the periodic table. The larger the star, the further up it went. Because there are fewer large stars, there are fewer heavy elements like gold, platinum, uranium, and so on."

"We have gold and platinum on Earth," Dwight noted. "We have every element in the periodic table on Earth."

"Nearly every element," Dr. Galatea corrected. "Elements with atomic numbers above 92 – Uranium's – have only been discovered in the laboratory since they decay to lighter elements in periods shorter than the Earth's lifetime. If they were present at the Earth's formation, we can't tell now."

"But, our star is of average size, right?" Dwight went on. "How come we have nearly every element here?"

"Because each time hydrostatic equilibrium is broken, and a star begins to collapse, it blows some of its atoms out into space. The more fusion cycles it goes through, the greater the variety of atoms that get thrown into the cosmos, there to be caught up in other interstellar clouds and coalesced into new solar systems, like ours."

"I thought elements were formed on Earth by volcanic activity or something," Mark said.

"Only stars can create atoms," said Dr. Galatea, "but molecules, atoms joined together by chemical bonds, can form on Earth. A carbon atom easily bonds with hydrogen, oxygen, or nitrogen, for instance, to form the basic building blocks of life - polymers, biopolymers, and protobionts - which evolved over the Earth's lifetime into plants, mammals, and finally human beings. And *that*, Jay," concluded the Professor with a self-satisfied smile, "is why we exist."

"So, we're just a bunch of atoms stuck together?" said Robbie. "That's what you're saying?"

The Professor shrugged as if to say, "It is what it is."

"Atoms made in stars, humans made of atoms," Mac marveled. "The Deists and William Paley were right. God the watchmaker set everything in motion with the Big Bang and left everything else to chance, the formation of stars, worlds, and life playing out on their own terms."

"Creatio ex Materia or Creatio ex Nihilo," rephrased the Professor. "Neither physicist nor theologian can honestly say."

"Theology picks up where physics leaves off," supposed Mac. "The unknown is a vacuum, nature abhors a vacuum, man fills the vacuum with religion."

"Aye," said Merrill, "and in man's distant past, *everything* was unknown, so theology was everything."

"Dr. Michener," Kyle said, "perhaps you could answer my question from a sociobiologist's perspective, given what you've been up to of late."

"Which is?" said Mac.

While one might look at Dr. Galatea and imagine him playing in the World Cup, one would look at Dr. Michener and imagine him spending all day in a library. The epitome of bookishness, he had a comfortable lived-in look about him. Stereotypically professorial clothes, gray and thinning hair, and Buddy Holly glasses. "Proudly following in the footsteps of the Leakey's and J.J., I took a sabbatical after his death to take his place on the Genomapping Project."

"Who was J.J.?" said Angela.

"Dr. Jonathon Joseph Kraeg," Mac answered, his voice deep and tinged with anger, "a paleoanthropologist and a good man. I first met J.J. when the Senate Foreign Relations Committee sent him, Dr. Michener, and Dr. Ingersaul to Camleton during my confirmation hearings to investigate whether I really was the last heir of Arthur. A few years ago, I joined him on safari in eastern Africa where he was working on the Genomapping Project."

"The Genomapping Project," Angela said, "is the world-wide effort to collect and catalog human DNA samples?"

"Yes," said Dr. Michener, "that's right."

"To what end?" said Mark.

"The history of a person's ancestors can be found in the markers of their DNA," answered Mac. "Markers are genetic errors that randomly occur when cells divide and get passed on from one generation to the next over time. A collection of distinct markers creates a haplogroup. The people of our Clan, for instance, were the Anglo people who settled in the British Isles 20,000 years ago, and they constitute a rare subgroup of the R1b haplogroup."

"Indigenous Africans," said the Professor, "have the most diverse genetic make-ups. The rest of the world has very little, meaning they came from a very small gene pool that walked out of Africa around 60,000 years ago."

"Adam and Eve thrown out of the Garden of Eden," kidded Robbie.

"That's pretty much what J.J. said," Mac chuckled.

The Professor continued, "Human migration can be tracked by following the markers that occurred at different places at different times. Each of us carries an evolutionary and geographic timeline in every one of our cells. For instance, the first marker that left Africa was M168. It went from Ethiopia to the Middle East 50,000 years ago, then M89 went from Arabia to the Caucasus 40,000 years ago, then M45 went from Kazakhstan to Western Russia 35,000 years ago, then M207 went from Western Russia to Europe 25,000 years ago, and finally M343 went to the British Isles 20,000 years ago.

"Interestingly, the Genomapping Project revealed that just one percent of our DNA accounts for *all* the evolutionary differences between races – skin pigmentation, eye color, hair color and coarseness, hairiness, and so on. In other words, the differences between races are little more than skin deep."

"Oh, my goodness!" said Angela. "That should deal a deathblow to racism."

"One can only hope," said Mac.

"If everything's already mapped out," Angela said, "why are you still collecting DNA samples?"

"To better identify and isolate the haplogroups of indigenous Africans," Dr. Michener replied. "Their extraordinary diversity and ability to thrive for millions of years may mean they have viral immunities and other genetic strengths that can be isolated and hopefully replicated. The less diverse a population is, the more susceptible it is to devastating diseases. Look what happened to the Native Americans after the Europeans arrived. Something like ninety percent of them were wiped out in a matter of decades by Old World diseases they had no natural immunities to."

"Is what you're doing in Africa dangerous?" said Angela. "Is that how Dr. Kraeg died?"

"No," answered Dr. Michener with a glance at Mac, "and no."

"J.J. was here in Geneva visiting," Mac explained, the anger returning to his voice, "and we decided to walk down to Petra's and Katrina's café for dinner. When we turned the corner at the bottom of the hill, there was a husky 20-something man with short-cropped blonde hair leaning against a lamp post across the street. He was wearing faded fatigue pants, black army boots, and a sand-colored hoody with a picture of something on it. Red and black lines in some sort of crisscross pattern. He started across the street and his right hand reached around his waist as if to pull up his trousers. When it came back around, he was holding a pistol."

"Oh, my!" said Angela.

"We were just outside Petra's window when the guy called out our names. J.J. turned and said, 'Do I know you?' and without another word the S.O.B. fired point blank three times."

Angela gasped and raised a hand to her mouth.

"The bullets hit J.J. square in the chest. He fell backwards into Petra's window and crumpled to the ground."

"I'd been watching through the window," said Petra, "and when I saw the gun, I grabbed the hunting rifle I keep behind the bar and ran for the door. I was too late to save J.J., but I shot the bastard before he could kill Mac."

"Petra dragged me inside, *literally*," Mac admitted. "I was so scared I couldn't *move*." He shook his head and looked down. "Terrible feeling, one I experienced twice more. Once in Lhasa with the Dalai Llama, and once on Cyprus, where I finally, uh, found Arthur, so to speak. Or he found me. Though I've been in tough scrapes since, I've fortunately never felt that paralyzing fear again."

Genevieve crossed her arms as if she were cold and Mac put his arm around her.

"Who was it that shot Dr. Kraeg?" Angela said.

"Some guy named Willie Cobb," T.J. answered. "Loner, apparently. Paranoid, end-of-the-world type."

Angela shook her head in disgust. "How inevitable it is that society creates such men."

"Does it have to be, lass?" Kyle said.

"Of course not, but the world would have to change, which is why we're here I suppose?" she said to Kyle.

"Aye, to change the world for the better," he said, and all eyes turned to Mac.

"Alright, people," Mac said with a dismissive wave, "nothing to see here."

The Keeper chuckled and said to the Professor, "Lad, let's hear more about tracking markers and our evolutionary timeline."

Happy to oblige, Dr. Michener rummaged through his satchel and pulled out a map with several broad arrows and numerous smaller ones sweeping between the world's continents. Setting it on the dining room table, he explained, "This is the genomap of marker migrations. Our descendants traveled north out of Africa during one of the Ice Ages when the deserts of the Sahara and the Middle East were savannahs." He tapped on an arrow crossing from Egypt to Arabia. "Imagine being in their footsteps," he said with a far-off look. "We're nomadic hunters following the animals we depend on for food as they migrate north into the new savannahs. Some of our clan settles along the banks of a great river that will eventually be called the Nile, but we move on, following the shorelines into what will one day be called Israel. There we settle, but our next generation moves further into Asia. Time and again our descendants migrate, some to double back into Europe, some to follow the shorelines into the Indonesian archipelago, some to settle in China and Japan, and the last to move across the Bering Straits into the Americas to create the newest, most uniform haplogroup on Earth."

"When we walked out of Africa 60,000 years ago," Duron supposed, "we were pretty much like we are today?"

"Mostly," said the Professor. "Our evolution from that point on was superficial. Merely adaptations to our environment, the one percent of our DNA I mentioned before. Most of our evolution occurred over the millions of years we lived in Africa, it's traces now buried in our junk DNA."

"What exactly is that?" said Dwight.

"Dormant genes that make up 97 percent of our chromosomes, thousands upon thousands of them, shunted away, turned off sometime in our evolutionary past as environmental factors changed and they were no longer needed. A modern human being is simply the three-percent of its 'on' genes. Its 'off' genes are its genetic story, what it evolved from, its less advanced ancestors, its evolutionary shadows."

"The Darwinists and Creationists have argued for two centuries over how we came to be," Mac mused, "and all along the answer's been inside us."

"The beast within," Mark joked.

"Quite literally," said the Professor. "Geneticists may one day find a Noah's ark of creatures inside us, falling backwards through the eons. They've already found base-pair sequences of human genes that are perfect matches with those of chimpanzees, mice, fish, flies, ringworms, even yeast and bacteria."

"Meaning humans share a common genetic ancestry with all of them?" Mark said in surprise.

Dr. Michener nodded.

Robbie said, "But, what if humans *haven't* evolved? What if God created us just as we are?"

"Like Aryans?" Damon quipped.

"Like, bite me?"

"Well," replied Dr. Michener, cocking his head, "in an ontological sense we haven't evolved. We're still animals."

"That's not what I meant," Robbie said.

"But it answers your question," Mac said.

"What? That God made us animals?" Robbie said impatiently.

"When Kyle, J.J., and I were on safari in the Kenyan savannah, we spent our time studying packs of wild dogs and colonies of apes. We saw *all kinds* of similarities in behavior between them and humans. For example, pups wrestle to prepare for the real fights they'll have as adults. Human boys wrestle, they play Cowboys and Indians, they pretend to be soldiers, they play all kinds of games and sports to prepare for what *would* have been adulthood in a hunter-gatherer society. Wild dogs chase down their prey. Humans have track and field, the Tour de France, NASCAR, and all kinds of other chases. One dog can't fend off or bring down a large animal, but a group of them can, so they live in packs. Humans have packs, too. Families, friends, social clubs, churches, workplaces, neighborhoods, cities, states, and countries. A dog pack has a hierarchy and a leader. So do humans. We have social classes and castes, republics and presidents, and so on."

"Churches and priests," added Dwight.

"Fiefdoms and lords," said Damon.

"Monarchies and kings," Duron said with a bow to Mac.

"Knock it off," he grumbled, and went on with his safari story. "The pack lived together on a piece of land they claimed and defended. Humans live in countries and defend them, but the packs do us one better. When rival dog packs approach each other, the alpha males step forward to fight, but *only* the alpha males. When one wins, the other pack retreats en masse."

"Survival of the fittest," Dwight commented.

"Survival of the *most*," Mac said. "Only two dogs fought. There's a lesson in that."

"Yeah. If our leaders want to go to war, then give 'em guns and let 'em shoot at each other, but don't make everyone else go to war, too," said Robbie.

"Here, here," Merrill agreed.

"Why shoot at all?" Kyle said. "Why fight? Why not reason? We need to resolve our differences without violence. Mind over matter. Words over warriors."

"Of course, Keeper," Merrill reluctantly admitted, "but t'would be enjoyable to see a scrum of politicians having it out, eh old friend?"

Kyle gave a reluctant smile, "Aye, that it would."

"There was something else I thought was very interesting," Mac added. "When one of our dogs was injured and couldn't hunt, the others brought him food until he was well enough to fend for himself."

"Do unto others, eh?" Duron said.

"As you would have them do unto you," nodded Dr. Michener.

"J.J. said it was a genetic instinct that helped the pack as a whole survive," said Mac.

Angela nodded. "It's an instinct driven by what researchers started calling the Dalai Lama gene."

"You mean the Jesus Golden Rule gene," Duron grinned.

"The Golden Rule didn't originate with Jesus, laddy," Merrill said. "The first written reference to it appeared in Egypt around 600 BCE, Buddhism around 400 BCE, Greek and Roman texts–"

"*Okay*," Duron said irritably. "Okay. The copyright goes to the Egyptians." He sighed in frustration and mumbled, "Isn't anything I learned as a kid true?"

"The Golden Rule, human altruism, quid pro quo, a Dalai Lama gene," the Professor ticked off. "They're as much an imperative as a conscious choice. We're driven much more by our DNA then we'd care to admit. It controls nearly all our actions. Our inherent need to be part of a group, our desire for advancement and recognition, our subordination to authority and our resistance to it, and so on."

"Like bosses and workers?" Mark supposed.

"Children and parents," Genevieve said.

"A penitent layman and his priest," Merrill smirked.

"A peasant and his king," Duron said, bowing to Mac again.

"Knock it off!" said the heir of Arthur, trying not to laugh.

Dr. Michener continued, "Our genetics drive our competitive-ness, our emotional need for love, our propensity for belonging and acceptance, our heterosexual or homosexual desires–"

"Whoa, whoa, whoa!" Robbie interrupted. "Being gay is *not* genetic."

"Five to 15 percent of nearly every mammal population is born homosexual," said Angela, "eight percent in *Homo sapiens*."

"Homosexuality's a choice and it's *wrong*," declared Robbie.

"Eight percent of us are homo Homos, huh?" sniggered Duron.

Damon rolled his eyes.

Mark groaned.

"Homosexuality's considered wrong simply because it's different," argued Genevieve. "Different is a threat, it upends the status quo, confuses conventional thinking, forces people out of their comfort zone, makes them wonder what else they've been wrong about."

"Alexis de Tocqueville's 'tyranny of the majority,'" Mac agreed.

"Sex is meant for procreation," Robbie argued, "not between two dudes or dudettes."

"I've known you since you were a teenager," said Duron. "If sex was just meant for procreating, you horn-dog, you'd have about 1,000 kids by now."

"I think Robbie meant to say pro-recreating," Mark grinned.

"If homosexuality's a sin, why did God create homosexuals?" Genevieve posed.

"He created liberals, too, and I don't know why the hell He did *that,*" Robbie grumbled.

"Funny," Damon said sardonically.

"Read *The Social Conquest of Earth* by sociobiologist E. O. Wilson," the Professor concluded, "and you'll be amazed at the ways animals and even *insects* act like human beings, or rather, *we* like *them.*"

Mac said, "J.J. told me everything we do starts from one of three basic motivations. Safety, sustenance, and sex. Nothing more, nothing less."

"What about after the towers fell on September 11th?" Genevieve suggested. "People from all the boroughs lined up at hospitals to donate blood. They physically sacrificed a part of themselves for others. If people can be that selfless, then surely we're more than just J.J.'s three S's."

"We're moving along a great arc of perfecting ourselves," Mac agreed. "Think of how much more punitive we were in the past. Read the Old Testament and the Koran, study the history of the Middle Ages, the Inquisition, the Crusades, slavery, the Final Solution. But amidst all that violence and war and oppression, we can find in our literature and art and legends a human ideal we've been striving to achieve, and gradually getting closer to."

"Arthur and Camelot," smiled the Keeper.

"The Five Nations," added Merrill.

"Which five nations?" said Dwight.

"Uh, oh," Mac smiled.

"Eight hundred years ago," the Elder grandly began to moans and laughs. "Eight hundred years ago," he repeated with feigned impatience, "the Seneca, Cayuga, Onondaga, Oneida, and Mohawk Indian nations were perpetually at war. Their cultures demanded that when a tribesman was killed, his nation was honor-bound to avenge him by taking one of their enemy's lives. In turn, the enemy's nation would be honor-bound to avenge *his* life and so it would go, generation after generation. But, then one day, a man named Deganawidah came and broke the brutal cycle of hate and death. It was said he was born of a virgin, became a shaman and a wanderer, and met a man from the Five Nations named Ayenwatha."

"Hiawatha?" Dwight said in surprise. "Longfellow's epic poem was based on a real person?"

"Aren't all legends?" Merrill replied. "Wasn't King Arthur and Camelot based on a real person and place?"

"I trust that was rhetorical?" Mac said drolly.

"Deganawidah and Ayenwatha confronted the powerful Onondaga warrior Chief Tododaho and asked him to cease his vengeful ways. But Tododaho considered peace so dishonorable that he ordered his warriors to kill Ayenwatha's daughter. And so, they did. Ayenwatha was then honor-bound to avenge her death, but in an act of supreme selflessness he refused. Word spread of his nobility and eventually the other four nations chose the path of peace. Deganawidah and Ayenwatha confronted Tododaho again and handed him an arrow. 'Break it,' Deganawidah told him, and the Chief did so easily. Then, Deganawidah tied five arrows together and asked Tododaho to break them. This the Chief could not do. Deganawidah said, 'Like the five arrows, the Five Nations will never be broken if they are bound together under the Great Law of Peace.' Tododaho finally understood and with his assent, the tribes came together as a single nation, forming a central governing body of representatives chosen by each tribe, and creating the first democracy in North America, one twice as old as the United States."

"Another example of our struggle to become better than we are," Mac said with a nod to Merrill. "Our animal within is gradually being subsumed by our intellect. The hands of Adam and God on the ceiling of the Sistine Chapel are drawing closer."

"From starbursts to biopolymers to human beings to gods," mused Angela.

"Uh, I don't know," Damon said apologetically. "It just doesn't quite make sense, going from less order to more, goo to gods. It's like it contradicts the Second Law of Thermodynamics."

"The universal law of increasing entropy," reflected Dr. Galatea. "Interesting point."

"What is entropy, anyway?" Mark asked.

"In a nut case," began Dr. Galatea, "it is—"

"Shell," Mac corrected him with a chuckle. "In a nutshell."

"Nutshell," the Professor said with a self-deprecating laugh. "In a nutshell, entropy is a measure of chaos or disorder. The entropy of a closed system not in equilibrium will tend to increase over time."

"Uh, yeah," Mark muttered, "clear as mud."

"All things tend to a state of greater disorder, not order," explained Damon. "Not formation, but disintegration. The Earth should tend towards greater disorder, which makes entropy and human evolution incompatible."

"A tornado in a junkyard making a 747," said Duron.

"So goes the allegory," nodded the Professor. "A closed system is like a capped Coke bottle. And in evolution's case, the Coke bottle is the Earth. Put a drop of dark red food coloring in a Coke bottle full of water and at first only a small portion of it turns red. Eventually, though, all the water reaches equilibrium and becomes pale coral."

"It would seem logical, then," Damon noted, "that if a random genetic fluke created a more sophisticated creature, it too would eventually become diluted, and fall back into a less evolved state."

"Genesis," agreed Duron. "God created Adam in His own image, meaning humankind started as a demi-god and devolved to what we are today."

"Meaning we're still devolving?" Dwight supposed.

"Next stop, Tarzanville," said Robbie.

"Paleontological evidence shows life becoming *more* ordered over the eons, though," said the Professor, "with Man appearing late in Earth's timeline."

"Which doesn't jive with the Second Law or Genesis," said Duron.

"Yes, but we're dealing with the law of averages and a very large Coke bottle here," replied Dr. Galatea. "Billions of random genetic errors naturally occur over time, a few get passed on, even fewer build on one another to create slightly more sophisticated bio-forms, and once in a great while a single organism reaches beyond 'dumb' evolution to Darwinism."

"By the grace of God," Duron smiled.

The Professor gave an indulgent smile and went on. "Once Darwinian evolution takes hold, organisms proactively seek out sources of energy and procreate in ways to increase their likelihood of survival. In other words, they fight against the Second Law, against entropy. The Second Law says the Earth Coke bottle *tends* towards greater disorder, towards equilibrium but it never has to fully achieve it. Parts of the bottle can become more ordered while others become less ordered. Humankind maintains a more evolved state because it consciously disorders its environment by killing animals, cutting down plants and trees, burning coal and oil, and so on."

"But, we can't go on doing that forever, can we?" said Damon. "Sooner or later, *everything* in our environment'll be disordered."

"Quite right," said the Professor. "If we consume our energy and other natural resources too quickly, if we let global warming get out of hand, if our rate of population growth continues exponentially," and he held up his hands in a gesture of futility.

"So we're heading towards *Soylent Green*," Damon said vexedly, referring to the 1970's Charleston Heston movie. "An overpopulated dystopic future where the world's main food source called soylent green is made from human beings!"

"Even *Soylent Green* couldn't last forever," the Professor pointed out. "All our eggs are in one basket. If we overfill it, our only hope will be to find a new home."

"Aye," agreed Merrill. "Never has the parable of the Garden Oasis been more apt."

"What's the Garden–" Mac started to ask. "Oh, no," he whispered.

"Once there was a beautiful garden oasis," the Elder began in his academic tenor, raising his voice to drown out the moans and laughs, "set amidst a great desert. There, a man and a woman lived in happy contentment within their Eden. Their love created a child and the oasis easily provided for all three of them. Soon came another and then another, multiplying their happiness. But, eventually their love bore too many children for the oasis to bear. The animals dwindled away, the trees and plants grew few in number, the family became hungry, and their clothes became rags, their homes hovels, and their nights cold. They began to fight over what little was left until one day a brother picked up a stone in anger and struck down his brother. As punishment, God sent them all into the desert. Some found other oases to live, some didn't. Those that lived multiplied again until their oases became barren, a brother picked up a stone and struck down his brother, and they were cast out once more. Again and again the cycle repeated until there were no more oases left. Death came and hunted them down one by one until only two lovers remained, hidden away in a secret Eden at God's side."

"Pretty bleak, old man," said Mac.

Mark quipped, "Better start passing out the birth control."

"There's truth in that, laddy. Decrease the birth rate or face a Malthusian catastrophe."

"Who's Malthusian? Some Greek god dude?" grinned Damon.

"Reverend Thomas Robert Malthus, an English cleric and scholar. He recognized that an increase in food and other resources led to greater population growth rather than a surplus of resources

NOVUM ORBIS REGIUM - The New World Realm

and a higher standard of living. Left unchecked, the population would someday outstrip resources, the world economy would begin to collapse, social structures would break down, physical infrastructure – gas and electrical distribution systems, transportation systems, clean water supplies – would fail, mass starvation would take hold, diseases would run rampant, wars would break out, and the population would collapse. A Malthusian curve shows the world's population over time and predicts when a collapse is likely."

"And there's one coming?" said Mark.

"Aye. It took 100 millenia for human beings to reach a population of one billion. That was in 1800. Today, just 200 years later, the world's population is seven billion. By 2100, it will be 14 billion. Think of the many thousands of beings that existed in the past but went the way of the dodos and Tasmanians. Think of the countless wars between nations. Think of *all* the violence that has *ever* plagued humanity, multiply it by 1,000, condense it into one generation, and *that* is what a Malthusian catastrophe will be like, unless we learn to live in balance with Nature."

"And in balance with the laws of thermodynamics," added Dr. Galatea.

"And their corollaries," said Mac. "Zero-sum and elemental-equivalency."

"Speak English," Mark grumbled.

"Zero-sum derives from the law that energy is neither created nor destroyed. It only changes its state of existence. Coal goes into a power plant and its energy comes out as electricity. The electricity goes to a house lamp and comes out as visible and infrared light. An old star loses its hydrostatic equilibrium and dies, its atoms are blown into space to be captured by interstellar clouds and condense into *new* stars. It's summer in the northern hemisphere, it's winter in the southern. It's night here, it's day there. The sun rises, the sun sets. Light, dark. Up, down. North, south. Plus, minus.

"Now think about life. We live, we die. We win, we lose. Good, bad. Laugh, cry. Love, hate. Everything has a cycle, and everything has an opposite. When they come together, they balance each other out. That's the zero-sum corollary. That's what living in balance with Nature requires. Give and take. Meeting in the middle."

"A good lesson for human relationships as well," Kyle said.

"Elemental equivalency derives from the fact that elements everywhere in the universe are born the same way in the same place. The stars. So, elements everywhere in the universe must have the same characteristics and obey the same laws of physics. And since man is made of elements, his every movement, sensation, and thought exists in harmony with, and because of, the laws of physics. We are of the universe and the universe is within us."

"Whoa! Far out, dude," Mark said in his best stoner voice. "*Way* out."

"Nature and man are the same. They're one. Breaking the balance between them hurts both."

"Again, we humans must live in balance with all livings things and each other if we wish to survive," said Kyle.

"There is one more corollary," Petra's daughter Katrina said excitedly, her English also spoken with a Swiss-German accent. An attractive brunette with soft brown eyes, she waitressed at her father's café between classes at university. "Simplism. It is an extension of the Second Law and reflected in the world of biology and genetics. Inside junk DNA are pseudo-genes turned off in the past, but whose remnants we can still see. Weevils that can't fly because their wings are covered by an outer shell, whales and dolphins that can't smell even though they have odor-receptor genes, humans with a coccyx, and so on, and so forth."

"Hey now, lass!" Merrill cried, crossing his legs. "I still want me cock-sis to work."

The others laughed, and Katrina blushed. "A coccyx is a tailbone," she explained. "Humans have four fused vertebrae under their skin at the base of the spine where other mammals have tails. A human tail actually forms in the womb but gets eaten away by the fetus's immune system. Sometimes, though, the pseudo-genes get turned back on and a baby is born with a tail as long as five inches complete with blood vessels, nerve fibers, hair follicles, and sweat glands."

184

"Whoa!" Mark exclaimed again.

"Nature's full of pseudo-genes. Snakes born with pelvises. Whales born with hind limbs, feet, and toes. I could cite all kinds of examples."

"Ah!" said Dr. Ingersaul, holding up a finger. Like Dr. Michener, he reached into his leather valise, pulled out an old biology book, and laid it on the dining room table. Though about the same age as Dr. Michener, Dr. Ingersaul was far more rugged looking with dark hair, brown eyes, tanned skin, and clothes only slightly out of fashion. "Biologists and paleontologists have used this chart for over a century," he explained, flipping pages until he found what he was looking for, and then turning it around so the others could see. "It shows how mammals evolved and hints at their pseudo-genes. The animals earlier on the branches remain in the DNA of the animals later on the branches." He reached back into his valise and pulled out yet another book, flipping through its pages to find another chart. "This one was created by comparing the genomes of mammals." Both resembled leafless hardwood trees lying on their side with branches stretching out in every direction and labeled with very small print.

"They're nearly identical," Mark noted.

"Where's Man?" said Duron, scanning the branches.

The Professor placed his index finger at the end of a tiny branch in the upper right corner of the diagram. "Here," and he traced it backwards to chimpanzees. "Our nearest living genetic relative who, by the way, has twenty-four chromosomes. We have only twenty-three. Two of our chromosomes fused together somehow in our evolutionary past. Maybe that mistake is what created the Hominina subtribe of primates. Maybe it helped us develop speech or spurred the development of our brains and led to our self-awareness."

Merrill studied the two diagrams' similarities. "How can there still be Creationists?" he grumbled. "The Scopes Monkey Trial is still being fought with too damned many William Jennings Bryans and not enough Clarence Darrows. All this evidence, yet half of you bloody Americans still believe the Earth is only 6,000 years old. More of you believe in angels than evolution!"

Duron cut him off. "'Anyone who will not receive the kingdom of God like a little child will never enter it,' and 'God hath chosen the foolish things of the world to confound the wise.'"

"Televangelists trot *those* out every chance they get," Merrill groused. "The last thing they want are followers who *think.*"

"Science is what science is," Robbie said, "and faith is what faith is."

"Faith and science can exist side by side if we value freedom of religion *and* the advancement of society," Duron added.

"Holy cow," Damon smiled. "You two possessed by liberal spirits or something?"

"Proverbs 14, 'A simple man believes anything, but a prudent man gives thought to his steps,'" Duron recited.

"Proverbs 19:2, 'A person without knowledge is no good,'" quoted Robbie. "Mark 4:22. 'For nothing is hidden, except to be revealed, nor has anything been secret, but that it would come to light.'"

"Words to live by, buddies," Damon said.

"It's everyone's responsibility to become as knowledgeable as possible about as many things as possible," stated Mac.

"As you have done," said the Keeper, "to a greater degree than any descendant before you."

"Careful, old friend," chided Merrill with a grin. "You'll give the lad a swelled head."

"Oh, we don't want that," Duron said. "He might start thinking he could become Secretary-General."

"Ha, ha. Let's get back to Katrina's Simplism Corollary, shall we?" Mac said.

She was more than happy to oblige. "The crux of it is this. Pseudo-genes and junk DNA make up 97 percent of our 35,000 genes. Everything we are comes from just the three percent of our DNA that's turned 'on.' The double helix structure of DNA – the source of inherited characteristics discovered by Francis Crick and James Watson in 1954 – is made up of just four base elements. A, C, G, and T. The twisted ladder of a double helix has rungs made up of only four kinds of base-pairs. A-T, T-A, C-G, and G-C. The number and placement of base-pairs along the ladder determines whether we're a ficus or a fungus, a worm or a whale, a dog or a dolphin, or a man or a mouse. Base-pairs produce only 20 different kinds of amino acids that drive our bodily functions, actions, and reactions."

"So, every living organism starts with one cell and a few percentage of 'on' genes that are made up of four base elements and four base-pairs that produce no more than 20 different kinds of amino acids?" Mac summarized.

Katrina nodded excitedly. "Yes! That is all it takes to make a human being. We are very simple creatures, hence the Simplism corollary, and it applies to everything. No matter how complex something appears, it is always simple at its most basic level."

"Why, I've never thought of it that way," said Dr. Ingersaul. "Well done."

She gave a little shrug. "I four-pointed biology."

"Of that I have no doubt," smiled the Professor.

"But, junk DNA seems antithetical to the Simplism Corollary," said Damon. "If we're simple, why do we have thirty-some-thousand genes that don't do anything?"

"You answered your own question," Katrina smiled. "The genes that are turned 'on' are very few, relatively speaking. Our 'on' genome is as simple as it can get. The genes that are turned 'off' are just refuse, the remnants of natural selection, our evolutionary history blinking on for a while and then blinking off as replication errors intermingle with our environment and move on to make something better."

"What exactly is a replication error?" Mark asked.

"Instead of an A-T, T-A, C-G, G-C sequence of rungs, a cell division ends up with a T-A, A-T, C-G, G-C sequence of rungs, for example. A person has six billion base-pairs and one out of every hundred million replications creates an error, meaning every person has 60 errors inside them. If even one of them gives the person an evolutionary advantage, then natural selection occurs."

"With that many replication errors, shouldn't we be changing like crazy?" said Mark.

"Only three percent of our genome is turned 'on,'" she reminded him. "So, nearly all replication errors occur in our junk DNA and don't matter. The rest are usually so minor as to be negligible. But, considering the billions of humans and the trillions of base-pair replications that have come and gone over the past 100,000 years, replication errors *have* collectively changed us."

"We are what we are because of our genes," Robbie said. "Genes have replication errors, errors advanced us evolutionarily. So, we are what we are because of errors?"

"Yes!" Katrina replied. "Humankind is a magnificent mistake."

"Well," drolled Damon, "that explains a lot."

"There's even a field of study called epigenetics which says we can *consciously* create positive human evolution by turning genes on or off with our lifestyles and the environments we choose to live in."

"Just what would positive evolution look like?" Duron asked warily.

"We could make humans less violent," Petra answered.

"More altruistic and empathetic," said Katrina.

"Perhaps more open-minded and less accepting of the status quo," added Dr. Ingersaul.

"More honest, forthright," Angela said, "maybe even self-tran-scendent."

"Meaning we'll all evolve into liberals," grinned Damon.

Robbie mimed throwing up.

"All the best attributes encoded into everyone's DNA. A world populated by perfect, god-like people," Mac said, "a single race of golden people with golden souls, as James Michener put it."

"A single human race," Robbie echoed. "How–" He struggled for the right word. "Horrible!"

"Horrible?" Damon said in dismay.

"Everybody the same? How would we know who's better?"

"A race of self-actualized, self-transcendent people wouldn't *care* who's better," answered Angela.

Robbie grumbled, "You intellectuals is so stupid."

After a respite of laughter, Katrina said, "Did you know there's a *genetic* basis for self-transcendence? A protein called VMAT2 that causes people to lose their sense of space and time, and more fully appreciate their oneness and interdependence with everything around them."

"Let's shoot the Republicans up with some of *that*," chortled Damon.

"The Republicans got something to shoot you with, too, buddy," said Duron.

"Certain drugs can create a temporary feeling of self-transcendence," Angela noted. "The Aztecs' peyote cactus, the Siberian shamans' psychoactive mushrooms, and the Native Americans' morning glory seeds, for instance. So, can extreme physical influences, like the dancing of the whirling dervishes, the deep meditation of the Buddhists, or the awe-inspiring magnificence of cathedrals."

"And epilepsy," Katrina interjected. "Fyodor Dostoyevsky wrote about the elation he felt just before he had a seizure."

"Right," said Angela. "So can—" She paused to look at Mac whose smile assured her it was okay.

Dr. Michener wondered what the glance and smile were about, but then recalled the confirmation hearings. "You tried to kill yourself," he said, realizing too late how impertinent he sounded. "Oh, uh, sorry, Mac."

"No worries, Doc, and I damned near succeeded."

"Oh, my!" gasped Katrina.

"While I was, you know, dead or dying or whatever, I felt this intense connectedness with my surroundings, as though I was completely a part of it and it of me. Like I never really existed alone, how none of us do. We're all part of a continuum of life."

"Your second brain was shutting down," Katrina told him.

"Exactly," Angela said.

"Mac might be smart, but *two* brains?" Robbie said with a smirk.

"He already thinks he's King Arthur, for crying out loud," Duron kidded.

"Our second brain is the cerebral cortex," Katrina explained. "It comprises nearly all of the brain's mass and function. Memory, planning, perception, sense of time, higher forms of reasoning, and self-awareness, for example. Our first brain is the limbic stem. It controls autonomic and reactionary impulses, basic emotions and anatomical functions. It's the animal at our core. When Mac approached death, the biochemical activity within his cerebral cortex began shutting down and his limbic stem began taking over."

"Our intellectual self disappears, and our core consciousness is exposed," Angela said.

"We become pure feeling," Katrina added.

"Jacob's ladder, Plato's Republic, Native American folklore, the Tibetan Book of the Dead," Angela ticked off. "They all described NDEs, probably generated by seizures, drugs or epileptic or otherwise, and misinterpreted as visiting heaven or communing with God."

"Voltaire," Merrill grumbled. "'If God did not exist, it would be necessary to invent Him.'"

"Only at the moment of death will we know whether God exists, or we invented him," Mac said as the phone rang down the hall. He sighed and said, "Back in a sec." It rang twice more before he reached the kitchen and picked up the receiver. "Guten abend?"

"Mac!" greeted an excited voice. "Is me uncle there?"

"Colin!" said Mac. "How've you been?"

"Look, mate," Kyle's nephew said impatiently, "is he there or not?"

Mac chuckled. "Yep. Where are you?"

"Casablanca. I, *Oi!* Put me uncle on!"

"Casablanca? Colin, you're not a field man."

"Just get me uncle!" he yelled.

"*Alright.* Alright. Hold on." Mac put the phone down. "Sheesh," he muttered, and walked back down the hall to get Kyle.

When he returned with the Keeper in tow, Mac pushed the speaker button on the handset.

"Nephew?" greeted Kyle.

"Uncle, I'm in Casablanca, see? And loads of people have seen foreigners out in the desert!"

"Just tourists," Mac said.

"No, mate. All Americans, all at night, and all in army transports."

It took but a moment for Mac to understand the implications. "Shit." And another moment to understand the risks. "Colin, get out of there! Go back to England and let me–"

"One more thing to check out, mate."

"Leave. Now," Kyle said.

"Just a quick trip, uncle," Colin told him.

"Get out of there!" Mac repeated.

"Bloody hell," Colin exclaimed. "Me bus is leaving. Ring you mates later," and the line went dead.

"Apparently, me nephew thinks he's James bloody Bond," Kyle said, "a delusion I'll be sure to assuage him of the next time I see him."

But, it would be a very long time indeed before they saw the young Clansman again.

ζ

"No tribal fictions need be rehearsed for us to realize that we
do, in fact, love our neighbors, that our happiness is inextricable
from their own, and that our interdependence demands that
people everywhere be given the opportunity to flourish."

– Sam Harris

"It is a far, far better thing that I do, than I have ever done; it
is a far, far better rest that I go to than I have ever known."

– Charles Dickens

Mac drove his red 1968 convertible Mustang up Raoul Wallenberg
Walk to the United Nations complex. Spotting an open parking
space in front of the General Assembly Building, he said to T.J.,
"Must be my lucky day."

"Let's hope," his friend said. "There's a hell of a lot riding on it."

Mac pulled into the open space and put the top up.

No sooner had they gotten out of the car and started towards
the Plaza of Flags than tourists surrounded Mac asking for auto-
graphs, selfies, and, most of all, to touch him. It was hardly the
first time, and he understood why. Whenever he visited a historical
place or a museum, he often felt a desire to reach out and touch
a relic. That's what he was, a living, breathing relic who dutifully
held out his hand and watched as the tourists reached back 1,500

years to close a temporal circuit between themselves, Mac, and Arthur.

When he and T.J. walked into the General Assembly hall, they saw that every ambassador was at their seat, even though only official delegates were required to attend. What's more, members of the press, families of the delegates, administrative staffers, and tourists lucky enough to get in were scrumming for seats in the gallery.

"I guess everyone wants to see if the rumors are true," T.J. said.

"What rumors?" Mac asked absently as he looked around the hall.

"That your delusions of grandeur have reached such stellar proportions that you're going to announce your candidacy for Secretary-General."

"Funny," Mac deadpanned. "You're a funny guy."

"On the other hand," T.J. said, "maybe they're just here for the fireworks."

Mac rolled his eyes. "What fireworks?"

"You and Boujeau duking it out."

"Ah. Well, I hope I don't disappoint anyone," Mac replied.

The President of the Assembly rapped his gavel.

"Just be yourself. That'll piss Boujeau off just fine," T.J. said with a half-grin as they walked down the aisle to their front row seats.

From the dais, the President of the Assembly announced in his pleasant, singsong Indian accent, "Our first order of business will be to elect a conference Chair. Do I have any nominations?"

The delegate from Tibet called out, "I nominate William Cameron MacCrarey!"

Applause filled the hall.

"I second!" shouted the Cypriot delegate.

More applause.

"Any other nominations?" he said, ignoring the Security Council delegate with his hand up. "Seeing none, I shall now call for a vote. A simple show of hands shall suffice," and every hand but one went up. "Congratulations, Mr. Chair," he said, waving Mac up onto the stage.

Obliging, Mac climbed the steps amidst tumultuous applause and exchanged brief pleasantries with the President beside the podium before accepting the gavel.

"Well, this is indeed an honor. Thank-you," Mac greeted the audience. "Today, together, we have the chance to change the course of history. With a coupe d'état of mind and spirit, we can give our nations and our people what they have waited for since 1948. True democracy, self-government, and freedom from those who believe they have the right to control our destinies simply by virtue of their economic and military might."

Cheers echoed about the hall.

"We're here today to speak with one voice and say might does *not* make right. Right is determined by the people, and *only* by the people. So, let us proceed with daring as well as humility and thoughtfulness as we debate the amendments to the Charter I am proposing." He held up a robin's egg blue folder with the UN logo on the cover. "Before each of you is a packet explaining the amendments in detail and their rationale. As we proceed, feel free to suggest improvements and new amendments to move us forward. *Always* forward."

To stage left, just out of view of the delegates, the man who had the most to lose by the conference, Secretary-General René Boujeau, paced back and forth, his fists clenching and unclenching. According to the Charter, the permanent members of the Security Council had the power to block whatever amendments the delegates came up with. But, he knew damned well that history repeated itself. Moses, Buddha, Christ, Luther, Jefferson, Gandhi, King, and others of equal greatness prevailed because of the basic human desire for self-determination and equality. If enough member states simply chose not to abide by the Charter and ignore the Security Council's directives, then the existing power structure of the United Nations would collapse as if it were made of nothing more than papier mâché. He'd be out on his French-Canadian ass and lucky to find a job as a washroom attendant.

What's more, the gossip mongrels were saying MacCrarey was going to run for Secretary-General, and his popularity alone might be enough for him to win.

Decades of careful planning, scheming, and coercion, billions of Euros secreted away, enough countries and military might to change the course of the future, and it would all be for naught if that bastard became Secretary-General.

"Never," he seethed.

"Over the past 70 years," Mac went on, "only four Articles have been amended. Three involved council memberships and the fourth weakened the power of the member states by raising the number of votes required to pass Charter amendments.

"If my amendments are adopted, every member state will be equal, and the Security Council will be simply an advisory body. We will be free to evolve into the world power for good and justice we were destined to become. Of course, all five permanent members of the Security Council and two-thirds of your home governments will have to ratify my amendments before they become part of the Charter, which could take years, if it happens at all." He paused. "Does that mean we shouldn't try? Does that mean we should just roll over and let the Security Council and Boujeau have their way?"

"No!" shouted the ambassadors.

Boujeau cursed and started forward.

"No, never. We must stand against all odds. We must send a message to the world that–" Mac noticed Boujeau making a beeline for the podium. "Ah! René, how nice of you to show your support for our conference," he said with gallant humor. "Or, perhaps you're here because of a rumor?"

"What rumor would *that* be?" Boujeau icily replied.

"Why, that I plan to announce my candidacy for Secretary-General," Mac said with feigned innocence and the chamber erupted in cheers. "Shall the campaign begin today with an impromptu debate?"

"Why not?" Boujeau said coldly. "I've never faltered in the face of a challenge, which is more than I can say for *you.*"

Mac raised an eyebrow. "Ah! You'll be taking the *high* road of campaign rhetoric, I see."

A ripple of laughter crossed the hall.

Along the left side of the hall were several floors of windowed rooms housing interpreters from around the world who translated the proceedings in real-time through headsets and laptops to the Ambassadors on the floor. English being the official language of the conference, the United States' office on the second floor was unoccupied. Or rather it should have been. In the darkened room crouched an anxious Colonel Randall Joseph Collins of the White Freedom Nation.

He raised his head above the sill of the sliding glass window to catch a glimpse of the stage. Boujeau and MacCrarey were talking, about what he couldn't tell, the former standing just to the left of Collin's line-of-sight with his back to the interpreter's office.

"Your desire to castrate the Security Council would deprive the Assembly of the Council's collective wisdom and patriarchal guidance!"

"Wisdom?" mocked Mac. "Patriarchy? All I see are five *bullies* who stand up for nothing but their own selfish interests.

Collins rested the deer rifle's long, black steel barrel on the windowsill and pressed the stock against his shoulder. He closed his left eye and peered through the scope with his right. Raising himself up until the scope's crosshairs settled dead-center on Mac's chest, he whispered, "Dead meat," and slowly began to squeeze the trigger.

A dark blur obscured his view. He cursed and opened his left eye to find Boujeau had taken a step to his right.

"Your ignorance astounds me," taunted the Secretary-General. The Assembly's job is to support the Security Council with votes of confidence no matter what they do." Boos and jeers wafted up from the audience. "You pretend to stand for the rights of others when all you really want is to turn the General Assembly into a 21st century version of King Arthur's round table and satisfy your delusions of grandeur!"

Mac noticed T.J. give a What-did-I-tell-you? shrug from the front row.

Boujeau stepped to his left again and Collins realigned the cross-hairs on Mac's chest. "Steady my hand, oh great and powerful Lord."

"Ironic that you should speak of delusions of grandeur, René, a man who desires nothing less than to run the world by his own leave."

"You will address me as Mr. Secretary-General! And I desire only to be the strong, disciplined leader the world's nations want and need, even if they're too ignorant to realize it. You, on the other hand, MacCrarey," enunciating his name with the greatest contempt, "are nothing but a media sensation, void of substance. A populist hero incapable of leadership whose ignorance and naiveté will lead the world into anarchy!"

"Die, you son-of-a-bitch," Collins breathed and pulled the trigger, just as his line-of-sight blurred again. The rifle's hammer struck the shell, detonating the gunpowder inside the casing. The slotted copper slug shot through the grooved rifle barrel and into the open air. The report thundered across the Great Hall as the fiery-hot piece of metal sliced through the back of Boujeau's skull, ripping through his brain and flattening out before exploding out of his forehead. The now mushroom-shaped slug crossed the space between the two men in a microsecond, slamming into the heir of Arthur's chest and hurling him backwards. Boujeau's dead body crumpled to the floor as Mac slid to a stop on the stage, blood pooling beneath him.

Even before the echo of the gunshot faded, Collins heard the click of a door latch behind him. He swung his rifle around, but before he could stand up, the heel of a boot slammed into the side of his head. Crashing into the windowsill, he collapsed to the floor as a tall, lean man with pale skin, blue-gray eyes, and blonde-white hair reached for the deer rifle. The Colonel struggled to hold on to it, but to no avail.

Schoen grabbed Collins roughly by the hair and slammed his head against the windowsill over and over with growing pleasure. Jamming the rifle barrel into the dazed Colonel's mouth, Schoen paused to relish the moment before pulling the trigger.

The flash of the muzzle pushed back the darkness just long enough to reveal a cloud of bloodied flesh and bone that had once been the back of Collins's head. Letting go of the man's hair with a shuddering sigh of pleasure, the Under Secretary-General wiped his fingerprints off the gun and placed it back in the dead man's hands.

A blinding flash of light and Mac found himself lying on the deck of his condo in Traverse, a tear running down his cheek, arms and legs growing numb, the stars above blurring as his eyesight dimmed. The world seemed to slow, and feelings of sadness and loneliness mixed with the sensation of a breeze from the bay rolling over the deck. Pine trees swayed and crickets chirped as he struggled to stay awake, his breaths fewer and farther between. Finally, the pain faded and along with it the stars.

"The world lost two of its most important men at the United Nations campus in New York City today," said National Public Radio's representative to the UN Charter Amendment Conference, veteran reporter Daniel Cohen, on *All Things Considered* that evening. "A day people around the world will look back on for a generation and remember where they were when they heard the news. One was a man who led the greatest governing body of nations in the world, the other a man who aspired to do the same. In a bizarre double-murder-suicide, a lone gunman shot dead the United Nation's Secretary-General René Boujeau and United States Deputy Ambassador William Cameron MacCrarey with a single bullet before turning the gun on himself. MacCrarey's stand against the Chinese in Tibet with His Holiness the Dalai Lama, his nearly single-handed capture of Pompous Zeda on Cyprus, his ending of the bloodshed in Brazil and his discovery of Little Deutschland had made him an international hero. His accomplishments earned him a long list of enemies as well. René Boujeau, Secretary of State Jake Tanner, Vice President Jack Abrams, and even President Mitchell Thomas have publicly denounced him in the past. Secretary of Homeland Security Johnny

Swaywell had even mounted a one-man crusade against MacCrarey, going so far as to label him the Beast of the Apocalypse.

"How the investigation will unfold, who the gunman was, and why he took the lives of two notable men is anybody's guess. That will be for the new Acting Secretary-General of the UN, Gerhardt Schoen, to sort out.

"It can at least be said that MacCrarey, the last living heir of the legendary King Arthur, did not die in vain. Moments after the two men were taken to Mount Sinai Hospital, the Charter Amendment Conference was hastily reconvened, and the delegates voted unanimously to ratify the amendments MacCrarey had proposed. Tomorrow, the full Assembly is expected to follow suit, removing the Security Council's unilateral power. This may be the start of a movement that not only turns the United Nations' power structure upside down, but the entire world's as well.

"As many of our listeners undoubtedly know, the new FCC has accused NPR of subversive and seditious reporting. NPR's attempts to defend itself in court have been blocked by judges appointed by President Thomas. History has taught us that a government treating free and honest speech as subversive and solid journalism as seditious is leading the nation down a road that one day ends in fascism, or in America's case, theofascism.

"Threats of violence against our reporters ginned up by the far right and the recent brutal murder of a member station manager last week in Houston has led NPR to the heartrending decision to suspend operations. If and when we return to the air will depend on whether we, as a nation, can return to civility and a respect for the truth. Until that day comes, this is Daniel Cohen reporting, perhaps for the final time."

On a windy winter day, dignitaries and politicians from around the world came to pay their respects to Secretary-General René Boujeau at his formal state funeral in Montreal.

Six hundred miles to the west, only friends and loved ones gathered around a grave to listen to the Keeper's eulogy. "The world dreams of a new Camelot, another Arthur," he said, though Genevieve wasn't listening. She held Cameron's hand and stood close to Father Hadley of the St. Aurelius parish in Traverse.

Cameron looked up at her weeping mother and asked again, "Where's Daddy?" But Mommy didn't answer. She couldn't. All she could do is kneel down and hug her daughter.

"Your father loves you very much," Father Hadley whispered.

Kyle went on. "Our Clan shall forge on, dedicating itself to the last heir and her descendants in the hopes of a future when peace, justice, and prosperity reigns for everyone."

Father Hadley took a handful of earth from the snow-dusted mound, held it out at arm's length, and slowly let it fall through his fingers into the grave. "From earth we come, to earth we return. The marks we leave behind are the memories of those who love us. May William Cameron MacCrarey rest in peace, and may we remember his nobility the rest of our days. Amen."

The others echoed their "Amens" and with one last look at the grave, Genevieve dabbed the tears from her eyes and turned away. "Take us home," she said to Michael.

"Of course," he said, touching Cameron on the cheek and leading them to the waiting limousine where Charles stood holding the door open. "I'll catch a ride with Kyle, Charles."

His valet-butler-chauffer and longtime friend nodded, closing the door behind Genevieve and Cameron. The elder Abrams watched them drive off and then walked back to join Kyle and Merrill. "What now?" he asked.

"Our last heir," the Keeper replied simply, though it sounded hollow even to him.

"Yes, of course," said Michael as Marion, T.J., Angela, Katrina, Petra, and Mac's friends joined them.

"What's that, lad?" said Merrill.

T.J. held up the folder in his hand. "Copy of the coroner's report."

"Throw it away," Michael ordered. "Let the UN investigators do their job. It doesn't concern us anymore."

"Yeah, well, maybe it should," Sean told him. "Maybe we should do a little investigating of our own. Schoen doesn't give a damn who was responsible."

"It's over," Michael said angrily and reached for the folder.

Sean made a grab for it too, and a three-way tug of war raged until Kyle commanded them to stop. They all let go at once and the folder fell free, opening like a butterfly's wings and sending papers and photos fluttering to the ground.

Sean tried to apologize as he knelt down, but the words wouldn't come. He covered his face and sobbed. Michael put a hand on the young man's shaking shoulder and said softly, "This too shall pass, my friend."

Dwight and T.J. helped gather up the papers, the former picking up the coroner's photo of the dead gunman. "Oh, geeze," Dwight said in disgust. "Like out of a slasher movie or something," and he handed it to T.J.

"Hold on," Sean choked out, reaching for the picture.

"Gross, huh?" said Dwight.

"No. I mean, yeah, but I've seen lots of gunshot wounds. *That*, though," and he pointed at the assassin's upper torso, "I've only seen once."

On the man's chest was a windmill-shaped tattoo with four triangles, each with two sides of equal length and right angles between them. The lines going from left to right and up and down were red, the vertical line longer than the horizontal one. The angled lines were black and formed an X. From each of its legs protruded equal-length black, dagger-like lines at right angles, a single drop of tattooed blood dangling from their tips.

"The gunman in Geneva had that on his shirt," Petra commented.

Mark stared at the photo and shrugged. "I don't get it."

"Watch," Duron told him, running his finger down one red line from the top of the tattoo to the bottom and then across the second red line from left to right. "A cross." Then he traced his finger along the black, zig-zagging lines. "And a swastika."

Mark scrunched up his face. "That's sick!"

"And to think," said Merrill wistfully, "the swastika was once a symbol of good fortune and prosperity to the people of the Far East."

"That was before the Nazis got hold of it, wasn't it?" said Duron.

"A second lieutenant I knew had a tattoo like that," Sean told them. "Bastard was always talking down anyone who wasn't a WASP like him. Bragged that he'd joined the Army to, 'Kill me some kikes, but I'd settle for a sand nigger or two.'"

"What happened to him?" said Katrina.

"Dishonorable discharge for punching an African-American drill sergeant."

"Where is he now?" said Mark.

"Either in prison or politics, probably," muttered Robbie.

"Prison," Sean answered.

"I was joking, dude."

"Not a prisoner. A prison contractor. The military used 'em in Iraq. He was assigned to Abu Ghraib and after it was closed for abusing inmates, he shipped out to Guantanamo. Still there as far as I know, probably one of the soldiers who waterboarded those prisoners."

"Son of a bitch," Robbie growled.

"So, what do we do now?" said Duron.

"Nothing," Michael told him.

Sean started to argue, but Kyle held up a hand. "Mac is dead. He is the past and Cameron is the future. Throw the picture away."

Soon, snow covered the graves, the news anchors moved on to the next crisis, the holidays came and went, and a bone-chilling winter gripped the Midwest. A poor little girl wearing a ragtag winter coat and what were once shiny, black leather shoes with white, sequined bows made her way alone along a dark Chicago street.

Little Dorothy Ann looked down at her cold, wet feet in sad amusement. How could they still be there? she wondered, unable to feel them anymore. The memory came to her again of how the shoes had been a gift from her mother the day before she'd disappeared. How long ago had that been – a few weeks? A month? Two? She couldn't say anymore.

The shy nine-year old, smart and quick to smile, had come home from school one day to an empty house. Dinner time came and went and still her parents hadn't come home. She called the university looking for her father, only to be told he'd left three hours before. She called her mother's friends, but no one knew where she was. She went to the neighbors who looked nervously this way and that before shooing her off their front steps and slamming the door.

She cried herself to sleep that night and awoke to the doorbell the next morning. Hope rising, she jumped out of bed, ran down the stairs, and flung open the door, only to find a stranger standing on the porch. A fair-complexioned woman with dark blue eyes and short brown hair looked down her short, pointed nose in disapproval. In her long-hemmed pale pink woolen dress and matching waist-length jacket and hat, she reminded Dorothy Ann of Professor Umbridge from the Harry Potter movies.

"I am from Christ Charities United," she said deliberately. "The government pays us to look after wayward children who've lost their parents."

Little Dorothy Ann put her hands on her hips. "My parents aren't lost."

The corners of the pink lady's lips curled slightly, and she took a little pink notebook out of her pink carpetbag purse. "I am required by law to ask you the following questions." Studying Dorothy Ann's dark wavy hair, brown eyes, and olive skin, she said accusingly, "You're part Greek, part Native American, and part Irish Catholic, yes? Your father wrote articles for the university paper criticizing our Christian government, didn't he?" She glanced at the black band with a silver zero Dorothy Ann wore on her left wrist. "Are you a Christian, child?"

Dorothy Ann hated that wristband. "Are you?"

"Answer my question!" the woman snapped.

Dorothy Ann planted her feet and crossed her arms. "What difference does it make? My mom says I can be anything I want."

"Your mother was *wrong*," the woman hissed. "Now *answer* my question!"

"No!"

Filled with the rage of the righteous, the woman drew her hand back and slapped the little girl hard across the face. "Answer me!"

Dorothy Ann stepped back, raising a hand to her stinging cheek. "No," she said, holding back her tears.

The woman leaned down and said with an unnerving calm, "Fine. The Lord giveth, and the Lord taketh away."

The next morning, Dorothy Ann awoke to the sound of a truck pulling up in front of her house. She looked out her bedroom window to see a moving van and a police car at the curb. In the driveway sat a VW station wagon. Out of the back seat hopped a blonde boy and girl around Dorothy Ann's age. Their mother got out and walked around the car to where the father stood looking up at the house. She was noticeably pregnant and smiled up at him adoringly.

Then, the other passenger door opened, and the pink church lady got out.

Dorothy Ann ran down the stairs and flung open the front door. "Go away!" she screamed through the screen door.

With a self-satisfied grin, the pink church lady came up the walk saying, "Your house belongs to *them* now." She gestured to the fair-haired family who seemed oblivious to what was happening. "You have five minutes to get out."

"No!"

From her pink purse, the woman produced an official-looking document with the words United States Department of Christianity printed across the top in bold letters, and a seal with an eagle holding a clutch of arrows in one claw and a cross in the other.

"It's our house!" yelled Dorothy Ann.

The officers got out of their patrol car. "Trouble?" the older of the two asked the pink lady.

"Why, yes," she said with a simper.

Dorothy Ann backed away from the door. Thinking fast, she opened the coat closet and rummaged around until she found a box half-full of wax candles. She and her mother had made them to take to the homeless people in the blast zone downtown, a ten-mile-wide and 20-mile-long swath of the city contaminated by the nuclear bomb's fallout. The cordoned off zone had no water or electricity, and the nearly one million victims of radiation poisoning inside were forbidden from leaving. The reason, her father told her, was that some people believed God wanted the victims to die a horrible death as a lesson to the rest of us, and since God ordained it, helping them was declared illegal. Still, many Chicagoans, including Dorothy Ann and her mother, showed up every day along the edges of the zone to bring food, bottled water, clothing, medicine, and candles to the condemned.

Dorothy Ann grabbed the box and ran to the kitchen. Rummaging through the pantry, she filled the box with Campbell's soup cans, a jar of peanut butter, saltines, and a bag of raisins.

Hurrying into the mudroom, she took her mother's overcoat from the wall hook and grabbed the first pair of shoes she saw, her new black leather pumps with the white sequined bows. She slipped them on, grabbed her mother's purse, and tried not to cry as she bravely walked back to the front door.

"Where am I supposed to go?" she said with a quavering voice.

"That's for the Lord to decide," the woman replied, yanking open the screen door and taking Dorothy Ann roughly by the arm.

Pulling away, Dorothy Ann escaped down the steps and ran across the snow-covered front yard to the sidewalk. She glanced back to see the Norman Rockwell family walk up the front steps to where the pink lady stood like a guard dog. Dorothy Ann turned away, and let the tears finally have their way.

Within the week, what little money she had was gone. After that, she sold candles on the street. Most passersby ignored her, even crossed the street to avoid her. One called her lazy and another screamed at her for trying to take hard-earned money away from decent people. One day a lady held out a dollar, but when Dorothy Ann handed her a candle, the lady's husband saw the wristband with the silver zero and snatched the dollar away.

"Martha," he warned, nodding at the girl's arm. "Put the candle back before they see us."

There were other symbols on wristbands, too, her father had told her. Yellow six-pointed stars for Jews, brown crescent moons for Muslims, black 3/5's for African-Americans, and silver zeroes for agnostics who were supposedly nothing in God's eyes. Dorothy Ann tried time and again to cut off the wristband, but nothing worked. So did other people, and more than once she'd seen a person with a stump where a hand and wristband used to be.

Her body trembled from cold and hunger as she shuffled past burned-out shells of abandoned buildings and the crumbled ruins of the Willis Tower. The filthy and torn clothes she wore hung loosely on her bone-thin frame, and the gently falling snowflakes covered her thick, unkempt hair. Taking a wide berth of the steel drum fires where the sick and dying gathered to stay warm, she carried the damp soot-covered box with the food she'd scrounged and the last of her candles to her new home.

Slipping through the doorless entrance of what had once been an apartment building, she made her way up six flights of stairs to the roofless top floor and down a burned-out, debris-filled hallway. She laid down on a pile of torn sheets and singed towels in the apartment at the end of the hall and looked up at the stars. A frigid draft swirled around her tiny body and with a shudder, she drew herself up into a ball and stared longingly at the box of candles. When another icy gust whipped about the room, she took a wooden match from the box, drew it down the charred wall, and touched flame to wick. A warm glow and flowery scent pushed the ashen blackness away. Warming her hands over the dancing flame, her shivers slowly gave way to a pleasant drowsiness.

Falling into it, she soon found herself in her grandmother's northern Michigan cottage toasting marshmallows with her parents in the fireplace to make S'mores. They ate and laughed over the gooey mess, and when it was time for bed, they unrolled their sleeping bags in front of the hearth and climbed inside. Dorothy Ann shimmied close to her mother during the night and when she woke in the morning, her father was cooking bacon, eggs, and hash browns over the fire.

The flame of the candle faded. Unseemly shadows crept closer and cries of the sick and dying echoed down alleyways. An icy chill shook her to the core and she drew another match down the wall, reached for a second candle, and lit it.

Once more the glow chased away the gloom and her grand-mother's cottage reappeared. A Christmas wreath hung above the fireplace and stockings dangled from the mantle. Thin red candles burned in brass holders and filled the room with the scent of peppermint. A Christmas tree decorated with strings of lights, tinsel, and ornaments stood in front of a window overlooking the frozen lake. She heard people talking and laughing in the next room and found her parents, aunts, uncles, cousins, and grandmother sitting around a dining room table. On the snow-white linen tablecloth stood a crystal vase of fresh flowers and long white tapered candles. A roasted turkey sat on a silver tray surrounded by a basket of fresh-baked bread and bowls of stuffing, mashed potatoes, creamed corn, and gravy, all steaming famously. She hurried around the table and sat down in the empty chair between her mother and father. Filling her plate, she ate and ate until her belly felt like it would burst, but still she made room for slices of pumpkin and mincemeat pies.

The flames of the candles spluttered, her parents began to fade, and the dining room grew dark and cold. A sickening, ravenous hunger clawed at her belly and the ashen walls of her apartment returned. She scrambled for another match and lit the last candle.

Joyously, she found herself sitting on the couch in front of the fireplace wrapped in her mother's arms. She felt a love so grand and timeless that even heaven itself couldn't be as wonderful.

"Mommy," she whispered, "take me with you before the candle burns out."

"I will," her mother answered, and the light from the fire grew brighter. "I promise."

"I love you, mommy."

"I love you, too," her mother said with a kiss.

"I missed you so much!"

Her mother held her tighter and said, "We'll never be apart again."

The light from the fire grew brighter and brighter, and the two of them rose into the air swirling around each other as if dancing on the wind. The cold and hunger, the hurt and sorrow faded. "I love you," said Little Dorothy Ann as their love and the light became one.

Never had a story affected Jan Roberts so deeply. When she'd worked the city beat for *The Times,* she'd filed stories about kids OD'ing, dying in car crashes, being abused by monstrous parents, and shot by gangs. Yet this girl, this little, "Dorothy Ann," she whispered, touched her to the core. On the computer screen before her was a one-paragraph article.

"The Chicago Police Department reported that the body of nine-year-old Dorothy Ann Athos was found late yesterday in a burned-out blast zone apartment building. Since coroner's reports for Zeroes are prohibited by federal law, no definitive cause of death was given. However, her demise was likely related to bitterly cold temperatures and malnourishment. Her body will be disposed of in the city incinerator within the required 24-hour period."

"How alone and desperate she must have been," whispered Jan, wiping a tear from her cheek. She looked again at the pictures, one a school photo of a beautiful dark-featured child, the other of a dirty emaciated corpse with open, lifeless eyes and an inexplicable smile etched on her face.

The sounds of an excited crowd in the street below wafted up to Jan's second-floor apartment window. She crossed the room and leaned out to see dozens of people heading towards Washington

Square. There'd been several rallies around the city in recent weeks, each becoming more daring than the last, and the reporter in her sensed a story. Drying her eyes, she grabbed her jean jacket and iPhone and ran down the stairs.

"Back in a bit!" she said to Tony the doorman as she hurried past.

"Sure ting, Ms. Roberts," the stocky Brooklynite said as he held the door open for her.

Joining the throng, Jan quickly learned that playwright and NYU Professor of History David Connors was about to give a speech in the square. Turning the corner at the end of her street, she saw hundreds of people converging on the park from every direction. Opening her iPhone video app, she sized up the crowd and waded in.

Testing a speaker system on a makeshift stage, a young co-ed from the university's AV department said, "Test, test, test," into a mic. Milling about in friendly comradery, the crowd carried signs and strung up banners while chanting slogans popularized on social media of late.

Professor Connors walked out onto the stage and the crowd roared.

With a sweep of his hand he said, "Hard to imagine looking about at these pricey brownstones, upscale apartments, and trendy shops that once upon a time this square was wilderness. The first Europeans settled down near Battery Park in the 1600's south of Wall Street, which was originally a street that ran along a wall meant to protect the settlers not from Native Americans, but from other Europeans. Nothing but forest, outcroppings of rocks, and the occasional Native American trail used for hunting and trading stretched north to here and beyond. Eventually, this became farmland and after a yellow fever epidemic in 1797, the city turned it into a potter's field for the dead. Still today, the remains of more than 20,000 poor souls lay beneath our feet."

That caused an unpleasant stir, quickly followed by tension-relieving laughter.

"In 1825, it became a military parade ground, in 1850 a park, in 1892 the city erected this," and he pointed up at the 80-foot tall

Washington Square Arch, "in tribute to George Washington's inauguration as President here in New York City a century before. At the time of his inauguration, the Constitution was only three years old, having replaced the Articles of Confederation, which had created a weak central government and strong, independent states which looked after their own interests, selectively enforced Congress's laws, and decided if and when they'd send the central government its tax revenues. The Articles were a complete and utter *disaster*, yet the far right is fighting *again* for strong states' rights and a weak federal government, so they can pick and choose which Washington laws and Supreme Court rulings to obey. They want to thumb their nose at progressivism. They want to cry 'religious freedom' whenever their medieval Christian values are challenged. Yet, history teaches us that only a strong Constitutional *central* government can guarantee equality, liberty, and equal protection under the law for *everyone*."

Cheers and applause rolled across the square and echoed back off the surrounding buildings.

"That's why we're here today. To tell those in power to respect our Constitutional rights. To counter the unconscionable acts committed by the White House and Congress that smack of Hitlerism!"

The crowd roared again as Jan moved about capturing the moment on her iPhone. Panning around the square, she noticed a clutch of reporters with press badges standing across the street. Why weren't they mingling with the protestors? she wondered. None held a tape recorder, a video camera, or even a notepad. She wondered how they were going to file a story. But then it hit her. They'd *already* filed their stories.

"Every great civilization falls," Connors went on. "It may take centuries as it did for Rome, or it could take mere hours as it did in the Arab Spring, thanks to the breakneck speed and power of social media."

A deep, booming *crack* sounded from behind Jan. She spun around looking for its source but noticed nothing out of the ordinary. When she turned back to the stage, she saw Professor Connors staggering backwards, a red stain spidering across his white shirt.

He regained his balance for a moment, but then collapsed face first onto the stage.

People began screaming and running this way and that. A troop of men and women dressed in Boy Scout-like uniforms marched into the Square from a side street. Freedom Patrollers, she realized, thugs who took freedom *away* from others like Hitler's Brownshirts did in the Thirties. They pushed into the panicking crowd, swinging their blackjacks and billy-clubs, the sound of their hard leather heels on pavement mixing with shrieks of pain.

More shots sounded, and a bullet whizzed by Jan's head. Forcing herself to stay calm, she stood her ground and panned the camera back and forth, back and forth until one of the thugs pointed her way. He shouted something to his comrades and they started for her.

Zooming in on them, she shouted, "Smile!" and took off at a run for her apartment building. Halfway down the block, she realized she'd never make it to Tony in time. Pulling her keychain from her purse, she sprinted towards her car parked down the street, pressed the FOB, and jumped in. Slamming the door closed, she pushed the FOB again and all four doors locked. A Brownshirt leapt onto the hood and pounded his fists on the windshield.

"Gimme your phone, bitch!" the bald-headed Patroller screamed.

Four more ran up and grabbed for the door handles.

"Do it!" one of them yelled.

A baseball bat came down with a crash and the rear window shattered. Jan turned over the engine, threw the transmission into first, and cranked the steering wheel hard to the left. Punching the accelerator, she let up the clutch and the car lurched away from the curb, fishtailing into the street.

The Brownshirt on the hood rolled off with a, "Bitch!"

Jan whipped the wheel to the right and gunned it. At the end of the block, she slammed on the brakes and looked back. The bald Patroller stood in the middle of the street pointing a gun at her. A sickening fear surged through her and just as she was about to punch the accelerator again, Tony sprinted out of the doorway to her apartment building and barreled into the Patroller, lifting him off the ground and flattening him against the side of a passing double-decker tour bus.

Jan rolled down the window, blew him a kiss, and drove away.

"Well, well, well, cub," Walt Jenson, her former newsroom editor, said as he sat down. "Been a long time. Now that you're a big shot and all, you don't have time for us little folk anymore?" He was hardly little folk, they both knew, producing a weekly primetime news show for a major broadcast network.

"I'd give anything to be a cub reporter again," she sighed and sipped her coffee. "Maybe America needs to be a cub again, too."

Walt's smile faded. "What happened?"

"The square," she said, holding back a tear. "They chased me."

"Washington Square? Geez, cub. You alright?"

"Yeah," she said with a forced smile. "Just shook up a bit."

"Tell me what happened," he said, and so she did.

"Then I crossed the George Washington Bridge," she finished, "parked along a quiet neighborhood street in Hoboken and fell asleep in my car. When I woke up, I found this place and called you." She reached over and squeezed his hand. "You're one of the few people in this city I can trust, Walt."

"I'm here for you, kid," he said, and meant it. "What d'ya need?"

"I've been working on a documentary and, it's really important stuff, you know? But, all my research is at my apartment and, and I don't–"

"Where and when, kid?"

From their table by the coffee shop window, they had a clear view of her apartment building down the street. After half an hour, Walt said, "I think it's clear," and threw a ten-spot on the table.

"Two men was lookin' for you's earlier, Ms. Roberts," Tony the doorman announced when they were in earshot. "I told 'em you was probably in Washington."

"Thank you, Tony," Jan said as they walked up to the door. "And thank you for yesterday."

Tony grinned and gave a dismissive wave of his hand. "You's kiddin'? I been lookin' for a chance to beat the crap outta one of them cretins."

Jan smiled and said, "Be back in a second."

"No problem, Ms. Roberts. No one'll bother you's. I promise."

Unlocking the door to her apartment, she stepped in and gasped.

"Jesus," Walt muttered, looking over her shoulder. "The bastards really did a number on the place."

She sniffled and started for the desk. "I need to get my files."

"Grab some clothes, cub, and let's get out of here. I'll get the files."

She hesitated, gave a nod and headed into the bedroom.

The drawers of the file cabinet and desk had been emptied, their contents unceremoniously dumped in a pile. Walt stood there, hands on his hips, wondering where to start.

"Cupcake recipes!" she called from the bedroom.

He gave a little laugh and said, "Been expecting this, huh, cub?"

By the time she returned with a garment bag slung over her shoulder, he had two cardboard boxes full of flash drives, printouts, and file folders labeled with names like Almond Poppyseed, Black Forest, and Blueberry Crumble.

"Let's go," he said and out they went, not bothering to close the door behind them.

Reaching the foyer, Jan gave Tony the doorman a kiss on the cheek. "You take care of yourself, okay?"

He blushed and touched the spot where her lips had been a moment before. "Where you's–?" He held up a hand. "Never mind. I don't wanna know. You's take care, too, Ms. Roberts," and he held the door open for her one last time.

In the end, 135 demonstrators had been beaten, trampled, or shot. Twenty-nine of them died. Only one of the reporters present that day filed a story even remotely close to the truth. Two days later, his newspaper was shut down by Homeland Security for purportedly, "Spreading seditious left-wing lies." In a written statement, the White House called the demonstrators in Washington Square, "drug-laced, licentious liberals." The President declared Professor Connors guilty of, "inciting a riot, damaging private property, threatening public safety, and corrupting the morality of America's youth." Under the newly enacted Liberty Laws, his death was ruled a legal execution. By week's end, Congress had banned all unauthorized public gatherings and extended legal immunity to Freedom Patrollers who injured protestors "in the line of duty."

Only a handful of close colleagues and personal friends knew what Walt Jenson and Jan Roberts were about to do. Shortly before airtime, they gathered the news team together in the control booth.

"You're not doing the show, people," Walt told them.

The crew looked at each other and then back at their stone-faced boss.

"So, what are we gonna do?" said Nick, Walt's AP.

"I'm running her documentary," Walt answered, pointing at Jan who was leaning against the controls console, "and she is going to host it, but here's the thing. This ain't just any documentary, and it ain't the same ol' crap that's been passing as news lately. It's hard hitting and it's gonna get the network in a lot of trouble, and I mean a *lot* of trouble. So, I'm telling you to leave."

Nobody moved an inch.

"Now," he told them.

Still no one moved.

"That's an *order*. Leave! All of you!"

They might as well have been pillars of salt.

"It's for your own good!" Walt yelled. "Go!"

"We talking *real* journalism?" Tiffany the broadcast supervisor said.

"Yeah. The truth, whole truth, and nothing but the truth, knock 'em down, investigative journalism. The stuff we all went to school for back when we were idealists. Now go!"

She looked at the others. "I'm in."

"Me, too," Pete the cameraman said.

"Hell, yeah," said Sam the lighting engineer.

"It's about fuckin' time we did some news again," Nick grumbled.

"I'm not going anywhere," agreed Frank the sound engineer.

A grudging but proud smile crossed Walt's tired face. "Let's get this show on the road," he relented.

"Yes!" cried Pete with a high-five for Sam.

Tiffany laughed in relief and Frank gave Walt a grateful nod.

"One minute!" Nick yelled, and everyone hurried to their places.

A flat screen computer monitor mounted to the window frame above and to the right of Walt's controls console displayed a real-time ratings website. The y-axis displayed the number of households tuning in, the x-axis the show's running time. The curve for the show airing before his sloped to zero as it wrapped up.

"Okay, people, we're live in…ten, nine, eight," and when Nick got to one, Walt pointed to Jan.

"Good evening, America. I'm Jan Roberts sitting in for Peter Murrow. Tonight, we'll be broadcasting a commercial-free documentary about America today. Not the one Washington has told you about or websites allowed to stay online describe, but the *real* America today. And let me warn you, it's not for the faint of heart."

The screen faded to black and a moment later the picture of a dark-complexioned little girl appeared, her mother and father standing to either side. The camera focused in on her eyes sparkling with the carefree contentment of youth, but then the sparkle faded into a blank stare, the camera pulled away, and she was curled up in a pile of sooty rags, snow dusting her frozen cheeks and black hair.

216

"This was little Dorothy Ann Athos," Jan Roberts' voice over began. "Last winter, she was found dead in a burned-out Chicago blast-zone apartment building. Her parents were reported missing shortly after the holidays and her home had been confiscated by a faith-based government contracting firm and given to this family." Up came a picture of the fair-skinned couple and their blonde, blue-eyed children. "The parents are generous tithers to the church that owns the contracting firm." The picture remained on the screen for another moment before a sequence of photos and video clips played of families forced out of their homes, people fired because of their beliefs, snapshots of wrist bands like the ones made popular years before to promote cancer research, but now engraved with images of a 3/5, a zero, an Islamic crescent, a Star of David, and an eyeball.

"Muslims and Jews have to wear a crescent moon or a Star of David. Former convicts, people on welfare, and anyone else Homeland Security deems morally suspect, have to wear a band with an eyeball on it. Three-fifths is a reference to the fact that our Constitution said an African-American slave was to be counted as three-fifths of a person. Though the 14th amendment did away with that clause, our new government reduces by one-fifth the votes of blacks and anyone of color on Election Day, on Juries, and in any majority-rules setting." Dorothy Ann's dead body reappeared, and the camera zoomed in on her black wrist band with the silver zero. "Atheists and agnostics have to wear this."

A choir sang *What a Friend We Have in Jesus* and the inside of a massive church sanctuary appeared. In front, several middle-aged white men in suits were handing out gold pins to parishioners coming up the center aisle. "Swearing in ceremonies like this one have been held in Christian churches around the country for men and women volunteering to join what are called, in Orwellian fashion, Freedom Patrols. Their members canvas their communities and report wrongdoers to local Homeland Security offices. Arrest records reveal a pattern of Constitutional violations, particularly for those wearing wrist bands." The video image froze. "The woman being handed a pin is the one who threw little Dorothy Ann Athos out of her home." The screen again faded to black.

"There have been other swearing-in's as well," Jan went on, "like this one in Dallas last month," and a video played of a federal appeals court judge taking an Oath of Faith. "'I hereby swear to perform the duties of my position and to uphold the Constitution of the Christian United States of America and the laws set down by the Almighty in the Christian Bible to the best of my abilities, so help me God.'" Pictures flashed past in rapid succession of municipal judges, city officials, public school teachers, Professors at state-funded universities, even executives of publicly traded corporations taking the same oath. Captions listed each person's name, title, and where they worked. A quick fade to black, and then another procession of photos, this time of people who *refused* to take the oath, showing their names and the dates they were reported missing.

The screen above Walt's head showed viewership passing the 10 million mark and rising fast. He rapped on the plate glass window and gave Jan a thumbs-up. She responded with a melancholy smile and he well understood why. This was the greatest moment of her career, but what would the government do to her once it was over?

A montage of photos appeared on the screen of President Thomas's Cabinet members. Jan's voiceover gave the professional qualifications, or rather lack thereof, of each. "The President's appointees come from the Christian National Separatists Political Action Committee, the ranks of the ultra-rich, major political contributors, businessmen, and pundits who made names for themselves by criticizing previous administrations and saying certain federal departments ought to be shut down."

A black and white photo appeared of a long conference table with Thomas and his Cabinet members seated around it. "You may recognize some of the leading evangelical ministers among those seated here. They have standing invitations to attend any White House meeting they wish. Ronald Reagan, who President Thomas refers to as Saint Ronald, started the practice, often hosting Jerry Falwell and Hal Lindsey at National Security briefings."

Next came a video of a military officer walking through the concourse of Washington Dulles Airport. The caption read, 'General Billy Boyd.'

"Why do you think President Thomas appointed you Chair of the Joint Chiefs of Staff?" a female reporter asked as she half-walked, half-ran to keep up with him.

"The President appoints whoever he believes will make America the Promised Land it once was."

"Wouldn't you admit there were more qualified candidates than you?" she said.

Boyd stopped. "I've been a United States Marine for 40–"

"Forty-three years, General, and in your acceptance speech you said, 'The strength of our country comes from the blessings of our Lord, Jesus Christ, and the might of our military.' But, the Constitution says–"

"I've seen the mighty hand of God, child," he said, pointing an accusatory finger at her. "And I know He respects strength When my Black Hawks in Mogadishu came under enemy fire, I saw the face of Satan in the clouds looking down on us. So, I prayed to God and the words of Daniel came to me and I cried out, 'Blessed be the God who has sent His angel and delivered His servants who trusted in Him.'"

"You *failed* to rescue the hostages, General," she pointed out.

"In Syria when–"

"Do you believe God elected Mitchel Thomas President and appointed you Chair of the Joint Chiefs of Staff?"

"Absolutely," the General answered righteously.

"You attend the Reverend-Secretary's Church of Eternal Vigilance in Alexandria?"

He nodded proudly. "The Reverend is a good man and our country needs more men like him during times of war."

"What war?" she exclaimed in exasperation. "We've pulled our troops out of every military theater and peacekeeping operation in the world! We've declared war on no one and no one's declared war on us!"

"The war against *terror*, young lady. The war against liberals. The war against atheism. The war to make the United States a decent, wholesome, Fatherland of God once again!"

"A war fought with minds or might? By civil rights or soldiers?"

Boyd leaned into her face. "Whatever it takes," he hissed.

"You'd be willing to kill Americans to make America a Christian nation?"

Another step forward.

"Being a murderer is being a Christian?" she taunted, taking a step back.

Boyd's face flushed. He grabbed her tape recorder with one hand and hauled back to punch her with the other. The picture started jumping around and a linebacker-sized arm appeared in the frame as the cameraman grabbed the General's jacket.

"The reporter interviewing General Boyd," Jan noted, "was reported missing by her station chief shortly after this interview."

The picture faded to black. A deep, thunderous rumble gradually grew louder and louder until the screen lit up and an F-22A stealth fighter jet appeared flying straight at the camera.

"All restrictions on arms dealing were lifted by Congress six days into Thomas's term. Free to peddle their wares to the highest bidder, the American arms industry is…making a killing. Fifty of these high-tech fighter jets were sold to an arms dealer in Morocco earlier this year. When asked how a dealer of second-hand rifles came across 40 billion Euros, the CEO of Lockhart-Mead said proudly, 'I don't care how people get their money. My job is to make money for Lockhart-Mead's shareholders.' When asked what the arms dealer intended to do with the jets, he huffed and said, 'Lockhart-Mead's in the killing business. What the hell do you *think* he's gonna do with his jets?'"

Pictures of other military weaponry panned across the screen. "Who's buying these weapons, and why, is anybody's guess. Profits and stock prices of arms manufacturers are at all-time highs. Shareholders are tickled pink, corporate officers are earning seven figure bonuses, and Congressmen are receiving six figure lobbyist checks."

Pause. "No one I interviewed in Washington seemed the least bit concerned."

The picture segued to a local TV station feed of a rally outside the United Nations complex in New York City. Protestors carried signs saying things like, "Out of the UN Now!" and "Armageddon is at Hand!" Several bore a picture of William Cameron MacCrarey with a hand-drawn goatee, Devil's horns, and pitchfork. "President Thomas cut off funding to the UN and terminated America's membership. Since then, the number of UN peacekeeping operations and humanitarian missions has been cut in half. With the U.S. gone, the Security Council is in deadlock and the only resolutions passed by the General Assembly have advanced Acting Secretary-General Gerhardt Schoen's personal agenda. In other words, the UN now runs completely by Schoen's leave. President Thomas has, in effect, handed Schoen the proverbial keys to the kingdom."

Forty million viewers and rising fast. "Geeze," Walt whispered.

"Six months ago, Roe v. Wade was overturned by the Supreme Court. No longer can a woman in America receive a safe, legal abortion, even if her life is in jeopardy." A cemetery with a freshly dug grave appeared on the screen. The dates on the tombstone revealed that the woman buried beneath was 19 years old when she died. "Women seeking to end pregnancies for either physical or emotional reasons are once again forced to find doctors willing to break the law, many of whom are unqualified or even unlicensed." The picture segued to another tombstone, this one of a woman 25 years old. "The death rate per one-thousand abortions has risen fortyfold." Another tombstone. Thirty-one years old. "An unmarried elementary school teacher, forced to resign when the school board discovered she was pregnant, found herself without the means to raise a child, blacklisted, and shunned by friends and family. She decided to have an abortion, but unbeknownst to her the abortionist had lost his medical license for self-prescribing amphetamines. He was high when he operated on her. She died at home, alone, three days later from internal bleeding." Jan paused. "For thousands of years, women have sought ways to end unwanted pregnancies, whether with drugs, surgery, or," another tombstone, 16 years old, "suicide.

"Pharmacists can legally refuse to sell condoms or fill birth control prescriptions," she continued as a picture of a chain drug store appeared on the screen, "if it conflicts with their religious beliefs. Companies can refuse to offer insurance policies that pay for birth control if it conflicts with the owners' or shareholders' beliefs. Laws have been passed prohibiting birth-control prescriptions for single-women and teens under eighteen. Funding for Planned Parenthood, and every other family planning service, has been cut off. Not surprisingly, unwanted pregnancies have risen sharply, caseloads for adoption agencies are skyrocketing, and opening orphanages is a booming business."

Next, images of homeless people huddled around drumfires, sleeping in cardboard boxes under overpasses, and standing in food lines slid across the screen one after another. "Congress began slashing federal spending soon after the election with the most vulnerable citizens paying the heaviest price. After speeches on the floor by congressmen vilifying the poor and unemployed as lazy sinners and a burden to society, bills were passed cutting nearly the entire budget for WIC, early childhood education, Medicaid, mental health care, homeless shelters, and food stamp programs. Since then, homelessness, malnutrition, and crime rates have soared. The number of families living in poverty, the number of children under-performing in schools, and the gap in life expectancy between rich and poor has risen sharply."

A frantic, grainy video of an assault on a woman by parishioners in a church sanctuary played next. Alone in the aisle behind her lay an older man bleeding and motionless. A child, at the urging of her mother, ran up and kicked the man in the head. Further on lay another motionless man surrounded by congregants. "A professor at a small Midwestern college recently appeared on a local TV show and accused the government of waging a war on truth. Invited to be a guest lecturer at a Sunday morning church service, he was walking up the aisle to the podium when he was shot six times by a parishioner. An off-duty officer at the service prayed for the Lord to steady her hand and shot the gunman. A moment later, *she* was attacked by parishioners for 'killing Christ's soldier' and beaten to death." Pause. "The Senate then passed a bill making it legal for 'patriotic soldiers of God' to kill anyone who defies the 'spirit of the Bible.'" Another pause. "No one from the church was charged with a crime, and the gunman who shot the Professor was honored posthumously in a ceremony held at the Capitol the day the bill was passed."

Fifty-five million viewers. Walt's heart pounded, pride and foreboding struggling for the upper hand.

A series of *New York Times* headlines panned across the screen. 'Gays Banned from Teaching in Public Schools.' 'White Gentiles Only, City Says.' 'Atheism Illegal in 41 States.' 'Darwinism Outlawed in Public Schools.' 'Death Sentence for Capital Crimes Mandatory Nationwide.' 'Hispanic Workers to be Electronically Tracked.' Meanwhile, the audio of a news story played. "Earlier this evening," the female news anchor said, "a suburban neighborhood became the site of a patriotic killing. After leaving work, a gay employee of a Disney Store was chased down in the parking lot by Freedom Patrollers, thrown into a van, and driven to City Hall where an impromptu public trial was convened on the front steps. The Patrol Captain declared the man guilty of breaking God's commandments and jeopardizing the morality of America. His men tied one end of a rope around the young man's neck and flung the other end over the limb of a nearby tree. The Patrol Captain shouted, 'Hoist the fag into the air!'"

An amateur video started to play, the camera zooming in on the face of the frightened young man. "Please! No!" he begged, tears running down his cheeks. His body lurched into the air, his legs kicking frantically and his hands clutching at the rope crushing his windpipe. When is body finally went limp, the onlookers cheered and patted each other on the back as the young man's dead body swung back and forth in the dappled, fading sunlight filtering down through the leaves.

"No government official condemned the murder and no preacher condemned the breaking of God's commandment not to kill. None of the Freedom Patrollers were prosecuted and the Patrol Captain is now the darling of Sunday morning evangelical services, Tea Party political rallies, and conservative talk shows." On the screen, a picture appeared of a tall, lean man of about 30 shaking hands with the Reverend-Secretary. The man had a blonde buzz cut and wore a crisply pressed brown uniform. Then, the picture morphed into an old mug shot photo. "Quite a change for a former skinhead acquitted by an all-white jury 11 years ago of killing an unarmed black teenager. Since then, he's been arrested three times for spousal abuse, and ticketed twice for brandishing a loaded weapon in public."

Eighty million viewers. "Amazing, Cub," Walt muttered to himself.

"Amendments to the United States Constitution have to be ratified by three-fourths of the States. Since the Bill of Rights was adopted in 1790, only 17 amendments have been passed. President Thomas recently issued an executive order requiring state legislatures to vote on his constitutional amendments within 90 days. And here they are." The text of more than two-dozen amendments scrolled down the screen. "One of them would change how redistricting of Congressional seats is determined. Instead of total population, only registered voters would be counted. To become a registered voter, a person would have to fill out a 10-page form, be finger-printed, and bring a photo ID and U.S. birth certificate to a Homeland Security office between Thanksgiving and Christmas. That is to say, *after* Election Day, and there are no Homeland Security offices in predominantly minority areas. It's estimated that if the amendment passes, the number of poor and minority registered voters will drop by 50-percent, allowing Whites to hold onto power indefinitely.

"Another amendment, euphemistically called the Sanctification Amendment, would make Christianity the national religion, mandate morning prayers at public schools, define marriage as being between two Christians of the opposite sex, declare desecration of the U.S. flag a capital offense, prohibit anyone not born on U.S.

soil from becoming an American citizen, forbid tax-funded scientific research, and replace the Preamble to the Constitution with a version presented to Abraham Lincoln in 1864." A video of the Speaker of the House reading the Preamble began to play. "'We the People of the United States, in order to constitute a Christian government, recognizing Almighty God as the source of all authority and power in civil government, and acknowledging the Lord Jesus Christ as the Governor among the nations and His revealed will as the supreme law of the land, and in order to establish justice, insure domestic tranquility, provide for the common defense, promote the general welfare, and secure the blessings of liberty to ourselves and our posterity, do ordain and establish this Constitution for a Christian United States of America.'"

Again the screen went black. The crackling and popping of a burning fire and the faint singing of *My Country Tis of Thee* could be heard. Dancing flames grew out of the blackness to reveal a crowd of people throwing books onto a bonfire. "Congress's new censorship law has made book burnings like this one common place." One after the other, book covers appeared followed by historical pictures of book burnings. "How history doth repeat itself."

Music played. "Imagine there's no Heaven. It's easy if you try."

"Songs like John Lennon's Imagine have been banned as well."

"Nothing to kill or die for, and no religion too."

"Some in Congress have claimed that John L-E-N-N-O-N was the illegitimate grandson of Soviet Premier Vladimir L-E-N-I-N." Pause. "Apparently, several members of Congress have reading disabilities, or perhaps they haven't read anything at all."

"Imagine all the people, sharing all the world!"

One hundred and twenty million viewers. Walt ran a nervous hand through his graying hair.

"Promising to create jobs, Congress overturned decades of regulatory laws enacted to protect consumers from dangerous products, pollution, fraudulent practices, and unethical behavior." Pictures of injured and maimed people appeared on the screen one after the other. "If they'd bothered to read the transcripts of past Congressional hearings, they would've known why the laws had been passed in the first place." Tombstones appeared next. "Corporate profits are up 25 percent, job growth is flat, the income gap between rich and poor is at an all-time high, tens of thousands have died, hundreds of thousands have been injured, and millions have gone bankrupt due to fraud, scams, and skyrocketing medical bills no longer paid by health insurance, Medicare, or Medicaid thanks to cuts in Federal funding."

The pictures faded, and Jan reappeared sitting at the news desk.

"I've mentioned this evening that several brave souls have gone missing. Since the Thomas Administration took office, hundreds of thousands of Americans have disappeared without a trace." A list of names scrolled down the screen. "Missing persons reports and interviews with families and acquaintances reveal that the missing came from every ethnic, cultural, religious, political, and professional background. Yet, they all shared one thing in common. They're our best and brightest, our unconventional thinkers, our moral guideposts, our outspoken critics, our selfless teachers, and our tireless defenders of free speech, religious pluralism, and human rights. In short, they are the ones totalitarian states fear the most, the people who see things most clearly, who march to the beat of their own drummer, who despise blind obedience, and who speak out in protest."

The scrolling list of names stopped when it came to Tula and David Athos. "These are the parents of little Dorothy Ann." The picture ever so slowly transitioned once again to the three of them together, and then to her snow-dusted face smiling in death.

The AP cupped his earpiece with a hand and listened intently. The color drained from his face and he gave Walt a panicked look. "TV stations are going off the air all across the country," he said anxiously. "FCC orders."

Walt's viewership numbers began dropping like a stone and he fell back in his chair. "Looks like we got their attention."

His AP cursed. "What do we do now?"

"Not a damn thing," Walt answered, watching Jan on the set. "In for a penny, in for a pound." Then he whispered, "I hope cub'll be alright."

"Over the past two months," she continued, "dozens of cities have hosted peaceful protests. Ordinary Americans who believe our civil rights are being violated and feel as though they're becoming outcasts in their own country have taken to the streets." Her footage from Washington Square played. "The last protest took place here in New York City. You haven't seen pictures of it until now." Brown-shirts moved into the square, the NYPD officers fell back, a gunshot, a scream, Dr. Connors fell to the stage, and people began running in every direction. "Americans are being murdered in the streets. Thousands upon thousands are disappearing. Little Dorothy Ann is dead." She paused. "What are you going to do about it?" She paused again. "This is Jan Roberts reporting."

A week later, a missing persons report was filed with the Chelsea, Michigan, Police Department by Ida May Roberts. Her daughter, Janice Marie, former New York Times journalist and recent freelance reporter, was nowhere to be found.

η

"Spend time with your loved ones, say a kind word to someone, give a warm hug to the one next to you, hold hands and cherish the moment. For someday that person will not be there again."

– George Denis Patrick Carlin

"History is replete with examples of strong-minded citizens well acquired of solid moral foundation without the assistance of organized religion. Churches or priests or rabbis. But it is risky for the nation as a whole to rely on the chance that its citizens will individually apply themselves to building a stable moral base without benefit of organized religion."

– James Michener

"Out of the shadows of night the world rolls into light. It is daybreak everywhere."

– William Wadsworth Longfellow

"They're coming," the conductor's hushed voice warned Dwight. "Woodward, Thirteen Mile, 12-B," and the line went dead.

By mid-afternoon, he was driving north on I-75 in a non-descript car with stolen license plates he'd found parked in space 12-B of a parking garage at the corner of Woodward Avenue and Thirteen Mile Road. He also found a manila envelope with a fake driver's license, social security card, birth certificate, and passport in the glove compartment. Protocol was to head for the border, but Dwight was driving north to Traverse to see about Genevieve and Cameron. On the seat next to him sat the postcard that arrived in the mail earlier in the day with the words, "Come to Traverse. I need you!" scrawled in a child's script.

Dwight knew all the conductors and knew what the call meant. He was being hunted.

So be it. He'd long ago resigned himself to one day joining the Disappeared. It would be the price he paid for helping those who feared for their safety. There'd already been a financial price, having spent every penny of his savings, home equity, and 401k, to clandestinely resurrect the Underground Railroad.

Half an hour from the Canadian border, he turned his Dearborn home into a safehouse, the first in 170 years. He drove families to the St. Clair River every night, ferried them across to Canada in an old Chris-Craft he'd bought, and recruited others to be conductors, safehousekeepers, and border runners.

The original Underground had been established by abolitionists who chose to use the terminology of the burgeoning railroad industry in their struggle to free slaves. Conductors were whites, free-born blacks, former slaves, and Native Americans who accompanied runaways from one station or safehouse to the next. The routes between stations were called tracks and conductors knew only their stretch in case they were caught. Runaways followed the tracks at night on foot or hidden away in wagons with false bottoms. Safehousekeepers were often Quakers, Congregationalists, or Wesleyans. Symbols of lanterns and the constellation Ursa Major, whose stars pointed north, were used to identify safehouses. The tracks ended in free states like Michigan where runaways could cross the border into Canada and be free of slave hunters.

All Dwight had to do was ask, and Robbie, Duron, Damon, and Mark became a part of the Underground as well. Robbie created an Underground website that made use of a complex mathematical algorithm designed by a U of M math professor to shift cloud host servers every few seconds, making it impossible for the government to shut the site down. Duron created digital maps showing the locations of tracks and safehouses that changed every day, along with a handheld app that randomly generated passwords for runaways to use on their journey from one safehouse to another. Damon kept the safehouses and conductors safe from Homeland Security and Freedom Patrollers by creating a network of informants. Many worked for the government, but most were members of churches that sponsored Freedom Patrols. Patrollers had a penchant for bragging, so informants often learned of planned disappearances the Sunday before they happened. Mark would contact the would-be-victims via a cell connection routed through GLOSAT and scrambled to avoid eavesdropping and put them on the next train out of town. When conductors like Dwight were the targets, he made sure they disappeared themselves.

Fiddling with the radio dial, Dwight came across a station in Sarnia, Ontario. *Imagine* by John Lennon was playing. He smiled to himself, remembering the note he'd left on the kitchen table.

With a wood-splitting crash, the Captain kicked open the front door. "Search the house!" he ordered his Freedom Patrollers. They broke into pairs, guns at the ready, and cautiously moved from room to room looking for Dwight-something-or-other, whose picture and address had appeared on the Homeland Security website that morning. He was guilty of criticizing the government and calling President Thomas "a theocrat barely more evolved than *Homo habilis.*" The Freedom Patrollers weren't exactly sure what a theocrat or a habilis were, but calling the President a homo was reason enough to bring the bastard in.

Rumor had it that Dwight-something-or-other was even friends with Public Enemy Number One, William Cameron Mac-Crarey. The Antichrist! For that, they'd slung a rope over the limb of an oak tree down the street and planned to use his swinging body for target practice.

The bulldog-of-a-Captain tramped across the living room and caught a whiff of something cooking. Detouring into the dining room, he discovered a table exquisitely set for six – the exact number of Freedom Patrollers in the house at that very moment. His nostrils flared, and he was about to order everyone out when he spied a note resting atop a china plate.

"I put a little something in the oven in anticipation of your arrival," it read. "I do hope you've been keeping to your schedule of rounding up so-called traitors. I'd be terribly disappointed if your meal was overcooked. And try not to be too destructive of my home. I'm sure the next occupants, a nice white Christian family faithful to your moral dictatorship, would appreciate it. As for me, I will continue burdening your kind with my supposedly godless ways until my country cares for all its people again."

Dwight had scrawled his signature across the bottom of the note along with, "P.S. Enjoy the music I took the 'liberty' of queuing up for your dinner."

The Captain crumpled up the paper and threw it aside with a curse. His curiosity getting the better of him, he plodded over to the bookshelf and pressed play on the CD player. A moment later, the gentle chords of *Imagine* by John Lennon wafted out of the speakers.

T.J. looked through the peephole. "Well, well, well," he chuckled, opening the front door of his eldest daughter's home in Queens. "Come on in!"

"Hey, Teej," Lieutenant Sean Kelly said, greeting his old friend with a tired smile and a hug. "Been months, man."

"Yes, it has. Mac wouldn't have wanted it this way," T.J. replied, taking Sean's coat and calling, "Marion! Taylor! Sean's here."

"Taylor's here?" Sean said in surprise.

"Got here just before you did," answered T.J., and led his friend down the hall. "Get something in the mail by any chance?" he smiled, glancing back over his shoulder.

Sean reached into his back pocket and pulled out a plain white postcard. "'Come to Traverse. I need you!'" he recited. "Nothing else."

"Marion and I got one two days ago. Taylor got his yesterday. No return address, no signature, nothing."

"Cameron?" said Sean.

"Maybe," T.J. shrugged. "Haven't been able to get through to Gen."

"We going?"

"Oh, yeah."

"Good to see you, my friend," said Taylor, setting his coffee mug down and standing up from the kitchen table.

"You, too, Taylor," Sean said with a hug for his friend.

Marion hugged him next and said in her motherly way, "Let me get you some coffee, dear."

"That'd be great. Thanks," Sean replied with a weary smile and settled into a chair opposite his former mission mate.

"I haven't seen you since the funeral," said Taylor. "What have you been doing?"

Marion set a cup of coffee down in front of Sean.

"Investigating," he answered, "and I think I've found something." He took a manila envelope from his backpack and pulled out a black and white photograph. "Randall Joseph Collins, before he blew the back of his head off in the interpreter's office at the General Assembly building."

"Looks like a redneck with a bad attitude," T.J. said. "Where was he from?"

"Hullett, Wyoming," Sean replied. "No local address, though. Post Office in town holds his mail for pick up. Probably a paranoid, fanatic type. That second lieutenant I told you about with the same tattoo was like that. He was White Freedom Nation. That's how I tracked Collins down."

"Collins. Same last name as the shooter in Geneva," T.J. noted.

Sean nodded. "William Louis Collins. Randall Joseph's son."

"Fuckin'–"

"Thomas Jefferson Makatu!" Marion cut him off.

"Sorry, dear," T.J. muttered.

"They really wanted Mac dead, didn't they?" Taylor sighed.

T.J. scoffed, "What'd Mac ever do to those backwoods mother–"

"Thomas Jefferson Makatu!" Marion cried. "*Get* our guests some cookies and muffins."

"Yes, dear," he sighed. Getting up, he walked over to the counter and dumped a tin of warm muffins onto a plate, stuffed a cookie jar under his arm, and carried them back to the table.

"I'm leaving for Gillette tonight," Sean declared. "I'll rent a car in the morning and drive to Hullett."

"Hold on, buddy," said T.J. "Whoever those people are, they won't take kindly to unwelcomed guests."

"I know that better than anyone, Teej, but I'm still going," he said stubbornly, stuffing a chocolate chip cookie in his mouth.

"No, you're not," Taylor insisted.

T.J. took out his cell phone, scrolled to a number he'd used many times before, and tapped it.

"I'm doing this for Mac!" Sean said, spitting cookie crumbs across the table.

T.J. pressed the speaker button and set the cell on the table. A click sounded and then, "Merrill MaGeah."

"Merrill, this is T.J. Sean's about to do something *really* stupid."

"Why aren't you here?" blustered the Elder.

"He's, you're, what?" T.J. stammered. "Where?"

"Traverse, y'daft fool!"

"You're in Traverse? I called Gen, but–"

"Get your bums up here! All of you. And that goes for Sean, too."

An airline ticket from Gillette, Wyoming, to Traverse sat on the seat next to him as the prairie passed by at 80 miles an hour and another black chimney of stone appeared on the northern horizon. The Bureau of Tourism brochure he'd picked up at the airport car rental desk said they were lava shafts from ancient volcanoes, each rising hundreds of feet into the sky, their ash cones worn away over the eons from wind and rain.

Cresting a rise, he spied the town of Hullett dead ahead and slowed as he approached the city limits. He drove the length of Main Street to get the lay of the land and then doubled back to angle-park his Jeep in front of a greasy spoon. Getting out, he took a moment to stretch and take in the 1950's timelessness of the town. Pickups parked in front of a general store, a mother and child walking into a five-and-dime, two old men smoking on a bench in front of a movie theater that doubled as town hall, a tumbleweed blowing down Main Street, the pleasing smell of freshly baked bread from the bakery across the street, and prairie grass crowding the town on every side.

Stepping into the restaurant, he sidled up to the white linoleum counter and sat down. A plump gum-chewing waitress in a pink uniform and a white apron walked over as he grabbed one of the menus stuck between a napkin dispenser and a bottle of ketchup.

"What'll it be, darlin'?"

Not bothering to look at the menu, he answered, "Farmer's omelet, hash browns, cup o' joe." Casually pulling a photograph of Collins out of his vest pocket, he set it down on the counter. "Ever see this guy?"

She blew a bubble, a momentary hint of recognition crossing her face. "You a cop?" she said.

"Nah, he's an old army buddy of my dad's. I was passing through, thought I'd stop by and pay him a visit."

She tore the order slip off her notepad. "Be about 15 minutes, hon," she said and walked over to the kitchen window. "Order!" she yelled and slapped the piece of paper down on the sill.

"That says something," he muttered and got up from his stool. He showed the picture to anyone who looked like a regular, but not surprisingly no one admitted to knowing Collins.

He sat back down at the counter and took a sip of his now-cold coffee. The tinkling of a bell above the front door announced the latest customer and in walked a beautiful young woman with dreamy dark, brown eyes, lustrous shoulder-length black hair, and full red lips, wearing a mid-thigh, black knit skirt and low-cut blue and white blouse that quite nicely showcased her shapely figure.

Laura Faraway slid into a booth by the window and promptly slumped down, crossed her arms, and assumed an I-deserve-better-than-this look.

"Excuse me, miss," Sean said, walking over and holding up the picture. "You ever see this guy?"

She rolled her beautiful eyes in annoyance, glanced in a bored-sort-of-way at the picture, and the same flash of recognition crossed her face. "Nope," she answered curtly and turned back to the window as if Sean had magically disappeared.

"Thanks," Sean said with a lopsided grin and strolled back to the counter.

Collins's people were nearby, alright. "Just gotta find out where," he said under his breath.

Taking another sip of cold Joe, he threw a 20 on the counter and left. Crossing the street, he walked two blocks west and stepped into the U.S. Post Office. After ringing the bell on the counter, a tall, thin, serious-looking man with graying blonde hair walked out of the back room.

"Afternoon," Sean greeted.

"Afternoon," Lars Robinson echoed. "What can I do ya for?"

"An old army buddy of my dad's lives around these parts. Don't have his street address, though. Thought maybe you could help me out."

"Sure thing," replied the Postmaster. "What's his name?"

Sean handed him the picture of Collins.

Lars' frowned. "You won't need an address, son. One of his folk'll be in shortly to pick up supplies," he explained, pointing out the window at Peterson's General Store.

"Uh, okay. Well, guess I'll just follow him back and surprise my dad's friend."

Lars chuckled darkly. "Son, you don't wanna be surprisin' *those* folks."

"Why not?"

"Let's just say they don't take kindly to strangers. Trust me."

"Okay," Sean said again, drawing out the syllables. "Who is 'they' anyway?"

"They're people you don't wanna ask too many questions about, son," Lars answered flatly and turned for the back room.

From the front seat of the Jeep, Sean sipped a fresh cup of coffee and watched a beat-up old F150 painted flat olive-green shudder to a stop in front of Peterson's. A man in fatigues and a black NRA baseball cap got out and anxiously looked up and down the street before hurrying inside.

"Bingo."

Setting the coffee down, he stuffed a donut into his mouth and grabbed the laptop off the passenger seat. Up-linking to GLOSAT, he typed in his ID and password, pulled up a satellite image of Main Street, and used the keyboard mouse to navigate the crosshairs over the olive-green pickup. After locking on to it, two sets of numbers appeared, 104 degrees, 44 minutes, 30 seconds west, and 44 degrees, 36 minutes, 10 seconds north.

A middle-aged man pushing a flatbed cart stacked high with hardware goods, barbed-wire coils, and wood posts came out twenty minutes later followed by the pretty girl from the greasy spoon pushing another cart filled with groceries. The soldier-wannabee loaded everything into the back of the idling truck and without so much as a nod, got into the cab, jammed the gear shift into reverse and punched the accelerator. The F150 lurched back, fishtailed to a stop and, with a gnash of gears, screeched off down the road.

Sean waited for a lone semi heading west to pass before backing into the street. Using the big truck for cover, he followed the F150 out of Hullett. At the first crossroad, the pick-up turned north and headed into the low rolling hills. The prairie grass and rarity of trees made it easy to follow from a distance with only the occasional curve or rise temporarily causing Sean to lose sight of the truck. The longitudinal coordinates on the laptop screen slowly clicked up until they hit 45 degrees, 0 minutes, 0 seconds north.

"Just like Traverse," he whispered. Was that a good sign?

Emerson, Lake, and Palmer played on the radio. "A bullet had found him, his blood ran as he cried. No one could save him, so he lay down and he died. Ooooh, what a lucky man he was."

In the distance, the F150 turned onto a rutted dirt road and disappeared into an old apple orchard. Sean followed, snaking his way through the trees until he found himself on the edge of a 50-foot-wide clearing of close-cropped grass. He hit the brakes and surveyed the tall, wood-framed barbed wire fence that ran a good 100 yards to his left and right.

Then he looked across the clearing at a gate and saw that just inside it was the soldier-wannabee leaning against his pick-up truck. He was staring back, arms crossed, and flanked by two fatigue-clad men brandishing rifles.

Cursing, Sean threw the Jeep into reverse and punched the accelerator. Cranking the steering wheel hard to the right with one hand, he pulled the Colt .45 from his shoulder holster with the other. Pointing it at the laptop screen, he fired and then swung the barrel around to get a bead on the gunmen, just as a fusillade of gunshots thundered across the clearing.

A cool breeze blew in off the water and swirled around the summer cottages lining the beach. It wound through the pines and birches blanketing the peninsula and up the hillside to the ridge where it curled over the decks and rolled between the homes overlooking Traverse Bay.

On a quiet cul-de-sac, the rear door of a black limousine opened and seven-year old Cameron Kristine Boujeau-MacCrarey jumped out. The breeze with its hint of spring brushed her face, and with a smile she ran to the front door.

"Wait for us, sweetie," Genevieve called out wearily as she followed her daughter up the walk, Kyle and Michael in tow.

"What a glorious day," the Keeper marveled.

Cameron struggled with the door handle and Michael hurried ahead. No sooner had he opened the door than she rushed into the foyer. "Hi, Uncle Merrill!" she called out and flew past.

"Hello, little one," the Elder chuckled as Genevieve came through the door looking spent. His smile faded as he wrapped his arms around her. "It'll be okay, lass," he said warmly.

"After all that's happened?" she snapped and pulled away.

Merrill's face reddened, and he looked down at the floor.

Genevieve sighed and put her arms around him again. "Sorry," she whispered.

"One never quite gets used to such things, lass," he said. "Me Clan knows that all too well."

Michael and the Keeper walked in behind her.

"I don't *want* to get used to such things," she said, trying not to sound bitter.

"Everything's squared away with the county Clerk and the death certificate," Kyle told his friend. "They won't go public for 30 days."

"Enough time," said Merrill.

"Hi, Uncle Dwight! Hi, Aunt Angela!" Cameron called through the screen door of the deck.

"Hey! No hug?" Angela called back as the last heir of Arthur ran to the kitchen.

"I'll be back!" she called over her shoulder.

"Mark and Damon are in town shopping," Merrill explained. "Robbie and Duron are flying in this afternoon. T.J., Taylor, and Sean should be here any minute."

Cameron ran down the hallway to the bedrooms next. Reaching the last door, she looked inside and cried, "Daddy!"

"Hey, sweetie," said a tired, raspy voice. "Come give me a hug."

She ran into the room and jumped onto the bed. Wearing blue-green scrubs and sitting up with his back resting against the headboard, he set the book he was reading down and wrapped his right arm around his beautiful daughter. His left was in a sling to keep the sutures that crisscrossed his chest from tearing open.

Genevieve looked in on them and noticed the smile as wide as Traverse Bay on Mac's face as he listened to Cameron go on about their trip into town. Tears came to her eyes.

"Mommy's crying *again*," he teased. "Let's give her a hug, too."

"Oh, you," sniffled Genevieve, wrapping her arms around the both of them. "I love you," she whispered.

"I love you, too," he echoed.

The doorbell rang and Merrill, who'd been watching from the doorway, wiped his nose on his sleeve and hurried back down the hall to the foyer. There he found Dwight ushering in T.J. and Taylor.

Merrill growled with invented anger. "Took you lads bloody-well long enough."

"The postcard," Taylor exclaimed, "is everyone alright?"

"Uncle T.J.! Uncle Taylor!" Cameron cried, running down the hallway.

T.J. beamed, kneeling down to catch her in his arms. "You okay?"

"Yeah. Why?" she answered innocently.

"Oh, well, uh—"

Genevieve came down the hall and Taylor noticed her tears. "You okay?" he said reflexively, and almost at once felt a stab of guilt. Of course she wasn't okay. Mac was dead, for chrissakes.

"Yes," she answered weakly, pulling a tissue from her purse. "Fine."

"We received these," Taylor said, holding up his postcard. "We came as—"

"You got it!" Cameron said, jumping up and down. "I wanted you to come see!"

T.J. tussled Cameron's hair. "See what, honey?"

"Daddy!" Cameron cried, throwing her arms in the air.

Taylor's heart sank, and he knelt down. "I'm sure Daddy's looking down on us right now from—"

"Heaven?" came a soft voice from down the hall.

"There he is!" she cried, pointing.

T.J. and Taylor turned to see the man they'd come to love and respect slowly walking towards them, the friend who'd been sorely missed, the leader they'd have followed to the ends of the Earth.

"My *God,* you're alive!" T.J. cried, unsure if he should believe his eyes.

"We thought, the news, the *funeral,*" faltered Taylor.

"The reports of my death were greatly exaggerated," Mac said weakly with a slight smile.

"A friend of the Clan is chief of surgery at Mt. Sinai," Kyle explained. "At my request, he issued a press release saying Mac had passed. Then, I arranged for a private ambulance to drive him to JFK where Michael's jet was waiting. He's been here recuperating ever since."

"The whole world thinks he's dead," Merrill told them, "and for the time being it needs to stay that way. Only those of us in this room know the truth. And 'those of us,'" he added looking around the room for effect, "should include Sean."

"He'll be here," T.J. told him. "He, uh, had a layover. Somewhere."

"What's going on?" the Elder demanded.

"He made a side trip to, to, uh, find something."

"Find out who sent me to Mt. Sinai?" Mac guessed.

T.J. sighed.

"Damned fool," growled Merrill.

"He'll be here," T.J. insisted, though it sounded to Mac as if his friend were trying to convince himself more than anyone else.

A long silence followed until Angela said, "Cherry crumb pie in the kitchen, everyone. Cameron, dear, help me put the coffee on."

Sitting in the living room after dinner, Mac felt tired but content. With his friends arguing and laughing, the love of his life resting her head on his shoulder, and Cameron asleep in his lap, he felt very fortunate indeed.

"We mustn't let time slip away," he said wistfully.

The Elders of his Clan, who were volubly debating who had really assassinated Julius Caesar, fell silent and the others followed suit.

"We should paint the canvass of our days with the brushstrokes of love and friendship, enlightenment and inspiration."

Duron snickered. "You reading a Hallmark card over there, buddy?"

"Nah," said Robbie. "He's got Cliff's Notes to one of those damned poetry books we had to read in high school."

"I'm sure I have no idea what Cliff's Notes are," Mac said pretentiously.

Everyone laughed.

"Seriously, though. We should live as though every moment might be our last and give our last moment so that others may live their lives to the fullest."

"Here, here," said Merrill, raising his mug of ale.

They all toasted their friend who once was lost, but now was found.

"What are you going to do?" T.J. said to Mac.

Kyle spoke up. "It's your decision and yours alone, lad. The Clan will not place you in harm's way again." He paused to reflect. "Perhaps we expected too much of this world, a world less noble than the one Arthur lived in."

"Whether it is or isn't," replied Mac, "I'll never walk away from the obligations of my heritage."

Merrill slapped his thigh. "I told you, old friend. I *told* you the lad wouldn't give up!"

"That you did," Kyle chuckled. "That you did."

"If you won't walk away, I won't walk away," said Robbie.

"Neither will I," Duron declared.

"Nor I," agreed Damon.

"That goes for me, too," Dwight said.

"And me," Mark grinned.

"Ditto," said T.J.

"Count me in," Taylor added.

Genevieve's tears came again.

"Someday," he whispered and kissed her hand.

"I know," she answered.

"Bugger," Merrill mumbled, pulling a handkerchief out of his pocket.

"You'll announce your candidacy for Secretary-General, then?" said Kyle.

"Of course."

With a smile, the Keeper got to his feet. "Well, then. Shall we have our last debate?"

A mix of laughs, Yes's, and good-natured moans were his answer.

"Won't we need the professors?" said T.J.

Merrill reached for the grip sitting alongside the couch and extracted a laptop. Setting it on the coffee table, he lifted the screen to reveal the familiar faces of the professors Skyping in from their respective universities.

"Rather presumptuous of you," Mac commented.

"Mmmm, rather insightful, I'd say," replied the Elder.

"Greetings, doctors," said the Keeper.

"Ciao," said Dr. Galatea.

"Good evening," Dr. Michener replied.

"Nice to be with you again," said Dr. Ingersaul. "Virtually, at least."

"If I recall," Duron noted with some hesitation, "this debate is to be about religion?"

"Oh, geeze," muttered Damon.

"Better hide the knives, Gen," quipped Mark.

"Better get some more wine," she replied, getting to her feet as the others laughed.

"At our last gathering," Kyle reminded everyone, "we asked the question, 'Why are we here?' and turned to the sciences for answers. Tonight, let us turn to religion."

"Genesis," replied Robbie with contrived boredom. "God created the Earth and the heavens and made man in His own image. Next question?"

"Ah!" grinned Dr. Ingersaul. "An Usshurite."

"Uh, is that a good thing or a bad thing?" said Robbie.

The professor chuckled. "James Ussher was a Church of Ireland Archbishop in the mid-1600s and a Biblical literalist who decided the Earth had been created on Sunday, October 23, 4004 BCE."

"What? No time of day?" Mark chuckled.

"How'd he figure that out?" Robbie said.

"He counted the number of generations from Adam to Darius, extrapolated a bit to New Testament times, and that was that. Of course, anthropology, paleontology, astronomy, and biochemistry all tell us differently."

"Taking the Bible literally is an act of foolishness," groused Merrill.

"Literally, perhaps," replied Dr. Ingersaul, "but taken more thematically, religious texts can provide us with a surprisingly accurate history."

"Off your rocker," Merrill proclaimed. "Completely bonkers."

"I'll take that as a challenge," said the good professor. "'In the beginning, God created the heavens and the earth. The earth was without form and void. And God said, 'Let the dry land appear.' Well, my friend, the oceans *did* form first and dry land arose from their depths as volcanoes gave birth to islands and massive tectonic plates crashed into one another to create the continents."

Merrill gave a dismissive grunt.

"'Let the earth put forth vegetation, plants yielding seed, and fruit, each according to its kind.' Through their seed, all living things are predestined by their DNA. 'Let the waters bring forth swarms of living creatures.' The oceans were the womb of life and everything that lives on the land or flies through the air genetically originated from some form of life that crawled out of the sea. 'The Nephilim were on the earth in those days.' Nephilim were giants and may well have been wooly mammoths, which survived in Eurasia until 8000 BCE, on St. Paul Island in Alaska until 6000 BCE, and on Wrangel Island in the Russian Arctic until 1700 BCE. Middle Eastern civilizations began circa 10,000 BCE, meaning they were contemporaries with mammoths."

"Whoa!" Mark said in amazement.

"'Let the earth bring forth living creatures according to their kinds. Let us make man in our image, after our likeness.' Man was God's last creation, and both Paleontologists and geneticists will tell you that humans came very late in Earth's history, evolutionarily speaking."

"Take that, old man," Mac said to Merrill with a smile.

"'Let *us* make man in *our* image,'" Duron repeated. "Who's 'us' and 'our?' Does that mean God wasn't alone? That there were other gods?"

"The Old Testament was written when Israel was surrounded by the Egyptians, Babylonians, and Greeks," said Dr. Ingersaul, "who had pantheons of gods. So, perhaps the God of the Jews was simply the chief god, or maybe He assimilated the powers and personalities of all the other gods, or maybe He was a spiritual pugilist who took on all comers and eventually came out on top, or maybe the notion of God simply evolved over the millennia in which the Biblical stories were passed down by word of mouth."

"Yeah, the last one," insisted Robbie, "we finally got to the right notion of God."

The professor continued without comment. "'Out of the ground the Lord God made to grow the tree of the knowledge of good and evil. The serpent said to the woman when you eat of it your eyes will be opened, and you will be like God.' Hasn't man not only eaten of its fruit, but over time climbed the tree of knowledge? Doesn't man's mastery of science, Nature, and technology today make him a god by comparison to people thousands of years ago? 'The Lord God said to the serpent, "Because you have done this, upon your belly you shall go."' Snakes evolved from four-legged creatures and only in more recent evolutionary times have they slithered on their bellies. 'All the fountains of the great deep burst forth, and the windows of the heavens were opened. The waters prevailed so mightily upon the earth that all the high mountaintops under the whole heaven were covered.' The last ice age was ending around the time Man gave up his hunter-gatherer ways and first settled in agricultural villages, often along coasts and rivers. As the polar ice caps melted, the water levels rose dramatically everywhere, which is why civilizations around the world have flood myths. In Europe, it led to the breaching of the Gibraltar isthmus by the rising Atlantic and the Bosporus isthmus by the rising Mediterranean."

"Many ancient villages have been discovered underwater," nodded Merrill, "including a 7,500-year-old village 12 miles off the Turkish coast in 300 feet of water. Perhaps whole civilizations were lost to the great flood, perhaps even the *first* civilization."

"Like Atlantis?" Damon grinned.

"Indeed," the Elder said with a Cheshire cat smile.

Mac caught an almost imperceptible shake of Kyle's head directed at his old friend, who in return gave a slight bow of unrepentant apology and said, "My point is that Dr. Ingersaul is correct about the Flood, and I concede his point of taking the Bible thematically but not literally."

"The Bible's the inerrant word of God," Robbie said impatiently. "End of story."

"Oh, really?" smiled the professor. "Then why has it changed?"

"It, it, *what?*"

"Nine-hundred years after the Jewish Exodus from Egypt to Palestine, Alexander the Great Hellenized the Middle East. A translation of the Old Testament from Hebrew to Greek was commissioned and legend has it that 72 Jewish scholars in Alexandria completed the translation in 72 days. Hence, it became known as the Septuagint, meaning 70 in Latin. The translators worked in parallel and pieced their translations together after they finished. But since ancient Hebrew has no vowels and a single word can possess different meanings depending on its context, the works of the translators contained several contradictions and inconsistencies. Later, gospels written by Christ's disciples, secondhand observers, early converts like Paul, and the Gnostics were cobbled together over several *centuries* to make the New Testament. The early church councils had to decide which gospels were authentic enough – that is to say, sufficiently inspired by the Holy Spirit – to include and which belonged to the trash heap of history. But, objectivity often fell victim to bias and politics, as it's wont to do. In 400 CE, Pope Innocent I established the Canon of the Latin Church. Three hundred years later, the Council of Aix changed it. Eight hundred years after that, the Council of Trent changed it again. Even individual verses were changed. In Mathew 28:18-20, for instance, Jesus says, 'All authority in heaven and on earth has been given to me. Go therefore and make disciples of all nations, baptizing them in the name of the Father and of the Son and of the Holy Spirit.'"

Robbie scrunched up his face. "So?"

"The Holy Trinity didn't exist until 300 years *after* Christ's death," answered the professor. "There's no way Jesus could have said that."

Robbie's jaw dropped. "What?"

"God didn't need a Holy Trinity until Emperor Constantine said He did."

"God created the Holy Trinity when he created the universe," Robbie said weakly. "Didn't he?"

"No, my friend," the professor answered. "The Council of Nicaea created it in 325 CE, and Constantine made it the law of the Empire."

Duron commented, "The Nicene Creed's all about the Holy Trinity, isn't it?"

Dr. Ingersaul nodded. "It says, and I'm paraphrasing, 'I believe in one God, the Father almighty, maker of heaven and earth, of all things visible and invisible. I believe in the Holy Spirit who proceeds from the Father and the Son, who with the Father and the Son is adored and glorified, and who has spoken through the prophets.' Then, there's the Athanasian Creed written not long after. 'We worship one God in the Trinity and the Trinity in unity. The Father and the Son and the Holy Spirit have one divinity, equal glory, and coeternal majesty.' Both were collectively composed by hundreds of bishops to quell a controversy within the Church."

"What controversy?" said Robbie.

"Arianism," Merrill replied.

"Aryanism?" Duron said in surprise. "Christians back then believed in Aryans like the Nazis did?"

"No, no, no," said Dr. Ingersaul with a wave of his hands. "Different spelling. Arians were followers of Arius, a priest from Alexandria who espoused that Jesus was merely a man made divine by God."

Damon shrugged. "How could that be controversial?"

"For many of the bishops, it was nothing short of heresy. It meant Jesus wasn't a god in his own right, a god who could perform miracles, miracles that gave the Church its authority. No miracles, no credence. No credence, no power over commoners and kings. Remember that back then the Church was competing for its life with Roman and Greek pantheism and countless pagan religions. At the time of the Council of Nicaea, only a few years had passed since Constantine made Christianity the official religion of the Empire. The Church was *in* favor, but it could just as easily fall *out* of favor. To survive, it bent over backwards to keep Constantine happy and corner the market on gods."

Merrill huffed. "Constantine knocked off political rivals and even a wife or two on his way to the imperial palace. As Emperor he was also the Chief Priest, or Pontifex Maximus, of the Empire, so after he made Christianity the state religion, he took control of the Church's wealth and power."

"The Pope is Pontifex Maximus," growled Robbie , "Constantine was the first Christian Pontifex Maximus...and Constantine was a greedy, power-hungry, murderer?"

"Aye," Merrill answered bluntly. "And what's more, Constantine wasn't even a Christian. He didn't convert until his deathbed."

"God would *never* let that happen!"

Merrill gave a blustery huff, but before he could say more, Dr. Ingersaul continued, "Prior to the Council of Nicaea, Bishop Arius was accused by his peers of being in league with Satan, corrupting the innocent, trampling orthodoxy, conspiring against Christ, etcetera, etcetera."

"Sounds like a Republican campaign," snickered Damon.

"Sounds like a heathen liberal," muttered Robbie.

"Constantine wanted the controversy quelled," the professor went on, "so the Church excommunicated Arius, his writings were burned, and anyone possessing copies of them could be put to death. Then, the Bishops wrote the Nicene Creed and Mathew 28:18-20 was changed."

"Were there other changes?" Dwight asked.

"Oh, yes, and contradictions. Many documented by Thomas Paine in the *Age of Reason*," noted Dr. Ingersaul.

"Shall we have a go?" Merrill said with a cocky grin.

"A verbal joust?" smiled the professor. "But of course. Lets' start with Esther, the only book, in its original form, of the Bible not to mention God. To lend it spiritual gravitas, in the Greek Septuagint translation, and later in the Catholic Vulgate, prayers offered up to God by the main characters were added."

"In Genesis 1, vegetation and animals were created before humans, yet Genesis 2 says humans were created before vegetation and animals," Merrill recounted. "What the bloody hell did we eat? In Genesis 4:9, God asks Cain where his brother Able is. Yet, in Proverbs 15:3 and Hebrews 4:13, God is everywhere, sees everything, and nothing is hidden from Him."

"In I Samuel 17:50," parried Dr. Ingersaul, "David kills Goliath. In 2 Samuel 21:19, David's brother Elhanan kills Goliath. To correct the inconsistencies, in a more recent translation 'the brother of' was placed before Elhanan's name."

"In many a verse," Merrill went on, "God is vengeful, jealous, angry, furious, and impulsive. In others, Old and New Testament alike, He's joy, peace, patience, kindness, and love. More than a wee bit bi-polar, eh?"

"In Genesis 6:4," said the professor, "there were Nephilim only before the Flood, but in Numbers 13:33 there were Nephilim after the Flood. In Genesis 6:19 to 22, 7:8 to 9, and 7:14 to 16, two of each kind of animal were taken aboard Noah's Ark. Yet, in Genesis 7:2 to 5, seven pairs of clean animals and one pair of unclean animals were taken aboard. In Genesis 16:15, 21:1 to 3, and Galatians 4:22, Abraham had two sons, Isaac and Ishmael, the progenitors of Judaism and Islam. Yet, in Hebrews 11:17, Abraham had only one son."

"God was seen by humans," Merrill continued, "including Adam, yet later verses say no one can see God's face and live. Some verses say children are to suffer for their parent's sins, yet in others they're not. Depending on the verse, God prohibits killing, condones it, and even orders it. The bloke can't make up his bloody mind."

"In Luke 1:26 to 27," the professor went on, "Jesus was conceived of a virgin, a parthenos according to the Greek translation. In the original Hebrew, though, Mary was simply described as an alma, a young woman. In Mathew 2:13 to 16, Joseph and Mary flee to Egypt. In Luke 2:22 to 40, they don't. In Mathew, Jesus's lineage was traced back to David's son Solomon. In Luke, it's traced back to David's son Nathan. In both books, Jesus's lineage is traced back from Joseph, but shouldn't it be traced back from Mary if she was Jesus's mother and His father was God?"

"I guess Jesus needs a paternity test," Damon kidded.

"Can you imagine," chuckled Dwight, "asking God for a blood sample? How would you send the court order? PopeExpress? Rocket ship?"

The professor continued with a smile. "The Septuagint translated Deuteronomy 32:8 as, 'When the Most High divided the nations, he set the bounds of the nations according to the number of the angels of God.' The Catholic Vulgate translated it as, 'according to the number of the children of Israel,' which Exodus 1:5 numbered as 70, Genesis 46:26 to 27 numbered as 66, and Acts 7:14 numbered as 75. Some New Testament books say to obey the laws of men for it is the will of God. Others say to obey God's laws, not men's. Between Mathew, Mark, and Acts, the New Testament disagrees on Jesus's last words and even on the names of the 12 disciples."

Merrill surrendered with a nod of his head. "Well done," he chuckled. "Well done. Let's call it a draw."

"Agreed," chuckled Dr. Ingersaul.

"By the way," Merrill said mischievously to the others, "that most Church traditions, rituals, and doctrines have no root in gospel or even in Christianity."

"Oh, come on!" Robbie said almost pleadingly.

"Christianity survived by cooption in its early days. Churches were built atop pagan temples, new rituals were created to replace olds ones, old ones were incorporated into new ones, elaborate ceremonies were devised to give the church gravitas, popular pagan festivals were coopted into Christian ones. Why do you suppose Christmas is celebrated on December 25th?"

Robbie crossed his arms and slumped in his chair. No one else bothered to venture a guess either, knowing Merrill loved to answer his own questions. He didn't disappoint.

"The Roman holiday of Saturnalia was celebrated on the winter solstice. Revelers binged, drank to excess, sang in the streets, ate human-shaped delicacies, and on December 25th sacrificed an 'enemy of the Roman people' to purge society of its decadence. Since Jesus was born to be man's salvation, and since Saturnalia was such a popular holiday, the church chose December 25th as His birthday."

"Singing in the streets and human-shaped delicacies, huh?" said Duron. "Caroling and gingerbread men?"

"Aye," smiled the Elder, quite pleased with himself.

"A side note," said the Professor, "Jesus's name derives from Joshua which means 'God is Salvation.' So was Jesus born to be man's salvation or was He just *named* salvation?"

Robbie winced.

"Was Easter coopted, too?" Mark said.

Merrill nodded. "Ēostre was the pagan goddess of spring. Her festival was celebrated on the first full moon after the vernal equinox. Since spring is when life renews itself, the dead being reborn as it were, the Council of Nicaea chose then to celebrate Jesus' resurrection."

"Shit," Robbie said under his breath.

"Constantine chose Sunday to be the Christian day of worship," said the Professor. "It was the day after the Sabbath and the day of the sun, the sun being the giver of life. So, he minted a coin with the image of Apollo the sun god on one side and Christ's initials on the other, equating Him with a Roman god."

"He'd already been equated with–" Merrill started to say.

"*The* God," interrupted Robbie, a tinge of desperation to his words.

Damon made a sound like a gameshow buzzer. "Sorry. Next contestant."

"Bite me."

"*Again* with the bite me. You got an oral fixation on something, buddy?"

Robbie laughed in spite of himself. "Just shut up, okay?"

"Yeah. Sure. All you have to do is ask. I mean, hey, I know when to shut up. When someone tells me to shut up, I shut up. They don't have to tell me twice. I shut right up. Shutting up is my middle—"

"SHUT UP!" everyone yelled and fell into a collective fit of laughter.

Merrill finally finished his sentence. "Dionysus. Jesus had been equated with Dionysus long before Apollo."

Robbie hung his head.

"True," said Dr. Ingersaul. "The hopeful story of Dionysus was well known to the Hellenized peoples of the Mediterranean by the time of Christ. According to Homer, Dionysus was the love child of Zeus and a mortal named Semele."

"And Jesus was the love child of God and Mary," said Merrill.

"As he grew older," continued the Professor, "Dionysus traveled about teaching his philosophy of life."

"As did Jesus."

"Dionysus was considered the god of wine and his festival was celebrated in the spring when the vine of the grape flowers. During his festival, three empty pots would be placed in a room and sealed. The following day, the room would be opened and the pots would be full of wine."

"Jesus's resurrection is celebrated in the spring," said Merrill, "and in John 2:1 to 11 Jesus performs His first miracle by turning jars of water into wine at the marriage in Cana."

"Dionysus was arrested in Thebes and brought before the king," continued Dr. Ingersaul.

"Jesus was arrested and brought before Pilate," said the Elder.

"Dionysus believed death was not the end of life, but a transition to a new one," concluded the professor.

"And the crucifixion of Jesus was a transition from Earthly life to one in heaven," said Merrill.

"Either Jesus's life just happened to parallel the story of Dionysus, or His life was made to parallel it. Regardless, associating an unknown teacher from a far-flung province with the beloved Dionysus, whose story was known everywhere in the empire, was a stroke of genius," explained the professor. "By doing so, the church took a big step towards getting Jesus accepted as a god and Christianity as a religion."

"Other New Testament mortals were associated with gods as well," Merrill pointed out. "In Acts *14*, Barnabas and Paul were preaching the word of Christ in the city of Lystra when they came upon, 'a man crippled in his feet, who was lame from birth and had never walked. He listened to Paul as he was speaking. Paul looked directly at him, saw that he had faith to be healed and called out, "Stand up on your feet!" At that, the man jumped up and began to walk. When the crowd saw what Paul had done, they shouted, "The gods have come down to us in human form!" Barnabas they called Zeus, and Paul they called Hermes.'"

"Sunday's the sun god's day, Easter's celebrated at the vernal equinox, and Christmas is celebrated at the winter solstice," noted Dwight. "The Jewish Rosh Hashanah is celebrated at the autumnal equinox and the Muslim Ramadan at the summer solstice. Strange how our holidays are tied to nature, don't you think? It's like we're pagan nature-worshippers or something."

"That's because our religions evolved from, and later co-opted, nature-worshipping religions. When the first agricultural societies began, there was only nature. Wind, rain, Earth, and fire. If nature was good, life was good. Stout livestock, cool flowing springs, gentle rains, abundant harvests, and wood for cooking fires. But, if hunters came home emptyhanded, or droughts wilted crops, or wells ran dry, or lightening set the savannah ablaze, or volcanoes buried villages under ash, then the people would cry, 'Why is this happening? Did we do something wrong? Are we being punished?' Since they knew nothing of Nature's workings, they found their answers in random coincidences. A man happened to follow the same routine twice before a hunt and found prey both times. Villagers sang a particular song or danced a certain dance and the rains came. They recited certain words before a battle and defeated their enemies. They threw out scraps of meat and rotten vegetables in the fall and crops grew in the same place come spring. Act and recompense. Nature demanded give and take. Man had to give something, pay homage, sacrifice in some way before She would sacrifice for him. So, he invented rituals to please Her, rituals that became ever more elaborate over time, from songs and dances, to prayers and totems."

"Totems?" Mark said.

"Figurines," explained the Professor. "Statues, paintings, and carvings."

"Like the Star of David, or a crescent moon, or the cross," Mac added.

"Yes, and after totems came physical sacrifices, like a fish, a bundle of grain, a lamb, even a human being."

"God told Abraham to sacrifice his son Isaac," Duron recounted.

"Life had to be ensured by death," said the Professor. "Plants die in the fall and are reborn in the spring, the aged pass away and babies are born, death traverses into life, the soul traverses from one being to another, hunters eat the flesh of their prey to take in their strength and cunning, warriors drink the blood of their enemies to take in their wisdom and courage."

"Drinking blood and eating flesh," Merrill said mischievously. "Taking in the virtues of the dead. Remind you of anything?"

Kyle and Dr. Ingersaul smiled knowingly but said nothing.

"What?" Mark asked.

"'Whoso eateth my flesh, and drinketh my blood, dwelleth in me and I in him.' John 6:54. Transubstantiation. The belief that bread and wine literally becomes the flesh and blood of Jesus Christ before they're consumed."

"Holy–" Mark started to say.

"Communion!" Damon finished for him.

"The Church infused with nature worship," Dwight reflected.

The Professor nodded. "Man hasn't advanced nearly as far as we'd like to think. We may have gone from hunter-gatherer to farmer to industrialist to information scientist, but we're still genetically a social animal who all too often unknowingly institutionalizes his inherited, primitive ways."

"Unknowingly," Mac echoed. "Unthinkingly. But, if we consciously imagine a state of grace, if we understand that our ultimate goal is to create a world where only the admirable is pursued, truth is sacred, and respect for everyone is sacrosanct, we can move beyond our DNA."

"Perhaps," Dr. Ingersaul hedged. "With conscious effort, compassion, and respect for facts."

"Our first step was Greek science and philosophy. The next was the late Renaissance when a new revolution of science and philosophy began with the aid of Johannes Gutenberg's printing press."

Merrill noted, "In just two generations, Europe went from one printing press to 1,000. The Bible was one of the first books to be printed. Once the lay people were able to read the Bible for themselves, they began questioning what the Church had been teaching them and a revolution was in the offing. In 1517, Martin Luther posted his *Ninety-Five Theses* denouncing Papal claims of authority and a whole new religion began. Protestantism."

Mac went on, "A generation after the *Ninety-Five Theses*, Nicolaus Copernicus declared the Earth revolved around the Sun, contradicting Psalm 104, 'He set the earth on its foundation; it can never be moved,' and Ecclesiastes 1, 'The sun rises and the sun sets, and hurries back to where it rises.' For that and the Church condemned him for heresy. Another generation and Giordano Bruno claimed there were other inhabited worlds in an infinite universe. For that, the Church burned him at the stake. Yet another generation and Galileo pointed his telescope to the stars to see moons around Jupiter, spots on the Sun, the phases of Venus, and mountains on the moon. He professed his belief in heliocentrism, the Church ordered him to Galileo refused, saying he didn't, 'feel obliged to believe that the same God who has endowed us with sense, reason, and intellect has intended us to forgo their use.' For that, the Church placed him under house arrest for the rest of his life. His death in 1642 marked the end of the Renaissance and the beginning of the Enlightenment, which culminated in 1789 with the U.S. Constitution and the French Declaration of the Rights of Man. During the century-and-a-half in between, scientists and philosophers explored new realms and pushed the boundaries of thought and knowledge. In the end, England and France created republics independent of monarchies. And France and America created republics independent of religion."

"Your quote of Galileo's," Duron said, "reminded me of Dr. William Jenner, inventor of the smallpox vaccine in 1796. His critics said if God wanted people to die of smallpox, then how dare we interfere, but Jenner believed if we can save lives with reason, we were morally obligated to do so."

"Where did you learn that?" Damon asked, feigning surprise.

"In a book," Duron answered defensively.

Pause. "You can read?"

"Can you read this?" Duron said.

"Merrill," Dwight asked contemplatively, "earlier you spoke of Apollo and Jesus, Jesus and Dionysus, Barnabas and Zeus, Paul and Hellenism and Christianity got mixed together."

"And Buddhism," the Elder nodded. "Cyrus the Great conquered the lands between the Greek Mediterranean and western India in 539 BCE. Everyone and every philosophy within his Empire was then free to travel between the Mediterranean and India, with Judea at the crossroads. By 500 BCE, the Buddhist concept of reincarnation had become part of Greek philosophy. By 400 BCE, Plato wrote in the Phaedrus of the soul and its immortality. By 300 BCE, Alexander the Great had conquered Cyrus's empire and over the next three centuries Hellenism worked its way into Judaism, then Christianity, including, the concept of an immortal soul."

"The borders of Cyrus's empire," Mac noted, "remained in place, under different rulers, for five hundred years, spanning the lives of the Buddha, Socrates, Plato, Aristotle, Alexander the Great, and the Ptolemies. Buddhism influenced Greek thought, Greek thought influenced Middle Eastern thought, and Jesus was therefore influenced by both. He said, for instance, 'Do not judge, so that you may not be judged,' and 'Why do you see the speck in your neighbor's eye, but do not notice the log in your own?' The Buddha said, 'Look not at the faults of others, nor at what they do or leave undone, but only at your own deeds and deeds unachieved.' Jesus said, 'If someone strikes you on the right cheek, turn to him the other also. And if someone wants to sue you and take your tunic, let him have your cloak as well.' The Buddha taught that one should, 'Win over an angry person with poise, a mean one with kindness, a greedy person with generosity, and one who speaks falsely with honesty.' Jesus said, 'Ye shall know the truth, and the truth shall make you free.' The Buddha said, 'Free of ignorance is free.'

"Nothing comes from nothing, and Christianity didn't spontaneously pop into existence. Something always comes before, and something always comes next. Christianity evolved out of Buddhist, Greek, and Judaic ideas, and Christianity evolves today in parallel with society and science. Some find solace in religion and a belief in an afterlife. Some become more giving and compassionate because of moral instruction from houses of worship. But, some have advanced to the point where morality is governed by intellect alone."

"You think the world will evolve someday to the point where we won't need God?" asked Mark.

"That implies there never *was* a God," Robbie said, "that He was just an invention."

"And if He was," Mac smiled, "what would that mean? I remember stopping in Florence once on a return trip from Rome. I had a few hours between trains, so I toured the Uffizi and afterward walked the streets where artists and intellectuals like Galileo and Da Vinci once lived and worked. Quite a humbling experience, I tell you. Well, eventually I came upon a low stone wall and to my left I could see the Ponte Vecchio, on a hilltop in front of me I could see the centuries old Medici palace, and below me I saw the Arno River. Its waters were running high and fast on their way to the sea, and in that moment, it struck me that our lives are like a river, always rushing and struggling forward, muddied by the effluence of trivialities, yet bound by the banks of societal norms and limited understandings all the way to the end. We never climb out to see what lies beyond, never stop to live in the moment, never accept that the past is past, the future is ethereal, and the present is all we have. So, we should live for today and *only* for today. We should revel in the freedom of knowing we don't have to live our lives like everybody else. We should explore and challenge, travel beyond, experience the new, and when the end comes we won't look back and regret what *might* have been."

"Here, here!" said Merrill, raising his glass, and everyone toasted to a life well lived.

"It was as much a criticism of me as others, I realized," Mac went on after setting down his glass. "So, I closed my eyes, calmed my mind, and focused on the moment. The birds singing, the rushing waters, the conversations of passersby, the sun and breeze on my face. I slowed my breathing, relaxed my body, pushed aside all conscious thought, and gradually became a primeval me standing before an ancient river. For a fleeting moment an amazing sense of peace filled me, only to be crushed a moment later by sadness. At first, I thought it must have been the loss of my brother and birth parents, but I'd come to terms with that long before. So, I had to keep searching further and further back until I reached my college days. That was when my history, philosophy, and science classes challenged my beliefs and forced me to admit that maybe I'd been wrong. Maybe there was no greater purpose to life, no One looking over our shoulder, that we're alone.

"But, life went on. Graduation, a career, long work hours, occasional romances. Nothing to challenge my belief in God again." He turned to Kyle and Merrill and smiled. "Then, I moved to Geneva and found a box of books on my doorstep. Homer, Socrates, Plato, Aristotle, St. Augustine, Leibnitz, Hume, Voltaire, Descartes, Kant, Hume. Dante Alighieri, Sun Tzu, Niccolò Machiavelli. Edward Gibbon, Benjamin Franklin, Thomas Paine, Thomas Jefferson, Alexis De Tocqueville, Winston Churchill. Robert Ingersoll, John Morris, Viktor Frankl, Bertrand Russell, Martin Luther

King, Karen Armstrong, Elaine Pagels, Madeleine Albright, His Holiness the Dalai Lama. Thomas More, Robert Louis Stevenson, Nathaniel Hawthorne, Alexandre Dumas, Walt Whitman, Henry David Thoreau, Herman Melville, Charles Dickens, Mark Twain. Victor Hugo, W. Somerset Maugham, Sinclair Lewis, Ernest Hemingway, Ray Bradbury, George Orwell, James Michener, David McCullough, Kurt Vonnegut, Charles Van Doren, Edward Rutherford, Ken Follett. Nicolaus Copernicus, Galileo Galilei, Isaac Newton, Charles Darwin, Albert Einstein, Francis Collins, Carl Sagan, Stephen Hawking, Stephen Jay Gould, E.O. Wilson. The Dhammapada, the Torah, the Bible, the Koran. Textbooks on law, economics, philosophy, humanities, psychology, the arts, world history, physics, biology, sociology, and political science. Four years I read. I listened to the news. I debated with my friends and Clansfolk. I found new ways of thinking and discovered new truths and realities."

"Maybe you think too much, man," Duron said with a grin.

Robbie agreed with a chortle. "No doubt, dude."

Mac replied, "Thomas Jefferson said, 'Fix reason firmly in her seat. Question with boldness even the existence of God. Because if there be one, He must more approve of the homage of reason than of blindfolded fear.'"

"Yeah, yeah. Whatever," Robbie muttered.

"A belief in God is a belief in a parent watching over us, and the fear of losing Him had stayed in my subconscious since college. As I stood beside the Arno, I realized I'd come to a breaking point. I had to consciously choose a path and commit to it fully. To go back and blindly believe in God or go forward and accept that this life is it. One chance, zero-sum. I made myself imagine a future without God where our fate is in our own hands, where we can make of our lives what we want, create whatever we want, be whatever we want. We could choose to be selfish and cruel, but wouldn't we realize that one person's selfishness means another's loss? Wouldn't we understand that all of us need to give and take in equal measure? Wouldn't we live by common decency to be treated likewise in return? And if we made our own fate, couldn't poverty, greed, war, totalitarianism, disease, famine, hate, naivety, discrimination, and ignorance be exorcised from the world forever? So, with adrenaline-fueled hope I cried out, 'God is dead! Long live the world of man!'"

With a half grin and a pained sigh, Mac said, "Unfortunately, an elderly Italian nun was passing by at that exact moment."

His friends roared with laughter.

"And apparently she understood English."

Even more laughter.

"She looked daggers at me," he said sheepishly. "So, with all the humbleness I could muster I said to her, 'May the sacrifices you've made for others give you peace, Sister, and may those with troubled hearts who seek peace in the Church find it.' The barest smile crossed her lips and with a slight bow of her head, she continued on."

"You are one lucky S.O.B., man," Duron said. "She coulda damned you right then and there."

"For sure," Mac chuckled.

"Yeah, just think," Dwight said sardonically, "if you'd been damned, people might be trying to kill you now!" and he started to laugh.

Mac winced and the room fell silent. Genevieve closed her eyes and lowered her head.

Realizing what he'd done, a mortified Dwight said, "Oh, geeze, Gen. I am *so* sorry. That was really insensitive of me."

"It's okay," she said softly with an obligatory smile and a tear. "It's okay."

For the umpteenth time, Merrill noticed T.J. frowning at his iPhone. "What in Hades have you been looking at all evening, lad?" he barked.

"Damned fool flew to Wyoming," T.J. grumbled.

"Sean?" Mac said.

"Logged in to GLOSAT this morning," nodded T.J., "but his GPS signal went dead just north of the 45th parallel. I've been checking passenger manifests ever since, but nothing. He's still there, somewhere."

Merrill growled, "The damned fool found what he was looking for."

"And it found him," Mac said, struggling to stand up. "Cyprus, Brazil, Chicago, a UN in shambles, an America I don't recognize. Well, no more. We're going to find Sean, we're going to end the White Freedom Nation's existence, we're going to extradite those responsible for killing Boujeau, and we're going to do it under the flag of the United Nations."

"Now you're talking!" said Duron.

"We're with ya, buddy," agreed Robbie.

"How soon can we have a strike team ready?" Mac said to T.J.

"Maybe half a day," he answered. "But–"

"Make the arrangements," Mac told him.

"There is *no way* President Thomas is going to approve a United Nations mission on U.S. soil. Not only hasn't it ever been done, but he thinks you're the incarnation of *Lucifer,* for chrissakes."

"Then we won't ask him," Mac said.

"Hooah!" shouted Robbie and fist-bumped Duron.

"Yeah, baby!"

T.J. began to say, "What about–" but Mac cut him off.

"We're not going to ask Schoen either."

"You can't just fly UN troops into Wyoming without somebody finding out!"

"That's the bloody point, Teej," Mac replied evenly.

T.J. let out a sigh of resignation. "Last known coordinates were 104 degrees, 44 minutes, 33 seconds west. Forty-five degrees, 0 minutes, 1 second north."

"Call Perry. Tell him to get us as close to those coordinates as possible."

"Us?" Duron said. "Get *us* close to those coordinates? You're not going, dude. You're still recuperating."

"Try and stop me."

θ

"*Let us cherish all creatures as a mother her loving
child. May our loving thoughts fill the whole world above,
below, across, without limit, a boundless goodwill.*"

– The Buddha

"*All for ourselves and nothing for other people seems, in every age of
the world, to have been the vile maxim of the masters of mankind.*"

– Adam Smith

"*Governments can err, Presidents do make mistakes, but the
immortal Dante tells us that Divine Justice weighs the sins
of the coldblooded and the sins of the warmhearted in a
different scale. Better the occasional faults of a government
living in the spirit of charity than the consistent omissions of
a government frozen in the ice of its own indifference.*"

– John F. Kennedy

They arrived at the Coast Guard hanger in Traverse just after midnight. Commander Ken Forston took Mac's duffel bag and helped
him into the cabin of the search-and-rescue helicopter.

"It'll take 20 minutes to get to Camp Grayling!" Forston
shouted over the sound of whooping props. "From there, you'll
catch a military transport bound for Regina, Saskatchewan!"

"What's in Regina?" Mac yelled back.

"Royal Canadian Air Force Base! The UN team is staging there!" answered Commander Forston. He stepped back, saluted, and slid the cabin door closed.

The chopper lifted off and banked over the city. Mac could see his house on the peninsula that divided Traverse Bay in half. Twenty-one minutes later they landed on a National Guard runway lined by birch and pine trees.

First Lieutenant Bill Holdsworth helped Mac out and led him to a massive transport jet sitting on the tarmac. Duron, Robbie, Damon, Dwight, Taylor, Mark, and T.J. followed.

"We'll be air-born in 10, gentlemen," Holdsworth said as they walked up the ramp into the tail section. "Then, three hours, 15 minutes to Regina." Pointing to a fold-down cot attached to the fuselage, he added for Mac's benefit, "Feel free to get some shut eye, sir. I'll wake you when we begin our descent."

"Thanks, Bill, but I've had plenty of shut-eye the past few months."

"Yes, sir," said the Lieutenant and gave his Mission Commander a salute before heading forward to the cockpit.

Mac and his team stowed their duffle bags and strapped in for take-off.

"We're beginning our descent now, sir," Lt. Holdsworth announced, coming back down the hold. "On the ground in 30."

"Time to suit up, gentlemen," Mac said, carefully standing up. He started to reach for his duffle bag but stopped. "Uh, Lieutenant, could you–"

The Lieutenant noted the mission commander's sling and said, "Of course, sir," and helped Mac off with his coat and shirt. When he saw the ghastly scar on the heir of Arthur's chest, the young lieutenant froze. Even though the shooting had been months earlier, large black sutures still crisscrossed blue-red blotches of torn skin, pieced together like a jigsaw puzzle.

"Looks worse than it feels, Bill," Mac assured the young man, wincing as he slid his left arm out of his shirt. "Hold that up, please?"

"Huh?" the lieutenant said, forcing himself to stop staring at the scar. "Oh, uh, yes. Of course, sir," and held up a black sweater for Mac to slip on.

Sliding his good arm into the sleeve, he said, "I can take it from here, Bill. Thanks."

Lt. Holdsworth stood at attention and gave Mac a perfectly executed salute before turning smartly on his heels and double-timing it back to the cockpit.

The jet rolled to a stop on a dark, cold, wind-swept tarmac stretching across the northern-most reaches of the Great Plains. The tail section unlatched, and massive hydraulic cylinders raised it high into the frosty air. It was nearly three a.m. Mountain Time when Mac walked out of the massive cargo hold wearing a black turtleneck, black khakis, and a black parka, its left side draped over his shoulder and sling. Colonel Perry Spencer stood at the end of the ramp waiting to greet his old friend.

"You're looking pretty good for a dead man!" he shouted over the roar of the north wind and the idling jet engines.

Reaching the tarmac, Mac gave his friend a one-armed hug. "Let's hope Sean takes my lead, eh?"

"We're about to debrief the team," Perry said and led Mac and the others to a waiting Humvee. "Hanger B," the Colonel ordered the driver and got in.

The private behind the wheel threw the truck in gear and off they sped. The outline of a large hangar gradually loomed out of the night, its huge doors open just wide enough for the Humvee to pass through. Inside were nearly 200 soldiers in camouflage make-up and black fatigues, seated in neat rows of folding chairs and facing two blackboards on rolling stands.

Through the Humvee's open window, Mac could hear Colonel Christopher Stone addressing the soldiers. "Self-proclaimed General Jonathan Robert Cobb is our main target. He's to be captured unharmed, if possible." He nodded at the truck coasting to a stop and added, "By the way, we'll have a special guest with us on our mission tonight."

The sight of a dead man stepping out of the Humvee sent a shock wave down the rows of men and women.

Walking over, Stone remarked with a smile and a casual salute, "I never thought I'd see *you* again."

"I had a few doubts myself," Mac replied wryly. "I'm glad to see you're in command, Colonel. Please, carry on."

"Yes, sir," Stone said and turned back to address his soldiers.

Perry led Mac and the others to the reserved front-row seats.

"It'll be pre-dawn when we air-drop into the Thunder Basin National Grasslands," the Colonel went on. "The White Freedom Nation residents'll still be asleep, but we don't have intel on which of these buildings are barracks." He pointed to the satellite photo taped to one of the boards. "Our best guess are the ones in the southeast corner of the compound here. Those'll be our primary targets. This large building here—" and he rapped on the board, "—near the gate is likely an assembly hall of some kind. All prisoners are to be taken there for interrogation. Infrared shows manned guard posts here, here and here. Red Team, you'll take 'em out as soon as Blue Team finishes setting up central command on the ridge overlooking the compound." He tapped on the photo again. "Green Team, your intel packets contain five-person squad assignments. You'll go in once the guard posts are secured. Every building in the compound *must* be secured at the *same time*. You've been issued live ammo for your sidearms, but your M-16 rounds are projectile syringes. Each one contains a nerve synapse inhibitor. Once injected into the body, it'll incapacitate the target in less than ten seconds.

"We don't need to make or become martyrs out there. Do your job, do it professionally, and bring everyone home alive. Any questions?" No one raised a hand. "Then, good luck and Godspeed," he concluded with a salute.

The soldiers of the strike team stood as one and saluted back.

"Load up!" Stone commanded.

A resounding, "Hooah!" and the soldiers double-timed out through the hanger door.

Mac and his friends followed.

A 10-seat jet prop rolled up alongside the dull green transport and Damon muttered, "That looks, uh…disturbingly small, by comparison."

"No shit," Dwight nervously agreed.

"You can always stay here," Mac replied.

"What, and miss all the fun?" Duron said.

"You Republicans," grumbled Damon.

The troop transport swooped low over the grassy Wyoming plain, leveling off 20 feet above the ground. While still traveling at 250 knots, the crew slid carbon-fiber sleds with Humvees and Jeeps anchored to them out the jet's tail. One after another they half-glided, half-fell through the frosty morning sky, slamming onto the grass-covered prairie and bouncing twice before skidding to a stop. Its payload delivered, the jet gradually spiraled back up to one thousand feet.

"Leveling off," announced Lt. Holdsworth.

The tail ramp lowered again, and Stone yelled, "Go, go, go!" He hooked his rip cord to the drop line and ran full tilt down the ramp, launching himself into the frigid, frenetic night sky. His soldiers dutifully followed with screams of "Hooahs!" and "Yeahs!" as they disapparated into the roaring torrent of air.

Touching down as the last Humvee was freed from its sled, Mac and his friends climbed out of the jet prop and into one of the trucks for a 30-minute ride to the bottom of a steep, treeless hill where Stone was busy directing the Humvees and soldiers. Mac got out and walked over.

"Everything's a go and we're on schedule," the Colonel reported. "Central command's up there," pointing to the ridge above them. "The Jeeps are busy carrying supplies, so you'll have to hoof it."

Just looking up the hill winded Mac. "Why don't you guys go ahead?"

Perry understood and nodded. "Come on!" he ordered the others and off they went.

Out of breath and chest aching, Mac reached the summit well after his teammates. The hilltop was broad, flat, and covered with knee-high prairie grass, reminding him a bit of Badon Hill. The sun was nearly up, the command post tents stood at the far edge, and the UN soldiers were readying themselves for battle. Walking across the field, the shallow valley beyond and the White Freedom Nation compound below gradually revealed themselves. The compound had guard towers at each corner and a dozen or so wooden one-story buildings. Steam rose from their furnace vents and the inhabitants were starting their day wholly unaware that their paranoiac nightmare of invading UN troops was about to come true.

Robbie handed Mac a pair of infrared binoculars. "Here, Bro. Green Team's in position."

"On your command, sir," Colonel Stone told his mission commander.

Mac lifted the spyglasses and scanned the compound. He thought of the countless self-deluded, hate-filled people who'd killed each other over the centuries in the name of God and country.

"Sir?" Stone repeated.

Mac shook his head in frustration and echoed the Colonel's own words. "Don't make or become martyrs down there, Chris."

"No intention to," said the Colonel and he lifted his radio. "Follow my orders to the letter and go! I repeat, go!"

The Red Team snipers took out the tower guards with syringe-bullets and Green Team converged on the compound from every direction. They cut through the barbed wire, silently poured through the fence, and surrounded the barracks.

"Go!" Stone ordered after a nod from Mac, and in they went.

Sounds of splintering wood, trampling boots, and screams of frightened women and children drifted up the hill, but soon all fell silent.

"That was, easy," Stone said, brow furrowed, watching the bewildered families of the White Freedom Nation being escorted out of the barracks.

"Too easy," Mac agreed, lifting the binoculars. Their infrared lenses made the body heat of the women and children being herded into Freedom Hall look like a parade of ghosts. Scanning the rest of the camp, something caught his eye near the main gate and a chill ran down his spine. Something giving off no heat at all was swaying from the limb of an oak tree.

He knew at once who it was. The shadowy remains of a man who once laughed and cried, dreamed and loved. A man whose wife and child would never again feel his embrace or hear him whisper, 'I love you.' A man Mac could see in his mind's eye proudly standing beside him atop a Cyprus mountain waiting to risk his life so that others might be free from tyranny.

"Damnit," he breathed, his fists tightening around the binoculars.

"What?" Stone exclaimed, casting an eye around the compound.

"The tree, by the gate," Mac answered through gritted teeth. "Find Cobb."

Stone squinted at the tree. "Son-of-a-bitch. *Yes,* sir. Captain!" he called. "We're going down!"

"Yes, sir!" said his aide-de-camp, starting for the nearest Jeep. A minute later they were lurching down the hill.

"Sergeant Helmbold," Stone said into his radio. "What's the count?"

"A hundred-seven, sir. All women and children. We're making another sweep of the buildings."

"Good work, Sergeant," the Colonel said. "Have you found Cobb yet?"

"Not yet, sir, but I will."

Impressed with the man's brass, Stone replied, "I know you will, sergeant. Over and out." He clipped the radio back on his belt. "I just hope he doesn't find you first, son."

"Helmbold's a good man, sir," the captain assured him.

"A hundred and seven women and children, the only men the ones in the guard towers. Where could the rest–" and then he recalled his history. Dread filled him. "Berlin. Iwo Jima. Waco. We've been thinking two-dimensionally!" He grabbed for the radio. "Green Team, get everyone inside the hall and take up defensive positions. Red Team, form a perimeter around the courtyard. Perry, follow us in. Sergeant Helmbold, find cover!"

The orders had barely passed his lips when the earth erupted. Cobb and his soldiers flung open sod-covered trap doors to underground bunkers and opened fire on anything that moved. Dozens of voices began shouting over the radio.

Stone cursed. "*Move*, captain."

"Bugger," Perry cursed under his breath. "Into the Jeeps! We're going down!"

The remaining UN soldiers headed off and Mac took charge of the command post. "Red Squad Two, you have four gunmen converging on the building in front of you," he said into his radio. "Green Squad Four, move to your nine o'clock position and take out the gunmen behind the mess hall. Red Squad Three, head north behind the buildings, break into two-man teams, then move south and pick off the shooters between the barracks. All squads in the hall, use your .45's and hold the bastards back."

Half a dozen White Freedom Nation soldiers ran towards the front gate. "Colonel, you're about to be pinned down by cross fire. Green Squad One, head due south to the fence line and follow it east. Perry, cut through the fence east of the gate and head west." Mac tossed the binoculars aside and shoved the radio into his breast pocket. "Stay here," he ordered his friends, drawing out his Berretta and starting down the hill.

"We're coming," Robbie told him.

"No!" Mac yelled. "You're not soldiers."

"You're not a soldier either, man," said Duron, "least not in *this* life."

They moved in front of Mac and formed an improvised V as they headed down the hill. "No!" he barked, coming to a stop. "Stay here! *All* of you."

Duron huffed, "I've known you since you were a pimply faced pudknocker. You think you can tell me what to do? I'll make my own damned decisions *and* mistakes, thank you very much."

"Damn straight," Robbie said.

Mac cursed under his breath, feeling pissed and proud all at the same time. "Well, get us a friggin' Jeep, then, will ya?"

"I'm driving!" Taylor called and ran off.

Mac walked back and bent over to pick up his binoculars. "Shit," he grunted in pain.

Duron picked them up for his friend. "Here."

"Thanks, buddy," Mac forced out as he straightened up.

"You don't have to go, Mac."

"I don't have to breathe either."

"You really are a stubborn son-of-a-bitch," Duron smiled.

"Look who's talking," muttered Mac.

Taylor drove up and yelled, "Everybody in!" and a moment later they were plummeting down the steep slope. By the time they crashed through the front gate, Green Squad One and Perry's unit were closing in on Stone's position. Taylor hit the brakes and the Jeep fishtailed to a stop. Mac and his team piled out into a soundscape of screaming orders, cracks of gunfire, and howls of pain. Bullets pinged off the Jeep so often it sounded like a pinball machine. Mac strode up to where Stone and Michaels were hunkered down behind a woodpile.

"Give me your sidearm, colonel."

"You trying to get yourself killed?" the colonel yelled. "Get down!"

"I've already been killed," Mac replied with a cold calm. "Your .45, please."

"I'm out of ammo!" Stone yelled back.

"I know," Mac said, grabbed the pistol out of the colonel's hand, and handed him the loaded Berretta.

Flashes of gunfire lit up the spaces between buildings. Lead slugs rippled through the heavy morning air. Tuffs of grass and dirt exploded as bullets slammed into the ground around him.

"Cobb!" Mac called from beside the hanging tree. "Come here!"

The gunfight continued unabated.

"Cobb! It's me!"

Above the din came a distant, "Hold your fire." Then more shots and another, "Hold your fire!" The fusillade waned, and an anxious voice called out from the shadows, "Who are you?"

"You know who I am, Cobb," Mac said with a disquieting calm. "Don't make me come get you."

A long moment passed before a paunchy middle-aged man clad in filthy fatigues and carrying an AR-15 cautiously emerged from between two barracks. Keeping the gun's barrel pointed at the stranger, Cobb strained to make out his face. "Who are you?"

"I am I," Mac answered with a chilling calm.

The General took another step forward. The stranger had one arm in a sling and a pistol held at his side. "I don't know you," Cobb called out.

"Yes, you do," Mac corrected him. "You've known me for a long time, and you've wanted me dead."

Cobb inched forward. "Dead?"

"Don't you recognize my voice, Cobb?" said Mac, but then it occurred to him that maybe the man had never actually heard Mac's voice before. Maybe he only knew what others like Swaywell wanted him to know.

"Tell me your name or I'll shoot you where you stand!"

"I am I," Mac said again, "the one," and stepped forward out of the oak tree's shadow, "the Antichrist."

As though evil itself had appeared before him, Cobb drew back in horror. "No! You…you're dead!"

"Dead," Mac nodded, slowly walking forward, "buried, and resurrected."

"No!" Cobb cried again and stepped back even further.

"The final battle between God and Lucifer is coming, my general, and I need you to lead my army of the damned." Another step and Mac was an arm's length away.

Cobb shook his head violently and lifted the rifle to his shoulder. "I'm a *Christian* soldier! I'm gonna *kill* you. Again!"

Mac laughed, deep and slow. "You can't kill a dead man, Cobb," he replied, bringing his .45 up and pointing it at the general. "It's time to join the eternal battle, my general."

The muscles in Cobb's legs gave way and he dropped to his knees. The rifle slipped from his hands and fell to the ground. "Please! Don't kill me!" he begged, clutching at Mac's parka. "I'll do anything. Anything!"

Mac slid his left arm out of its sling with a grimace and clutched Cobb's neck. The sutures in Mac's chest ripped open as he lifted the general to his feet. Fiery needles of light shot across his field of vision and he felt the warmth of his blood spreading across his chest and down his abdomen.

"Tell your men to surrender," he forced out, face crimson from pain, and pressed the .45's barrel against Cobb's forehead. "And as true as the steel of my gun upon you, I shall set your families free in the lands of my choosing."

"Yes. *Yes!*" Cobb cried. "Surrender," he screamed. "*Surrender!*"

One by one, the defenders of the White Freedom Nation came out of their hiding places, guns in hand.

"Tell them to lay down their weapons," Mac rasped.

"Put 'em down!" the General ordered, gesturing with his hands. "Put 'em down!"

His soldiers reluctantly did as they were told, and Stone's men moved forward.

"This," Mac whispered, his eyes wild with pain and anger, "is for Sean." His finger slowly drew back the trigger.

"*No!*" Cobb screamed.

Mac pulled the trigger and the barrel slide released with a loud *click!* The sound echoed across the courtyard and Cobb's head jerked backwards. The brave general collapsed to the ground like a rag doll, the hero of the White Freedom Nation having fainted dead away.

A makeshift honor guard wrapped Sean's body in an army blanket and carried it to a waiting Humvee. Mac and the others stood in reverence as the truck drove off.

"Search the compound," he told Stone.

"Yes, sir," replied the Colonel.

"Robbie," Mac said, his hand on his chest, "tell Merrill I'd like the Clan to set up a trust for Sean's family."

"Sure thing, bro," he said.

"Duron, contact the local authorities and make arrangements to send the families back to wherever they came from. Pay for their transportation and assign each family a probation officer."

"Will do," his friend answered.

"T.J., extradite Cobb to The Hague and make sure he appears before the International Court of Justice."

"My pleasure," he replied.

"Let's get back to central command," Mac told everyone and started for the hill.

When they reached the ridge, T.J. gestured to Mac's chest and told him, "Gen made me promise to take care of you, as if that were possible, so go get that looked at."

He smiled and said, "Oh, well, I wouldn't want you to get in trouble," and turned for the MASH tent. "I don't want to get in trouble with her either," he mumbled to himself.

Inside the tent he found the cots full and stretchers filling every inch of ground. Medics and nurses were working frantically to save those in grimmest need. Mac's torn sutures seemed so insignificant by comparison that he felt ashamed to even be there.

He took off his jacket and asked the nearest medic how he could help.

"Why are you helping me?" the frightened young man said. "You're, you're *him*."

The air of urgency in the MASH tent had long since passed and Mac knelt beside a cot applying a fresh bandage to the abdomen of a White Freedom Nation soldier.

"The Antichrist?" Mac replied with a half-grin and a shake of his head. "There's no such thing. Don't accept what others tell you at face value, son. Challenge what you're told, gather your own facts, come to your own conclusions," Mac finished with the bandage, "and then live and let live."

The young man seemed to struggle with his thoughts for a moment and then turned away. Mac patted him on the shoulder and said with a resigned smile, "One day you'll understand," and stood up to find a UN medic standing next to him.

"Let's take a look at your chest, sir," she said and guided him to a cot just vacated by a bull-of-a-sergeant hobbling out of the tent and trying to master his new crutches. With a nurse's help, the doctor cut off Mac's sweater and began injecting a local anesthetic around the jigsaw-like wound. After a dozen shots, she pulled the torn sutures out of Mac's chest and began sewing him back together.

"You'll need to take it easy for a while," the doctor told him, "though I doubt you're going to heed my advice."

"Maybe someday, doc," Mac smiled and half an hour later he walked out of the tent to find Colonels Perry and Stone locked in conversation.

When they saw him, the latter said, "I think we've found what you're looking for."

He followed them to a waiting Jeep and got in with a grunt of pain. "Remind me never to get shot again."

"Bloody well duck next time," Perry said.

The heir of Arthur laughed and grunted again.

"Sorry, ol' boy," grinned the colonel.

At Freedom Hall, Stone led Mac into a rustic office and said, "Take a look," pointing to the far wall. Behind an Army-surplus metal desk hung two framed letters. The one to the left was from several years before.

> *Dear General Cobb,*
>
> *The Reverend Johnny Swaywell and I have been close friends and confidants for many years, and it warms my Christian heart to know there are good white Americans like you still out there standing up for God and country. I am proud to notify you that effective immediately your HDF unit has been activated. I must stress that your unit's activation is a singularly unique event. All knowledge of it must be kept secret at all costs. You are to report directly and only to me. My private telephone number is below. Call me to receive your orders. With your help, general, our way of life will be preserved.*
>
> *God Bless you,*
> *Senator Jack Abrams*

The one to the right was from the prior summer.

> *Dear Colonel Collins,*
>
> *I heard from my good friends the Reverend-Secretary Swaywell and Vice President Abrams of your terrible sacrifice. Please accept my belated condolences for the death of your son, and know that whatever God has willed to happen, it is for His greater glory. While I am sure you are comforted in knowing he died in service to his country, I know your soul will never be at peace until your son's killer is brought to justice. Given your sacrifice, I hesitate to ask for your help again, but I must. You see, we have unfinished business, you and I. The Antichrist, William Cameron MacCrarey, the murderer of your son, the heir of a king born under the*

Empire that killed our Lord Jesus Christ, still lives. He is plotting to overthrow Secretary-General Boujeau and take over the United Nations, but you and I can stop him. I have the power to hand you justice and you have the power to be God's mighty sword on Earth. Call me at my private number below and I will explain what the Lord has in store for you.

Your fellow soldier of Christ,

Under Secretary-General Gerhardt Schoen.

"The letters, combined with what we've learned from the White Freedom Nation residents, should be enough to bring charges against Abrams, Swaywell, and Schoen for the murders of J.J. and Boujeau," said the Colonel.

"The first domino," Mac whispered as he turned for the door. On the landing, he called, "Teej! Is the press release ready?"

T.J. held up a "hold on" finger and finished his conversation with a White Freedom Nation family, directing them to a UN soldier near the gate. Jogging over, he said, "Yeah, it's ready, but I really don't think—"

"Release it," Mac ordered and called over his shoulder. "Perry!" The colonels came through the door. "Run the United Nations colors up the parade ground flagpole for me, would you? *Above* the stars and stripes."

"Righto," said Perry.

"Mac, Mac, Mac," T.J. groaned. "Once your press release hits the wire, we'll have reporters swarming all over this place. Now you're gonna give 'em a picture like that? The President and right wingers'll have a *field* day."

"I'm counting on it," Mac replied.

Pulling up behind the empty limousine parked in the circular driveway, Mac shifted his old Mustang into park, grabbed the folded copy of *The Washington Times* off the dashboard, and tucked it under his arm. He and T.J. got out and walked up to the oaken front doors of Michael Abrams' mansion.

Punching the security code into the digital keypad on the wall, Mac said, "They'll be in the solarium."

Entering the cavernous three-story entrance hall, they found themselves surrounded by staircases and hallways leading off in every direction.

"Uh, okay. So, which way is the solarium?" T.J. asked.

Mac shrugged. "Hell if I know."

Michael's man Friday emerged from a hallway to their left and said, "Lost are we, gentlemen?"

"I'll assume that was a rhetorical question, Gerald?" Mac replied.

"This way," he said with an undertone of exasperation and headed back the way he'd come.

The heir of Arthur whispered to T.J., "Sir John Gielgud," referring to the iconic English actor who portrayed an arrogant but caring butler in the movie *Arthur*.

"Thank you," Gerald said, a hint of boredom in his voice.

Mac cringed, and T.J. laughed. A few minutes later, Gerald left them outside a set of double glass doors.

"You understand what I'm about to do?" Mac said to Michael.

"Completely."

Mac led the way into a large, greenhouse-like room with floor to ceiling windows and a domed glass roof. Ornamental trees and beds of flowers crowded twisting fieldstone walkways leading to dozens of island patios. On the nearest, Jack Abrams stood beside a glass-topped wicker table and four matching chairs looking out at the blossoming apple trees. Atop the table sat a tea service.

"The second domino," Mac whispered.

Jack ignored the approaching footsteps.

Mac stopped two paces away. "Look at me."

The Vice President took his time turning around. Mac drew his arm back, hand clenched into a fist. Jack flinched and stepped back, but Mac's wide right hook caught the man squarely on the jaw, spinning him around like a top and dropping him to the stone floor. "That's for J.J. Kraeg, you son of a bitch."

"You're supposed to be *dead*," the Vice President spat, rubbing his chin.

"Why does everyone keep saying that?" Mac muttered, grabbing Abrams by the arm and helping him to his feet. "Read," he said and shoved the newspaper into the VP's hands.

Next to a photo of the UN flag flying above the American colors read the headline, 'UN Troops Attack US Citizens.' Jack paled straight away.

"Out loud," Michael commanded as he walked over.

"'For the first time since Pearl Harbor, a foreign power attacked U.S. citizens on American soil. A press release issued yesterday morning by the United Nations led Federal authorities to the compound of an anti-government, neo-Nazi group called the White Freedom Nation. UN soldiers raided the compound early this morning, killing several members and extraditing their leader, Jonathan Robert Cobb, to The Hague. The U.S. State Department issued a press release in return saying the UN's actions were conducted without the consent of the White House. In a hastily called press conference, President Thomas expressed shock and sadness over what he called, 'the unprovoked murder of U.S. citizens by Godless UN troops.' UN representative, T.J. Makatu, said a number of UN soldiers died as well and that documents handed over to local authorities prove that the White Freedom Nation was involved in the double-assassination of Deputy UN Ambassador William Cameron MacCrarey and Secretary-General René Boujeau last fall. Oddly, several White Freedom Nation soldiers reported seeing the late MacCrarey during the raid. In an official statement, Acting Secretary-General Gerhardt Schoen denied any foreknowledge of the attack and blamed rogue fighting units loyal to MacCrarey.

"'Numerous video tapes of Christian Vigil sermons, Nazi paraphernalia, newspaper clippings about MacCrarey, and personal letters from Acting Secretary-General Gerhardt Schoen and Vice

President–'" Jack paused to look at his Grandfather. "'Vice President Jack Abrams were among the items found in the compound. Black Hills County Sheriff–'"

"Enough," said Mac, taking the paper back. "Thomas and Schoen know the game's afoot. As of this moment, you're under house arrest by the United Nations, and by the end of the day Swaywell will be, too. The day after tomorrow, Michael will escort you to Schoen's swearing-in ceremony at the General Assembly Building, after which you'll be flown to The Hague."

"Go to hell," said the VP.

"Jack, you're my only grandchild and heir," said Michael, "but even if it breaks your grandmother's heart, I'll leave every damned penny I have to the Clan Camulodunum if you don't do exactly what Mac tells you."

A look of loathing and panic crossed his grandson's face, and like an unrepentant delinquent, he forced out a, "Yes, sir."

"Now, you're going to tell me everything, and I mean *everything* you know about what Schoen's up to," Mac said.

Alone in his office, the President stared at the front page of *The Washington Times*.

The army of the Beast killing God-fearing Christians on U.S. soil. How could this be happening? The Antichrist is dead, isn't he? America is a Christian nation again and his friend Gerhardt Schoen will be Secretary-General soon, won't he? They'd stopped the End Times from coming, hadn't they?

He needed answers and wanted words of comfort. "Get me Johnny!" he called to the open door.

A middle-aged woman in a plain ankle-length dress and a peroxide blonde bouffant peaked in. Reluctantly, she said, "Mr. President, the Reverend is tapin' his weekly sermon at the Crystal Cathedral this mornin'."

"Then, get me Jack!"

She took a step back. "The Vice President is, uh, he, well, his grandfather–"

"His grandfather *what?*" yelled Thomas.

Another step back. "He won't let the Vice President leave his house, sir. He's grounded."

"Grounded?" the President bellowed, pounding his fists on the desk. "I wanna know what the Lord wants me to do, damn it!"

Michael's limousine came to a stop in front of the Church of Eternal Vigilance at the end of a four-lane divided boulevard flanked on either side by a massive, rambling asphalt parking lot. A six-car tram pulled up behind the limo and dropped off a load of latecomers dressed in their Sunday best.

"When in Rome," Mac said, getting out of the car to follow the churchgoers. He didn't get two steps before his friends formed up around him. Robbie and Duron at point, T.J. and Dwight to either side, and Damon taking up the rear.

"You guys worry too much."

"Yeah, this coming from a guy who's been shot at how many times?" Duron muttered.

Mac growled and continued on to the bank of glass doors.

Once inside, they found themselves standing in a vast rectangular atrium the size of a football field circumscribed by restaurants, a fitness club, a family counseling center, a café, a gift shop, a book store, and a Christian reading room. In the atrium's center stood a large rectangular granite fountain with a 12-foot tall white limestone statue of Jesus. Hands raised to heaven, jets of water streamed out of His fingers to shower down on 11 of His disciples kneeling in a circle around Him. The 12th, poor Judas, cowered in a corner, damned to eternal dryness.

"Guess Swaywell never read the *Gospel of Judas*," Mac muttered.

"Which is?" Mark said absently, studying the statue.

"Gnostic text from 280 CE which says Christ purposefully fulfilled the prophecies by asking Judas Iscariot to betray Him to Pilate. Judas reluctantly agreed out of love and respect for his teacher."

"Don't think that was in the Bible," said Robbie.

"Didn't make the cut," Mac replied as he turned to study an illuminated map of the building with an index of offices and functions. "Administrative Offices, Admissions Bureau, Agency for Overseas Ministries, Charitable Giving Office, Copy Center, ah! Here it is. Crystal Cathedral, B-17." He took his bearings. "That way."

His friends formed up around him again.

"Good grief," he grumbled.

Outside a travel agency stood a rack of pamphlets about places like a creationist museum near Cincinnati where Adam and Eve frolicked with dinosaurs, an observatory in Georgia with a telescope that could see heaven, and the Center for Creation Studies at Jerry Falwell's Liberty University. There were dozens of others and Mac picked up one about a Florida theme park called Genesis Adventure Land. Opening it, he discovered that God purposely buried dinosaur bones and ruins of ancient cities to make the world *seem* much older than it really was, just to test our faith.

He put the brochure back on the rack.

They passed tables of Christian knickknacks, necklaces with wooden crosses, bracelets with Bible verses, T-shirts with "Out of the UN Now" on them, Jesus fish appliqués, Calvin & Hobbes decals with Calvin praying before a cross, posters of the Holy Land, home schooling educational games, bumper stickers of NASCAR numbers and slogans like "I Love Christians," "Right to Life / Right to Guns," "Don't Tread on Jesus," "Honk If You're Going to Heaven," and "No Taxation without God's Representation."

Passing the book shop, Mac glanced through the plate glass window at the shelves crowded with Christian videos and paperbacks with titles like *A Guide for Christian Political Activism, Conquering the Evil Left, Genesis Geology, Home Schooling for Dummies, The Homosexual Agenda, Why Liberals Hate Christmas, Intelligent Design & UFOs, The Right Christian, Politics and the Church, Monkeys and People: The Darwin Conspiracy, Restoring States' Rights,* and *America: The New Holy Land.*

Mac stopped to look at a poster hung on a pillar of the 39-story glass and marble UN Secretariat Building in New York City. Beside it stood a 39-story tall Jesus Christ knocking on its side as if it were a door.

"Oh, geeze," he sighed in frustration.

The others gathered round.

"Does that mean–" Damon began to ask.

"That the UN is anti-Christian?" Duron supposed.

"Because Mac's supposedly the Antichrist?" Mark added.

"Because the UN represents all faiths and all peoples?" Dwight said.

"Because it doesn't automatically defer to the U.S.?" asked Robbie.

"Yes to all of the above," Mac replied with a scowl.

A plump woman with too much makeup and overly done hair hurried by. As she did, she recognized Mac and let out a gasping shriek before dashing off down the concourse.

Mac sighed again. "Come on."

At the far end of the concourse, brilliant white light illuminated the open space beyond a bank of glass doors. Drawing nearer, they could make out dozens of high-wattage lights mounted to a domed ceiling and rows of seats. Reaching the doors, they peered down into the immense Crystal Cathedral, laid out like a vast Shakespearean Globe Theater with a round stage in the center and concentric rings of seats leading up to the glass doors.

A hundred feet wide, brightly lit, and slowly rotating, Mac guessed the stage could make a full revolution every 20 minutes. Atop it stood an olivewood altar, a multimedia pulpit, a massive pipe organ, a two-story stainless-steel crucifix, and risers for a choir that could give the Mormons a run for their money.

"The telecast'll begin in a sec," Mac said. "Once Swaywell's on stage, we go."

An announcer's voice boomed out, "Ladies and gentlemen. The Church of Eternal Vigilance in Alexandria, Virginia, is pleased to present another hour of the Christian Vigil. Prayers, teachings, news and its meaning as revealed by America's most influential biblical scholar and Secretary of Homeland Security, Dr. Johnny Swaywell. And now, *heeeeerrre's* Johnny!"

A spotlight illuminated a swaggering Reverend-Secretary coming down one of the many aisles leading to the rotating stage, waving and shaking hands as he went. Dressed in a perfectly tailored light blue suit, he mounted the stairs to the stage as quickly as his portly frame allowed and sauntered over to the pulpit.

"Welcome!" he thundered into the microphone. "Welcome. The Lord has been busy this week as I will reveal to you this morning, but first let's begin with a passage from Acts."

"Let's go," said Mac and in they went.

A wave of gasps, hushed words, and an occasional cry of fear followed Mac as he led the others down the aisle. When the commotion became too much to ignore, Swaywell halted his reading and looked up in irritation. No sooner did he recognize Mac than the Reverend began vigorously shaking his head and backing away.

"No!" he cried. "It can't be! He's, he's dead!"

"Again with the dead thing," groused Mac. Reaching the stairs leading up to the stage, he took them two at a time.

"Stop him!" Swaywell beseeched his acolytes, the music director, the choir members, even the altar boy, but no one dared move towards the man who'd risen from hell itself.

"Devil! Demon! Antichrist!"

"Come with me, Johnny," Mac told him with barely concealed ire.

"Never!" the Reverend-Secretary screamed and cast another pleading look at those around him.

Mac reached for Swaywell's arm, but the Reverend-Secretary fell to his knees, raised his eyes to heaven, and with quavering voice recited, "'The Lord is my shepherd, I shall not want. He maketh me lie down in green pastures.'"

Mac reached for his arm again.

"No!" Swaywell screamed, trying to stand and back away at the same time, only to lose his balance and fall with a thud on his broad rump.

The congregants gasped, and one brave soul shouted, "Leave him alone!"

"God save him!" cried another, and Bibles flew through the air, tumbling harmlessly across the stage.

One slid to a stop at Mac's feet. He picked it up, dusted it off, and set it on the pulpit. Then, he waved Robbie and Duron up to the stage to take Swaywell away.

Emboldened by cries of protest from the congregants, the Reverend said tremulously, "Keep your evil hands off me!"

"Relax," Robbie said coolly as they each took an arm.

"Time to pay the piper, old man," said Duron, and they led him down the stairs to taunts and jeers.

"Who's gotta gun?" yelled a congregant

"He wants to take *away* our guns!"

"He wants to destroy America!"

"Go back to hell, beast!"

"Death to the Antichrist!"

"Revelations!"

The words of Luke 23:34 came to Mac's mind. "Forgive them, for they know not what they do." He stepped up to the podium and said into the microphone, "When everything is said and done, when we look back and reflect on our lives, how will we judge ourselves? On what scale will justice be meted out by your God or the Fates? Will we be, *shouldn't* we be judged by how we loved one another? And not just those like us, but everyone? What we did to show them how important they were to us? That we valued them more than ourselves? That we helped them live a life with purpose?" His voice grew ever more urgent as he talked. "For the rest of our lives, shouldn't we build up and bring together instead of tear down and divide? Shouldn't we reach out in love and friendship, rather than push away with prejudice and intolerance? I ask this not just for the sake of others, but for the sake of your souls. Calm your mind, still your heart, reflect on those you hurt, who you called sinners and considered inferior. Think about the consequences of your words and deeds. Understand their lives and why they are the way they are. Ask their forgiveness and do everything in your power to set right what's been made wrong. Do unto others as you would have them do unto you, for nothing is more important than that. Nothing."

And with that he walked down the steps and up the center aisle with his friends and Swaywell in tow to the sounds of deafening silence.

Jack Abrams and Johnny Swaywell sat at the wicker table in the solarium, each holding a framed letter addressed to the White Freedom Nation.

"What do you want from me, Son of Satan?" the latter demanded, trying to sound braver than he looked.

Mac leaned over the table. "First, I'm not the Son of Satan, I'm not the Antichrist, and if you had even an *ounce* of common sense you'd know that! Second, you're gonna tell me what your involvement's been with Schoen and how you ended up as Mitchell Thomas's Secretary of Homeland Security."

Swaywell paled.

"If you don't, I'll hand you over to the people you've belittled and vilified all these years – gays, feminists, Jews, Muslims, atheists, immigrants, minorities – and let them do with you what they will."

The reverend shuddered at the thought of it and turned pleadingly to Abrams who'd apparently found something very interesting in the bottom of his tea cup. Swaywell let out a long, resigned breath, ran a trembling hand through his ruffled graying hair and began, "Almost three years ago, Gerhardt called me. He wanted, uh, he wanted–"

"He wanted to kill me?" Mac said, pushing over the third domino in his mind.

"We'll be in New York by early evening," Mac said to Michael as the Mustang merged onto the interstate. The others, including the

Reverend-Secretary and the Vice President, followed in the limo. "We'll be staying with the Penn's in the Village."

"I'll take Jack and Johnny to my apartment on the Upper East Side," replied the elder Abrams.

"The swearing in ceremony's at the General Assembly Building tomorrow at noon," said the heir of Arthur. "Have your grandson and Swaywell sit where I can see them. When it's over, bring them back to your estate in Virginia and keep them there."

"Will do," Michael answered. "You'll be bringing charges against them?"

Mac nodded. "But not for a while. We need to keep them incommunicado a bit longer. I want to keep the President off balance."

Michael chuckled. "He'll be a basket case inside of a week."

"I'm counting on it."

"When you're ready, I'll get you in to see him."

"Unannounced?"

"But, of course."

Taylor, Perry, Lynn, Dave, and Mac sat at the kitchen table with Merrill and Kyle, who'd flown in the night before. Mark, Damon, Dwight, Duron, and Robbie leaned against the counters, plates in hand, laughing and arguing as usual. All were in good spirits and with good reason. Brilliant sunlight filtered in through the tall narrow windows and the kitchen seemed electric with anticipation.

"'Tomorrow and tomorrow and tomorrow,'" Merrill gleefully recited from *Macbeth*.

Mac recited another of its lines. "'Life's a walking shadow, a tale signifying nothing.'"

"Ah," Merrill sighed, "perhaps not quite apropos, eh?"

Kyle chuckled and said, "A toast! To Mac, to the blood of our ancestors, to the once and future Camelot!"

"Here, here!" chimed the others.

Mac gave a slight bow and raised his mug. "To luck!"

"To luck!" cried the others and then broke into laughter.

The man from Traverse got to his feet. "Thanks for standing by me, Keeper. And to you, Merrill. You took a broken man and gave him a reason to live."

"A thousand lifetimes, a thousand times I'd do the same," the Elder replied with uncharacteristic warmth.

"We're very proud of you," said the Keeper.

"We all are," said Lynn.

Mac declared in his best mission commander voice, "Colonel, you're in charge of the convoy."

"Yes, sir!" Perry exclaimed, snapping to attention. "What are you waiting for?" he barked at the others, "Fall in!"

More laughs as they marched out of the kitchen single file.

Lynn gave Mac a peck on the cheek. "Genevieve just texted. They're landing at LaGuardia now. Charles will bring them straight to the General Assembly Building."

"Wonderful. And thank you again for being our hosts."

"Go change the world, buddy," Dave said with a hug.

"Come, m'boy," Kyle said proudly, "the world is waiting."

The limousine turned onto Raoul Wallenberg Walk and approached the General Assembly Building, Dag Hammarskjold Library, and Secretariat Building.

"Ready?" Perry said from behind the wheel.

Mac's friends replied with enthusiastic variations of "Yes."

"I was talking to Mac, you tossers."

"As I'll ever be," he answered.

Perry drove up to the UN campus security gate and lowered the window.

A gruff-looking guard stepped out of his hut. "Name and purpose of your visit," the Schwarzenegger-sized man asked with a mix of contempt and boredom.

"Here for the swearing in," Perry told him with the no-nonsense manner of a career officer.

The guard gave Perry's RAF uniform a once over, his eyes lingering momentarily on the colonel's eagles, and replied a bit more respectfully. "I'll still need to see everyone's ID and official invitations, sir," he insisted.

Mac lowered the rear window. "You don't need to see our identifications."

The guard turned, ready to tell whoever had interrupted him to take a flying leap, but when he saw who it was, he bolted upright.

"Jesus, Mary, and Joseph!" he blurted out, stumbling back into the hut and slamming his palm down on the red mushroom-shaped button marked Open. Stepping out again, he faced the limo and stood at attention, saluting as the car drove on.

Robbie sniggered. "Did you see the look on that guy's face?"

"Focus," Mac said, suppressing a smile.

"Go focus yourself," Robbie replied with a dismissive grin.

"Classy," Mac muttered. "Real classy."

Their car pulled around to the General Assembly Building's loading dock along the East River. "He's here," Perry told the person on the other end of the car phone and clicked off. By the time they piled out, a detachment of UN security guards in *Men in Black* sunglasses and black suits were waiting.

"Wow," said Mac, "just like the movies."

"Focus," Robbie mimicked.

"Go focus yourself," Mac told him.

A waiting elevator took them up a floor and opened to reveal not 20 paces ahead the double-doors to the stage where Mac's life had nearly ended.

He stopped cold.

"Alright, lad?" said Merrill, putting a hand on the heir of Arthur's shoulder.

Mac steeled himself and took a breath. "Follow me," he said, willing himself to take a step forward. The next took a little less effort and the one after even less. Reaching the double doors, he took another breath and gently pushed open the one to the left. Standing just out of the audience's line-of-sight was Michael Abrams listening to the President of the Assembly's last-minute instructions.

Mac slipped through the door. "Where are they?" he asked.

"Front row. Right of the main aisle," he answered. "They'll meet us back here after the General Assembly adjourns."

Mac gave the friend of the Clan a skeptical look.

"Not to worry. Jack'll do whatever I tell him and Johnny follows Jack around like a puppy dog."

"And once the votes are electronically tallied," the President concluded, sounding none too happy, "we shall have a new Secretary-General."

During the perfunctory applause, Mac asked, "Where is he?"

"Schoen's to the left of the aisle with a handful of dignitaries he probably had to bribe to sit that close to him."

Mac chuckled while the President gathered up his papers and added somberly, "Before we vote, our Acting Secretary-General would like to say a few words."

Schoen rose from his seat and stormed the stage. Seizing the podium, he declared, "You will see the *end* of your precious United Nations, if I am not elected Secretary-General."

In the moments that followed, one could have heard the proverbial pin drop.

"You, the General Assembly, naively chose to follow that *fool* MacCrarey! You voted to strip the Security Council of its powers and *now* look. We are impotent! The laughing stock of the world! But," he said, his lips curling into a foul grin, "the world will laugh no longer. I will re-cast the United Nations into its proper order, the order of destiny, the order of God and Nature!"

Rumblings of shock and anger began spreading through the hall.

"Is he talking about being elected Secretary-General or taking over the world?" Mac said facetiously.

"Yes," Michael answered in disgust.

"William Cameron MacCrarey poisoned your minds!" Schoen continued. "His antiquated ideals of honor and chivalry stirred within you the fires of revolution, and for that he was *killed.*"

A smattering of jeers and boos rose up.

"In his ignorance, he failed to understand that there is no honor among thieves and inferiors, only among the strong and *masters* destined to rule others!"

The Ambassadors began taunting and shouting, but then suddenly fell silent when someone appeared to stage left. Someone who looked very much like…

But, no, it couldn't be! They'd seen him shot dead before their eyes, right on this very stage!

Someone began clapping, an ambassador cried, "Thank, God!" and the Assembly rose to its feet. A roaring applause and a cheer went up as Mac strode up to Schoen and stopped an arm's length away.

"Step back," Mac demanded.

Schoen stood stock still, his mind caught between disbelief and a rekindling hatred so intense it made his skin crawl. He wanted nothing more than to strike down this man whose veins carried the blood of Arthur, this heir of his ancestors' enemy, but knew he couldn't. Not here. Not now. The primacy of becoming Secretary-General had to win out. And there'd be time enough for killing later.

He forced himself to step aside and another cheer went up.

Mac stepped up to the podium. "If you'll have me, I'd like to be your new Secretary-General."

The Assembly roared with applause.

Schoen pushed Mac aside. "You are insane!" he screamed at the Ambassadors. "This man is mentally *unfit* to be Secretary-General! He tried to kill himself, he was committed to a mental institution, and he was a failure as a Mission Commander!"

Mac listened indifferently as Schoen ranted on.

Then, a little voice called out, "Daddy!" from stage left and he turned to see Cameron running towards him. He held out his arms and she threw herself into them.

"I missed you, daddy," she said.

"I missed you, too," he smiled, hugging her tightly.

Genevieve hurried over, followed by Michael, Merrill, and Kyle, and wrapped her arms around the both of them. "I love you," she whispered.

"I love you, too," Mac echoed. "Both of you."

"That man lives in sin with that *whore*," cried Schoen, pointing at Genevieve. "She gave birth to his illegitimate child! The morality of the Secretary-General must be beyond reproach. But this immoral, pathetic, *failure* of a man," and he flicked a contemptuous hand at Mac, "is nothing more than a manic-depressive, suicidal, hedonist, and she, the *niece* of the late Secretary-General Boujeau, is nothing but a slut and mother of a bastard!"

Murmurs rolled through the assembly and Genevieve gave Mac a crestfallen, "I'm sorry" look.

"You've nothing to be sorry for," he said with a smile and handed Cameron to her. "I'll be right back," he added casually, though she could plainly see the fury in his eyes.

"Withdraw your name from consideration," Schoen demanded, "or—"

Mac drew back his arm and paused just long enough for the Acting Secretary-General to understand what was about to happen. Schoen took a step back, but the heir of Arthur's fist slammed into the Aryan's face, sending him stumbling back before crashing to the stage.

"That's for Genevieve and Cameron," Mac said through clenched teeth before pulling Schoen to his feet. "And I'll see you in prison for what you did to J.J., the soldiers under my command, and the Amerindians." He straightened his jacket. "Now, I've a world to change," and he turned for the podium.

"Before I kill you, MacCrarey," Schoen hissed, "I will make your life a living hell."

"I've already been there," Mac said coolly.

The soon-to-be-former Acting Secretary-General took a menacing step towards Cameron.

Mac spun on his heels, but Michael, Merrill, and Kyle had already formed a line in front of her.

"Should any harm come to her," the Keeper declared with such forceful nobility that Schoen halted at once, "you shall have *me* to answer for it."

"And me," echoed Merrill.

"And me," said Michael.

"And us," said Duron as Mac's friends joined the line.

Schoen glared at the lot of them, gave Mac one last hate-filled look, and stormed off the stage to tumultuous cheers and applause.

Mac held out his hand for Genevieve to join him at the podium. Taking Cameron from her, he said, "Say hi to everyone, sweetie."

She gave a little wave and buried her head in the nape of Mac's neck. Salutations in dozens of different languages greeted her in return.

"Yes," Mac said to the Assembly, "Genevieve is the mother of my child, and for that wonderful gift, I'll spend the rest of my life trying to make her and Cameron as happy as they've made me. And yes, she is the niece of René Boujeau. Her mother died when she was young, and her father became an alcoholic, lost his job, and moved his family to the not-so-nice side of town. She ended up getting involved with drugs, dropping out of high school, being taken advantage of by men void of nobility and humanity, and all the while, her uncle, René Boujeau, did *nothing* to help her. She faced a life few of us could imagine, much less overcome, but overcame it she did. She earned a GED, a Bachelor's and Master's Degree, and now she works as a counselor helping teens and adults overcome the sorts of problems she faced."

The Assembly gave her an acknowledging round of applause.

"Yes, there were military and civilian deaths during my field assignments, some because of my fear and inaction early on, but all due to the grave threats posed by the dictators and military thugs bankrolled by Boujeau and Schoen. Proof of this along with evidence of the Reverend-Secretary Swaywell's and Vice President Abrams's involvement in the deaths of Dr. J. J. Kraeg and Rene Boujeau, and two attempts on my life will be posted on the United Nations' website later today."

Shocked murmurs rose up from the Assembly.

"Should I be so fortunate as to be elected your Secretary-General, I will work with you to create a new age for the world, a *Novum Orbis Regium* – a worldwide democracy watched over by peacekeepers and peacemakers. A world of wisdom, not superstition. Altruism, not materialism. Neighbors, not strangers. And opportunities, not obstacles. A world where we provide a social and intellectual foundation for every child and adult and grant them the self-respect and self-sufficiency they deserve. Where unbiased laws apply equally to everyone. Where tolerance and respect reign supreme. Where living without hate, without ignorance, without greed, without war, without poverty, without hunger, without pestilence, without overpopulation, without ecological devastation, and without *borders* is no longer a dream but commonplace.

"If we do this, then schoolchildren a thousand years from now will read of us in their history books and marvel at our wisdom and fortitude. I wish only for the chance to lead us into such a noble future."

The Assembly rose to their feet and applauded.

He stepped back from the podium, took Genevieve's hand, and walked over to stand with his Clansmen and friends.

The President of the Assembly hurried over and, dispensing with formality, proclaimed, "All those in favor of electing William Cameron MacCrarey our new Secretary-General raise your hands!" Every hand but those of two Security Council Ambassadors shot upwards. "I hereby declare, with the authority granted the General Assembly by the newly amended Charter, that William Cameron MacCrarey is the world's new Secretary-General of the United Nations!"

Cheers and roaring applause greeted his pronouncement.

Beaming, Mac embraced Kyle and Merrill. "This world and Arthur's are now one," he said to them.

"Aye, laddy. Now lead as Arthur would," said Merrill.

"Be wise and just," added Kyle.

"I will," Mac promised. "I will."

"I'll miss you," Genevieve said as she undressed for bed.

"I'll miss you, too, but it'll just be for a week," Mac told her, loosening his tie. "I'll get my transition team in place, do the PR thing, try and find us an apartment, and I'll be in Geneva by the weekend to help pack. I promise. By this time next week, we'll be New Yorkers."

"Well, it's *closer* to Traverse, at least," she said, undoing her bra and tossing it aside. "Now, come to bed, Mr. Secretary-General."

Mac threw his tie over the headboard and put his arms around her waist, just as his cell phone rang. He made a sound like a growling sigh and said, "Hold that thought."

She giggled, slipped off her panties, and crawled under the covers. He sighed again and punched Accept.

"Mac." A pause. "Hey, Teej. Um, can this wait? I have some, uh, pressing business to attend to." Another giggle from the beautiful woman waiting for him in bed. The smile on his face faded the longer he listened. "Where is he now?" Pause. "Order security to pick him up when he lands. Then fly him to The Hague. I'll meet you at the Secretariat in the morning after I take Genevieve and Cameron to JFK." Another pause. "You, too, Teej. My best to Marion." He pressed End, set the phone down, and stood for a moment lost in thought.

"Something wrong?" said Genevieve.

"It's Schoen. He, he left the country. Headed for Germany."

"Why?"

"No idea," Mac answered and sat on the edge of the bed. "You and Cameron are everything to me. And my Achilles heel."

"You won't lose us," she promised, taking his hand. "Ever."

"Promise?"

"Promise," she answered, a playful smile crossing her lovely face. "Now, come to bed."

It had been a long, long week, his days and evenings full of meetings, public appearances, press conferences, sit-downs with foreign dignitaries, interviews with potential appointees, and dashing across town to look at apartments whenever he had a free hour. Finally, Friday evening arrived, and Mac settled into his seat for a five-hour trans-Atlantic flight to London. There, he'd have a four-hour layover at Heathrow before catching a connector to Geneva. With any luck, he'd arrive in time for brunch Saturday at Petra's with his two favorite ladies.

"Beverage, sir?" the passing flight attendant said.

"Microbrew, if you have one," he answered, and by the time she returned he was fast asleep.

Genevieve woke with a start.

Sitting up, she listened, unsure of what had awakened her. A bad dream, perhaps. The wind. A car rattling past in the street.

Then, she heard one of the Clansmen below her window yell for someone to stop.

She threw back the covers and as her feet touched the floor, a deep *crack* sounded outside, then another and another before everything fell unnaturally silent.

She ran to Cameron's bedroom, wrapped her in blankets, and whispered, "We have to go."

"What's wrong, mommy?" Cameron said with a yawn.

Genevieve lifted her out of bed. "We have to be quiet as mice, sweetie. Okay?"

"Okay," yawned Cameron, curling up against her mother and closing her eyes.

Genevieve hurried downstairs to the kitchen, grabbed the car keys off the counter, and pulled open the back door.

Standing on the stoop was a man silhouetted by the light from the neighbors' windows, panting like a wild animal, the sharp smell of burnt gunpowder hanging about him like a black veil.

She screamed and stepped back. The dark figure tore open the screen door, rushed in, and struck Genevieve hard across the face.

Stars bloomed in front of her eyes as she stumbled backwards holding on tight to Cameron. Again, he hit her, harder this time, and she fell to the floor. The dark visage bent down and grabbed for the bundle of blankets. A stray beam of light from the kitchen window slashed across the man's pale face and blonde-white hair.

"No!" she cried, holding on to Cameron for dear life.

Gerhardt Schoen drew back his arm, his hand balled into a fist.

What seemed but a moment later, a touch of a hand woke him.

Stretching, Mac yawned and said to the flight attendant, "Yes?" wondering what time it was and how long he'd slept.

"The Captain has a satellite call for you, Mr. Secretary-General. You can take it in the forward cabin."

He nodded wearily and followed her up the aisle to find the co-pilot waiting outside the cockpit door, phone in hand. "Congratulations on your election, sir."

The heir of Arthur gave the man a tired smile. "Thanks," he said, glancing at the man's nametag. "Captain Williams."

"David." He held the phone out. "And today I'm first officer."

"Call me Mac," he said and took the phone. "MacCrarey here."

"Patching your party through now, sir," the UN operator said. A click and Genevieve's near-hysterical crying sounded over the line. A shiver ran down his spine.

"He…he took…her. Gerhardt…Schoen took…her," she said through heaving sobs.

A dread-induced surge of adrenaline wracked Mac's body. His hand gripped the receiver so tightly it creaked. "Is she okay?"

"I…don't know," she cried, holding a bloody compress to her face.

Mac sensed what she wasn't saying. "Did he hurt you?"

"I'm…fine. I'll be fine. Mac…he killed Benjamin and Liam. They were on night watch."

Mac struggled to keep some semblance of composure. "Get to T.J.'s house and stay there," he forced out. "Promise me."

"Okay," she sniffled. "Please…bring her home."

His heart pounded. "I will," he said as confidently as he could.

"I love you," she said with another sob.

"I love you, too. I'll call from London."

She started crying again. "I love her so much."

"So do I, Gen. Very much."

"Hurry home. Please."

"I will. Now go," and he pressed End.

Punching in a number from memory, he hit Send. The line rang twice, a click, and the voice of Perry Spencer said, "United Nations Command, First Battalion."

"Schoen has Cameron," Mac told him.

Perry pushed his chair back from the command desk and stood up. "What do you need?"

"Put a GLOSAT lock on me. Use my iPhone to triangulate my coordinates." Mac took the phone out of his jacket and turned it on. "Schoen'll call to tell me where to meet him. Get your team ready and follow me from a distance." Lifting a shaking hand, he rubbed his eyes. Barely above a whisper, he added, "Perry, if things go badly–"

"I'll find the son-of-a-bitch myself, sir, and bring her home."

"Thank you, my friend."

"We'll be right behind you. Don't worry."

Mac clicked off and handed the phone back to David. "My daughter, she's missing."

"Come with me," said the co-pilot and knocked on the cockpit door. "Mitt. David."

The door unlocked, and they stepped inside.

After explaining the situation, the pilot said with cocky self-assurance, "Consider this your private jet, Mr. Secretary-General." He flipped the PA switch on. "This is Captain Mitt Bennett speaking. I've just learned the Secretary-General's daughter is missing. I'd like to get him home as quickly as possible, which means diverting our flight from London to Geneva. That'll put us behind schedule a good four hours." He paused. "Do I have your permission?"

David leaned towards the open door. Mingled voices of passengers and crew rolled forward from the aft cabins. A moment later the head flight attendant came through the curtain.

"Permission granted, sir."

"We'll have you home inside of three hours, sir," Captain Bennett said.

"Call me Mac, and thank-you," he said, putting his hand on the good man's shoulder and turning to David. "Both of you."

Stepping out of the cockpit, he said to the head flight attendant, "Whatever they want," nodding to the passenger cabins, "it's on me."

No sooner had he pulled up the Internet photos than Colonel Perry Spencer understood why Gerhardt Schoen chose to lure Mac to Castle Neuschwantstein. It sat atop a rocky evergreen-strewn mountain in the heart of the Bavarian Alps, three of its sides surrounded by a clear blue mountain lake and the fourth by nothing but a narrow land bridge with a single-lane road leading down to a sleepy little hamlet.

Pointing out the cockpit windshield, Perry told the helicopter pilot, "Put her down by the farmhouse."

"Aye, sir," she answered.

The chopper began its descent and Perry made his way back to the crew cabin.

"Landing in five," he told the strike team. "We'll have a kilometer to hoof. Once at the castle, pair up, take positions at the entrances, and await my orders. No military insignia. Concealable weapons only. Hands-free radio. Understood?"

"Hooah!" they roared like caged lions.

"There are hundreds of rooms and countless hiding places," Perry warned. "It's mid-afternoon on a Saturday and the place'll be crawling with children and tourists, many fair-skinned and blonde like Schoen and Cameron. No heroics, no rash moves, and be damned careful. Understood?"

"Hooah!"

Deep beneath the castle, oil lanterns dimly lit a dank windowless stone chamber carved into the ancient rock. Accessible only by a labyrinth of stairwells and long, lonely corridors, the low-roofed rectangular room had once been the castle's chapel. Few tourists even knew it existed and fewer still took the time to find it.

The heir of Arthur pushed open the battered wooden doors. Beyond, the flickering red-orange light lent the chapel a surreal feel and the wall painting of Wagner's *Parsifal* imbued it with a sense of malevolence.

"Apropos," Mac muttered, recalling how Parsifal, or Percival, was supposedly a Knight of Arthur's roundtable.

The word had been spoken no louder than a breath, yet it rolled unimpeded along the stone walls to the end of the grotto. A desperate, terrified "Daddy!" echoed back out of the shadows beyond the stone altar and the hairs on the back of Mac's neck stood on end.

Out of the shadows stepped Gerhardt Schoen clutching Cameron's long blonde hair with his talon-like hand. With a malevolent grin, he slowly lifted her off the ground.

Cameron's screams pounded against the rock walls. Her feet kicked at the dank air as she tried in vain to tear his fingers from her hair.

"Let her go!" Mac roared, starting for the altar.

Schoen's other hand swung up and the light of the lanterns glinted off the jagged blade of a hunting knife. "Stop!" he bellowed, jabbing the tip of the blade into Cameron's side just enough to break the skin.

"No!" Mac cried, sliding to a stop, her screams of pain almost too much for him to bear.

Schoen gave a deep, slow laugh. Pulling the knife back, he gestured with the blade to the chapel. "It is apropos, ja? An ancient pagan temple, a sacrificial altar, and the last two heirs of Arthur."

Mac's blood ran cold and every muscle in his body tensed with fear and rage. Cameron dangled helplessly in the air, tears rolling down her cheeks. "It's going to be alright," he said to her in a quavering voice.

"My Aryan ancestors sacrificed to their gods on this very altar," Schoen went on, seemingly oblivious to her screams.

"You have what you want, Schoen, now let her go!" Mac shouted.

"Ja, I do," he hissed and slowly swung the knife back to Cameron.

Mac took a step forward. "Let her *go*, damn you!" he yelled.

"At long last," Schoen said as if in a macabre trance, "I shall feel the warmth of Arthur's blood pour through my fingers," and he slid the knife into Cameron's side.

Screams of agony permeated every corner of the foul cave.

"No!" Mac cried, bounding for the altar.

A deafening *crack* sounded and the dank air shuddered. A plume of red exploded from Schoen's right shoulder and he howled in pain. He let go of Cameron and she fell in a heap onto the stone floor. Staggering backwards, Schoen clutched his blood-splattered shirt, his eyes fixed on the gunman sprinting down the aisle and taking aim. He bayed with rage, stepped back into the shadows, and disappeared.

Mac reached Cameron and fell to his knees. She lay on her back, body trembling and tears rolling down her cheeks.

Perry Spencer flew past.

"Get a doctor!" Mac called to him.

The colonel slid to a stop, staring hungrily at the darkness beyond. Holstering his pistol, he turned back and knelt down beside Cameron. Lifting her nightshirt, he inspected the gash and pressed Mac's hand over it to stanch the flow of blood. "Keep it there. I'll be back." Perry stood and ran up the aisle.

"Stay with me, Cameron," Mac pleaded.

"I kept calling you, Daddy," she said, barely above a whisper, "but you never came. Why didn't you come?" Her body shuddered. "Where will I go when I die, Daddy?" she said weakly.

"You're not going to die," Mac choked out.

Her breathing slowed, and she stared up at the ceiling in shivering wonder. "Daddy! I can see angels!"

Mac scooped her up in his arms. "Please don't leave me, Cameron."

"Angels," she breathed, "they want me to go with them." Her eyes closed, and her body began to go limp. "Never let me go, Daddy," she whispered.

"Never," he answered as the tears came. "I'll never let you go and I'll love you forever."

l

"Here I stand. I can do no other."

– Martin Luther

"The true neighbor will risk his position, his prestige, and even his life for the welfare of others."

– Martin Luther King

"The line between dissent and disloyalty, between harmful revelations and vital ones, is murky. But I would argue that the judicious questioning of the conduct and morality of war is an expression of deep patriotism."

– Richard Stengel

The winding stone staircase led down to a placid black pool deep inside the mountain. Its surface shimmered with the light of a single lantern hanging from the stern of an old inboard motorboat moored to a rickety wooden dock. A smoky mist and the faint scent of burning oil and gasoline hung in the still air.

Schoen stumbled at the bottom of the stairs, grunting in pain and clutching his bloodied right shoulder. Regaining his balance, he half-ran, half-staggered down the footpath and out onto the dock, the rotting boards creaking under his feet. Pulling the mooring line off the piling, he eased himself into the boat, took hold of the wheel with his left hand, and with a cry of anger and pain, slammed the throttle forward with his right. The engine whined, the hull shuddered, and the bow lifted out of the water. He steered towards a tangle of hanging roots and vines on the far wall of the cave and careened into them at full throttle.

A moment later, the boat shot out of the cave's mouth, skimming effortlessly across the waves of a crystal clear alpine lake. All around him, snow-capped mountains reached majestically up to a cloudless blue sky, their peaceful beauty at odds with his rage. He let out a furious cry and punched the dashboard over and over until the bones in his hand would liked to have broken. Breathing heavily, his fury satiated for the moment, he pulled a smartphone from his pocket, pressed the GLOSAT icon, and entered his security code. A digital button appeared with the word EXECUTE glowing in red letters. With a grim smile, he pressed it and the word RECEIVED flashed and then slowly faded away.

Four thousand miles to the west, a desktop computer on the top floor of the Secretariat Building in New York City whirred to life. Encrypted deployment plans began uploading to GLOSAT and a few minutes later they were streaming across a chain of satellites and down to identical computers in the palaces of Schoen's military dictators.

By nightfall, millions of soldiers were on the march and trillions of dollars' worth of military hardware were being mobilized across Northern Africa, Eastern Europe, the Middle East, and the Caucasus. By sunrise, the second most powerful fighting force on the planet would come into existence, the President of the first having recently withdrawn his country from the world stage.

Well before dawn, two American-made F-22A stealth fighter jets and an air tanker took off from an old Soviet airfield. What the air base's night commander didn't know was that Kazakhstan's two most valuable and lethal jets weren't being piloted by Kazakhstanis. The two pilots had emigrated from Tibet and volunteered for military service in their late teens. Though born into a society of Buddhists, the light of passivity had long since been extinguished from their souls by the brutality of Chinese occupation. Their hearts had been so deadened to compassion by hate and militarism that the Dalai Lama's return to their homeland and the current negotiations for independence from China were meaningless to them. All that mattered now was revenge. And the money wired into a Russian bank account for them by the former Acting Secretary-General.

The filed flight plan said the three planes would follow Lake Zaysan east towards the Altai Mountains, refuel in mid-air, and mirror the Mongolian border south before returning to base. Instead, after the refueling they throttled up and held to their easterly vector into the mountains and down into a long, deep valley until radar contact with their base was lost.

"Off screen," the mission commander relayed to his wingman. "Confirmed."

"Stay close," said the commander.

"Roger."

The commander manually navigated through one valley after another until they reached the Gobi Desert. There, he locked into an east-by-southeast vector and went to autopilot. Three hours later, the pilots took control again and dropped through the cloud cover to find the city of Beijing stretching in every direction below them.

"Arm missiles," said the commander.

"Roger. Missiles armed."

When the on-board computer told them they were within range, the commander ordered, "Fire!" and both pilots loosed their payloads.

At 0600 GMT, another pair of F-22As took off from a desert airbase near Casablanca, Morocco. Armed with a full complement of missiles, they banked northwest and headed out to sea. Flying at speeds exceeding Mach one, the pilots navigated around the Iberian Peninsula and then locked into a northeasterly vector. An hour later, they were over France, Morocco's former colonial master. An hour after that, they throttled down and dropped to 200 feet, scanning the banks of the meandering Seine looking for their target. Finally, amidst the circuitous streets and geometric parks, they saw it. The tallest structure in Paris, gleaming dark gold in the rich yellow morning light.

The mission commander adjusted his altitude and vector. "Arm weapons," he ordered.

"Confirmed," answered his wingman.

The equivalent of an 81-story building, the 1063-foot Eiffel Tower was so renowned, so iconic that it had long-since become part of France's collective psyche. Built for the World's Fair in 1889, the tower had been the world's tallest structure for half a century until the Empire State Building stole the title away.

The mission commander flipped up the safety guard on the firing switches and whispered, "I avenge my people."

"We have two very disturbing reports for you," the harried anchor said as an amateur video of missiles arching overhead appeared on the screen. "One from China and the other from France.

"The world's largest palace came under attack this morning in Beijing. Two unidentified military aircraft fired air-to-ground missiles into the Forbidden City late this afternoon local time."

A state television feed showed bronze lions, peaceful shady arcades, lily pad covered pools, marble balustrades, and colorful dragon statues in the foreground, while in the background brightly painted buildings were engulfed in flames as people frantically ran to and fro.

"Government officials report that much of the Forbidden City, including the Throne Room and Treasure Hall, were destroyed. Who's responsible for the attack and why remains a mystery."

A live feed began to play from a security camera mounted atop the Palais De Chaillot across the Seine from the Eiffel Tower. It showed four graceful lattice structures curving purposefully upwards from the surrounding gardens and then dissolving into torn and twisted strands of smoldering iron.

"The French government reported that two unidentified military aircraft flying at nearly Mach two entered French airspace mid-morning local time. Air force interceptors were unable to reach the jets in time to prevent the pilots from launching four missiles, one at each of the Eifel Tower's legs. Within seconds of the strike, the Tower's spire collapsed towards the Pont d'Lena bridge.

"The air strikes in Beijing and Paris occurred less than an hour apart in GMT time, leading many to believe they were coordinated. French President Francois de Mars declared the attack an act of war and he and Chinese Premiere Xiang Cho have placed their militaries on full alert, as has nearly every other nation on Earth."

Early the following morning, a phalanx of aircraft – bombers without bombs, air tankers without fuel, troop transports without troops, and cargo planes without cargo – took off from bases in 20 different countries, overwhelming radar and satellite warning systems across half the globe. Among the hundreds of diversionary aircraft, however, were five fully loaded F-22As.

The Serbian pilots dropped below the thick cloud cover on approach to Moscow. Imagining themselves national heroes for what they were about to do to their former communist masters, they unhesitatingly armed their missiles.

The commander reminded his wingman of their orders. "Only St. Basil's," referring to the iconic Russian orthodox cathedral with its multi-colored onion dome spires, "is to be spared."

"Understood," the other pilot acknowledged.

"Vector in from the Moskva River and fire at the Communist Palace of Congresses. I will bank in from the north and fire at the Presidential residence and administration buildings."

An urgent beeping sounded in his headset.

"Incoming MiGs," he reported. Studying the radar image projected on the canopy, he added, "They'll never stop us in time."

A lone Syrian pilot flew in low over the Dead Sea. The radar warning system beeped insistently as four Israeli interceptors appeared on the 360-degree holographic radar image projected on the cockpit's windshield. Noting his speed and relative position, he calculated his chances of reaching the target. Eighty-percent likelihood of success, 100 percent likelihood of his death.

So be it. Allah would bless him with virgins from now until doomsday for this.

The Holy City came into view and he dropped to roof-level, hoping the interceptors wouldn't fire on him here and risk civilian casualties. Lining up with the gold Dome of the Rock, he whispered the words spoken by the martyr Sayyid Qutb, "'Brother, push ahead, for your path is soaked in blood.'"

Beneath the mosque was the foundation of Herod the Great's Second Temple, excavated on one side to reveal the massive white limestone bricks – some weighing as much as 100 tons – of the Western Wall. The First Temple had survived 410 years before being destroyed by Nebuchadnezzar in the sixth century BCE. The Second was razed to its foundation by the Romans in 70 CE, along with the rest of Jerusalem. The great Jewish Diaspora followed and nearly two millennia passed before a new Israel came into existence. Numerous Muslim armies had attempted to destroy her since 1948, but all had failed.

"The God of the Jews is powerful," thought the pilot, "but so is Allah."

His targeting computer beeped, and he flipped up the trigger guard.

There was a blinding flash and his jet lurched to the left. He heard the sickening shriek of tearing metal as his right wing buckled and sheared off. The jet began to spiral and with a prayer for a quick death, he armed his missiles and held onto the shaking stick, aiming the plane at the great stone wall dead ahead.

The commander did his best to keep his two jets at 100 feet. Their blockers had long since left to rendezvous with air tankers over the North Sea, but for him and his wingman this was a one-way trip. The on-board radar was already tracking four RAF fighter jets inbound. Never again would he see his beautiful Crimea.

Melancholia began to well up inside him. "Concentrate!" he chastised himself. "Succeed and honor your people."

The altimeter told him to adjust his wing flaps slightly as he banked left to mirror the course of the Thames River valley.

"My valley of death," he whispered.

The suburbs of London were crowding the river's shores now. Just three more minutes and they'd be within range. Two. One. And rounding a bend in the river, he spied Westminster.

A royal residence for nearly 500 years beginning with William the Conqueror in 1066, its many regal and gothic halls now housed the Royal Courts of Justice, the House of Lords, and the House of Commons.

He never dreamed it would have such majesty. He'd seen pictures, of course, but he'd never seen it in person nor had he ever set foot in England. All he knew of England was that her people had killed his ancestors in a war barely remembered by the outside world, but never forgotten by his. Only military strategists gave the war any thought today, and only for its innovative use of then-new technologies and methods, such as railways, telegraphs, photography, and modern nursing practices at the hands of Florence Nightingale. Alfred Lord Tennyson immortalized the Crimean War between the Brits and Ottomans in his epic poem, the *Charge of the Light Brigade*. Ordered to take the enemy's position, the Light Brigade unquestioningly obeyed, even though every officer and soldier knew it would be suicide. French Marshal Pierre Bosquet called the charge magnificent, "but it is not war," he said. "It is madness."

"Arm weapons," the pilot said and flipped up the arming switches on the control panel. The computer acknowledged its preprogrammed targets. "GPS locked on."

"Confirmed."

"Fire!" he ordered. Both F-22As let loose their complement of missiles and then arched up and left, out of harm's way. The first two missiles bore down on Westminster Bridge, detonating on impact, and hurling cars, trucks, and even a double-decker bus high into the air before they rained down into the Thames along with the pulverized remains of the bridge and bloodied pieces of bodies.

Four more missiles slammed into the long, gothic stone façade of the palace overlooking the west bank of the river. Grand halls and elegant rooms with their tapestries, paintings, and medieval furnishings disappeared in a monstrous conflagration. Stone and debris blasted out over the water, falling unceremoniously onto passing ships and barges. The building's flying buttresses crumbled and the roofs between the four eastern towers collapsed, crushing to death those who'd survived the initial explosions.

The last two missiles arched gracefully through the pale blue sky, their steam trails hinting at what was next. The hearts of horrified onlookers sank when the first missile slammed into the four-sided face of Big Ben, blasting it into a thousand flaming pieces. The second struck the middle of the centuries-old clock tower like a boxer landing a punch. With aching slowness, it toppled over as screaming Londoners below scattered in every direction.

"'Ours is not to reason why,'" the commander whispered as he flew aimlessly off, echoing Tennyson while two air-to-air missiles wound their way towards him. "'Ours is but to do or die.'"

The British had killed his ancestors, he'd avenged them by killing British citizens, and now he was about to be killed by British pilots. Perhaps one day his people would avenge *him*.

But, then the British would want to avenge themselves again, wouldn't they? And his people would want to avenge *them*selves again, and on and on it would go, a never-ending cycle of pride, ego, revenge, and murder.

In the face of death, when nothing else remained, when everything was lost, only then did he realize that living life hating others, trained to kill by people who were supposed to teach you right from wrong, isn't living at all.

To hate is easy. To kill is easy. But, to forgive, to give and take, to live and let live – that takes strength of will and a spirit at peace with itself. If everyone could understand that, then perhaps there'd be peace among all people.

A missile struck the tail section of his wingman's plane and it disappeared in a blinding ball of flame. A second slammed into his fuselage just behind the cockpit.

"I forgive you," he said, and the words, "I hope you forgive me," flitted through his mind, but there was no time left to whisper them aloud.

Colonel Perry Spencer sat in his office at the Air National Guard base in Traverse transfixed by the images on his side-by-side computer screens. Two nights before, United Nations field operatives reported massive troop movements in countries across northern Africa and around the Black Sea. Each country's actions were seemingly unrelated, yet all had begun within hours of each other. Using images from seven different GLOSAT satellites over a 72-hour period, Perry had confirmed military mobilizations out of 23 separate countries into neighboring states. The 3 a.m. BBC broadcast reported fighting in dozens of countries.

Downloading the images to his iPad, he gathered up his things and told the base's Commanding Officer, "I'll be at the Secretary-General's home."

"Can you believe this shit?" exclaimed the CO, standing in front of a wall of PC monitors, radar screens, and TV sets. "The other side of the world's goin' fuckin' nuts!"

"You don't know the half of it," Perry muttered to himself and hurried out the door.

Just after 6 a.m., Perry let himself in the front door. Mac kept it unlocked, a habit for northern Michigan residents, and told his friends to come and go as they pleased. His home was their home.

From the foyer, the colonel listened for anyone who might be awake, and heard the sounds of sobbing coming from the bedrooms upstairs. His heart sank, and he bounded up the steps three at a time, nearly running into Mac and a doctor coming down the stairs.

"She'll be fine, Mr. Secretary-General," she reassured him, closing her medical bag.

Mac ran a hand through his disheveled hair. Face drawn and eyes bloodshot, he half-asked, half-pleaded, "You'll be on-call if we need you?"

"Of course," she smiled reassuringly. "I live just up the peninsula, but she'll be *fine*."

"What happened?" Perry said, backing down the stairs.

"A little trouble breathing," Mac told him. "I, I guess I overreacted."

"I heard crying," said Perry.

"Genevieve," Mac said. "Out of relief. Marion's upstairs with them. Doctor, this is Perry Spencer. Perry, this is Dr. Sonya Michaud."

"Ah! Colonel Spencer," the doctor exclaimed, "Cameron's hero."

Perry blushed. "My medic's the hero."

"You're *both* heroes," Mac said, putting a hand on the colonel's shoulder. "Coffee you two?"

"Love some," the doctor answered.

In the kitchen, they found T.J., Taylor, Robbie, and Duron leaning against the counters, and Damon, Dwight, Mark, and Merrill sitting quietly around the table. All of them had tea or coffee cups in hand. Ever since Cameron had been flown home on a military medivac, they'd been ensconced at the condo.

Everyone tensed when the Doctor appeared in the doorway.

"She's fine," Dr. Michaud assured them.

A collective sigh of relief filled the room. Mac started for the coffee, but Robbie grabbed two cups and with a shaking hand picked up the pot.

"Duron, do me a favor and turn the TV on in the living room?" asked Perry, taking out his iPad.

"Sure thing, buddy."

"What's up?" Mark asked.

"You've heard about the terrorist attacks the last two days," the colonel said. "World-renowned sites in China, France, Israel, Russia, and England. Tactical similarities and compact timing, all with American-made F-22As." Turning the iPad around so everyone could see, he said, "These satellite pictures were taken three days ago. And these," he said, pulling up a new set, "were taken today. Same locations." He pointed at several sites. "Massive troop movements. Air, ground, and naval, covering an area the size of the United States, all heading for the same place."

"Where?" T.J. said.

Perry pulled up a Google Earth photo. "The armies in the Balkans are moving southeast," and he drew his finger down from the upper left corner to the center of the screen. "The armies in the former Soviet Black Sea states, southwest," and he drew another line with his finger from the upper right corner of the screen to the center. "The armies in North Africa, due east," and he dragged his finger from the left side of the screen to the center."

"The Middle East," said Mark.

"Oil," Robbie added. "If he gets control of the greatest concentration of oil on Earth—"

"He could wreak havoc on the world economy," Dwight finished for him.

"Uh, guys?" Duron called from the living room. "You better come take a look at this," and he turned the volume up on the television.

The voice Mac heard made his blood boil. "Bastard," he growled and stormed out of the kitchen.

"Video," Duron told Mac and the others, pointing to the TV. "Schoen emailed it to every major news network in the world."

"I trust by now it is *painfully* clear," the former Acting Secretary-General said with icy menace, "that I have the power to strike anywhere I choose. The Eiffel Tower, the Forbidden City, the Western Wall, Westminster, the Palace of Congresses, even the Willis Tower."

Duron cursed.

"But, they were *nothing* compared to what I am about to do. Alexander the Great, Caesar, the Khans, Bonaparte, and Hitler will become mere *footnotes* to history when *I* am finished."

"The man's insane," Robbie said.

"Bloody nutter," Perry agreed.

"What rightfully belonged to the Third Reich will become my *Viertes* Reich," Schoen went on. "The time of the Aryan Übermensch is now at hand, and the peoples of the world must be set to their proper use according to their genetic caste."

"Here I go back in chains," muttered Dwight.

Duron huffed, "Get in line with the Jews, Muslims, and atheists."

"Resign yourselves to your fate. If you resist, may God have mercy upon you. For I will not." He snapped his heels and raised his right arm in a Nazi salute. "Sieg heil to God!" he shouted. "Sieg heil to Der Viertes Reich!" and the video ended.

The dumbfounded news anchor reappeared, and Duron muted the volume.

Perry told the others, "Judging from my photos, he has at least three million soldiers on the march. Thirty countries are under siege and if he conscripts fighters from the nations he conquers, his army could double in size within *weeks.*"

"The sites he attacked," Mac noted, "were all in permanent Security Council member states."

"And by destroying those particular sites," Merrill added, "he destroyed a part of their nations' souls."

"Hold on," Mark said. "The Western Wall's in Israel. That's not a Security Council country."

"Der Viertes Reich," Mac reminded him. "Schoen's resurrecting the Nazi empire, anti-Semitism and all. He wants the Middle East not just for its oil, but for its Jews. Hitler armed Muslim countries in the 30's and told them to attack the Zionists in Palestine. Schoen's going to do the same and earn the favor of Muslim nations. He'll destroy Israel and slaughter the Jews."

"How do we stop him?" said Mark.

"No one will stand up to him now," said Mac.

"Whadya mean?" Damon exclaimed. "Of *course* they will."

"Schoen attacked Westminster and the Kremlin while Parliament and the Russian Politburo were in session, killing hundreds of elected officials in the blink of an eye."

Damon hung his head. "So now politicians the world over won't dare convene their legislatures for fear of being slaughtered."

"No one's gonna do anything?" Duron said in disbelief. "They're just gonna *kowtow* to that bastard?"

"Only a leader with the testicles of Taurus would stand up to that madman now," Merrill replied. "And he or she would need the might of America to do it."

"And Thomas is in Schoen's back pocket," Robbie sighed.

"Is there no leader bold enough to stand up to Schoen?" Dwight said despondently. "No other nation strong enough to defeat him?"

"No single leader or nation," came a voice from across the living room.

Everyone turned to see Genevieve standing at the foot of the stairs, arms crossed as if trying to keep warm and eyes red from crying.

"Only the leader of the *united* nations can."

Mitchell Thomas stood beside his bed in pajamas and a bathrobe trying to make sense of what he'd just seen on the television.

"Why is Gerhardt doing this?" he said to his Secretary of State.

Jake Tanner stood watching the foreign affairs experts on the TV debating that very question. "I don't know, sir."

General Billy Boyd knocked on the open door and Tanner turned down the volume. "Well?"

"Middle East," the General said, handing Tanner a two-page report. "Four days, maybe five."

"What about the Middle East?" said Thomas, turning to look at them.

"We never should have gotten into bed with that son-of-a-bitch," muttered Tanner.

"Who?" said the President. "What are you talking about?

"Schoen. His army's heading for the Middle East."

"But, but," stammered the President, "why does he even *have* an army? And why would he lead it to–" He gasped, and his face lit up with joy. "Revelations! The Holy Land. He's heading for the Holy Land!" Thomas fell to his knees. "The final battle at Armageddon. It's coming!"

"Uh, okay," said Tanner.

Boyd slowly backed out of the room.

The President clasped his hands together and looked up at the ceiling. "Gerhardt is leading his Army to defeat the Antichrist at Armageddon!"

"Yeah, sure he is," Tanner said with a placating tone. "Look, I'm gonna call someone to help, okay?"

"The End Times!" cried the President, hobbling over on his knees and grabbing the Secretary's coat sleeve. "The Beast will call upon the kings of the world to assemble for the final battle between good and evil. The Antichrist will lead his armies to the Holy Land, his *United Nations* armies! We must stop him. We must help Gerhardt stop him!"

Tanner pointed at the TV. "You wanna help that bastard?" he said in disbelief. The phone on the bed stand rang. With a growl, he stomped over and picked it up. "What?" he barked.

"Give me Mitchell," the icy Germanic voice ordered.

A shiver ran down Tanner's spine. Could this get any worse? "Your good, God-fearing friend must have ESP," he said, handing the receiver to the President.

Thomas snatched it away like a drowning man reaching for a life-preserver. "Gerhardt, I know what you're doing, and the great might of the United States is at your beck and call!"

Gerhardt Schoen stood in the cement-gray bunker his grandfather had built to hide the artwork and other valuables stolen from the Jews he'd sent to Bergen-Belsen. Many Nazi elites had bunkers or secret rooms behind false walls or Swiss safe deposit boxes. The Nazi Party itself had warehouses, mines, and caves to store what it stole from banks and museums. But when it became apparent the war was lost, the party elites booked passage on ships headed overseas to abscond with their ill-gotten riches.

Remodeled with a floor-to-ceiling bank of computer monitors and TVs, wall maps, satellite feeds and banks of phones, Schoen's bunker now served as the command center for his private war.

"Stand down your army, Mitchell."

The President's mien dimmed. "But, Gerhardt, I can help. I *want* to help."

"Then, pray," he replied. "Tell your people to pray for the Lord to be victorious."

"I will, Gerhardt," Thomas promised, "but I can–"

"Do as I say!" he snapped, and the line went dead.

Thomas stood like a statue, receiver in hand.

"What did the bastard want?" Tanner grumbled.

"Stand down our military," Thomas said softly. "And tell my Chief of Staff to declare a national day of prayer."

Tanner's jaw dropped. "Are you fucking–"

"Get me Johnny!" cried the President jubilantly. "I must tell him about Armageddon."

The Secretary grimaced. "Swaywell's with Jack."

"I was told Jack's grandfather won't let him leave his estate."

Tanner rubbed his temples. "He won't let Swaywell leave either."

The bearish stock market in the wake of the nuclear attack on Chicago had become steroidally bullish in Thomas's first year in office, thanks to his pro-business, anti-regulatory rhetoric. Folks with 401ks or a little money in the market believed the worst was behind them and started spending again, ending the recession. Prices for everyday goods and services like health insurance soared at the same time businesses slashed real wages and benefits to increase profits. In Thomas's second year, the wealth gap grew into a canyon and most people discovered they could barely cover their mortgages and supermarket bills. Spending collapsed, personal bankruptcies became commonplace, and the recession returned with a vengeance. Five days after Schoen's war began, the Middle East's oil wells and refineries were his. Oil exports ceased, prices quadrupled, a gallon of gas rose to ten dollars, and the stock market crashed.

Now, all indications pointed towards a full-blown depression, and still no nation stood up to Schoen.

In the weeks that followed, the world held its collective breath as GLOSAT images revealed an ever-growing army under his control. Eleven million soldiers in fifty-two countries and counting, half amassed in the Balkans and Caucasus poised for an invasion of western Russia and Europe, the other half staged in defensive fortifications around the Middle East.

On a snowy New York day, William Cameron MacCrarey once again addressed the General Assembly.

"The peacekeeping forces of the United Nations were never intended nor of sufficient number to fight a war of this magnitude.

To be victorious, our member nations must combine their armies, navies, and air forces under a single command."

But, the world's leaders feared Schoen's retribution too much to heed Mac's advice. They obsessed over the costs of war and their collapsing economies, they dreaded their best and brightest coming home in coffins, and above all they were afraid of opinion polls and losing elections. Mac's emissaries visited the world's capitols in hopes of arranging the transfer of armed forces to the UN. But in the end, everyone chose appeasement.

It was history repeating itself, Mac knew. Chamberlain and Hitler writ large. Disgusted with their lack of honor, he called a press conference and took his case directly to the people.

"Regardless of race, gender, ethnicity, or religion, and regardless of national sovereignty, wealth or politics, we are all citizens of Earth," he admonished. "The threat of eleven million soldiers, limitless conscriptions, and trillions of dollars' worth of weaponry under the control of a megalomaniac like Gerhardt Schoen is a threat to everyone. If the world chooses to do nothing, then we deserve what is to come. Totalitarianism, enslavement, ethnic castes, eugenics, exterminations, all these followed the appeasement of Adolph Hitler. Sixty million lives were lost in six years at a time when the world's population was a *third* of what it is today. They had only telegraphs, radios, prop planes, and guns at their disposal. Today, we have radios, TV, the Internet, supersonic jets, satellites, nuclear weapons, and intercontinental missiles. The losses will be unimaginable!

"Well, I for one refuse to follow the path of appeasement. If you're willing to stand with me, if you believe we have the right to choose our own fate, if you believe in honor and nobility, then become Patriots of the world. Future generations shall build monuments to you, and history books shall call you heroes!"

Replayed on every news station, cascaded through social media, and printed in every newspaper, Mac's speech galvanized support among a growing number of people, though governments around the world officially condemned his call to arms as provocative and reckless.

In the weeks that followed, his every waking hour was spent working out the three C's of war-time logistics. Communications, consolidation, and conveyance. He made no public appearances, gave no speeches, and remained incommunicado, so much so that rumors began to circulate that he'd changed his mind and skipped town. Of course, in the case of a looming world war, he'd of had to skip Earth.

But then a new United Nations website appeared online. It directed Patriots to predesignated seaports by specific departure dates where supplies and armaments would be waiting. Battalions would be formed by country and training begun at sea. Since the home governments of the volunteers remained officially hostile towards Mac's efforts, international waterways would be the routes of conveyance.

There was only one problem. The United Nations had no Navy, which meant no naval transport ships and no means to protect them. Fortunately, the British Prime Minister, several high-ranking officers in the Royal Naval, and key members of Parliament were, by no mere happenstance, friends of the Clan. So, despite Great Britain's official policy of appeasement, the command of the Royal Navy's battleships, troop transports, destroyers, and supply ships, everything but aircraft carriers and submarines which were needed to defend the British Isles against possible invasion, were quietly placed under Mac's command.

And to their credit, most other governments looked the other way while their roads, railways, and airports were used by supply convoys, Patriots, field nurses, and medics making their way to the seaports. Only the United States turned Patriots into criminals, made supplying them a crime, ordered the Coast Guard to blockade the coasts, and sent the National Guard to occupy the United Nations complex in New York City.

Yet, its efforts amounted to naught. Americans, whether brand new immigrants or descendants of colonists, despised despots like Gerhardt Schoen, and the U.S. Patriots outnumbered those of every other nation combined. They said goodbye to their loved ones, left the safety of their homes, followed the Underground Railroads to Canada and Mexico, and poured into the seaports by the millions to become part of the greatest naval invasion force in history.

Four months to the day after Mac's speech to the General Assembly, the United Nations armada, led by Mac's flagship the HMS Victory, approached the African coast just before dawn. The war against Viertes Reich would begin by taking Morocco and driving eastward across Africa as the Allies had done in World War II.

Like caged and hungry lions, his battleships prowled back and forth while the Victory sailed into the mouth of Casablanca's harbor. Its shores were lined with shipping docks, warehouses, high-rise apartment buildings, office towers, and resort hotels. Beyond, shop-lined streets, mosques, markets, and whitewashed homes spread out as far as the eye could see. A bluff rose up amidst the sprawl and atop it loomed President DeMorte's Palace.

Mac wondered whether President DeMorte was still there or whether he'd chosen to leave like most of the city's residents had in anticipation of the armada's arrival. Satellite photos from the day before showed makeshift tent cities sprouting up in the desert to the north and south while Moroccan army units moved in to take up position around the bluff.

Of course, the UN wasn't really attacking Morocco. The UN was there to depose a despot in bed with Gerhardt Schoen.

On the bridge of the HMS Victory, Mac told Admiral Allan Frampton, "Please give the command."

"Aye, sir," said the tall, lanky admiral with graying red hair, neatly trimmed beard, and bright blue eyes that exuded a confidence born of great and terrible experiences.

He relayed the order and a moment later the ship's big guns fired in sequence. A munitions warehouse along the waterfront disappeared in a cloud of flame and debris. A naval dock and tethered corsair went next. Camouflaged canon batteries along the beach opened fire on the Victory, but the ships guns quickly dispatched them. The guns continued to fire until all the predesignated military targets within a mile of the harbor were destroyed.

"Cease fire," Mac ordered, and the guns fell silent. He stood motionless at the railing of the bridge wondering if anyone had been killed in the explosions, whether they had families who'd be waiting forever for their loved ones to come home. How sickening war was, yet how frustratingly inevitable it had always been.

He shook his head in regret and said, "Begin the landing."

By mid-day, the UN held the harbor. Transport trucks, tanks, light-assault vehicles, Humvees, and Patriots disembarked and began staging for the coming campaign. At a beachfront command post in an old warehouse, Mac unfurled a map of the city atop a clutch of oil drums.

"We can't get bogged down in a bloody, block-by-block fight," he told Perry and Colonel Stone. "We need to avoid civilian casualties, and we need Casablanca as our main supply port and military headquarters for the coming campaign. So, we go for the serpent's head."

"Understood," Stone agreed. "And the Moroccan army units surrounding the bluff?"

Mac turned to Admiral Frampton. "Can you pin them down long enough for me to get a battalion up to the palace?"

"You can damned well count it, sir," he replied.

"Now, that's an answer," grinned Mac.

Mac, the admiral, his officers, Perry, and Stone again studied a map, this time in much finer surroundings. The topographical map of Northern Africa lay strewn across a long, polished wood table, the map's corners fluttering slightly in the warm, dry breeze drifting across the white limestone veranda of the Presidential Palace and in through the open doors of the ornate dining room.

"The Moroccan forces have fallen back to the desert," Frampton informed everyone, pointing to a spot on the map east of Casablanca. "To here."

"Take half our battalions and drive DeMorte's troops east towards Algeria," Mac told Stone. "No need to capture them. If they surrender, take their weapons and send them home. Otherwise, keep them moving east. Perry, you and I will lead the other battalions southeast into the Atlas Mountains along the Moulouya River to the Algerian border here," he explained, tapping the map. "The Algerian army is taking up position around Algiers on the Mediterranean coast. We'll sweep up through the desert and attack from the south as your battalions," he said to Stone, "attack from the west. Flanked by the sea to their north, the Algerians'll have no choice but to fall back to the east. Again, no prisoners. Just keep 'em moving east."

"Why east?" Stone said.

"Schoen controls the Middle East. The gateway to the Middle East is Israel. The gateway to Israel," and Mac tapped the map again, "is through the Negev Desert, Africa's only land bridge to the rest of the world. The Negev's narrowest point is the Israeli-Egyptian border, 120 miles of arid no-man's land from the Mediterranean Sea to the Gulf of Aqaba. That's where the bulk of Schoen's southern army is dug in to defend the oil fields and repel an attack from the west."

"Will the Europeans and Russians mount an attack on his northern forces if we engage the army in the Negev?" said Stone.

"No. They can't coordinate a large enough attack without Schoen's intel ops discovering and countering it. We're on our own and Schoen's getting stronger by the day. Our only hope is to get to the Negev as quickly as possible, defeat him, and drive north to take on the rest of his army."

"Understood, but you still haven't told us why we're driving the African armies east."

"To give us an edge. We'll drive the retreating African soldiers – hundreds of thousands of them – into Schoen's Negev line and overwhelm his positions before we attack."

Perry was impressed, but said, "It'll be a long haul."

"But, if we pull it off," Stone interjected, "it'll be something for the history books."

Mac nodded. "As long as our supply lines from Casablanca keep up with us, we can mount a long-haul campaign, and they only have to get us to the Suez. Once we take the Canal, we can bring supplies up through the Red Sea."

"Will we have air cover after that?" asked Stone.

Mac shook his head. "Our Achilles Heel, I'm afraid. We have no aircraft carriers and the air forces of the North African and Gulf States are in Schoen's hands."

The Colonel grimaced. "We're taking one helluva a risk."

"No argument," Mac replied. "All I can say is we have Patriots, they have conscripts."

Perry wasn't quite sure that would be enough, but he was damned sure he wasn't going to underestimate his friend who'd defied the odds more than once. "What's become of DeMorte?" he said.

"Turned tail and ran, as far as we can tell," the Admiral answered. "Palace staff said he was heading to some resort called Viertes Reich, but that's what Schoen's calling his future empire, isn't it?" He shrugged. "All rather confusing."

"Viertes Reich?" Mac echoed and started to laugh. "Well, we better tell our people in Little Deutschland to expect some company."

The column of soldiers and trucks stretched for miles along the northern bank of the Moulouya River heading east into the Atlases. They passed serene orchards of date palms, forests of cedars with Barbary apes swinging from the branches, scattered hillsides terraced with small farms, and occasional mud-walled Berber houses with their customary low door obliging visitors to stoop low as they entered.

The lead Jeep flew the blue and white flag of the United Nations from its radio antenna. Mac sat in the front passenger seat studying the approaching Casbah of Kaliffe brooding over its mountain pass.

"Casbahs were built during the Ottoman and Berber Empires, which dominated this area a thousand years ago," he said to his driver. "The word's a mistranslation of the French word for citadel. Most are abandoned now, though a few are used as trading posts or safe havens for nomadic Berbers traveling their ancient trade routes."

"Yes, sir," the indifferent corporal replied.

Mac smiled to himself and pondered whether he was becoming another Merrill-the-Professor. Two of the casbah's outer walls ran up the hillside from the Moulouya to the parapets of a fortress, the third crossed the top of the ridge, and the fourth flanked the old Roman road that ran along the riverbank. Each had to be a half mile long at least. At the corners where the walls met stood flat-topped, sandstone guard towers upon whose roofs families of storks had set up housekeeping. Within the walls were hundreds of buildings made of brick the same khaki pallor as the surrounding mountains. A cobblestone street wound its way between the buildings, running from the massive wooden gate along the river up to the fortress perched on the ridge.

Mac nodded at the wispy spires of smoke tinted burnt-orange by the setting sun. "Supposed to be abandoned," he mumbled, furrowing his brow.

"Supposed to be, sir," the corporal agreed. "Cooking fires?"

Mac realized the man was right and the word, "Stop!" was on the tip off his tongue when the rim of the casbah's western wall lit up with flashes of light, followed seconds later by sharp cracks of rifle fire rolling across the desert plane. Bullets slammed into the ground in front of them, sending up plumes of sand that drew closer as the gunmen adjusted their aim. The corporal slammed on the brakes, threw the Jeep into neutral, and leapt over the seat like a fox from the hounds. Kicking open the Jeep's back gate, he hit the ground running and never looked back.

Mac chuckled and opened the passenger side door. A bullet pinged off the doorframe, another slammed into the ground in front of him showering his pant legs with sand, a third tore through the loose cloth of his uniform, creasing his skin just below the rib cage.

Seeing the blood seeping into the shirt, he cursed. "Again with the stitches."

Perry Spencer's Jeep slid to a stop next to Mac, blocking the casbah's line of fire. "You alright?" his friend called out.

"Fine, fine," pressing a hand against his side. "Might need a few stitches."

"Again with the stitches?" said the Colonel.

The Casbah of Kaliffe lay quietly in the morning shadows of the Atlases.

"Still asleep," Mac said to Perry.

"Wake 'em up?" replied the colonel.

"Yes," Mac said with a wry smile. "Let's."

"Fire when ready," the Colonel told his Second-in-Command, Major Robert Michael, on loan from Colonel Stone.

The major relayed the order and a moment later two artillery guns opened up, their shells exploding along the casbah's lower wall.

"Knock on the door, Major," Perry said.

Another gun fired and the gate in the lower wall disintegrated into a flaming ball of sand and splinters.

"Let's go," Mac told the others and climbed into the waiting Jeep.

As they approached the casbah, Perry leaned forward in his seat, staring intently at the cloud of settling sand. "Uh," he began in a bewildered tone, "looks like we have some company."

The major squinted into the haze. "Well, I'll be damned."

"We just fall through a black hole and go home?" said Mac.

"Maybe *your* home," Perry replied, "not mine."

"Stop the truck," Mac ordered.

They piled out and watched as a melting pot of the world's people materialized from the shroud of sand. Waving and shouting in American English, men and woman, young and old, black and white, European and Native American, Hispanic and Asian, Middle Eastern and Indian hurried towards them. Their clothes were filthy and ragged and everyday in appearance as if a moment earlier they'd been walking to campus, driving to the office, sitting in a restaurant, visiting the mall, working around the house, reading a book in a café, standing on an assembly line, or eating popcorn in a movie theater when some great hand from the sky picked them up and plopped them down behind the walls of Kaliffe.

A 30-something woman drew near wearing a torn and faded jogging suit that hung on her shapely though overly thin frame. She had long, tangled auburn hair and large brown eyes, and when she called out, "Deputy Ambassador MacCrarey!" Mac knew at once who she was.

Without taking his eyes off her, Mac said to the Colonel, "Let's make sure these people get some decent food and clean clothes. Better bring up the field medics, too."

"Of course," replied Perry.

"Ms. Roberts, I presume?" Mac said, stepping forward to greet her.

"Thank God you rescued us, Mr. Deputy Ambassador," TV reporter and free-lance journalist Jan Roberts replied in a tone that conveyed gratefulness for being freed and bitter anger over being imprisoned. "You have no idea what we've been through."

"It's Mr. Secretary-General now, Ms. Roberts, but please call me Mac."

Surprised and saddened, she sighed. "I really *have* been gone a long time, haven't I? What else have I missed?"

"You'll never believe me."

The Patriots set up tents and a mess, the medics helped the sick, the cooks did their best to keep up, and the quartermaster gathered clothes, bedding, and personal items as best she could for their new guests. Plans were being made to transport the newcomers back to Casablanca where Admiral Frampton, ensconced in the Presidential Palace, would arrange to ship them home. A quick census revealed that some 4,000 people walked out of the casbah, but stories abounded of the many who hadn't. Perhaps 16,000 had been imprisoned in Kaliffe at one time or another, all thanks to the Freedom Patrols back home and the Administration's moral purification campaigns.

"And those were the ones who stayed," Jan said. "I'll bet 100,000 passed through, like we were a clearing house. They'd stay a night or two and then get trucked into the mountains, maybe to be executed or left up there to die or taken to another prison. We had no idea, until last night when the commandant told us the Atlas Mountains are riddled with casbahs like Kaliffe. He said they were, 'Only following orders,' but 'orders' can't account for the horrible way they treated us."

"How many times have crimes against humanity been excused with those words?" Mac said angrily.

"Give me a battalion," declared Perry, "and I'll free everyone in every casbah I find."

"You got it," Mac replied, the pride and respect he had for the man obvious in his words.

Jan looked across the plane at silent Kaliffe, its lower wall lost in the evening mist rolling off the river. She thought of the abuse they'd suffered at the hands of the guards and remembered the men and women she'd come to know and later had to help bury. "What if there are casbah-like-prisons in other countries, too?" she said, dabbing her eyes.

"Then, we'll find them," Mac assured her. "Every last one."

She had no doubt he would. "I want to go with Colonel Perry," she said, "and report on what we find."

"If you wish," Mac said.

"Sir!" a burly young Sergeant called as he approached. He was gripping the arm of a small, thin-framed man with a ruddy complexion and dark tussled hair. The angry captive struggled fiercely to break free, though his efforts did nothing but annoy his captor.

"I don't believe it," the Secretary-General said to himself.

"Excuse me, sir," said the Sergeant, "but this guy insists he knows you."

"He does," Mac admitted.

"Sod off, ya bloody tosser!" snapped the scrawny man who tried yet again to pull free, but this time the Sergeant all too gladly let go Colin stumbled sideways, tripped over his own two feet, and fell spread-eagled on the sand.

Mac chuckled and shook the Sergeant's hand. "I'll take responsibility for this, uh, gentleman."

The Sergeant gave a quick salute and made a hasty retreat.

"Cockney Colin Dunham," Mac said, helping him to his feet. "Thank goodness you're alright. Kyle's been beside himself with worry."

"Yeah, well," faltered Colin, caught between his usual bluster and concern for his favorite uncle.

"Guess you found what you were looking for, eh?" Mac remarked.

"That's bloody obvious, idn't it?" the young man groused.

Mac thought back. "You called, what? A year ago?"

"Took you bloody-well long enough to get here, mate. Enjoyin' bein' king, are we? Forgettin' all about us little Clansfolk?"

Mac laughed despite himself.

"Clansfolk?" Jan said. "What Clansfolk?"

"Like I'd bleedin' tell a reporter," huffed Colin.

"I'll explain later," Mac promised and invited everyone to sit down at a nearby camp table. "Colin, tell us what happened."

The younger Dunham didn't have to be asked twice and launched into a colorful story while Mac grabbed a coffee pot out of the coals of a cooking fire. "Brewed from beans grown right here in the Atlases," he said, pouring the rich brew into tin cups and handing them out.

"You gonna keep interruptin' me?" griped Colin, greedily sipping the hot brew.

Mac blew into his tin cup and shook his head. "Go on."

"So, I was in Fez, right? Askin' questions about Americans in the desert. What they was doin', where they was goin', and what not, when a car pulls up and two tossers jump out. Americans, mate, and the big one throws a bag over me head and chucks me in the back seat, like we was in one o' them old gangster movies. Took me to a warehouse where I sees dozens o' people all trussed up like me! Next day, we gets loaded up on trucks and driven into the desert. Thought I was a goner, mate. But, they kept drivin' until we got dropped off in front of them wooden gates you blokes blew up."

Mac asked several questions of young Colin and finished with, "Would you be willing to go back to Casablanca and comb through the records in DeMorte's palace? See if you can find a connection between him, Schoen, the United States, and these casbahs?"

"O' course, mate. Anythin' for me Clan. Even die if I had to. Not that I want to, o' course. *You* can bleedin' die every other day, mate, but not me."

"Funny. Real funny," Mac said drolly. "I'll issue orders giving you carte blanche to come and go from the Presidential Palace as you please. Anything you need, alright?"

"You're a good man, Colin Dunham," Jan Roberts said, and his ruddy face ruddied even more. When she leaned over to kiss him on the cheek, he dropped his coffee cup.

"You okay there, buddy?" Mac said, trying not to laugh.

Colin got up from his chair, swayed a bit before steadying himself with the table, and mumbled, "I've gotta, uh, um, pack me things." Of course, no one from Kaliffe had 'things' to pack. Staring at Jan and backing away, he bumped into a couple holding hands, mumbled "Sorry, mates," and hurried off.

"Mac, this is Tula and David Athos, formerly of Chicago," Jan said, giving them each a hug.

"And not from anywhere anymore," Tula said sadly. "None of us are."

"Terrible what happened, the *Shkhara* and all," Mac said with sincerest empathy.

"They lost a child after the attack," Jan explained, stepping between them and putting her arms around their waists. "Little Dorothy Ann," and by the time she'd finished explaining what happened, David was wiping his eyes with the back of his sleeve.

"We heard you were going to send us home," he said, trying to pull himself together and not sounding the least bit pleased with the news.

"Yes," Mac replied, puzzled. "As soon as we can make arrangements."

"We don't *want* to go home. We want to *fight*. Tula, me, everyone!"

Mac couldn't believe what he was hearing. "You, you've been here for a year? Year-and-a-half? Victimized, humiliated, starved, and you don't want to go home?"

"I was a father and a professor, my family was torn apart by ignorance and prejudice, my daughter died a terrible death," he said, standing tall. "I was an *American*, but my government said I was worthless and sent me here. You think I can just go home, resume my old life, and pretend none of that happened? You think I'm going to do *nothing?*"

Mac told him, "To be willing to fight, David, is to be willing to die."

David reacted as if Mac had slapped him across the face, "I'd have died a *thousand times* if I could have saved my daughter's life, Mr. MacCrarey. To fight – and yes to die – is the *least* I can do for her now, and for my country."

Mac felt like a fool and held out a hand with an apologetically proud smile. "Welcome to the fight, my friend. Now I know our side will win."

ια

The transports bound for Casablanca carried those too young, too old, or too ill to fight. Colin Dunham climbed into the last truck looking both determined and ashamed.

"We all have our path to follow," the Secretary-General told him as the transport lurched away, "and yours is to find out how these people ended up here at the end of the world."

Young Colin understood and gave a resigned nod.

Mac watched the convoy drive off and said to the person standing next to him, "Tomorrow, it'll be you and Perry leaving."

"Off to liberate casbahs," Jan Roberts nodded, and they turned to head back to camp.

Stopping along the way to watch the Exiles go through their drills on a makeshift parade ground, Mac explained, "Perry'll arm and train any Exiles you come across. When they're ready, he'll bring them, and you, to the front lines."

"So, it isn't goodbye, then," she replied.

"No. It's until we meet again." Tula and David Athos marched past, rifles over their shoulders. "Basic training takes eight weeks," Mac sighed. "They have two days."

"God help them," Jan whispered.

The next morning, Mac led his battalions into the Moulouya River pass. By dusk, they'd reached the far side of the mountain range and before them lay the vast Sahara. The undulating hummocks of sand resembled nothing so much as motionless waves on a timeless sea, achingly barren of life but for a single Berber caravan on a far-off dune. Half a millennium ago its camels would have been laden with spices and indigo, nuggets of gold, and ivory tusks bound for Moroccan seaports and tall masted ships.

A Jeep pulled up beside him and Major Michael leaned out the window. "Your orders, sir?"

"Tindouf," Mac answered.

The major looked to the horizon. "Four-hundred miles."

"Due east across blistering sand," Mac acknowledged, "then due north."

Michael nodded absently, his eyes fixed on the endless dunes. "To engage the Algerian army at Algiers."

Mac's battalions attacked from the south, the Casablanca battalions from the west and the Algerian army fell back into the eastern desert just as Mac had predicted. The day before the battle, Algerian President Hadi had left aboard his private jet bound for a South American resort called Viertes Reich, his palace staff explained.

Mac said to Stone with a chuckle, "Better tell our team down there to expect some more company."

Then came the real surprise. Thousands of Algerians showed up at the palace to join the UN Army. They wanted to exact their revenge for Hadi's quarter-century of cruelty, but since he'd gone AWOL, Schoen's *other* dictators would do just fine.

"They've earned the right," Mac told his officers. "Arm and train them like we did the Exiles."

The same pattern played itself out in every country they liberated. Battles won, capitols surrendered, dictators fleeing, soldiers retreating, and freed citizens volunteering to fight. At Suez, the battalions met their UN supply ships and the quartermasters readied everyone for the final campaign. There, in a communications lorry, Mac pointed to a spot on the recon officer's computer screen and said, "That place. On the Israeli border, what's it called?"

She zoomed in and then checked a geo-political map of the region. "No name, sir. Just a plateau in the desert. Maybe a tel."

"A tel," Mac echoed wistfully, the word taking him back to his studies in Geneva. "Derived from Arabic. Refers to a tall man-made earthen mound created by the repeated occupation and abandonment of a city over hundreds or even thousands of years. A settlement begins near a natural well, evolves into a city, gets destroyed by war or wanes into abandonment and gets covered in drifting sands. Later, another settlement begins on top of the last one and the cycle starts over. Eventually it's abandoned forever, and the desert reclaims it, leaving nothing but a flat-topped mound of sand and the ghosts of long-ago cities and civilizations. Ever since I read James Michener's *The Source* I've wanted to go on a dig at a tel. How tall is it?"

"Maybe 200 feet."

"Perfect. Let's make that our field command post. Call it New Megiddo."

"New Megiddo?" she repeated with a suspicious grin. "Revelations, sir?"

He smiled and cocked his head as if to say, "Why not?"

She folded her laptop. "I'll let the others know, sir," and she got up to leave. Reaching the door, she turned and said, "We will win. Won't we, sir?"

Mac's smile faded. Though his troops had doubled in number since leaving Casablanca, engaging Schoen's massive army in the Negev would be far from easy. And if they failed, their bleached bones would litter the desert for all eternity.

"We have to win," he said simply.

"Yes, sir. We do," she replied and saluted before disappearing through the door.

A moment later, the long-lost Colonel Perry walked in.

"New Megiddo, eh?" he chuckled. "You really like buggering people, don't you?"

Mac shrugged. "Just some people," he said with a hug for his old friend. "Good to see you. How'd your hunt for casbahs go?"

"Found two dozen more," answered the colonel. "A hundred-thousand new Exiles ready to fight."

"The American spirit's alive and well, eh?" Mac grinned.

"Wild West bravado and all that rot, eh? Well, ol' boy, my country had that spirit 1,500 years before you even *had* a country."

Mac reminded his friend, "I think I may have had a relative in your country back then."

"Ah, yes," Perry replied, "you're a descendant of Arthur *and* an insufferable American."

Mac laughed and asked, "How's Ms. Roberts?"

"Fine, fine. Catching up with the Athos' now. What's the plan from here?"

"Break camp in the morning, disperse our battalions along the 120-mile long Israeli border from the Mediterranean to the Gulf of Aqaba, set up command in the center at New Megiddo, and drive the retreating soldiers from the countries we liberated into Schoen's line. Then, we attack."

Mac, Perry, and the other commanding officers stood on the observation platform mounted to the roof of the communications lorry. From their vantage point atop Tel New Megiddo, the team had a good 30-mile view in every direction. Having already driven the retreating North African soldiers into Schoen's defensive positions, Mac ordered his Patriots and Exiles forward. Watching the battle unfold via a GLOSAT real-time satellite feed, the colonel announced to the team, "UN battalions engaging enemy positions along the entire line."

"Order the left and right flanks forward," Mac told Perry, and the order was relayed.

Mac began pacing back and forth on the platform, the satellite feed showing the battle line slowly morphing into a claw.

"Pincer movement taking shape," Perry called out. "Flank battalions are—"

"Incoming!" the radar officer yelled from inside the lorry. "North by northeast!"

Perry cursed and swung around, raising his binoculars. "There!" he said, pointing to a row of tiny black dots emerging from the only bank of clouds in the sky. Steam trails unfurled from the jets like the legs of a giant ghostly spider reaching for the ground.

"Shit," Mac breathed as he and the others watched helplessly as the air-to-ground missiles found their targets.

"Our left flank is halting its advance," Perry announced, one hand holding the laptop, the other cupping his radio earpiece.

"Come on," the Secretary-General willed. He knew his troops could make it through the barrage if they just hunkered down until the jets exhausted their munitions.

Perry cursed again. "They're retreating! Both flanks!"

Mac swore under his breath.

"More incoming!" the radar officer yelled. "Southeast!"

A string of F-22As rose out of the black, undulating band of heat along the eastern horizon. More steam trails appeared, wending their way down toward the retreating UN line. Once their missiles were spent, the spiders morphed into stinging scorpions, strafing the UN soldiers with machine gun fire. Two of the jets broke off from the pack and dove for the tel, sending the officers around Mac scrambling over the sides of the lorry.

"Come on, you bastards," Mac growled, pulling out his Beretta. He took aim and fired, knowing full well how dangerous and futile it was to shoot at a supersonic jetfighter with a pistol, but to turn-tail was dishonorable and to do nothing was unthinkable.

Hands already on the top rung of the ladder leading down from the platform, Perry cursed, pulled his .45 out of its holster, and walked back over, saying, "So, you don't think you're King Arthur after all, eh?"

"What are you talking about?" Mac said distractedly. *Blam! Blam!*

Perry took aim and fired. *Blam!* "You don't think you're King Arthur." *Blam!* "You think you're George bloody Patton."

Mac Laughed. "Let's show these poor dumb bastards how to die for their country!" he growled with a pathetic impersonation of George C. Scott.

"Yes, sir!"

Tula and David Athos ran past the tel, the lorry just above them. Tula slid to a stop, staring up in disbelief at the magnificent madness of their commanders. For the sake of little Dorothy Ann and the others back home being victimized, she shouted to her comrades-in-arms, "Look!" and pointed at the lorry.

Tula's husband stopped running and looked up. With sad understanding, he gave his wife a loving smile, hoping against hope that they'd soon see their lovely daughter again. He waved for the other Exiles in his unit to follow and yelled, "Let's go!"

With a war cry, they turned and charged for the line. Nearby units heard the cry, saw the two men on the lorry, and without hesitation gave a war cry of their own and joined in the charge. Just as they reached the battle line, a thunderous low-pitched scream rolled in from the west. Mac feared another squadron of enemy jets were bearing down on them, but instead two air-to-air missiles cruised in low over the Exile's heads and rose up in pursuit of the two F-22As. With deafening twin explosions, the jets disintegrated in mid-air and rained down in pieces to the desert floor. A deep, growling roar followed and the silvery shape of an F-16 Phantom raced in from the west low and fast. Another silvery shape rose up behind it, then another and another. More air-to-air missiles streaked overhead and the F-22As disappeared one after another in balls of white-orange flame.

The crackling of static sounded over Mac's radio and a swaggering voice said in a flat, Midwestern accent, "USS Enterprise, reporting for duty, *sir!*"

Mac beamed. "'Fate protects fools, little children, and ships named Enterprise,'" he said into his radio, quoting an old Star Trek movie. "Whoever the hell you are, you're my new best friend."

The man laughed. "Captain Jonathan Sleeping Bear, Mr. Secretary-General."

"Native American?" Mac said.

"Yes, sir. Chippewa."

"Well, Captain Sleeping Bear, I'm immensely appreciative, but by helping me you've just committed treason against the new United States," his enunciation of 'new' dripping with derision.

"Some things are more important than country, sir," the confident captain replied. "And besides, if I'm now a man without a country, you'll take me in, won't you, sir?"

"I love this guy," Mac said to Perry. "Captain, call me Mac, and right now I, too, am a man without a country."

"Call me Jonathan, and let's damned-well make one!"

"I'm with ya, buddy," Mac said. "All units, advance!" he ordered into his radio. "I repeat, *advance!*"

A cheer rolled over the desert sands. Perry holstered his pistol and grabbed the laptop as the other team members climbed back up to the platform. "Pincer attack recommencing," he announced.

"Hooah," Mac whispered.

Just before dusk, Schoen's army commander in the Negev radioed his surrender.

Mac refused to accept it. "Men of honor meet on the field of battle to negotiate terms," he radioed back. "We must serve as examples of civility for our peoples."

The commander agreed, and he and his officers met with Mac, Perry, Colonel Stone, Major Michael, and Captain Sleeping Bear atop the tel at daybreak. All were in dress uniforms. "Your soldiers will be disarmed, given food and supplies, and sent home. Those are my terms," Mac stated. "Are they acceptable?"

Schoen's officers were speechless. They would have accepted anything short of *execution*, given the sort of brutality Schoen's dictators doled out. To them, the man standing before them seemed nothing short of a living, breathing miracle.

"Are they acceptable?" Mac repeated, a bit more forcefully.

"Yes!" exclaimed the commander. "Yes, sir!"

Mac smiled. "Very good. And may the Age of Peace soon be at hand."

A large tent sat on the tel, its sides rolled up, the communications lorry long gone. Inside, UN officials, political and economic strategists, renowned PhDs, respected diplomats, and noted world leaders sat cross-legged on Persian rugs in an impromptu circle. To one side of the circle stood Perry, Colonel Stone, Major Michael, and Captain Sleeping Bear. To the other stood Merrill, Kyle, Michael, T.J., Jan Roberts, and Mac's old friends.

A convocation the likes of which the world had never seen was about to begin. "A month ago, on this very tel," Mac explained, slowly circling the attendees, "I accepted the surrender of Gerhardt Schoen's southern army." A warm desert breeze wafted through the tent, gently rippling his sand colored khaki pants and loose-fitting white cotton shirt, its sleeves rolled half way up his tanned forearms. "The following week, the United Nations' army liberated Israel and Palestine, the week after that Lebanon and Syria, and two weeks later, Turkey. As the news of our mounting successes spread, Schoen's conscripted soldiers began disserting in droves. By the time we reached the Balkans and Caucasus, we hardly had to fire a shot, and yesterday the last country Schoen controlled was liberated. All of his puppet dictators have been captured in Viertes Reich and after this convocation, I will publicly declare a cessation of military operations and the end of the war."

With a cheer, the gathering gave Mac and his officers a standing ovation.

The Brazilian President asked, "Is Schoen in custody?"

"His whereabouts are still unknown."

"How do we find the tosser and put an end to this?" said the British Prime Minister.

"He and I shall meet soon enough."

Murmurs of incredulity wafted about the tent.

"Take me at my word," Mac told them. "I invited you here for something far more important than to talk about Gerhardt Schoen. I am tasking you with the creation of a new form of government that we can give the countries we liberated. The UN now holds them in trust. Fifty-two nations in all. Twenty-three that Schoen's dictators controlled and 29 they took over during the war."

"New? As in never before tried?" the French President wondered. "Or simply new to the 52 countries?"

"Both," he answered. "We need a single governing structure that will preside over all of them." "If it can be dreamed and willed, then it can come to pass," he insisted.

"You're proposing a single sovereign UN country," said the Canadian Prime Minister, "made up of 52 former nations?"

"I am."

"Replace 52 governments with a new United States," accused the Russian President.

"No. I'm not advocating for a world-wide America. I'm not advocating for a global Euro-Zone. I'm not advocating for *any* current form of government. History has taught us that every one of them has fatal weaknesses. Monarchy and free market economies end in revolution. Communism collapses from economic stagnation. Nationalism ends in bloody warfare. Few last more than a handful of generations before decay, rebellion, invasion, or civil war brings them to their knees. Even Egypt, Greece, Rome, Persia, the empires of Great Britain and France, and now the United States, only lasted a few centuries.

"I want you to create a *new* government that will stand the test of time. One that won't fail because it ceases to respect human rights, one that doesn't fall prey to religious persecution, racism, xenophobia, militarism, social inequity, greed, and classism. We need something original and purely of the people, by the people, and *for* the people. Leave the borders of the 52 former nations intact for now and hold democratic elections to pick *local* leaders to handle day-to-day affairs. Then, hold a second election to adopt a supranational constitution for a borderless government, elect federal legislators, and choose a head of state."

"How would power be shared between the supranational government and the former nations?" a diplomat and historian from Greece asked. "What sort of legislature should there be? How should the judiciary be organized? Will there be—"

"Figure it out. Use history as a guide. Create a form of governance that can work for *every* nation on Earth. Start with the fundamentals. Clean and plentiful drinking water, readily available food supplies, healthy and sanitary living conditions, reliable sources of energy. Then, move on to what it takes for everyone to live a safe and happy life. Accessible and affordable healthcare, roadways and efficient transportation systems, K-through-college education, adequate self-defense, a fair yet successful economic system, equitable laws, pluralism inclusive of everyone, a just judiciary, law enforcement that bolsters close and peaceful communities rather than division and fear."

"While we're working on all that," the Indian Ambassador said with a smile, "what exactly will *you* be working on?"

Mac replied with his trademark cocky grin. "Something the world has never seen before."

"What?" the Israeli Secretary of State asked eagerly.

"Meet me in New York and find out."

"New York?" the Nigerian Prime Minister said in surprise. "The United Nations complex is occupied by your National Guard."

"No one is permitted in," a Professor from Mexico added and then smiled. "Especially the Antichrist."

Sympathetic laughter filled the tent.

"Well then, I guess I'll have to do something about that, won't I?" Mac replied.

"What?" the French President said excitedly. "What are you going to do?"

"Come with me," Mac answered and walked out of the tent.

The bewildered dignitaries dutifully followed and upon reaching the far side of the tel gave a collective gasp, for looking up at them from the desert floor were hundreds of thousands of Patriots and Exiles. Perry handed Mac a head mic and clipped a transceiver onto his belt. The setting desert sun's rays imbued the Secretary-General's clothes with an almost golden radiance.

"To you, the noble citizens of the world," his voice boomed out through the banks of speakers set into the western face of the tel, "I salute you!"

The vast sea of men and women cheered.

"You fought bravely, freed millions from brutal tyranny, and defeated the most dangerous man since Adolph Hitler. I am prouder to call myself an American today than I have ever been."

Cheers rose up again.

"Our country is far from perfect. She's made mistakes and lost her way many times over the centuries. Yet, she always returned to the path of liberty and equality because Americans uncompromisingly believe in our Bill of Rights. We stand tall when standing for something is the most difficult. We fight for freedom at home and abroad. And when a ruling party takes away our Constitutional rights, we rise up and fight against tyranny! So it is that I ask you to accompany me on one last crusade, a crusade back to our home, a crusade to make her the Promised Land once again, a crusade to restore our Constitution! Will you join me?"

The Patriots and Exiles cheered one more time.

Mac raised his fist in the air and declared, "Tomorrow, we sail for America!"

"I'm Jan Roberts, reporting to you live." Pale and thin, she stood in front of a gun-gray steel wall in loose-fitting fatigues, her long auburn hair whipping about in the wind. "In the coming months, I'll be reporting on the progress of a grand experiment Secretary-General MacCrarey and world luminaries have undertaken. The melding of one-quarter of the world's nations into a single, supranational government. At Tel New Megiddo–" and she gave a summary of Mac's speech to the convocation, finishing with, "–'Something the world has never seen before,' promising to reveal it in a worldwide broadcast from New York City."

Walking to her right, the wall behind her ended and the frenetic gray-green waves of the vast north Atlantic appeared. Extending to the horizon were chevrons of battleships and destroyers steaming towards a distant shore.

"In the meantime, MacCrarey will be dealing with matters in the United States." She paused. "This is Jan Roberts, reporting live from the bridge of the USS Enterprise," and the picture faded to black.

"Perfect," Mac said, taking the mic from her and handing it to the Royal Navy videographer. "Download the video-file to a flash drive and give it to Mr. Makatu in the comm center. He'll know what to do with it."

"Aye, aye, sir," the ensign replied, packing away his equipment.

"T.J.'ll transmit the video via GLOSAT to the BBC," Mac explained. "They'll broadcast it tonight."

"Mac, you won't really attack the United States, will you?"

He took her by the arm and led her to the railing. "I want Thomas to think I will."

"Aren't you running the risk of Thomas attacking first?"

Mac grinned. "Fundamental rule of warfare and poker. Stack the deck in your favor."

"How do you intend to do that?"

"It's already done. The President and I just need to have a little chat."

"Oh, okay. You're just going to waltz into the Oval Office and say, 'Hey, Mitch, gotta sec?'"

"Yep. Pretty much."

The following morning, the UN armada reached the outer perimeter of U.S. territorial waters. Every ship held its position but one. The USS Enterprise. She steamed on to the mouth of the Chesapeake Bay where a U.S. Air Force helicopter landed on the ship's foredeck just long enough to refuel and take on four passengers. She lifted off again, banked north, and an hour later set down on the south lawn of the White House.

The former head of the Joint Chiefs of Staff, General Curtis Powell, greeted Secretary-General MacCrarey, Captain Jonathan Sleeping Bear, and Colonels Perry Spencer and Christopher Stone halfway between the helipad and the West Wing.

"He's in the Oval Office!" Powell shouted over the whooping of the helicopter blades.

President Thomas sat on the divan reading, a steaming pot of coffee on the low table in front of him. Beside it rested a silver tray of Danishes, donuts, breads, and muffins. No bagels, though. *Never* bagels. "Jews made bagels and Jews killed Jesus Christ," he'd told the kitchen staff his first day in the White House.

A knock sounded at the door. "Come in," he said without looking up.

The door opened, and he was vaguely aware of footsteps crossing the room.

"Hello, Mitchell," said a dreadfully familiar voice, a voice the President never expected to hear again.

A shiver went down his spine, his head jerked up, and there standing on the opposite side of the coffee table was William Cameron MacCrarey. Dropping his Bible and clambering to his feet, the President cried, "Help me!"

"No one's going to help you now, Mitchell," Mac said calmly.

"I've seen to that," added Powell.

Thomas turned to the General, mouth agape, and cried, "Traitor! Judas!"

"Sit down, Mitchell," Mac told him in a bored sort of way.

"Devil! Son of Satan!"

Mac pushed the President back down onto the divan. "There's no such thing as the devil, I'm not the Antichrist, the United Nations isn't evil, and you're about to resign."

Thomas huffed. "Resign? You're mad! God gave me the Presidency and only *God* can take it away!"

"Resign and save the country the embarrassment of an impeachment," said the General.

"Congress'll *never* impeach *me!* I made America *great* again. I made her *Christian* again. I *saved* her!"

The heir of Arthur held out his iPhone. "Look."

The President gingerly took the phone as if it might explode. On the tiny screen, gaunt, dispirited-looking men and women stared blankly into the camera. Behind them stood the crumbling hovels of Kaliffe and on a distant hillside sprawled a graveyard. "Your Exiles and their prison," Mac said, the anger in his voice plain. "And for many, their final resting place."

Thomas paled and dropped the phone. "They, they deserved their punishment," he said lamely. "Their kind made our country weak and sinful. We had to take our country back from them."

"Back from whom," Mac snapped, "the people? And who did you give it to? Bigots and billionaires? Nationalists and nihilists? And what have they done with it since? Hoarded the nation's wealth and power? Turned the clock back to the 50's, moral McCarthyism and all? Decided which people were good enough to be free and which weren't?" He picked up the phone, started a new video, and showed it to the President.

The Exiles were charging across the battle line in the Negev, and then the picture morphed into the horrific images of the bloody aftermath. "How much death have you and Schoen wrought together?"

"God punished them," the President whispered tremulously.

"No, Mitchell," Mac replied. "*You* and Schoen punished them. Soldiers and citizens don't deserve the wars created by politicians, theocrats, and megalomaniacs like Schoen. And the Exiles sure the hell didn't deserve the prison sentences you and your cohorts gave them." Mac turned to Perry. "Give it to him."

The Colonel handed the President a sheet of paper. "That's the speech you'll be giving to the White House press corps in five minutes. In it, you admit to creating the Exile camps, ask for the American people's forgiveness, tell them to respect the opinions and beliefs of others, and announce your resignation. This evening you'll be flown to The Hague to stand trial with Jack Abrams, Johnny Swaywell, and Jake Tanner."

Thomas snorted and tossed the paper aside. "Never!"

Mac leaned down until his face was just inches from Thomas's. "On my ships are the American Patriots you alienated and the Exiles you imprisoned. And they're just dying to meet you, Mitchell."

The President shuddered and shrank into the divan.

"Give the speech or you'll be spending some quality time with my new friends."

"And don't think for a moment he won't do it," said Perry.

"I hope he does," grinned Captain Sleeping Bear.

"Go ahead," Powell told Mac. "I won't stop you, and I've already ordered the U.S. military to stand down. The UN forces'll face no resistance whatsoever should they choose to land, Mr. President. But, if you read this speech," he picked the piece of paper up off the floor, "MacCrarey's ships'll stay only long enough to disembark the Exiles and Patriots. Once ashore, the Underground'll escort them back home."

"The USS Enterprise will be the only ship to remain behind," Mac added. "She'll sail to the port of New York tonight and drop anchor in the East River beside the United Nations complex. When I'm confident the United States has restored the Constitutional rights of her citizens, *all* of her citizens, Exiles and Patriots included, I'll give her back to the U.S. Navy."

The President turned his head and gazed longingly at the portrait of Ronald Reagan hanging on the wall opposite his desk.

"He wouldn't even recognize America today," the heir of Arthur told him.

"Resign, Mr. President," Powell insisted, holding out the speech. "Let this be over."

Thomas reluctantly took it, his hand shaking with helpless, self-righteous anger.

"Good choice," Mac told him. "Perry, ready the chopper. General, please escort the soon-to-be-ex-President to the press room. And Mitchell, get yourself a good lawyer. You're gonna need one."

"Oh, by the way, you'll have company on the flight to The Hague tonight," Michael Abrams mentioned to his two dinner guests as he cut into his steak. "Former President Thomas."

The Reverend Johnny Swaywell dropped his fork and slumped in his chair.

Jack slammed his fist down. "This is so, so," he struggled for the right word but could only come up with, "unfair!"

"Unfair?" Michael replied indignantly. "Were people dying because of your policies fair? Was forcing people to wear wristbands and taking their rights away one by one fair? Was life in a casbah fair?"

Jack looked down at his plate. "We were making America great again," he said quietly.

"We were doing the Lord's work," the Reverend meekly proclaimed. "We were making America Christian again."

"You call what you did 'great' and 'Christian,' do you?" challenged Michael.

"Look," Jack replied, "I didn't agree with everything he," hoisting a thumb at Swaywell, "and Thomas did. But, we had to do *something*. The country needed to be stronger, to ready itself against our enemies, and to put down the growing socialist tide."

"To take back our religious freedoms," Swaywell added, his voice regaining some of its former pulpit pomposity, "to silence the science sinners and liberal liars!"

"Shut up!" Jack yelled at him.

"You coalesced power unto yourselves by taking away the rights and even the lives of those you decided were worth less than you," Michael retorted.

Jack pushed his chair back and stood up. "We had the guts to do what needed to be done to save this country. You're a *fool* for not seeing the necessity of it and you're a *hypocrite* to talk of taking away people's rights and then imprisoning us here!"

"Well, then, why don't you leave?" said Michael, cutting into his steak again. "Go on."

Swaywell looked from Jack to Michael and back again. Jack eyed his grandfather warily. "Fine," he said defiantly. "We will."

"Yes, leave. Both of you," Michael said, taking a sip of wine. "Goodbye."

Swaywell quickly got to his feet, but just as the two of them reached the door, Michael added, "Oh, did I mention the first of the Exiles were brought ashore this evening?"

The would-be escapees froze.

Tapping the side of his head, the elder Abrams said apologetically, "Must have forgotten. Mac brought a few dozen or so up the Potomac to a nearby Underground station."

Jack yanked the door open.

"And," his grandfather casually added, "my estate just happens to be that station."

Jack's eyes closed.

Swaywell spun around. "They're here? Now?" he gasped, his eyes darting around.

Michael nodded. "Patrolling the grounds, I expect." Another sip of wine. "Please feel free to leave, though. I'm sure they'd be happy to arrange a trial for you right here. In fact," another sip, "I should think they'd rather prefer it."

A chill ran down the Reverend's spine.

Jack let out a sigh.

And the two would-be escapees shuffled back to the table, heads down.

ιβ

"*The purpose of getting power is to be able to give it away.*"

– Aneurin Bevan

"*The higher the level of knowledge and power, the
greater must be our sense of moral responsibility.*"

– His Holiness the Dalai Lama

"*The person who is harmonious amid the hostile, peaceful amid the
violent, free from grasping amid the greedy, that one I call superior.*"

– The Dhammapada

William Cameron MacCrarey noted the time. "Okay. Here I go," he
said, giving Genevieve a kiss and kneeling to hug his daughter. "Wish
me luck, sweetie."

Cameron, still thin and pale, kissed him on the cheek. "Good
luck, Daddy."

Mac walked out onto the stage and everyone in the packed
assembly hall stood to cheer and applaud. In the moments it took
him to reach the podium and the ovation to subside, he reflected
back on the people he'd met and the places he'd been to since that
fateful, wintry night in Traverse. There'd been Dr. Angela Fuentes
and his time at the State Hospital. Merrill and his stories of Arthur
during their walk from Bath to Mons Baddonicus. Kyle and the

clansfolk on his first visit to the old hall in Camleton. Michael introducing himself at the confirmation hearings. Meeting T.J. in the offices of the UN Secretariat Building before they left together for Geneva. Evenings and weekends in Petra's and Katrina's café reading books by the greatest writers and thinkers of every age. The fearless Dalai Lama standing before the Chinese soldiers in Lhasa. Long, thought-provoking conversations with Drs. Kraeg, Ingersaul, Michener, and Galatea. Sean running through the rain-drenched olive grove on a Cyprus mountaintop, and the timeless days sailing up the coffee-brown Amazon with him and Taylor. The proud settlers of Monte Misme fighting off the soldiers from Little Deutschland. The gun battle at the White Freedom Nation compound. The American Exiles walking out of Kaliffe. Captain Sleeping Bear's F16s thundering across the desert. And now here, with his friends, Genevieve, Cameron, Merrill, and Kyle, about to address the world.

"There are those who believe I am here to herald the end of the world and the beginning of the Apocalypse," he began when the applause subsided. "Well, perhaps, in a matter of speaking, they're right. Apocalypse comes from the Greek 'apokalypsis,' meaning the revealing of truth. And the truth is, our world is on the verge of a momentous change, a change that will lead us into the next great age, a change that will take its place beside such momentous human events as the Mesopotamian transition from nomadic bands to city-states, the cultural achievements of the Egyptians, the intellectual advances of the Greeks, the daring innovations of the Renaissance, and the bold secular leaps of the Enlightenment. Here, today, we shall take the first step into the Age of Peace, of a one-world democracy, of a *Novum Orbis Regium* where the responsibility to protect those who cannot protect themselves is sacred, where providing a positive social and intellectual foundation for everyone is paramount, where ensuring self-respect and self-sufficiency is recognized as a basic human right, where unbiased laws apply equally to all, where living without hate, without greed, without war, without poverty, without hunger, without pestilence, without overpopulation, without ecological devastation, without ignorance, and without borders is no longer a dream but commonplace."

Heartfelt cheers and rousing applause filled the hall.

"Churchill once said, 'If you're not a liberal at twenty you have no heart. If you're not a conservative at forty you have no brain.' Well," Mac chuckled, "I choose to have a heart *and* a brain. If you do as well, then together we can solve any problem, destroy every tyranny, and create a Utopia far beyond any ever imagined. The nations we liberated from Gerhardt Schoen now have transitional governments in place, administered by experts brought in by the UN. The citizens of those countries will soon participate in elections to establish a supra-national government called the United Republics of Earth, or URE, a form of government that takes the lessons of history and embraces ten ethical promises. We will correct our past mistakes, we will always move forward, we will respect individual freedom in all matters, we will take to heart the importance of human rights, we will ensure secular and religious inclusivity, we will enforce fiscal responsibility, we will respect the scientific method, we will do no harm to others, we will live and die by the timeless motto, 'do unto others as we would have them do unto us,' and we will answer in the affirmative these questions posed by James Michener in his book, *This Noble Land.* Does the government have a stable monetary system? Does it have a political system that guarantees the peaceful transition of power between parties? Does it give the elected party a clear understanding of the people's needs and the tools to meet them? Does it provide its citizens with health services? Does it provide publicly funded schools, colleges, and technical training? Does it provide adequate employment opportunities? Does it maintain a strong manufacturing base? Does it fund research into new technologies and processes? Does it allow collective bargaining? Does it allow equal pay for equal work? Does it establish a livable minimum wage and ensure good paying jobs for experienced workers? Does it instill a work ethic and a sense of accomplishment? Does it foster a sense of inclusion? Does it provide financial assistance for displaced workers and help them transition into new fields and places of employment? Does it encourage a frugal though enjoyable lifestyle, small families, charitable giving, and respect for others? Does it have a legal system that provides only the necessary level of restraint over the lives of individuals and the conduct of business? Does it have a taxation system designed to keep the gap between the very rich and the very poor to a fair and economically beneficial level? Does it motivate the lower economic classes to strive for a better life without causing resentment and social unrest? Does it foster a large, economically vibrant middle class? Does it respect the freedom of religious choice, including the choice not to be religious, and provide churches and secular forums to advocate moral principles and positive lifestyles? Does it provide recreational opportunities to promote good health? Does it provide museums, symphony halls, parks, zoos, libraries, and theaters? Does it embrace gender, cultural, ethnic, and racial equality and pluralism? Does it balance local, national, and international views in social matters, politics, and economics? Does it treat its very young and very old with respect? Does it empower the elderly and the ill to control how they live and die? Do women have control over their reproductive and economic lives? And, is the liberty of the individual fairly balanced against the needs of the many?

"To achieve all this, the URE must begin with informed legislating. Technology will aid us in this by guaranteeing the right of one person, one vote, *and* by giving the people the opportunity to weigh in on legislation being put forth by elected officials *before* it becomes law. Bills will be posted online, the citizenry will electronically vote for or against them, and the results will be electronically tallied and given to the legislators to guide *their* votes.

"Minimum qualifications for holding elected office will be established, such as age, years of relevant experience, level and type of education, and so on. Those interested in running will be pre-qualified by an impartial board, and political candidates will have their positions on relevant issues vetted by subject matter experts and the free press.

"PACs and political contributions to candidates by parties, corporations, churches, and non-profits will be banned. Such legal entities will *never* have the same constitutional rights as 'We the People' do in the URE, and only 'We the People' will be allowed to make political contributions. And those contributions will be capped at a level everyone can afford. In this way, no one person or entity will be allowed to exert disproportional influence on an election or a candidate.

"How will the government fund itself? Well, as Benjamin Franklin put it, 'Nothing is certain except death and taxes.' So it must be in the URE."

Gentle laughter wafted about the hall.

"The URE's tax structure will be non-progressive for businesses, non-profits and churches. Yes, non-profits and churches will be taxed the same as businesses. No tax code will exist, only a single tax rate set by a panel of non-partisan experts at a level that funds the government. Corporate and personal tax breaks, accounting games, the shifting of income overseas to tax havens, tax inversions, and the like will be banned, and violations will be considered a capital crime.

"'From everyone who has been given much, much will be demanded,' says a good book, and so it will be in the URE. The *personal* tax rate *will* be progressive, meaning the more one makes, the more one pay in taxes. The purpose of this will not be to redistribute wealth, but to recognize that in a capitalist system the owners, shareholders, and executives of businesses profit from those who buy their products, products that are priced at more than what they cost to make. Today, prices and laws are set such that one percent of the world's population controls 50 percent of its wealth. That is a crime against humanity, an inevitable reality of capitalism, the institutionalization of greed, a modern day feudal system that breeds political corruption, legal bribery via campaign contributions, inequality, alienation, resentment, hopelessness, desperation, and if left to fester, crime, riots, and even rebellion. There must be something better, something that provides the motivation to work hard while at the same time creating a stable, vibrant economy that benefits everyone, not just a privileged few." He paused and admitted, "I have no idea what that something *is*."

More gentle laughter.

"But, it must be conceived of and when it is, the URE will adopt it.

"Businesses will be encouraged to provide products and services for the poorest two-thirds of the world's population, which collectively holds five trillion dollars in spending power. Economies of scale, scope, and size, will make selling products to the poor both socially *and* financially beneficial. The URE will grade businesses on their social responsibility so consumers can make well-informed decisions when buying products and services.

"A public-private partnership will bring together corporate researchers, public strategists, and responsible politicians to creatively apply new ideas and technologies.

"To support trade with countries outside the URE, all but the most critical trade barriers, import duties, and tariffs will be eliminated. Any that remain or are erected in the future will benefit the people, the URE, and its businesses, in that order.

"Each URE region will grow whatever produce its climate is best suited for, mine whichever resources are most abundant, and manufacture what it's best able to. Regardless of which region they live in, the workers will earn a decent wage.

"To encourage stable communities and a growing middle class, property ownership will be achieved via investment cooperatives. In contrast to home mortgages from banks or credit unions, investment cooperatives allow persons with decent credit to buy a home with *no* mortgage and *no* interest payments. This is done by representing home values as shares of stock, and persons looking for a new home simply buy as many shares as they can reasonably afford. The rest of the shares remain with the investment cooperative for other investors to buy and sell. In lieu of monthly mortgage payments, the homeowner buys more shares when they can afford to. When the homeowner decides to sell, they simply cash in their shares and move on. Such a form of home ownership saves homeowners thousands of dollars a year in interest expense, money they can spend on goods and services to spur the economy.

"'A rising tide lifts all boats,' goes the saying, but over the past four decades only some of those boats have risen. The disparity between rich and poor is the highest it's ever been. Even America, the wealthiest nation on Earth, spends 10 percent of its budget to help feed and house people with jobs that pay so little they can't afford a decent place to live and a full belly. That, too, is a crime against humanity, and within the URE, corporations will pay their fair share and no longer be allowed to increase their profits by preying on the desperation of the poorest workers in the poorest places by paying them paltry wages."

The assembly thundered with approbation.

"Too often, the better-off in society believe that people on welfare are lazy and greedy. The far right of every country sees the higher-than-average levels of crime in poor communities and thinks the people who live there must be immoral. By thinking this way, they can guiltlessly do nothing to help. They ignore the fact that their own capitalism, greed, and prejudice *lead* to the poverty, inequity, and urban blight that *creates* hopelessness, desperation, unemployment, and ultimately crime. Forty-seven percent of crimes are born of social and economic desperation. Theft, burglary, prostitution, drug and alcohol abuse, and so on. Only five-percent of crimes involve physical violence, and only the perpetrators of violent crime should be imprisoned. Jailing people for crimes of desperation solves *nothing* if desperation is allowed to continue generation after generation. To counter this, the URE will criminalize the practices of the well-off that leave people on the edge of financial destitution, a paycheck away from homelessness, suffering from poor nutrition and unhealthy living conditions. Those arrested for non-violent crimes in the URE will be sentenced to tether programs and assigned probationary counselors. When necessary, they'll be given additional education or skilled trade training. The result will be less crime, smaller police departments, fewer courts and jails, and lower taxes.

"In the 1920's, alcohol prohibition did nothing to end drinking and instead created speakeasies, bootleggers, and organized crime.

Drug prohibition has done the same. Nearly a third of the people in prison today were sentenced for drug crimes or crimes related to alcohol abuse. The URE will decriminalize recreational drugs for those of age and offer conditional amnesty for farmers, smugglers, and peddlers of drugs who legally become licensed as producers and distributors and then taxed as businesses. Any who violate the terms of their licensed amnesty will be placed under house arrest. Tether programs, probationary counselors, substance abuse treatment programs, life-skills training, and anti-drug public relations campaigns will be paid for with tax revenues from drug sales. The remaining revenues will be used to reduce taxes.

"In many nations, insufficient retirement savings and lack of pension plans have resulted in a large number of elderly living below the poverty line, dependent on welfare and social security just to get by. The URE will require companies, non-profits and churches to provide a base level pension for their workers who in turn will be required to invest a percentage of their wages in retirement plans like 401ks. By doing so, no retirees will live in poverty and the Social Security system will remain solvent in perpetuity.

"The URE will require companies to provide healthcare insurance at no cost to their employees for annual doctor appointments, health screenings, vaccinations, and emergency and curative care. The URE will do the same for the unemployed and retired. The public will be educated on the importance of frequent examinations, early diagnosis, healthy lifestyles, and clean living conditions. Greater investments will be made to eradicate communicable diseases in a manner affordable to everyone. End-of-life care alternatives, including the right to die on one's own terms, will be shared with everyone facing serious illnesses. All existing healthcare providers will become part of a URE-wide consortium of privately operated clinics, hospitals, pharmaceutical companies, and medical equipment manufacturers. Over time, redundancies will disappear, inefficient processes will be streamlined, economies of scale will be achieved, Medicare and Medicaid will remain solvent in perpetuity, and healthcare costs will go down.

"Patient health histories will be maintained in a secured online database available to every healthcare provider in the URE. Doctor fees and drug prices will be based on pre-established wage and cost schedules set to ensure positive patient outcomes, affordability, and cost containment, in that order, as determined by a panel of qualified experts and patient advocates.

"The URE will fund research into the human body to learn what makes us sick, what makes us better, and how we can avoid illnesses in the first place. We will delve into the human genome and our findings will be placed in a publicly available genetic diagnostics and treatment database. Any custom genes and gene therapies developed as a result of the research will be licensed to the private sector and the license fees used to offset taxes.

"The URE will ban pharmaceutical and other patents that create monopolies and allow companies to make extraordinary profits at the expense of the citizenry.

"The URE will limit work weeks to 40 hours, prohibit overtime, and mandate retirement at 62 to create more jobs for younger workers and lower the unemployment rate.

"The URE will enact laws to balance the rights of workers, unions, and employers with the affordability of goods and the vibrancy of the economy.

"The URE will create a highly advanced software model to analyze economic, sociological, military, political, meteorological, geological, and ecological trends around the world to predict problems far enough in advance to take effective actions.

"The URE will aggressively address global warming and foster the use of renewable energy sources.

"The URE will fund research in the various fields of science, engineering, and manufacturing to develop low-cost, high-yield processes and products. Everything invented with public monies will be competitively licensed to the private sector and the revenues used to offset taxes.

"The URE will offer incentives to businesses that build factories, warehouses, and offices in economically challenged areas and hire local workers.

"The poorly educated face perpetual economic hardship and can be easily misled by business leaders, politicians, and pundits with ideological and economic agendas at odds with the general welfare of the people. Thus, the citizenry will be given a broad liberal arts education in philosophy, the humanities, world history, literature, the sciences, economics, composition, art, and music.

"The URE will grade colleges and universities on their curricula, graduation rates, and post-graduation employment levels. As grades go up, so will the grants and scholarships awarded to students accepted by those schools to offset tuition costs.

"A URE World University will be founded with campuses around the globe that offer baccalaureate degrees tuition-free to anyone who gives four years of public service to the military, government, or humanitarian organizations. A URE vocational school that teaches mechanical, electrical, shop-floor, computer, artistic, and graphic trades will be founded under the same terms.

"But being well-educated means much more than just a diploma, certification, or degree. It means having an open mind that continuously learns, a mind that benefits society in countless ways. Thus, continuing educational requirements for adults will also be required for as long as they wish to vote, work, or receive government benefits.

"The URE will pass a Homesteading Act to encourage people who want out of blighted areas and unrelenting poverty and are willing to live and work on the world's frontiers. While remaining environmentally conscious, free tracts of land will be given to individuals who economically and motivationally qualify. That is to say, those from lower-to-middle income brackets with needed skills, educational backgrounds, or experience levels. Whole new communities will be built from the ground up. Public works projects will be sponsored to develop the necessary infrastructure to reach and support the new communities. Roads, water and sewer systems, electrical grids, gas lines, etcetera. Those projects will in turn create opportunities for people to *establish* the experience levels and *learn* the skills they need to qualify for their *own* tracts of land.

"The URE will ensure that the world's natural resources belong to the world's people. No handful of nations, private persons, or businesses will ever again control what the Earth has provided to all of us. A nation's border is little more than an arbitrary line drawn on a map once upon a time by politicians or generals, so why should some nations find themselves with great wealth by the randomness of history while others are left with nothing? In the URE, licenses for the extraction and refinement of oil, natural gas, precious metals, minerals, trees, land and fresh water will be competitively awarded. License fees and revenues from the sale of natural resources will be used to offset taxes.

"The URE will meld the world's space programs into one global URE Space Administration. Its short-term mission will be to mine the asteroid belt between Earth and Mars for valuable minerals. The revenues from their sales will fund the Space Administration's longer-term mission of developing advanced propulsion systems and extended mission spacecraft for manned missions to planets similar to ours in other solar systems." He smiled. "Kind of like the Starship Enterprise, eh?"

Polite laughter.

"Some may say this is an extravagance or a waste of money, but the fact of the matter is we have no choice. All our eggs are in one basket. If the Earth falls victim to a comet collision or a massive solar flare, then we could be wiped clean from the cosmic record books. Our very survival depends on establishing other homes in the Milky Way.

"Here's something else we have no choice about. All I've just proposed will be for naught if the world's population continues to grow at an exponential rate. Natural resources will be exhausted, poverty and desperation will become endemic, crime rates will soar, wars will become so commonplace as to seem mundane, and disease and pestilence will run rampant. Taming our population growth must begin with ensuring a woman's right to control her own body and choose if and when she becomes or remains pregnant. We must also encourage, even mandate if necessary, the use of effective forms of birth control until a couple, married or unmarried, chooses to start a family. And when they do, they must have no more than two children on average. Those who choose to remain childless or have only one child can voluntarily put up for adoption a child-yet-to-be born for couples who can't conceive or want more than two children."

That was a bit much for some, but most of the gathered applauded.

"I mentioned to the convocation at Tel New Megiddo that when next we met I'd have something to show them that never existed before. Something crafted to lead us into the *Novum Orbis Regium.*"

The hall suddenly became electric with anticipation. Rumors about what Mac had been working on in the weeks since Jan Roberts's broadcast from the USS Enterprise had run rampant.

"A World Constitution."

Everyone in the great hall stood and cheered.

"Hmmm," he muttered, shuffling through the papers on the podium, "I thought I had one here."

Laughter and more shuffling.

"Ah! Here it is," and he pressed the remote control he'd been secretly palming.

The large screen behind him lit up with a list of constitutional articles.

"The United Republics of Earth shall consist of three levels of government, federal, state, and municipal. State borders shall be drawn using rivers, oceans, lakes, mountain ranges, and deserts as demarcations, and natural population distributions as size delimiters. Historical precedence, ethnic groupings, and religious beliefs shall *not* be considered.

"The states and municipalities shall govern their own affairs, hold their own judicial proceedings, and pass their own laws, insofar as they're Constitutional and comply with URE laws concerning civil rights, the sciences, and education. The military, the macro-economy, foreign trade, treaties, and humanitarian affairs shall be the purview of the federal branches of government, of which there shall be four, the Legislative, the Judiciary, the Executive, and the Advisory.

"The first three shall heed the insights, findings, and recommendations of the fourth. The Advisory shall serve as the counterbalance to democracy's two greatest weaknesses – the ability of extremists and the wealthy to irrationally sway popular opinion, and the inability of elected officials to make difficult decisions during difficult times. The Advisory shall consist of subject matter experts from various fields and disciplines and may be appointed by any number of current Advisory members, representatives of the other three branches, or the public. The length of Advisory members' terms shall be dependent on their expertise and the issues facing the URE at a given point in time. As appointees, members of the Advisory may be removed by a majority vote of their peers, or by a public referendum, but not by officials of the other three branches of government.

"The Legislative branch shall consist of a World Senate and a House of the People with the power to assess taxes, create budgets, confirm appointees of the President, approve trade pacts, pass legislation, initiate proceedings for impeachment of the President or Vice President, and generally conduct hearings on matters of public interest. The General Assembly of the United Nations shall become the World Senate, its membership consisting of two representatives freely elected from each sovereign country that becomes part of the URE. The House of the People shall be analogous to the House of Commons in the UK or the House of Representatives in the U.S. with its members freely elected in districts created by natural population distributions of one half of one million people.

"The Advisory shall endorse or reverse the Legislature's vote for impeachment of the President or Vice President.

"The Judiciary shall consist of local district courts, state courts of appeals, federal district courts, federal courts of appeals, and a URE Supreme Court. The members of the Judiciary shall be appointed by the Advisory and confirmed by the Senate. Judges can be removed from office for misconduct by a majority vote of the

Advisory members, or by public referendum, but never by elected officials. Appeals of verdicts dealing with the interpretation of the World Constitution or matters affecting more than one state may work their way up to the Supreme Court whose rulings shall be final. Cases filed by or affecting the public shall be heard by publicly funded courts, but cases between businesses, non-profits, or churches shall be mediated only by privately-funded arbitrators whose decisions must be endorsed by Advisory-appointed judges. Unendorsed decisions shall be remanded back to the arbitrators.

"The Executive branch shall consist of a President and Vice President, each voted into office by the people independently of the other. The President shall have defined veto powers and shall abide by all rulings of the Supreme Court. He or she shall be empowered with the right to issue executive orders dealing with matters not addressed by the law, set policy, make treaties, and appoint cabinet members. The Vice President shall be empowered to preside over the House and Senate, cast deciding votes in cases of ties, appoint ambassadors and consuls, perform various diplomatic duties, and fill the office of the Presidency in the event of the President's death or incapacitation. The Vice President shall also be required to endorse the President's Executive Orders before they can go into effect.

"The terms of office for members of the Legislature, President, and Vice President shall be four years. One-third of the House and Senate shall be elected every two years. The President and Vice President shall be limited to two terms, the Legislature four. The Advisory shall vet those who choose to run for office, taking into consideration their age, credentials, experience, and education. Its findings shall be posted online three months prior to election day.

"The government shall not establish an electoral college, or the like, and election to office shall be solely and directly based on a popular vote of the people. Voting districts shall be created by the Advisory branch, not elected officials, and gerrymandering of any kind shall be considered a capital crime, punishable by imprisonment.

"Voting for office holders shall be held in official government buildings, public libraries, and online via an official government website. Voter identification shall be biometric, and elections shall be conducted over a one-month period in October every second year. When vacancies in the Legislature occur, the affected voting district shall hold an electronic election to fill the remainder of the vacated term.

"The government shall never, under any circumstances, establish a religious, ethnic, or racial requirement to hold office, to vote, to testify in a court of law, to serve on a jury, or to become a URE citizen.

"When taking office, an elected official shall publicly make the following affirmation, 'I do solemnly affirm that I will faithfully execute the duties of my office to the benefit of the people, and will to the best of my ability preserve, protect, and defend the Constitution of the United Republics of Earth, and if for any reason I am unable to uphold this oath, I will resign from my office.'

"The URE shall never under any circumstances reference or invoke the name of a deity or religion at any official URE event or in any oath or pledge, nor shall it include the name of a deity or religion on any official URE document or unit of currency.

"The government shall ensure that the right of citizens 19 years of age or older to vote is never denied or abridged based on gender, sexual orientation, race, ethnicity, wealth, genetic make-up, handicap, religion, or previous citizenship. Only a citizen's mental incompetence, failure to pay URE taxes, or prior conviction for insurrection, treason, or serious crime shall supersede their right to vote.

"Similarly, only these same considerations shall deny a new resident the right to become a URE citizen. Beyond that, everyone living within the borders of the URE, born on URE soil, or born to a citizen of the URE outside its borders shall be a citizen and have the freedoms and rights delineated herein, strictly and consistently enforced by all branches and levels of government.

"Beholden to the President as Commander-in-Chief shall be a standing army, navy, and air force to be used solely for defense. Soldiers shall be chosen by a draft without consideration of class, social status, wealth, profession, religion, ethnicity, race, sexual orientation, or gender. All individuals 19 years of age or older shall be subject to the draft once in their lifetime. Individual states shall not be allowed to have standing militias but shall have local police forces beholden to a federal Agency of Law and Security to ensure public safety, enforce statutes and regulations, suppress terrorism, and safeguard civil rights.

"The standing army, navy, and air force shall also be used to end hostilities between battling parties outside of the URE. Once hostilities are ended, a peace negotiation shall immediately commence under the mediation of the URE. No war and no clash of armies shall ever again be allowed anywhere on Earth."

Again, the Assembly cheered and applauded.

"The government shall ensure that the production, ownership, and use of deadly arms by the people is reasonably regulated. Arms owned by the people shall require permits and be stored in a central community armory. The owner shall be allowed to temporarily keep such arms in their homes or on their persons for the purpose of hunting wild game, safety training, or self-defense in life-threatening situations. Removal of arms from an armory, as well as the sale or trading of arms, shall require an official permit. Local law enforcement agencies may advise local governments regarding the issuance of permits but cannot itself prohibit them. The sale, trading, or possession of deadly arms without a permit shall be punishable by imprisonment. Permits shall not be issued for weapons capable of inflicting mass casualties, and the possession of such weapons shall be considered a capital offense. Permits shall also not be issued to persons convicted of a felony or who are of questionable mental competence and stability.

"The URE shall not sell arms of any kind to other nations, nor allow any businesses within its borders to do so.

"Terrorism in every form – killings, kidnappings, intimidation, incitement, slander, coercion, etcetera – shall be considered a capital offense. Spying, drone strikes, state-sanctioned espionage, and the like shall also be considered a capital offense.

"The President shall have the power to declare war, but a three-fourths majority vote of the Legislature along with the concurrence of the Advisory may override the President's actions. The Legislature shall have the power of the purse to fund military actions and the Advisory shall establish rules concerning prisoners thereof. In the event of a declaration of war, and this is important, the President, the Speaker of the House, and the Majority Leader of the Senate shall be immediately drafted and assigned to forward combat units."

All present rose to their feet and applauded.

"The government shall be in session perpetually and shall perform their duties virtually to the extent possible to expedite their completion and minimize expenditures, although a physical capitol may be established with the concurrence of all four branches.

"Every bill brought before the Legislature shall be vetted by the Advisory whose findings shall be posted online. The public shall then be given the opportunity to electronically vote for or against the bill, and their tallies forwarded to the legislators before *they* vote on the bill. Bills passed shall be presented to the President for signature or to be remanded back to the Legislature. A two-thirds vote of the Legislature shall override a remanded bill and make it law.

"The Legislature shall have the power to levy taxes and fund the operations of the URE. The gross annual revenues of all persons, businesses, non-profits, and churches shall be taxable at rates set by the Advisory. Operating budgets shall be prepared annually, critiqued by the Advisory, and signed or vetoed by the President.

"A Treasury Department independent of the Legislature shall collect tax revenues.

"The Legislature shall have the power to borrow money, establish a common URE currency, set its value with the assistance of the Advisory, and regulate commerce.

"Vessels traveling between URE states and the URE products they carry shall not be subject to import or export tariffs, taxes, or duties, though products and services coming in from non-URE countries may be subject to excises at the Legislature's and Advisory's discretion."

"The URE shall not grant businesses, non-profits, or churches the rights delineated herein, which are reserved solely for the people.

"The URE shall not infringe upon, nor shall it pass laws, even in times of war or states of emergency, that detract from the rights delineated herein.

"The URE shall ensure that anyone in a position to sway public opinion shall adhere to facts, reason, and real-life conditions. Severe penalties shall be imposed for conveying falsehoods.

"Concerning a free press, the government shall ensure that the media is unbiased and subject to peer review. Schools of journalism and media outlets shall be certified, and journalists shall be licensed. Any knowingly false or misleading reporting shall result in a certification or license being revoked and possible criminal prosecution.

"The URE shall not infringe upon the rights of the people to freedom of speech, of the press, of expression, to peaceably assemble, or to present the government with a list of grievances.

"The URE shall establish and fund a public library system and provide public day care, pre-school, and primary and secondary educations to its citizens.

"The URE shall establish and fund a World University and Trade School for its citizens.

"The URE shall not provide public monies to non-public institutions, including private educational organizations and religious establishments.

"The Legislature shall make no law respecting a particular religion. The people shall retain the right to express or practice their religion or non-religion without interference or restriction by the government, but no person shall have the right to interfere with or restrict the expression of religious or non-religious beliefs by others under penalty of criminal prosecution.

"The Legislature shall not pass any law that provides for cruel or unusual actions or punishments. Law enforcement and punishments for crimes shall be applied equally to all peoples. The President, Vice President, and members of the Advisory, Judiciary, and Legislature shall be held to the same letter of the law as are the people and shall be subject to the same punishments.

"The Legislature shall not pass any law that would retroactively change the consequences for actions or crimes committed prior to the enactment of the law.

"The Legislature shall make no law abridging the people's freedom from unreasonable searches and seizures.

"The Judiciary shall issue warrants only upon probable cause and when supported by oath, affirmation, and reasonable details of where to search and who or what to seize. Such oath, affirmation, and details shall be public information.

"Neither the Judiciary, the military, nor any government branch or agency shall operate out of the public eye, and none can delegate their responsibilities to private entities.

"The people shall have the right to petition the government for information concerning its actions.

"The Judiciary shall not convict or incarcerate individuals without proving their guilt in a public court of law. Terms of incarceration shall be standardized and approved by the Advisory and only clear extenuating circumstances shall vary them.

"The Judiciary shall not allow the death penalty to be imposed as punishment for any crime.

"The Judiciary shall not incarcerate a person or persons for crimes that do not pose a physical threat of harm to others. It shall instead place them under house arrest and electronic monitoring.

"The Judiciary shall not infringe upon the people's right to cross examine witnesses against them, compulsorily obtain witnesses, or obtain the timely assistance of competent, publicly funded defense counsel.

"The Judiciary shall not infringe upon the people's right to a fair, impartial, and timely trial by one's peers.

"The Judiciary shall not twice place a person or persons in jeopardy of life or limb for the same offense, except in cases of appeal being heard by higher courts due to irregularities in an earlier trial, constitutional interpretation, or new evidence.

"The Judiciary shall not compel a person or persons to be a witness against themselves.

"The Judiciary shall not infringe upon the people's right to be free from excessive bail or fines.

"The URE shall not allow discrimination in any form beyond objective intellectual or skills-based merit.

"The URE shall not deprive a person or persons of liberty or property without due process of law and just compensation.

"The URE shall not infringe upon the people's right to be free from slavery or indentured servitude in any and all forms, including bondage, prostitution, human trafficking, excessive work hours, and earning substandard wages. Violation of this right shall be considered a crime against humanity and subject to the severest of penalties.

"The URE in its exercise of power and commerce outside its borders shall also grant the rights delineated herein to the citizens of other countries affected by said power and commerce.

"The URE shall not grant titles of nobility and no person holding elected office shall accept same from another nation.

"The URE may have a flag if the Legislature and the people so choose, but no official allegiance to it shall be required.

"Amendments to the World Constitution may be proposed by the people, the Legislature, or the President, but they must be endorsed by both the Judiciary and the Advisory before being put to a vote of the people. Amendments shall become part of this Constitution if and when ratified by three-fourths of the people.

"And finally, the enumeration of the rights herein shall not deny or disparage *other* rights reserved to the people."

Mac pressed the remote in his hand again and the screen went dark.

Passionate cheers and fervent applause resounded through the hall as once again the gathering rose to their feet.

"A draft of this Constitution will be posted on the UN website for public comment. I invite your nations to take part in a series of Constitutional Congresses meant to debate and amend what I've presented. The first will be convened three months from today here in New York. Subsequent ones will be held on different continents until a final Constitution is ready to be voted on by the citizens of the URE. Africa, South America, Asia, Australia, and Europe, in that order. My sincerest hope is that one day *every* nation on Earth will adopt this Constitution as their own."

Mac's mien noticeably dimmed during the applause that followed, and when it subsided he said gravely, "Gerhardt Schoen, I now address you alone. Mons Baddonicus, dawn, two days."

And with that, Mac walked up to the edge of the stage, spread his arms wide as if to embrace the Assembly, and jumped down to the main floor. Everyone roared with approbation as he was engulfed by those who wished nothing more than to tell their friends and family that once they touched the man who united the world.

ty

"It's the end of the world as we know it, and I feel fine."

— REM

*"Until God grants us the ability to read the future, all human
wisdom is contained in these two words – wait and hope."*

— Alexandre Dumas

At an out-of-the-way inn in the old part of Bath, Merrill and Kyle
recounted stories of the Clan and tales of Arthur well past midnight,
and then shared with his second-to-last heir a heartfelt goodbye,
knowing it might be their last. After, Mac walked along the damp,
misty streets alone, wishing Merrill could have joined him as he had
all those years before, but this walk Mac had to take alone.

The night held firm though the dawn was mounting its charge
as the centuries-old shops gave way to cottages, the cottages to
groves of trees, and the trees to open fields broken by the occasional
field stone wall. As Mac walked on, the road gradually faded into
a footpath winding its way into green rolling hills still ashen with
moonlight, and the silhouette of Mons Baddonicus rose above the
northern horizon.

He finally left the path and strode through the dew-dampened
field grass, the morning mist swirling around him like ghosts in a
cemetery. The long-ago cries of his kinsmen carried on the wind,

the scent of long-ago cooking fires filled his nostrils, and the Earth shook with the pounding of horses' hooves. His breathing grew long and deep, his heart beat faster, and a mix of exhilaration and trepidation fueled his ascent up the steep slope of Mons Baddonicus.

Breaching its crest, he took in the broad, flat, treeless peak with one sweep of his eyes, its knee-high grass awash with the reddish glow of dawn, and not more than 100 paces away stood Gerhart Schoen. Dressed in black fatigues and hunter's sweater, everything about the man – from his stance to his stone cold unblinking eyes to the Lugar clutched in his hand – spoke of murderous intent. Mac reached inside his jacket and drew out his Beretta. When a mere 20 paces separated the two, they raised their guns and slowly began circling each other.

"My grandfather was chosen by Der Führer to purge the Reich of those who refused to submit themselves to Aryan ascendancy," Schoen proudly revealed. "Any people with an ideology or self-identity that would keep them from kneeling before the Master Race had to be eliminated. People like the Jews who clung to their Hebrew God. And your Clan who clung to the dream of another Arthur."

"How did your grandfather even know of our Clan?" Mac said.

"He'd always known, as had his father and his father before him," answered Schoen. "My people always knew of you. We were told of Arthur when we were old enough to sit on our father's knee. Not of knights or acts of chivalry, but of the *truth*. Of how Arthur had *stolen* what was rightfully ours and *murdered* our people!"

"Stole what was rightfully yours?" mocked Mac. "Murdered your people? You're mad! England was always ours and always will be."

"My ancestors were the first race in a *thousand years* to defeat the Romans," he declared. "We won every battle, took for our own the lands of the dying Empire, and conquered every foe. Until Arthur." He waved his hand at the surrounding field. "Until here. Never again did we rise to such power until Der Führer, only to be defeated *again* by you damnable Brits and your American bastards."

"We," Mac reflected aloud, and then it struck him! "You're a descendant of the Saxons that Arthur fought here."

"I am *the* descendant. I am Oesc of Kent's last heir!"

Mac couldn't believe what he was hearing! Yet, at the same time, it seemed to make twisted sense. The book of lineocide in Little Deutschland. His bloodline nearly ending. The attempts on his and Cameron's lives. "Your ancestors kept the bitterness of their defeat alive for 1500 years," he said, trying to reconcile the facts while continuing to circle his nemesis in a macabre, ritualistic dance.

"My ancestors took a blood oath to destroy every vestige of Arthur," Schoen said. "Only then could we fulfill our Saxon, our *Aryan* destiny of dominion over the world. Boujeau was merely a means to that end. Then he died, and you became Secretary-General. There was nothing left but to release my blitzkrieg, avenge Oesc and my people, and give life to my glorious Viertes Reich!" He stopped circling and slowly pulled back the Lugar's hammer, the fire of his perverse reverie fading until only a bitter hatred remained. "But, *you*, Arthur reincarnated, thwarted my people yet again! By killing you, here where it all began, I will end your bloodline forever!"

Mac, too, stopped circling and shook his head slowly. "Cameron's still alive, Gerhardt."

The Aryan stared back unblinking, his face turning crimson. A primal, raging scream burst forth sending an involuntary chill down Mac's spine.

"My Clan will protect her, Gerhardt," he said. "They'll follow her as they did me. So will others who believe in what's good and right."

"Your Clan didn't save your brother," Schoen bit back, "and they won't save *you*."

"Clark," Mac whispered, the memories of that terrible day nearly bringing him to his knees.

Schoen breathed in Mac's pain and laughed slow and long before twisting the proverbial knife. "My father ran him down in the street like a dog, and when you're dead I will do the same to your daughter."

Mac would gladly have sold his soul for the barest chance of wrapping his hands around Schoen's throat. His hand tightened around the Berretta's grip and he said through gritted teeth, "In this moment, here on Mons Baddonicus, I still live. Arthur's blood courses through my veins and his nobility infuses my mind." He turned his body at a right angle to Schoen's. "But if you long for my death, then I give you leave to shoot. And if there be a God, may He have mercy on your soul."

Schoen's eyes flared. He cupped his right hand in his left to steady the Lugar and aimed.

"*Fire,* damn you!" Mac yelled.

The Aryan pulled the trigger, the barrel flashed, and the Lugar bucked in his hand. The bullet sliced unseen through the heavy morning air, ripped through the front of Mac's jacket, and tore a gash across the just-healed skin and muscle of his chest before careening off into the tall grass beyond. Without so much as a gasp of pain or a flinch, Mac whispered, "My turn," and pulled the trigger. The Berretta kicked hard, a bright red-orange plume exploded from the barrel and the slide snapped back to reload the chamber.

The bullet slammed into Schoen's right shoulder and sent him staggering backwards. He looked down to see a hole in his sweater, but no blood. The ache of the impact faded and with a devil's grin he raised the Lugar to fire again, just as a searing pain ripped through his torso and radiated into his limbs. He let out an unbidden cry of agony and sank to his knees.

"It wasn't a bullet, Gerhardt," the heir of Arthur said, blood dripping down the front of his jacket as he slowly walked towards the Aryan. "It was a tiny, hypodermic needle filled with a poison the Cuari use for hunting, encased in a hollow, polypropylene shell. You remember the Cuari, don't you, Gerhardt? The Amerindians you enslaved in Little Deutschland? Not to worry, though. The poison won't kill you, only paralyze you long enough for a trip to The Hague."

With a tormented moan, Schoen fell back onto the ground, his body growing rigid.

"Hurts, eh?" Mac said, unable to keep a slight grin from crossing his lips as he knelt down beside his nemesis. "It's over, Gerhardt. Forever, it's over."

Mac sensed the presence of someone else close by and jumped to his feet. He swung the Beretta around and pivoted in a full circle to find a host of men and women, young and old, encircling him. He tensed for a fight, but then recognized one of them.

Clarice! Then, he noticed Kyle and Colin, Merrill and Michael, and from somewhere a young girl cried, "Daddy!"

Pushing past the Elders, Cameron broke into a run. Mac holstered the Beretta just in time to scoop her up in his arms. "Hey, sweetie. What are doing here?"

"Me and mommy came to help you!"

"You're bleeding," Genevieve said worriedly as she hurried forward.

"Yeah, that seems to happen a lot."

"Again with the blood?" said Perry, turning back. "I'll get some help."

"I'm fine," Mac assured him. "Nothing a few stitches won't fix," he grinned.

T.J., Marion, and Mac's old friends were among the throng of Clansfolk approaching as well.

"How'd my speech go over, Teej?"

"Media's on your side," he replied with a tussle of Cameron's hair. "Polls show the public is, too. More than half the countries have already named their delegates to the Constitutional Congress. Looks like you're gonna have a world to run, Mr. President."

Mac laughed and the gash in his chest felt like it was being pried open with a rib spreader. "I'm far from being President, Teej," he forced out through the pain.

His friend shrugged and smiled. "That's not what the *polls* say."

"So, what do we do with this guy?" said Duron, nodding at Schoen.

"Take him to Bath," Mac answered, "then get him on the first flight to The Hague."

"You got it," said Robbie, the two of them grabbing an arm and lifting Schoen to his feet. "Time to pay the piper."

"Hey, old man," Mac said to Merrill, and to the Keeper, "*Novum Orbis Regium*," and gave each of them a one-armed hug.

"*Novum Orbis Regium*," Kyle echoed with a smile. "So, laddy, if the Constitutional Congress decides to establish a URE capital, where might you recommend it be?" Then, he added quickly, "Not that it matters to me."

Mac knew what the Keeper wanted to hear and decided to have a little fun. "Traverse would be nice. Don't you think, Gen?"

"Oh, yes," she played along. "*Very* nice."

"Laddy!" Merrill cried. "You wouldn't!"

"No," Mac chuckled. "I wouldn't. Camleton is where it belongs, and Camleton is where it shall be."

Kyle breathed easy, clapped Mac on the back, and said, "Come back with us, all of you, and spend some time with the Clan."

"That sounds great," Mac answered with a weary smile.

Merrill took Mac by the arm. "Half a mo, lad?"

"Uh, okay," Mac answered warily, handing Cameron to Genevieve.

"*Only* a moment, Merrill," she chided, "I'd like to have him to myself for a little while before you give him to the world."

"Aye, lass," he promised, and the three Clansmen meandered towards the edge of the field.

"There's something we need to tell you," said the Keeper.

Mac sighed. "I hate it when you say things like that."

"Everything turns out alright in the end," Merrill said with an innocent shrug. "Doesn't it?"

"Yeah," Mac muttered. "Sure."

"Remember when we took you into the catacombs under Camulodunum?" the Keeper asked.

"Of course," Mac answered, "to see the tombs of Arthur and Genevieve."

"Aye, as well as the soma of Alexander the Great," Merrill reminded him.

"Yes," Mac replied, his curiosity getting the better of him. "Why?"

"And the airlock," Kyle went on.

"Yes," Mac said again, "with what's left of the Library of Alexandria. What are you two getting at?"

"Well," Kyle said, "you see, there's something *in* the Library."

"What?" Mac said with growing unease.

The Keeper took a deep breath. "The Holy Grail."

The End

"Sooner or later, the sands of the mariner's clock run out...and even Odysseus' ship must dock."

– James Michener

The characters in Novum Orbis Regium *and in* Traverse *are entirely fictional. Any similarities to real people, alive or dead, to other texts, or to institutions are purely coincidental. The names of Mac's friends are the actual first names of friends of mine, though their characterizations are fictional. Where I have referred to real places, I have often taken liberties with my descriptions for purposes of the story, and when I have referenced historical and contemporary facts and figures, I have tried to be as accurate as my sources allowed while still advancing the book's fictional plot.*

About the Author

W. A. Holdsworth was born in Chicago in 1961 and lived in several states before settling in Michigan. He spent his summers in Traverse City and still vacations there every year, as does the protagonist of his novel Traverse. Mr. Holdsworth attended the University of Michigan and Oakland University, earning an engineering degree and serving as President of the engineering school's honor society. After two years with General Electric, he enrolled at Michigan State University and earned an MBA. The following 30 years were spent working first as a management consultant and then as a Director for one of the largest counties in the U.S.

Not much of a reader as a youth, he began listening to Books On Tape during business trips. He soon became an avid reader of classic and contemporary adventure novels, and indulged his life-long interest in history, science, philosophy, and religions. It wasn't until his late thirties that he began writing while working and raising a family. A fan of the Arthurian legend, he wanted to bring the story of Arthur and Camelot into the modern world with a novel that was both exciting and meaningful. The result was Traverse, and its sequel Novum Orbis Regium. He is now writing the next book in the trilogy.

43383051R00227

Made in the USA
Middletown, DE
26 April 2019